Pamela Taylor

I0590682

Upon This Throne

Second Son Chronicles - Volume 4

Black Rose Writing | Texas

ISBN: 978-1-68433-606-7
PUBLISHED BY BLACK ROSE WRITING
www.blackrosewriting.com

Printed in the United States of America
Suggested Retail Price (SRP) $19.95

Upon This Throne is printed in Book Antiqua

*As a planet-friendly publisher, Black Rose Writing does its best to eliminate
unnecessary waste to reduce paper usage and energy costs, while never compromising
the reading experience. As a result, the final word count vs. page count may not meet
common expectations.

This series is dedicated to the hope that thoughtfulness, compassion, respect, and rational dialogue can triumph over bigotry, greed, mistrust, and self-righteousness to create a world that is truly a better place for all of humankind.

I'm particularly grateful to Linda Kirwin for her help and guidance. Though her project started as a beta read with critique, she quickly grasped what I was trying to do in this series and became a valued editorial consultant. Thanks also to the members of the DFW Writers Workshop who listened to readings and offered their food for thought. And a very special thank you to Jeffrey — himself a second son — who was my first reader and who encouraged me in the early days, when I was unsure if my vision was worth pursuing.

Praise for The Second Son Chronicles

Second Son

"A fine-grained and emotionally satisfying medieval adventure."
— *Kirkus Reviews*

"Overall, this was a lovely read that shows Taylor's skills as a wonderful storyteller – one that knows how to lure the reader into wanting to continue with Alfred's tale. I certainly will be!"
— Karen Brooks, author of *The Locksmith's Daughter* and *The Chocolate Maker's Wife*

"In the genre of historically inspired fiction, Taylor has done a marvelous job of combining fact, history, and fun."
— *IndieReader*, 4-star, *IndieReader Approved*

"Historical fiction lovers will enjoy this tale of knightly adventure."
— *Sublime Book Review*

Finalist, Historical Fiction, 2020 Eric Hoffer Awards

My Father, My King

"Written in elegant prose, with an intricate storyline that is woven together like a fine medieval tapestry."
— *Authors Reading*

"An absolutely sensational renaissance novel filled with dry humor, heartfelt moments, and exceptional characters."
— *Sublime Book Review*

"An intriguing… enchanting… fictional take on ancient ruling family, and its traditions."
— *Indie Reader*

2019 PenCraft Awards, 2nd Place, Fantasy

Pestilence

"Taylor deftly depicts the fragility of a society in the grip of a madman… the next installment promises a massive emotional payoff."
— *Kirkus Reviews*

"… deceptions, triumphs, passions and bloodshed will grip readers from the first page to the last page."
— *Authors Reading*

"… a well-written and well thought out book filled with courtly intrigue and drama."
— *IndieReader 4-star, IndieReader Approved*

"This is another winning addition to the Second Son series for fans of well-written, captivating historical fiction."
— *Sublime Book Review*

The Royal Family

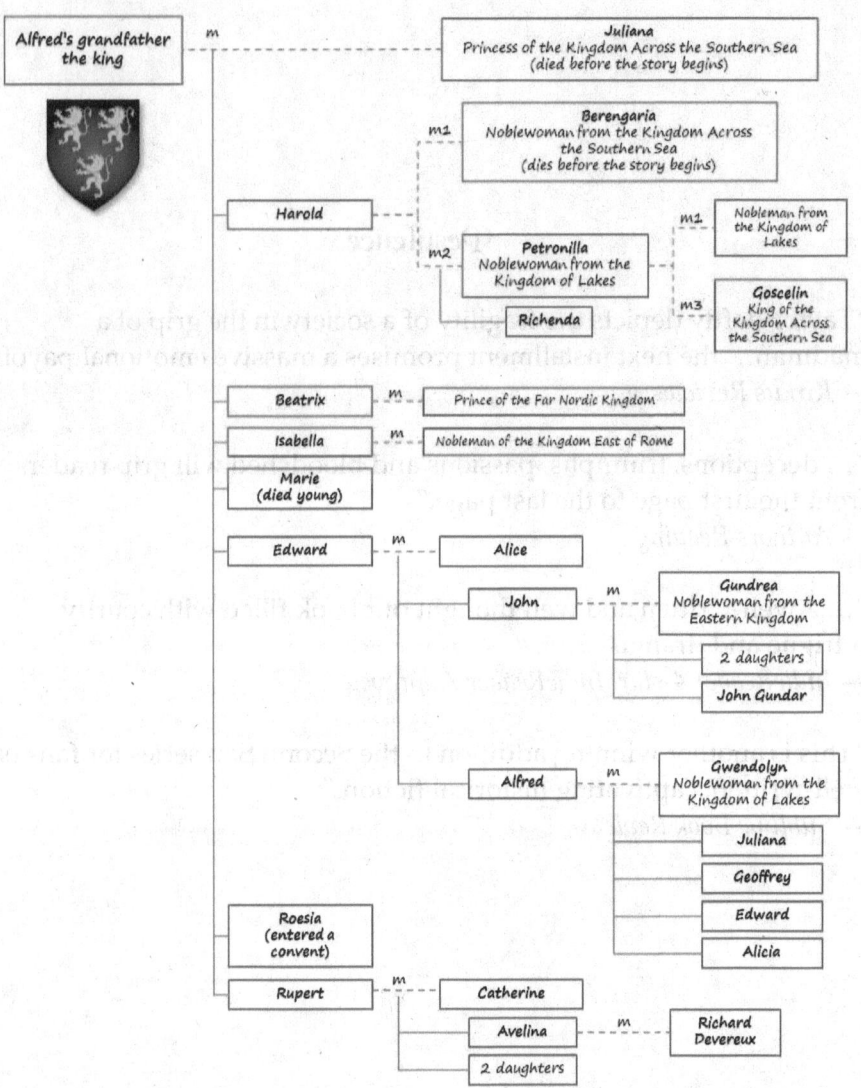

The Nobility

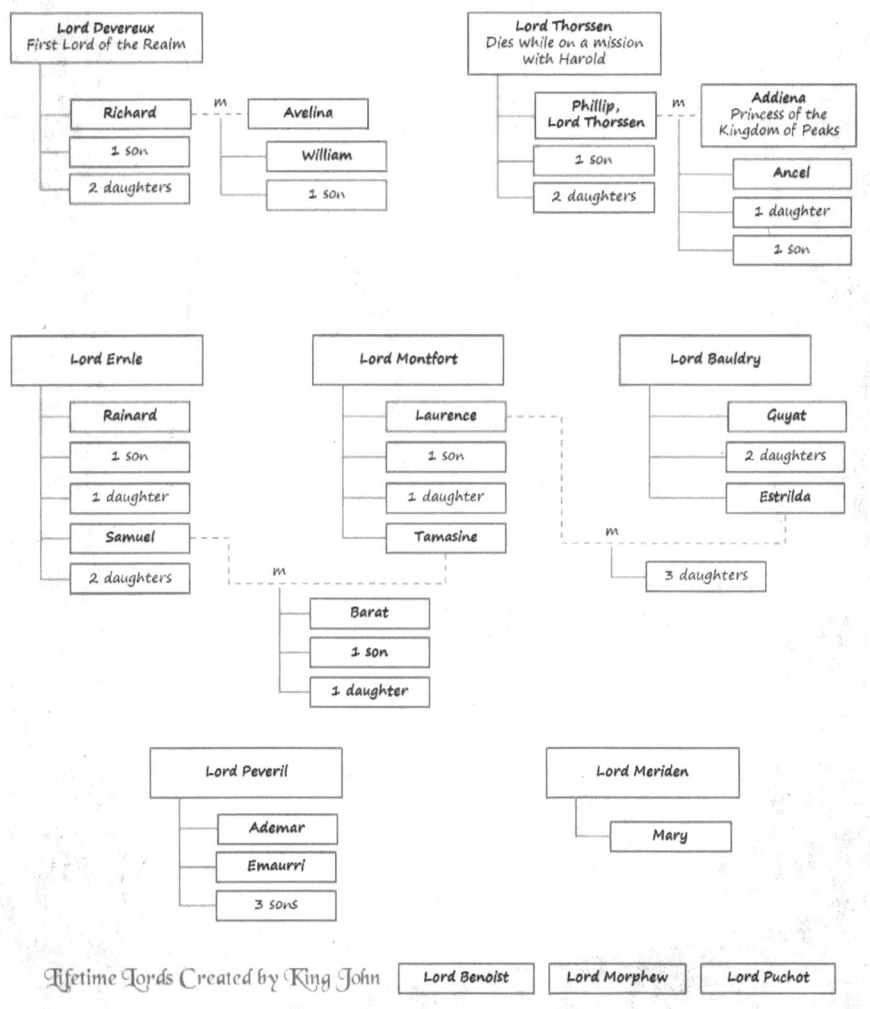

Lord Devereux
First Lord of the Realm

- Richard — m — Avelina
  - 1 son
  - 2 daughters
  - William
    - 1 son

Lord Thorssen
Dies while on a mission
with Harold

- Phillip,
  Lord Thorssen — m — Addiena
  Princess of the
  Kingdom of Peaks
  - 1 son
  - 2 daughters
  - Ancel
    - 1 daughter
    - 1 son

Lord Ernle

- Rainard
- 1 son
- 1 daughter
- Samuel
- 2 daughters

Lord Montfort

- Laurence
- 1 son
- 1 daughter
- Tamasine

m

- Barat
- 1 son
- 1 daughter

Lord Bauldry

- Guyat
- 2 daughters
- Estrilda

m

- 3 daughters

Lord Peveril

- Ademar
- Emaurri
- 3 sons

Lord Meriden

- Mary

Lifetime Lords Created by King John   Lord Benoist   Lord Morphew   Lord Puchot

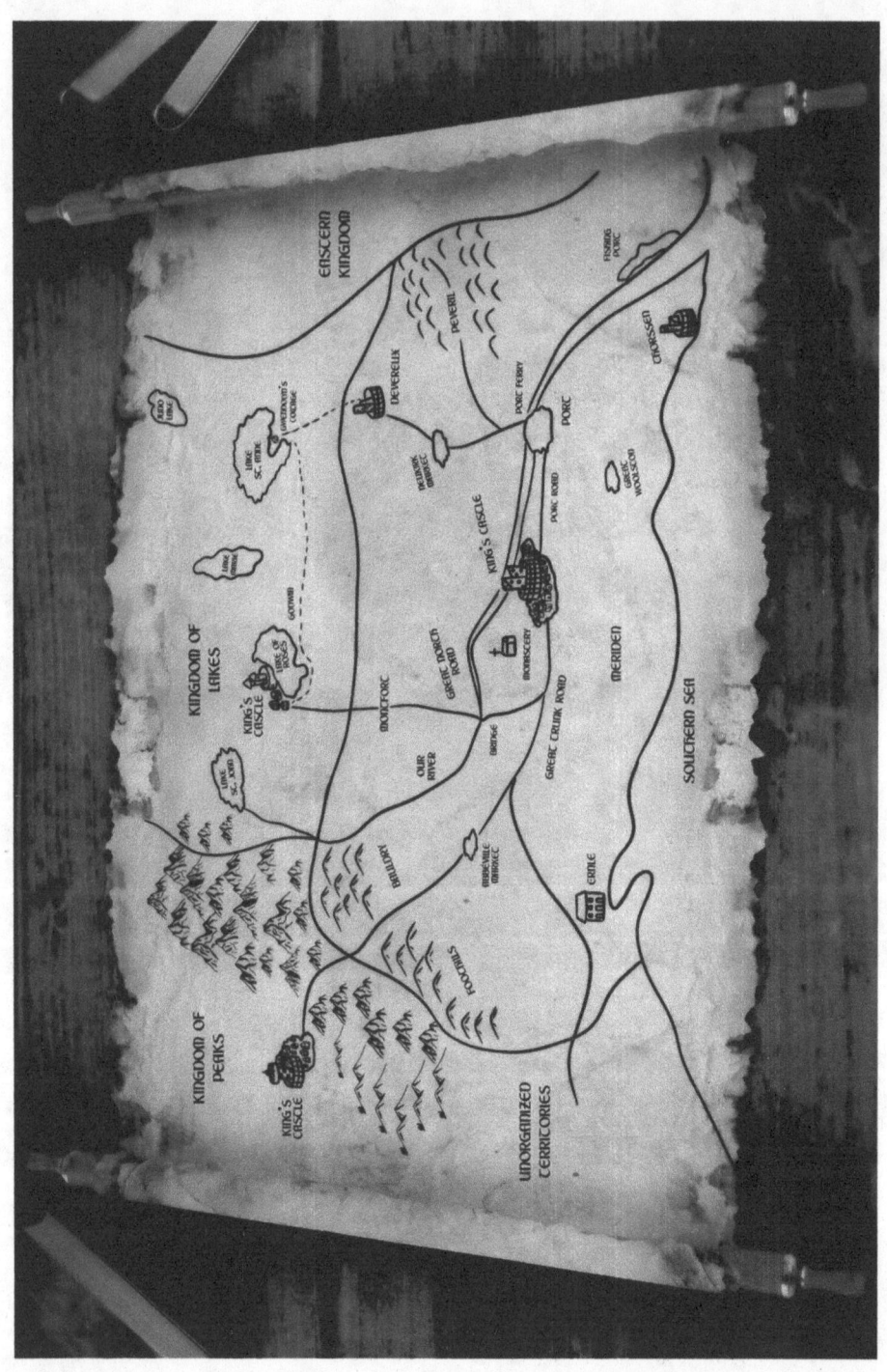

Upon This Throne

The soft light through the window wakes me gently from a very deep sleep, and I open my eyes to survey my surroundings. I'm in an unfamiliar bed in a room I've never seen before. Across the room, beside the window, a man in priestly garb dozes in a chair. Trying to raise myself up to get a better view, I discover I'm almost too weak to do so. My stirring brings the priest immediately alert.

"Ah," he says quietly. "I see you have decided to come back to us." Crossing the room, he sits beside me on the bed and places one hand on my forehead. "And the fever has not returned. That is good – very good indeed."

"Where am I? What is this place? And how did I get here?"

"I shall leave your first two questions for others to answer. As to how you arrived, I am told that your horse brought you." I must look puzzled, for he continues, "Yes, I know that sounds silly since that is how men go places. Yet I am told that when you arrived, you were delirious with fever – barely able to stay in the saddle and clinging to your horse's neck – and that the horse brought you here and called out for help."

Vague recollections. Of endless rain. Of giving Star Dancer his head. "You say there are others. Are they sick as well?"

"They are not. Nor do I think they will be, and for that I credit your lady wife." So it wasn't a dream! "She realized immediately that you had the sickness, so she made everyone leave the room, including herself. Anyone who had touched you – she made them strip naked and have a hot bath – fresh water for each bath. She ordered all the clothes burned, including her own. Then she banished everyone to the other side of the house and sent for me."

"She thought I was dying?"

"Quite the contrary, my son. She wanted to be sure you would survive. You see, I spent some years with the monks of St. John's Abbey where I learned their medicines and their methods of healing. They are by far the most skillful of any in this land. So you might say that I am a healer of men's bodies as well as men's souls." His speech has the sing-song rhythm of the Kingdom of Lakes though he speaks my tongue with ease. Wherever I am, it must be somewhere in Gwen's homeland.

"How long have I been here?"

"Today marks the fifth day. When I arrived you were still in the grips of the fever. I was able to rouse you enough from time to time to drink the infusion of herbs I had prepared. We know not why, but this infusion helps to keep the throat from swelling, which is the most dangerous part of this sickness and what usually causes death. When I could no longer get you to drink, I kept a steaming pot of the infusion by your bedside. Strangely enough, breathing the vapors – while not as good as drinking the draught – can also have a beneficial effect."

A steaming pot of his mixture sits on the table beside the bed. I sniff it cautiously. Surprisingly, it doesn't have the stench so typical for medicinal preparations, instead smelling slightly floral but also oddly pungent.

He continues. "Two days ago, your fever broke and you fell into a deep sleep from which you could not be roused. Some think this is the spirit deciding whether to go on to the next world or stay in this one . . . and perhaps sometimes it is. But the monks taught me that often it is merely the body's way of taking the time it needs to heal itself." He hands me a cup of water. "Drink. We must begin to replenish what the fever took away from you." The water is fresh and sweet.

"Now," he says, "we must clean your body and cleanse this room before anyone else can be allowed to enter." From behind a screen, he pulls a tub partially filled with water to a spot near the hearth then takes an enormous kettle from the hook above the fire and pours steaming water into the tub and into a large pitcher nearby.

Coming back to the bedside, he says, "Let's see if we can get you into the tub." Again, I'm astonished at how little strength I have, but he manages to get my nightshirt off and practically carry me into the tub.

Though a slight, wiry man, he's remarkably strong. "Bathe yourself as best you can while I attend to a few other matters."

He removes all the bedclothes and piles them on the floor. Then he removes his own cassock, adds it to the pile along with my nightshirt, and ties the whole lot into a big bundle that he tosses out the window, followed by the pillows and the top mattress from the bed. "We will burn that lot." Holding his hands out the window, he pours water to cleanse them. Next, he retrieves a fresh cassock from the large corner cupboard, prepares the bed with clean sheets and new pillows, and lays out a clean nightshirt.

Those tasks complete, he returns to make sure I have a proper bath. Getting me to my feet, he pours the pitcher of now-warm water over me to wash away any remaining soil from the bathwater, helps me out of the tub, and wraps me in a blanket to ensure I don't get chilled while getting dry. Finally, he pulls the nightshirt over my head and helps me back into the bed, propping me up on the pillows. I'm utterly exhausted from even this small exertion. Satisfied that I'm comfortable, he pulls the tub back behind the screen, taking great care not to spill anything. "I will deal with that later when I have someone to help me.

"The final thing before I let you rest. We must cleanse your mouth." He hands me a different cup. "This is vinegar with a little water. Swish it around your mouth and gargle, but do not swallow." I fill my mouth from the cup – vinegar, for certes – and follow his instructions, spitting it all out into the empty pitcher.

"Now for some nourishment." He makes for the door to the corridor. As he opens it, the room fills with the outside air coming through the window. "I shall leave this open to draw in the fresh air. It has healing powers of its own."

He's not gone long, returning with a tray containing a bowl of hot broth, a small piece of bread, and a fresh cup of water. The broth is delicious and after a few mouthfuls, I reach for the bread. "It would be best, my son," begins the priest, "if you would . . ." While he's speaking, I tear a piece off the bread and soak it in the broth before putting it in my mouth. "Ah! It seems you know what to do."

I smile at him. "I once had to recover from near starvation, Father. It seems the monk who cared for me then must have learned skills similar to yours."

"Then it seems you have been twice blessed, my son." The hint of a smile appears on his face. "The broth and water will restore what the fever took away. And tomorrow we will add a bit of porridge."

"Perhaps with some honey, Father?"

"Why not? Honey also has healing properties. By the way, you should know that for the first day or two, your piss will be dark – perhaps even brown. Do not be concerned. That is actually a good thing – your body ridding itself of the poisons left behind by the sickness.

"Today, you should rest. Then tomorrow you should begin walking around a bit, to start getting your strength back. After that, you can be the judge of how much to eat and how active to be. Your past experience will be a good guide."

While he's been talking, I've finished my meal. "I'm surprised how hungry I feel, but that's enough for now," I tell him.

"Indeed," he replies, placing the tray on the window ledge. "You can have more later. Right now, there is someone who has been waiting patiently to see you and whose patience, I fear, may be coming to an end." He goes to the door and beckons. Gwen hurries to the bedside and lays her head on my chest. No amount of weakness can keep me from wrapping my arms around her and holding her tightly. The priest retrieves the tray and makes for the door. "I will return these to the kitchen and see to the burning of the bedclothes."

When at last we release our embrace, Gwen strokes my hair and says, "Thank God and all the saints, Alfred. We've been *so* worried about you."

"And you? Are you alright? No sign of the sickness?"

"We are all well, my love. Father made us all drink his brews on the first day. He said if there was no sign of a fever by the third day, we were no longer at risk. And as you can see . . ."

"And the baby?"

"The baby is fine, Alfred." She strokes her belly. "Though she seems to enjoy keeping me awake at night."

"She? You think it's a girl?"

"I hope so."

"So where are we? I surmise from the priest's accent that it's somewhere in the Kingdom of Lakes, but what is this place? And why did you come here?"

"My family's cottage on Lake St. Anne," she replies. "Tomorrow, when you're stronger, I'll tell you all about our journey and how we came to be here."

"Star Dancer? From the little I remember and what the priest told me, that horse saved my life."

"Osbert's been taking care of him. And there's no doubt he brought you here. But Father Bartholomé says it was most likely the rain that saved you – it kept your fever from getting too high. He says the first day is critical – if the fever gets too high, it can boil your brain and then there's nothing anyone can do.

"The children want to see you, but I've told them they have to wait until tomorrow when you're up and about a bit more. And tomorrow, you can move from here into our room – Osbert has unpacked your clothes that we brought from the manor. We'd only been here two days when you arrived, so we're still settling in. But for today, rest and get your strength back."

Father Bartholomé returns. "Quite right, my dear."

"Before I leave, Father, there's someone else who I think is going to have an apoplexy if he has to wait any longer." She goes to the door, and Osbert follows her back in.

"They say ye be better, m'lord, but I just have to see fer meself."

"Much better, Osbert. And so very glad you were at the manor to take care of things rather than off with me in the army."

"All be just as ye'd want it, sir. I be riding Star Dancer a bit every day, and Father say I can start taking care of ye again tomorrow."

"You may have to exercise Star Dancer for a few more days while I finish getting my strength back."

"Dinna' ye be fretting about that, sir. I be happy to keep him fit and ready fer ye."

"Very well, then," says the priest. "Let's not tire him too much this first morning. Come back this afternoon for a bit, my dear." And he shoos them out of the room and returns to his chair by the window.

For the rest of the day, I alternately nap, talk with Father Bartholomé, and eat the broth and bread that he brings up twice more. By the time I finally need the chamber pot around sundown, I'm able to manage it on my own.

During the afternoon, I asked him about the sickness. "I've been puzzling over how I got it, Father. It wasn't in the west, so it wasn't among the army. We didn't encounter it on our journey east until two days or more after we crossed the border. And, as you know, it wasn't among the people of the village where my family started their journey."

"An isolated case like yours is indeed unusual," he replied. "But then you've had an unusual journey." He proceeded to tell me everything he knows about the sickness. "It was known about even in Roman times, you see, but back then, they knew no way to treat the sufferers. No one knows where it comes from. It just appears, ravages a population, and then vanishes as quickly as it came. And it may not return for decades – sometimes even for a century or more. It's been longer than that since it was seen in this kingdom or yours.

"We know disease can spread through the air or through sharing food and cups with sick people. Sometimes it can spread through touching the sick and handling what they have handled. There seem to be other ways sickness spreads that we don't understand. The monks of St. John's believe vermin like rats may be involved somehow. They have observed that when people practice cleanliness and keep their food and grain secure from vermin, there is less sickness of any kind."

"My grandfather believed in the importance of cleanliness," I told him. "Perhaps he read some of the same writings as the St. John's monks – he was, after all, an avid reader who collected a great library of books."

"Your grandfather was a wise man. One thing we know for certain – anyone who gets this sickness and survives will never succumb to it again. I survived it when I was a very young man studying in Rome for the priesthood, so I was in no danger while attending you. Now you are forever safe from its grasp. Perhaps that is why it disappears so quickly – it takes its victims but cannot infect the survivors again and so it dies its own death.

"Now tell me everything about your journey here – every detail. How you came to be infected may be something that seemed completely innocuous at the time." So I told him about my flight with Donal from the war in the Unorganized Territories, about arriving home to discover my family had fled in fear of the sickness, and all the details of my ride north in search of them. When I finished, he scratched his head. "It seems most likely you came in contact with it at the port."

"And yet, my family passed through the port only a few days earlier and suffered no ill effects."

"Did you cover your mouth and nose?"

"No. I'd intended to ride through, cross the ferry, and be away from there quickly."

"Hmmmm," he pondered. "In a place like that, with so many dead and dying, you could have simply breathed it in from the air. Or perhaps when you were splashed with the river water. Or perhaps the oars of your boat were splashed or had recently been handled by someone ill. Perhaps even the rope you found. When you took food from your pack to eat as you rode along, your hands could have passed the infection to the food and thus into your body. We will never know for sure, though I think the port is the most likely source. But why such great concern about how you came to get the disease?" He had sensed my deeper worry.

"I spent a night at Devereux Castle, Father. I'd be utterly devastated if it turns out I had taken this sickness to the people there."

"I cannot tell you with certainty, my son, that you did or did not. Perhaps you can take comfort in the fact that you had no fever when you were there. We know not why, but it seems this sickness spreads most easily in the presence of those who have the fever. I will pray for your friends that they have not become ill and, if they have, that they may survive." Small comfort, especially as I've no idea how I'll ever find out.

The next morning, I wake feeling remarkably refreshed. Osbert shows me down the hall to the master's chamber where a bath, a shave, and fresh clothes make me feel even more like myself, and I emerge from the dressing room to find the promised porridge waiting. Gwen lingers while I eat. She seems . . . distracted? Apprehensive? I can't quite put my finger on what's troubling her, so finally I just ask.

"I said I'd tell you today how we came to be here," she begins and then hesitates. "Promise me you won't fly into a rage."

"Have you ever known me to fly into a rage?"

"No," she admits. "But then I've never had to tell you something like this before."

"It can't be all that bad." Outwardly, I'm all reassurance; inside, I'm not sure whether to be curious or apprehensive myself.

She walks into her dressing room and returns with her blue cloak – the one she convinced Letty not to leave behind when we moved from the castle to the country manor. Sitting beside me with the cloak in her lap, she takes a pair of sewing scissors and starts opening the stitches that attach the lining to the cloak. Then she pulls a folded page from inside the lining. Curiosity is winning over apprehension in my mind.

"When we were betrothed – before we even met for the first time – my father gave me this cottage." She hands me the paper to read. "He wanted to be sure I'd have a safe place to go should something go wrong with our marriage."

I hereby grant to my daughter Gwendolyn, in her own right, all rights and privileges to our cottage at Lake St. Anne and the property on which it is located. It is hers to use as and when she sees fit for her lifetime. Upon her death, these rights and privileges revert to whoever holds the title of Lord of our estates at that time.

It's dated and signed by Godwin, and his seal is affixed. I hand the document back to her as she rushes to add, "Don't misunderstand, my love. Father didn't think we would be unhappy – he was only guarding against the uncertainties of life. In fact, I'll never forget his words: 'It is my greatest hope that the cottage will become your family retreat and never be put to use as a refuge.' In the early days of our marriage, I, too, guarded against uncertainty, intending one day to share this with you and fulfill my father's dream.

"I was on the verge of telling you and then your father died. As I watched John puffed up with power and how he schemed against you, I became convinced that one day we might both need a refuge. So I kept my secret – even from you – and when we had to flee, I still kept the secret, though it broke my heart to know you might not find us. I knew I had to keep Geoffrey and Edward safe." She looks down into her lap where her hands fidget nervously with the document. "I only hope you're not angry."

When will my wife cease to surprise me? I take the document from her and slide it back into its hiding place in the lining of her cloak. Then I take her hands and bring them to my lips, covering them in kisses. "How could I possibly be angry with the woman who had the courage to protect my sons' lives even in the face of not knowing if she'd ever see me again?"

"But I kept this from you for so many years," she continues to protest.

"And that turns out to have been a most fortuitous decision, my dear." I put my arm around her and can feel the tension drain from her body. "My supposition was that you had gone to your parents. I'd spent all my lucid moments looking for a track or road leading west. But I never found one."

She laughs, though I've no idea what I've said that's so funny. "It seems I owe my good fortune to the fact you were too sick to see it and Star Dancer just kept walking on. The road west turns off just a mile south of here."

Then she continues in a more serious vein. "Alfred, we're completely safe here . . . well, as safe as it's possible to be. Besides the servants who live on the property, the only people who know we're here are Father Bartholomé and my parents. I swore Father to the sanctity of the confessional before I would even let him see you, and my parents would go to their graves before they'd betray us. Even the people in the village across the lake have no idea we're here. Hamon – our steward – you'll meet him later – can bring in food from different towns and villages so there's no pattern. We'll be isolated, but we'll be safe."

"Why such extremes?"

"When you're feeling better, you'll realize, Alfred. The minute you deserted the army, you became a traitor. If John could find you, he'd have no scruples about dragging you back to be hanged. I shudder to think what he might do to your sons. Don't forget – Ralf's wife and sons were found even in a remote part of this realm. So we must do absolutely nothing to make that any easier."

It's beginning to dawn on me just how much my life is changing . . . has already changed. We are, indeed, safe for the time being. But how will we know what's happening in the rest of the world? To the people we care about? What of the outcome of the war? How will we know if John is defeated or victorious? If he's defeated, is he killed or taken prisoner? Is our kingdom overrun by the lords of the Unorganized Territories? If John is alive and the kingdom intact – drastically reduced in size though it may be now that the lords have withdrawn their loyalty and their lands – how will we know what's happening? When might it be safe for us to venture further abroad, even just to visit Gwen's parents? And then I'm drawn back to the truly mundane. "How will we be able to live here? What will we do for money for the bare necessities?"

"I brought what money was in your strongbox."

"That won't last long."

"I know," she says, reaching once again for her cloak and sewing scissors. This time her snipping is on the hem of the garment. When she puts down the scissors, she reaches into the compartment she'd opened and produces a gold coin. "There are more. Enough to last us for at least a year – perhaps a bit longer if we're careful."

"Another gift from your father?"

She nods her head. "I thought more than once about retrieving a few of them to invest with the banker, but something held me back. Now I'm ever so glad it did."

From her sewing box, she takes needle and thread and begins repairing the stitches she'd snipped, locking her secrets back into her cloak. "Alfred, no one knows about this but us . . . not even Letty."

"I thought you trusted Letty completely."

"I do. She's as loyal to me as Osbert is to you. But what she doesn't know, she can never be coerced or tricked into revealing. Sit with me while I finish this; then we'll go down and you can meet the servants. Hamon is our steward, Lora the housekeeper. I'll let them introduce the others."

"You said they all live here?"

"Lora is Mother's assistant housekeeper. For years, she's been ready for a housekeeper's job in a grand house, but she's so loyal to Mother she's turned down every opportunity. When the news about John going to war reached my parents, Mother sent Lora here to get the house ready for us."

"She was that sure we'd be coming?"

"Lora's instructions were to open the house and stay until Christmas. If we hadn't come by then, Lora was to close up the house and return home.

"Hamon looks after the property whether anyone is here or not. He and his family live in the caretaker's house. When we're in residence, he's the steward. The rest of the servants are his family – unmarried sons and daughters. They were far too young to serve when we came here in the summer as children with my parents, so Mother would bring some servants from home and hire others from the village. But as Hamon's children grew, there was less need to hire the villagers. There are ten of them, so there are still enough unmarried ones at home to help us now."

"You said earlier that your parents know we're here."

"Well, right now, all they know is that we might be here. Mother worked it all out. When we arrived, Lora was to send a letter saying that her sister still needed help to care for the children. Lora has written the letter, but I've changed the plan a bit. Father Bartholomé has addressed it in his own hand. He'll take it with him when he leaves today, seal it with his seal, and send it from the village as his own correspondence."

"How did you know about Father Bartholomé?"

"The summer before we were betrothed, my family came here for a month, as we did every summer. For some reason, I forgot to bring a book to read, so I approached Father after church one Sunday to ask if he had anything I might borrow. He'd only just been assigned here after his stay at St. John's Abbey, so his selection was small – a volume of verses and songs of the troubadours and a text on medicines and healing.

"Naturally, I chose the volume of poetry – far more romantic summer fare," she laughs. "But when I returned it, I asked him about the medical text and why he would have such a thing. That's when he told me about his sojourn at the abbey and how he had learned healing from the monks. There." She holds up her finished work. "All back as before. Let's go meet the servants and see Father Bartholomé off."

I follow her out, getting the lay of the land on this floor at least. It's odd to be learning my way around a new home. The master's chamber is at the end of the corridor, spanning the entire width of the floor – a large bedchamber and sitting area combined, with small dressing rooms on each side. Along each side of the corridor are other rooms of smaller proportions, judging by the placement of the doors. The main staircase descends from the center of the corridor toward what I learn, following Gwen downstairs, is the front entry hall, where Father Bartholomé is waiting.

"Ah, my son, I am pleased to see you looking so well." He shakes my hand. "I know your lovely wife has given you assurances of my discretion, but I would like you to know that my route home will in no way betray where I have been."

"Thank you, Father," I say. "For everything. I'm a lucky man indeed to have both you and this lovely lady looking out for me. I hope one day to find a way to repay you."

"Live a long and good life, my son. That is all the repayment I need. Now, I should be on my way if I am to be home before Evensong." As he opens the door to leave, I see his pony cart, hitched and ready, with a case that I assume must hold his herbs and medicines already stowed securely for the journey. "Send for me, my dear, if I'm needed for the birth," he calls to Gwen, then clucks to his horse to walk on.

Next, it's into the parlor to meet the servants. Gwen introduces Lora first, who curtseys and says simply, "M'lord."

Hamon is far more effusive. "Your Lordship, we are *so* pleased you're finally here. Lady Gwendolyn has always been a favorite hereabouts, and we so longed to meet her very special husband. And we are terribly glad you recovered from your illness. You were quite a fright that night when you first arrived."

"I must admit, I felt quite frightful as well, but I'm on the mend now, thanks to Father and some excellent broth and porridge from the kitchen here."

"My wife, Agnes, Your Lordship – your cook."

"I look forward to enjoying what comes from your kitchen, Agnes. And Hamon, in our family we tend to reserve the lordship address for formal events and visiting nobility. I'll be quite content with a simple sir . . . or a m'lord when you feel that's necessary."

"Thank you, sir," Hamon replies, bowing. "Thank you very much for that, m'lord," then turning to Gwen, "m'lady." I'm unaccustomed to this much deference and effusiveness from our servants. Most likely, though, Hamon's manner this morning stems from nervousness at meeting a new master for the first time. He seems more relaxed as he introduces his children who make up the rest of the staff.

These formalities taken care of, Osbert and Letty join us as Agnes and her children leave to get on with their day. Lora and Hamon remain. Gwen seems to have some other household business that requires attention. "Since we've had no time to work out the household arrangements before and since Alfred is now able to move into the master's chamber, I thought now would be a good time to sort things out. The dressing rooms in the master's chamber here are much smaller than we're used to and have no separate exit to the corridor. That makes it awkward for Osbert and Letty. Nurse is soon going to be very busy with the new baby in addition to young Edward. And Geoffrey has been railing at Nurse for several weeks now that he's a grown lad who can dress himself." This gets a laugh from everyone, especially Letty and Osbert who apparently are familiar with my eldest son's little outbursts.

"So here's what I propose. The front room next to ours becomes the nursery. Nurse can manage there with Edward and the new baby. Juliana gets the room next to ours on the back of the house, and Letty can sleep with her. Letty, you can help her if she needs anything before you come to me in the mornings. Geoffrey will share the next room on the back with Osbert. Geoffrey can dress himself to his heart's content, though I'd appreciate it, Osbert, if you'd see that he looks reasonably presentable each day and takes a bath like he's supposed to."

Osbert laughs. "I be a boy once meself, m'lady. I think mayhap he be much happier to listen to me than to someone he have to call Nurse." Which produces another round of laughter.

Gwen continues. "We'll use the corner room on the back for the school room. The one Alfred's been in should be aired out and made ready for whenever it's safe for us to welcome visitors. Does that suit everyone?" This is the first time she's actually been mistress of her own house. Watching and listening, I can see how well the role suits her.

"Very well, that's the easy part taken care of. Now I have to go mediate the debate among the children as to which dog sleeps with whom. Come, my love." She takes my hand. "I've no doubt some fatherly wisdom will help."

The terrace is the usual bustle of children and dogs at play – including a puppy. "Three dogs?" I ask Gwen.

"I didn't know how long we might be here or what havoc John might wreak with the kennel. So I sent Brother Eustace to bring back a young male of Brother Adam's choosing against the possibility we might have to stay here permanently or rebuild the kennel later."

Hearing our voices, the children immediately stop their play and surround me with squeals of "Papa, Papa!" Hugs and kisses complete, I sit on the steps with them. "I see we have a new member of the family."

"His name is Brumby," Geoffrey volunteers, "and he's a boy dog. Mama says that when he grows up maybe he and Primrose can have some puppies. I think that would be great fun."

"Well, we'll see when the time comes," I reply, tousling his hair.

Juliana sits next to me. "I'm so glad you're well now, Papa. Why didn't you get back in time to come here with us?"

"Well, dear, a man can't just leave the army whenever he wants to. It has to be at the right time. But we're all here now and that's what matters."

"I want to hear all about the army and the knights and the war," announces Geoffrey.

"Well, a lot of it is very boring or just hard work, Son. You ride all day, but you can't ride any faster than the archers can walk. And if the roads are dry and you're at the back of the column, you're always breathing the dust that the horses in front of you stirred up. Then you camp at night and eat food that isn't very good. And the next day you do the same thing all over again."

"Hmph." Geoffrey isn't impressed. "But then when you got where you were going, did you fight?"

"No, Geoffrey, my troops didn't fight. Our job was to watch the rear and the flanks to make sure no one sneaked up on us that way."

"That sounds boring."

"Actually, it's very important. It keeps the rest of the army from being surprised or surrounded. When you start your knight's training, you'll learn all about tactics and then you'll understand just how important the rear guard is." I'm doing my best to steer him away from talking about the fighting – he's far too young to hear about the terrible sights and sounds and smells of battle.

"So when I got back home and Uncle Rupert told me you had already left, I had to hurry to catch up." And I tell them the tale about my journey in search of them, making it seem, for their sakes, like I was just following to catch up. I make a very big deal of my adventure at the port – leaving out all the sickness and death – and when I come to the part where Star Dancer leapt into the river, they all squeal and laugh and clap their hands.

Young Edward tugs at my sleeve. "Papa?"

"Yes, Edward?"

"Papa, can I jump in the lake on my pony like that?"

I chuckle. "I don't think that would be a very good idea. You see, the river is very deep at the port, so Star Dancer couldn't get hurt. But the lake here is very shallow near the shore, so your pony could hurt himself very badly if he tried to jump in."

"Oh." He seems disappointed but satisfied with the explanation.

"Papa?" Geoffrey this time.

"Yes?"

"Osbert told us Star Dancer was so smart he brought you here all on his own when you got sick."

"Well, Star Dancer is smart alright. You see, he knows that where he sees light at night, there's probably a building. And he knows that where there's a building, there are probably people. And he knows that people give him oats. So he saw the lights in the windows here and thought to himself, 'I think I'll go get some oats.' And I came along for the ride."

"Papa?" Juliana.

"Yes?"

"Papa, do you have to go back to the army?"

"No, Juliana. We're all going to stay safely here for now. Things will be a bit different than they were at the manor. We don't have a village close by, so there won't be festivals or markets to go to. But there are lots of things we can do together, and we'll have a grand time."

"Papa," she continues, "did you know we're going to have a new baby brother or sister sometime soon?"

"Indeed we are. And we'll have to choose a very special name for the baby when it arrives. Now I think your mother has some more news for you." Gwen tells them about the new bedroom arrangements.

"We really get our own rooms, Mama?" asks Juliana.

"Well, you must share with Letty and Osbert, but you're old enough now to move out of the nursery."

"And I can dress myself," announces Geoffrey proudly.

"You can dress yourself." Gwen gives him a motherly smile. "But we have to decide which dog sleeps in which room."

"I want Brumby," Geoffrey doesn't hesitate. "We should have an all boys room. Me and Osbert and Brumby."

Gwen looks to her daughter. "Juliana? I didn't know if you wanted to train the puppy."

"I can train him anytime, Mama. It's Primrose I want to sleep with me."

"Well, that's nice," says Gwen, "because I think Willow is the perfect nursery dog. She practically raised young Edward."

"But I want a boy dog," Edward whines.

I pick him up and set him in my lap. "I'll tell you what. If Primrose ever has puppies, you can have first choice of the one you want. And in the meantime, you can go on pony rides with Osbert while your brother and sister are doing their schoolwork. What do you think of that?"

"I like pony rides," he beams, dogs temporarily forgotten.

"Now, I think we've tired your father enough for this morning," admonishes Gwen. "Back to your play."

The rest of the day is spent getting to know my new surroundings. There's a small study across from the parlor and a bright dining room with a view onto the terrace and the back garden. A path from the back of the garden leads into the woods – and presumably down to the lake.

Wandering over to the stable, I find that Osbert has just brought Star Dancer back from his daily exercise. The horse nickers softly at my approach, and I stroke his nose. "No apples today, I'm afraid, old friend, but it won't be long before we have nice fresh ones."

"There be oats in that barrel in the corner if ye be wanting to give him a handful."

As I walk back with a handful of oats, Osbert is removing Star Dancer's saddle. "It be all cleaned up fer ye now, sir. 'Twere a right mess after being out in the rain all that time." Not to mention going for a swim in the river, I think to myself. "But now I be thinking it look as good as new."

"That it does, Osbert. I must say, I don't know how you do it." I continue to stroke the horse's nose as Osbert finishes brushing him down. This magnificent beast - a gift from my grandfather for my fifteenth birthday - really did save my life. He could just as easily have stopped where he was when I fell asleep lying on his neck - stopped and waited for me to tell him what to do next. But instead, he kept on going, taking us both to safety. I'm reminded of what Lord Egon of the Territories said when I made a gift to him of one of Star Dancer's colts. "A man never knows when he will have to trust his life to the abilities and instincts of his mount. So we must earn their respect against such a day."

Tonight we retire early. "Now," says Gwen, snuggling close to me in our new bed, "tell me everything that's happened since the last time we were together like this."

And so I recount the whole adventure, including all my careful planning to find an opportunity to escape the king's clutches. When I come to the part about Samuel assuming the disguise of a monk - complete with tonsure - to carry my message to Egon, she laughs out loud. "Oh, my, I do so wish I could have seen the expression on Tamasine's face when he returned home."

"Tamasine won't know the nature of Samuel's errand - only his choice of disguise. It's safer that way," I remind her.

I tell her of John's inept military tactics and the cost it was taking on our troops, though I spare her the horrific details of the battle. I tell her how I took the third watch on the night before my troops were to lead the next day's charge so Donal and I could slip away in the dark, desertion being the only way I could keep my promise to Egon not to raise my sword against him. I tell her how we found more and more of the sickness as we rode east and how we began staying clear of the villages to avoid becoming ill ourselves. I tell her of my fear when I arrived home only to learn my family had left, telling no one where they were going. And unlike the story I spun for the children, I tell her all the grim details of my desperate ride north in search of them, including the clue that Osbert managed to leave with Richard despite not really knowing their final destination and being sworn to secrecy by Gwen. "I hope you'll forgive him for that."

She smiles. "I've no need to forgive what I was hoping he would find a surreptitious way to do."

As I tell the tale, I marvel at just how remarkable it was that all the small things necessary for me to make good my escape fell into place as and when I needed them – and how fortunate we are to have this refuge to ride out the storm of the remainder of John's reign. Our lovemaking this night is gentle and tender, reminding me in some ways of our wedding night – two people making a new life together in this, our new home. For how long, I know not . . . for several months . . . for a few years . . . perhaps even for the rest of our lives.

If I were cynical, I would long ago have concluded that the mysterious special destiny envisioned for me by my grandfather is nothing more than a continual progressive isolation from the affairs of the kingdom and the role of a scion of the royal house. The isolation imposed by my brother, King John, when he banished from court all the nobility save me and my family. Living at the royal manor as a guest of my Uncle Rupert, my only connection to events in the kingdom being through my mother's correspondence. And now, hiding in a foreign land, with only two people in the larger world knowing where I am.

When I occasionally lapse into total self-absorption – consumed by the feeling I've done nothing of any value since my father's death – Gwen is quick to remind me of the history of John's reign that I've been writing and the friendship I've begun with Lord Egon of the Territories. And while she's absolutely correct and it does lift my mood to acknowledge those achievements, I can't help but wonder if any of them can be maintained in the current circumstances or if they'll simply atrophy with time and continued isolation.

•　　•　　•　　•　　•

Shortly after I recovered from my illness, when Letty and Osbert were unpacking the last of the trunks, Gwen brought me the collection of things from my strongbox. Looking through the documents, I asked, "What about the chronicle?"

"I sent those pages to André for safekeeping, since he already had the earlier chapters. Brother Eustace took them when he went to fetch the puppy."

"Exactly what I would have done." And then I came across my father's letter — the one he'd left for me to read after his death. "Have you read this?"

She didn't answer directly. "When I was at my lowest - utterly unsure if what I was planning was the right thing - your mother encouraged me to read it. She said it would strengthen my resolve. I admit I thought about it, but in the end, I declined. Just knowing there was something in your father's words to give your mother confidence in my decision was enough to keep me going down the path I'd chosen. There was no need to intrude on the privacy of his last words to you."

I handed her the letter. "Your secret may very well have saved our lives. My secret may reassure you how very important that was. I think you should read it."

"Are you sure, Alfred?"

"I'm certain."

When she finished reading, she refolded it slowly and carefully and handed it back to me, her eyes brimming with tears. "I'm not sure I've ever told you how much I came to love and respect him. Like my own father, in fact." One of the tears escaped and ran down her cheek. As she reached to wipe it away, I took her in my arms, and we held each other tightly for a very long time.

And so, determined not to let my own lack of diligence leave future generations wondering what happened, I'm adding to the history, recording what I witnessed firsthand of the war and the sickness and the dissolution of the kingdom by the lords' withdrawing their loyalty pledges and reclaiming their hereditary domains. The kingdom over which John now reigns is vastly reduced in territory and population from the one in which I grew up. It retains the central area of what was once the larger kingdom - which includes the castle town, the port, and the monastery - and a narrow corridor along the Great Trunk Road leading to the border with the Kingdom of Peaks. The port is an invaluable asset, and Abbéville Market, which lies on the Great Trunk Road, will almost certainly remain the commercial and trading center for all the western domains. But I suspect John's lack of interest in commerce - believing it to be beneath the dignity of a king - means he'll never grasp the position of strength these assets provide and will continue to reduce their value by making access to them difficult. It's a recipe for conflict with our neighbors and more ruinous warfare. Thinking about it serves only to remind me that I may be unable to fulfill my father's exhortation to protect his and my grandfather's legacies.

Over the howling protests of both Geoffrey and Juliana, Gwen has insisted that each morning be devoted to schoolwork, though it's still summer. With the new baby due to arrive just before the harvest moon – the normal start of the school year – she knows it's unlikely there'll be time for a full day of schooling then. So she softened the blow by assuring the children that doing some schoolwork now means they'll have their afternoons free for play all the way until Christmas. But I've no doubt this is merely a way to get them used to some school year-round to keep their minds sharp despite living in isolation.

And while the children do their schoolwork, I do my own, trying not to forget the bits of the Territorial language I'd begun learning from Brother Eustace. Gwen brought many pages he'd prepared, including a small lexicon of words in both languages and written sentences of useful conversation with translations. I've started inventing imaginary conversations and attempting to conduct them in this new tongue – but it's slower going in the absence of an expert speaker.

Even young Edward is starting to learn his letters and numbers. One day he showed me very proudly how he could write his name. Shortly after this, Gwen mentioned, "I really think we need to stop referring to him as 'young Edward.'"

"It's probably time, but I'm curious what brought it up just now."

"He asked me the other day why it is that when he writes his name, he just writes Edward but when people talk about him they call him young Edward. 'Don't I need to write it all?' he asked. So I told him that Edward was also his grandfather's name and that when his grandfather was alive, we needed to know which Edward we were talking about. Apparently, he's been listening in on Juliana's history lessons, because his answer was, 'Oh, you mean King Edward. So does that make me Edward the second?' It was all I could to do keep a straight face and give him an explanation he would like."

So from now on, my younger son is simply Edward, tempted as I am to replace young with precocious when referring to him. I'm convinced he's going to give both Geoffrey and Juliana some serious competition in their studies.

As the warm days of summer progress, the children beg to be allowed to go to the lake for a swim or to go boating, but Gwen has strictly forbidden it to all but Hamon's family. "The villagers fish all up and down the lake from the last frost in spring until the first one in the autumn. And in summer, others come from the towns to the village for a bit of holiday. There are boats on the lake from early morning until nearly sundown. It would be far too easy for someone to get wind of our presence here if anyone unfamiliar is seen on the shore or on the path in the vicinity of this cottage."

In fact, even Hamon keeps close reins on which members of his family are allowed to venture beyond the immediate grounds around the house. Hamon buys food in the village, just as he's always done. He manages to get a bit extra now and again, but never so much that it would look like more than a bit of a splurge for his children. Hamon or Lora or Agnes go to the nearest town from time to time to buy whatever else we need. They don't go every market day, and it's not always the same one that goes. Sometimes Hamon goes alone; other times he takes one of the women; and occasionally, he drives both of the women there, but lets them do the shopping alone. We have food from our own kitchen garden as well, and Hamon, Osbert, and I occasionally go hunting to provide additional meat. So far as we can tell, we're succeeding in our efforts to avoid drawing attention to ourselves.

Summer has begun to wane and the equinox is just a few days away. Though she's never had a problem delivering her children, Gwen has been rather apprehensive about the impending birth. It will be the first time without the presence of midwives and the close proximity of the monastery's infirmerer. Agnes has done her best to allay those fears. "You rest easy, m'lady," she said one day. "I'll be with you; and I've birthed ten little ones, so I think I know a thing or two about getting them into this world safely. And don't you worry . . . Father Bartholomé's just across the lake if we need him." When the time comes, all Gwen's apprehension seems to fade away.

Osbert and I take the children for a long ride in the woods, down the track I'd followed on my journey here. At midday, we find a pretty grove and stop to enjoy the meal Agnes had packed for us. As a treat, I let each of them have a taste of small ale. Juliana wrinkles her nose at the unfamiliar flavor. Geoffrey pretends to like it, trying to appear grown up – though I can tell from the fact that he doesn't ask for more that it really is pretense. Edward screws up his face and spits his out on the ground.

Juliana wants to know the names of all the trees. "That one be an oak," Osbert points up to the canopy of the huge specimen closest to us. "'Twon't be long afore all this ground be covered with acorns and the squirrels be scurrying about hiding 'em away fer winter."

"Are they the same kind of acorns you had to eat when you were walking back home, Papa?" she asks, referring to my foraging as I made my way home from captivity so many years ago.

"Indeed they are."

"What do they taste like? Can we try one sometime?"

"You wouldn't like them when they've first fallen. They're really bitter. But after the autumn rains – when they've ripened a bit – some of them aren't too bad, especially if you've nothing else to eat."

She points out some other trees and Osbert identifies beech, elm, hawthorn, and a beautiful stand of ash. Edward starts running from tree to tree, leaning against the trunk and asking, "What's this one, Osbert?" When it begins to look like he'll never tire of the game, I call him back.

I get him to sit beside me and point to a smaller oak nearby that's already started to drop a few leaves. "Look up there. See all those things that look like balls of twigs up in the branches?" It takes him a moment to figure out what I'm talking about, but then he nods vigorously. "That's mistletoe. And at Yuletide, one of Hamon's sons will climb a tree and fetch some of it for us to hang in the house."

"Why, Papa?" he asks.

"Well, for one thing, it's very pretty."

"But it's for kissing too," Juliana chimes in. "If a gentleman sees a lady standing under the mistletoe, he has to kiss her."

"Ewwww." Geoffrey grimaces. "You won't catch me anywhere near the stuff. We won't have it in every room, will we, Papa?"

I chuckle. "That will be up to your mother and Lora, I'm afraid. Now, all of you go wander around the grove a bit. See what you can find."

"I want to climb a tree," whines Edward.

"Go with Osbert. I'll bet he can find you a small one to climb."

Juliana heads toward some late-blooming wildflowers she sees in the distance. Typically for a lad his age, Geoffrey is far more interested in the animal spoor. "There've been rabbits here," he pronounces before he's gone a dozen steps. "Come see, Papa." He doesn't wait for me to join him but charges on into the trees, then stops. "What's this?" He points to the ground near his feet and to a trail of small, oval-shaped black pellets leading deeper into the woods.

"Deer. Quite a herd of them, by the looks of it. We'll have to remember this grove when it's time for the harvest hunt."

"Can I go on the hunt too, Papa?"

"Let's wait until you're a little older and we can do a small hunt first – just you and me."

We follow the deer spoor for a bit, hoping to spot the herd, but at this time of day, they're most likely bedded down somewhere. When we return to the clearing, Juliana has collected a bouquet of flowers – "For Mama," she says – and Edward runs up squealing, "I sat in a tree, Papa. I sat in a tree." The sun has begun to lower in the western sky, so we have no choice but to mount up and head back to the cottage. I only hope we've been away long enough. Babies have their own, entirely unpredictable arrival schedules.

This one, however, seems to have come with very little fuss or bother. "She was here by midday," Lora greets us at the door. "Would you children like to meet your baby sister? You'll have to be nice and quiet, 'cause she might be sleeping, and we don't want to wake her up, now, do we?" They follow her up the stairs, surprisingly subdued.

Once the sibling introductions are complete, I go up to Gwen. Nurse has just brought the baby in for feeding. Gwen looks absolutely radiant – motherhood agrees with her.

We name her Alicia Marguerite, to honor her grandmothers. "Shouldn't it be Margaret Alicia?" I'd asked. "After all, we call Juliana after my grandmother, so shouldn't we honor your mother by calling this little one Margaret?"

"You forget," Gwen replies. "Two of my sisters already have daughters they call Margaret. One more would just be too many Margarets running around, and ours would wind up with some ridiculous nickname to distinguish her from the others. I'm sure Mother would agree."

So we call her Alicia. And as Gwen gives me the tiny creature to hold and I look at her beautiful face, I wish there were some way to let my own mother know that we've welcomed her namesake to our family. Her christening will have to wait until Father Bartholomé pays us a visit.

●　　　●　　　●　　　●　　　●

Autumn is especially colorful, living here surrounded by forest. Juliana makes a collection of leaves in the complete rainbow of the season. The apple trees are generous, and there is ample fruit for everyone, including Star Dancer. We have a successful hunt – Hamon and his sons, Osbert and me – and Agnes and her daughter dry and cure enough to take us through the coldest part of winter. With Christmas approaching, the cottage begins to take on a festive look as bits of holly and evergreen make their way inside and Hamon's sons drag home a large section of a fallen tree to be our Yule log. Gifts are sparse this year. Hamon has managed to find a small toy for each of the boys in one of the Christmas markets; Lora has embroidered a new kerchief for Juliana; we give a silver coin to each of our loyal servants. Our celebration consists mostly of a special feast prepared by Agnes and her daughter that we all enjoy together – most especially the scrumptious fruit pies that Agnes managed to keep as a surprise for everyone.

Even though the New Year has passed and Twelfth Night is just two days away, there has as yet been very little snow. There are still patches of it on the ground in places where the anemic winter sun doesn't easily reach, but much of the ground is clear. The trees of the forest, bare of their summer canopy, look like an army of tall, dark sentries standing guard around our cozy cottage, and we can see for greater distances in every direction between their still, silent forms. Today being sunny, it seems a good time to take Star Dancer out for a bit of late morning exercise while the children are using the schoolroom as a winter playground and Gwen helps Nurse with the baby.

I'm halfway down the stairs when the front door bursts open and Hamon's youngest son rushes in. "Papa! Papa! Come quick!" He's clearly been running some distance. Hamon and Lora are there in an instant, as I bound down the last of the steps.

"Horsemen, Papa." He gasps for breath. "On the western road. Three of them. Moving fast. This direction."

I don't hesitate – we haven't much time. "Lora, upstairs. Get everyone into the master's chamber and lock the door. Open it to no one but me. No one, d'you understand?" She nods her head, already starting up the stairs. "And tell Gwen to do her best to keep the baby quiet."

"Osbert!" He nearly runs over Lora in his haste to get down the stairs. "My sword and dagger. Get them and meet me upstairs. Bow and some arrows if they're handy, but there's no time to waste.

"Alright, Hamon. Calm as you can be, try to send them on their way. If they want to know why the house is open, you're expecting Lord Godwin and Lady Margaret and have gotten things ready for them."

"Aye, m'lord, but what if they start looking about and find the carriage in the barn?"

"Very well, Godwin and Margaret are here for Christmas but have gone to the village for the day. Can you manage?"

"Aye, m'lord."

"Osbert and I will be upstairs in the guest room listening. If you can't get rid of them we'll think of something. Just be as calm and as normal as you possibly can. Take your time opening the door." As I dash up the stairs, I can hear the faint but unmistakable sound of hoofbeats in the distance growing louder with each passing moment.

The hoofbeats stop below us. Then the sound of boots on the front steps followed by a loud knock on the door. Hamon's measured pace making his way from the kitchen. The slow turning of the latch and the sound of the door being partially opened. Hamon's voice, surprisingly calm, "Good day, gentlemen. How may I be of service?"

Then a voice that is oddly familiar. "May we come in, Hamon?"

Hamon's reply shows he's clearly flustered. "M'lord? What? Who are these men with you?"

Again, the oddly familiar voice. "Friends, Hamon. All is well."

And then a voice I would know anywhere, raised to be heard throughout the grounds, "Alfred, it's Samuel. We know you're here. Are you planning to let Richard and me – not to mention your father-in-law – freeze to death on your front steps?"

Followed by, "Come on, Alfred." Richard's voice this time. "A glass of brandy or some hot cider would go down well to warm us up just now."

Still wearing my sword and dagger on my belt, I quickly leave the guest room and go to the stairs. "It's alright, Hamon. I do know these two renegades and am pretty certain they haven't taken Lord Godwin hostage."

Clearly relieved, Hamon opens the door widely and invites our guests inside as I descend. He then calls for his sons to take charge of the horses as the new arrivals begin to shed their gloves and cloaks.

"I'm sorry to have given you such a fright, my son," says Godwin, "but the news these two brought me couldn't wait for a secret message from Margaret to Lora."

"The king is dead," says Samuel solemnly. Before I can even take this in, both he and Richard go down on one knee, heads bowed, and Richard says, "Long live the king."

I'm stunned. Completely and utterly speechless. The little tableau is finally disturbed when Osbert comes down the stairs asking, "What yer mates be doing on their knees, m'lord?" shaking me out of the stupor that had temporarily overtaken me.

"That, Osbert," I reply with a grin, "is a most excellent question. Get up, you two. I'm going to need some time to grasp all this, but first I need to free Gwen and the family from captivity in our bed chamber."

Turning to Godwin, "Sir, if you'll show them into the parlor, I'm sure Hamon can find some of that brandy or cider Richard was carrying on about."

I take the stairs two at a time, fumbling with my dagger and sword, trying to remove them, followed by Osbert, who's trying to collect them. My hand shakes as I raise it to knock on the door. "Gwen, it's alright. You can let everyone out now." She must have been standing at the door listening, for the key immediately turns in the lock, and she opens the door a crack, making absolutely sure there's no one behind me in the corridor.

"Was that Father's voice I heard?"

"It was. Richard's and Samuel's as well. Leave the children with Nurse. You need to hear this."

"Hear what, Alfred?"

"I'm not even fully sure myself, but it was enough for your father to bring Richard and Samuel galloping here without even sending us a message to let us know they were coming. Let's go down and find out."

As we enter the parlor, Gwen rushes to embrace her father. "My dear," he says, "you are undoubtedly more beautiful every time I see you." She moves on to Richard and Samuel, kissing each of them on the cheek.

The steward has served brandy all around and offers me one as well. "Thank you, Hamon. I think I just might need this."

"Hamon, do you think Agnes can accommodate three more hungry mouths for the midday meal?" asks Godwin.

"Aye, m'lord. Will you be wanting to eat in here, sir?"

"I think that's probably an excellent idea if Gwen has no objections," Godwin replies. "My dear?"

"None at all," she answers.

"And Hamon – the nicest wine you have in the cellar."

"Aye, m'lord." And he's off to see to the arrangements, closing the parlor door behind him.

"Very well, Richard . . . Samuel. I'm still struggling to take all this in. Why don't you start from the beginning."

"It's true, Alfred," Richard begins, then hesitates. "Can I still call you that?"

"Don't be ridiculous. Of course you can. We'll worry about formalities of address when the occasions demand, but right now I need to be talking to friends."

Gwen looks around, totally perplexed.

"It's true," Richard resumes. "John's dead. Stabbed twelve times in his bed in the middle of the night, the twelve daggers left on the bed beside the body."

"Have the perpetrators been found?"

"No one has any idea who did it. No one claims to have even heard of a plot."

"What about the daggers? Who did they belong to?"

"There's no way to know," Samuel replies this time. "All the knights were searched and all were in possession of their daggers."

"The King's Own Guard? Where were they in all this?" I ask.

"They were searched too." Samuel again. "And every man had his full complement of arms. Where they were when the killing happened is a complete mystery.

"It's really no surprise, though, that no one is missing a dagger. There were so many arms brought back from the battlefield – far more than would be needed by the corps of knights who survived. Those twelve daggers could have been taken from the stores without anyone ever noticing."

"So John survived the battlefield," I remark.

"Yes," answers Samuel. "But not victoriously. His army – what was left of it by then – there were so many desertions after the dissolution of the kingdom – anyway, his army was routed and then pursued as they retreated back across the border. They came home in utter defeat."

"We've heard," says Richard, "that John was ruthless with his captains, demoting or dismissing all of them."

"I can't say I'm surprised," I comment. "He refused to listen to them on the battlefield, but I'm sure he would never admit the defeat was in any way his fault."

"Even though he wasn't killed in battle," Samuel picks up the thread again, "he was very happy to let everyone believe that you were."

"Well, he certainly wouldn't have wanted it known that I'd deserted, though he couldn't have failed to be aware of it since I was supposed to lead the forward elements in that day's attack."

"It also explains why he did nothing to look for you," says Richard. "There's no need to search for a man who's dead, and a brother who's dead can't threaten one's position or power. So when the king was found murdered, the bishop sent for Lord Rupert, believing him to be the heir."

"What about John Gundar?" I ask.

"Dead of the sickness."

"Are you certain?" I have to be sure.

"Absolutely," Richard replies. "When the sickness began to abate in the port and people started venturing about a bit, there were repeated complaints about a horrible smell in the vicinity of the queen's house. The undertaker and his helper broke in and found the bodies. Four men, presumably the guards. A fifth man in priest's garb. A woman dressed in black from head to toe. Three children. Apparently the servants had fled when the sickness appeared. The occupants of the house had been dead for quite some time, it seems.

"A crowd had gathered in the street, and when the undertaker said he intended to remove the bodies, the crowd took over, throwing stones through the windows and torches through the broken panes. They didn't stop until the whole interior was engulfed in flames. There's nothing left there now but the stone shell of the building. I saw it, Alfred, as I passed through the port on my way to meet Rupert."

"Oh my God!" Gwen gasps, the implication of everything she's just heard dawning on her.

"Yes, my dear," says Godwin. "It seems that Alfred's destiny is to rule, as did his father and his grandfather before him."

She reaches for my hand, and her own is shaking, much as mine was earlier.

Samuel picks up the story. "Lord Rupert sent messengers summoning Richard and me to meet him at the castle. By the time we arrived, he had convinced the bishop that we had to be absolutely sure you hadn't survived before declaring the next king. The day we arrived was the day of John's funeral. Rupert gave him a proper burial, but without any ceremony other than the religious rites. Then he sent us off in search of you."

"He was certain," Richard says, "as were Father and I, that you'd gone to Gwen's parents, so that's where we headed. Fortunately, Rupert thought to provide us with a letter from the bishop confirming John's death, else we might not be here today."

Godwin chuckles as Richard continues. "This fine gentleman," inclining his head toward Godwin, "wouldn't even admit to us that he had any idea if you were dead or alive until his own bishop verified the seal and read the letter."

"I'm grateful, sir," I tell Godwin. "I'd trust these two with my life – as I have you – but you'd have had no way of knowing that."

"Well, once I was sure, I couldn't get them here fast enough. It seemed like it took twice the normal time to get here, even though we pushed the horses as much as we dared."

"And now we need to get you and your family back home," says Richard, "so that you can be properly crowned."

"All in good time, my friend. I need more than just these few minutes to absorb the enormity of what this means. Rupert will have everything under control at home, and we need to plan properly for the family's journey. After all, we do have a rather small one whose needs we'll have to consider."

Godwin's eyes light up at the mention of the baby. "Ah, yes, my newest grandchild!"

"A girl, Father," Gwen supplies.

"And when do I get to meet the little princess?"

My daughter a princess? This is definitely going to take some getting used to.

Just then, Hamon, Lora, and Agnes arrive with the food and wine. While Hamon pours and Agnes arranges things on the sideboard, Gwen speaks to Lora, "Would you ask Nurse to bring the children down? Including the baby? Tell them they're getting a few minutes to greet their grandfather and then they can have their meal."

We're soon invaded by the full menagerie – happy squealing children, three dogs, and Nurse carrying a whimpering bundle. "She just waked up, m'lady, so she's hungry."

The older children crowd around Godwin, all three trying to tell him everything at once, including the fact that they have a new baby sister. Gwen walks over to her father and hands him the baby. "Your newest granddaughter – Alicia Marguerite. We call her Alicia."

"Thank heaven!" Godwin chuckles. "We couldn't manage yet another Margaret in the family. Your mother will be relieved."

Alicia is quiet for a bit, studying this strange new face above her. Then hunger wins out over curiosity and she lets out a demanding wail. "I think she wants her mother," says Godwin, handing the baby back to Gwen.

"I'll just step across to the study and feed her. Now children, you'll have plenty of time later this afternoon to tell your grandfather everything you've been up to since we've been here. Go along with Nurse now and have your meal. I won't be long, gentlemen, but do help yourself to some food."

Though I put food on a plate, I'm not the least bit hungry. The others are ravenous. After the first sip of wine, Godwin pronounces, "This stuff just keeps getting better with age. Hamon certainly knows how to manage a cellar."

"Hamon and his family – Lora too – have been a godsend, sir. They've looked after our needs and protected us when Gwen and I both felt the most vulnerable ever in our lives. I must tell you though, it was your daughter who got us here safely and in complete secrecy and who's been like a mother bear protecting cubs when it comes to maintaining that secrecy. None of us have even been down to the lake.

There's no doubt I owe my life to her and to your incredible foresight. I've no idea how to express the fullness of my gratitude."

"Be a good king, Alfred . . . like your father. That's all the gratitude I need."

Suddenly it dawns on me. Richard is here, hale and hearty. "Speaking of survival, Richard, did the sickness ever come to Devereux Castle?"

"We were lucky," he replies. "It made it to Neukirk Market but seemed to stop there. We saw no sign of it at the castle or in the village below."

"That's an enormous weight off my mind. I contracted it on the second day after I left you and have been fearful ever since that I might have been responsible for bringing it into your midst."

"You had the sickness and survived?" Samuel sounds incredulous.

"Thanks to a remarkable priest and his amazing knowledge of healing."

"Ah," says Godwin. "Father Bartholomé. A remarkable man indeed."

"Is it still rampant in the kingdom?" I ask.

"Amazingly, no," answers Richard. "It raged through the spring and most of the summer and then just disappeared. We've not heard of a case since . . ."

"At least since the equinox . . . perhaps a bit earlier," Samuel supplies.

"That's exactly what Father Bartholomé said would happen. And he said we won't see it again for decades – perhaps even a hundred years or more. One less problem facing us, thank heaven."

Gwen returns, serves herself some food, and rejoins the conversation. "I've been thinking. You need to get home as soon as possible, Alfred. You should go on with Richard and Samuel. Father, would you mind too terribly much staying here a few more days and then traveling back with us as far as your manor?"

"I would be delighted, my dear."

"Osbert can stay as well," I interject. "You'll need him for the rest of the journey."

"You'll need him too," she says. "Hamon's sons can come along with us. Now that we don't have to worry about John's agents, they'll be quite sufficient to our protection. One of them can drive the carriage and the other can drive a wagon to carry our baggage. Since we'll be taking Lora and Father back home, the carriage is going to be even more crowded than on the trip here."

"Alfred," says Godwin, "if your party leaves just at midday tomorrow, that will put you in a town with an inn for the night. Unless the weather suddenly turns foul, you should then have an inn each night. Your mates here know the best ones, and you yourself know the journey south."

"Then it sounds as if we have a plan," I agree. "Best we ask the servants in and let them know what's up."

It's obvious Hamon has already broken the news—everyone is all bows and curtseys as they come in the room. "Thank you for that," I tell them. "But we're no different now than when you helped us start our day earlier this morning. There'll be formal occasions when those rituals will be necessary, but you're part of our family, and that's not going to change."

Osbert speaks up. "I be talking with Donal back when we be together, m'lord. He be telling me everything I be needing to know to be squire to a king. See, we both be thinking even then that ye be king one day."

I clap him on the shoulder and give him a big grin, "Well, it seems you and Donal and my grandfather had things all figured out." It's time to go tell the children we're going home.

"Papa?" asks Juliana. "Does this mean we can't call you Papa any more?"

"Of course not, my dear. I am still and always will be your Papa."

"Papa?"

"Yes, Geoffrey?"

"Does this mean I'm a prince now?"

"You and Edward are both princes and your sisters are princesses." Telling him any more than this right now would just cause him to lord it over his brother. I'll have to introduce him to his new role slowly and carefully. "And when you're sixteen, people will begin calling you Lord Geoffrey."

"Does that mean Juliana will be Lady Juliana before I'm Lord Geoffrey?"

"It does indeed. But you'll be called Lord before Edward is. That's just how the rules work." He seems satisfied.

This is all a bit beyond Edward's comprehension, but he nevertheless has a question. "Do I get to be Lord before Alicia gets to be Lady?"

"That's right."

He crosses his arms over his chest in a gesture that's a combination of pride and smugness. "Good. I'm glad I'm not last anymore."

"Alright," says Gwen, "no more school until we get back home." Which pronouncement is met with cheers of joy. "We need to start packing up to travel. Nurse will tell you what you need to do."

"Mama?" asks Juliana.

"Yes, dear?"

"Will we ever come back here?"

Gwen glances at me before answering, and I give her a smile and a nod in response. "I'm sure we will, dear. It's a very pleasant place. And the next time we come, we can go down to the lake and maybe even take a boat across to the village on the other side."

By bedtime, we're both exhausted from the sheer emotional toll of the day. "I'd like to use the remainder of the silver coins we brought from the manor to make gifts to Hamon and Lora," ventures Gwen.

"Of course. Is there enough for a donation to Father Bartholomé's church as well?"

"I think so. I'll leave a small purse with Hamon to take to the good Father next time he goes to the village." She snuggles quietly for a moment, then, "Alfred?"

"Yes, my love?"

"Do you think we really will be back here from time to time?"

"I certainly hope so."

We fall asleep in each other's arms. Tomorrow our new lives begin in earnest.

When we let the horses run like they want to – they're frisky in the cold winter air – conversation is impossible. We slow them to a trot or a walk frequently, though. I don't want to overtax Star Dancer, who's older than either Richard's or Samuel's mount, and we want to ensure they don't break into a sweat that would chill them excessively.

They both want to hear how I managed to escape John's clutches and wind up in the cottage on Lake St. Anne. Without a word passing between us, Samuel and I both omit our parts in warning Lord Egon, mentioning only that Samuel was doing a private errand for me as a reason for his monastic disguise. Richard roars with laughter as I describe it.

"Please let's just keep this to ourselves," Samuel pleads. "Tamasine made me wear a hat everywhere – even a nightcap in bed – until my hair grew out. Said she couldn't sleep with a monk . . . not even a pretend one. I'd just as soon she were never reminded of that little episode." His extremely effective way of making sure no one starts asking inconvenient questions.

"Your secret is safe with me, Brother Samuel," Richard replies playfully, but we both know he's serious.

Samuel wants to hear about the conduct of the war up until the time I deserted. He nods knowingly when I describe Egon's blocking force in the narrow valley and my assumption that the larger army was arrayed on the plain below. "How could John not have used his scouts properly?" asks Richard.

"For the same reason he refused to listen to me, to his commander, or to his captains," I reply. "Convinced he knew best. Focused only on what was right before his eyes."

We ride along in silence for a bit, my mind processing what I've heard over the last two days. Finally, I broach the topic that's been bothering me. "Samuel, you said John convinced everyone that I'd been killed in battle."

"That's right," he replies. "I had no idea you might still be alive until Rupert told me."

"That must mean, then, that every man in both my troops was slaughtered that day." They acknowledge my assertion in silence. "They were good men, Samuel. Loyal to their captain – loyal to their king. They would have fought well and many would have survived if there'd been a better battle strategy. They didn't deserve their fate."

"Nor did any who lost their lives on that misbegotten mission," says Samuel quietly.

"Mourning the fate of your men does you credit, Alfred," says Richard, "but you mustn't forget one important thing. John's *intent* that day was that you be among the dead. The men who were lost could not have rebuilt the kingdom. You can." We ride on in a sober mood until we reach the inn.

By the next day, my mind has started to grapple with some of the urgent things that will need attention. Rebuilding the kingdom – even one as small as what remains – will require money and people I can trust. "I have no idea what all those knights and armaments and supplies for the invasion cost – not to mention what it must have cost to feed them all beforehand. I'm really worried about what state the Treasury might be in," I tell my friends.

"Richard, I know it's asking a lot – especially since it's no longer a Devereux concern – but could I persuade you to stay long enough to help sort it out? You can figure out where we stand and what needs to be done much more quickly than I could either do it myself or find someone capable."

"Don't give it a second thought, Alfred. Of course I'll help you."

"You could send for Avelina and the children if you like. There'll be plenty of room at the castle."

"Let's just see what we find and then decide."

"I'm going to need your advice, too, Samuel. Most urgent – before Gwen and the family arrive would be my preference – is the matter of the King's Own Guard. I'll have none of those in John's Guard, and Mauger has to go, of course."

"There's someone I want you to meet," says Samuel. "When Rupert told me what had happened, I sent for Sir Tobin. He should be at the castle by the time we arrive."

"That name sounds vaguely familiar."

"It would. He took over from me as commander of the garrison. When John ordered the two garrison troops into his invasion force, he put Tobin in charge as captain.

"Tobin's the son of one of Father's tenants. Followed me into the knighthood . . . three, maybe four years later. He's the only captain who abandoned the fray after the dissolution of the kingdom. We talked at great length when he returned. He was in terrible turmoil about his decision to come home. On the one hand, he felt he'd dishonored his rank; on the other, he brought quite a number of Ernle knights and many foot soldiers out with him and felt he'd done right to save their lives. The thing he said to me so often was, 'Such a terrible waste of lives . . . and for a purpose none of us understand.' Father put him in charge at the garrison. He's a good man, Alfred, who would choose good men to surround you."

"I'll speak to him straightaway . . . just as soon as we've dealt with the formalities.

"The next thing I'm going to need is a few good engineers. We have to get the port back in operation. If it's continued to deteriorate from what I saw six months ago, the equipment will need refurbishing, the docks may need repair . . . who knows what else may be necessary. Your father and I will have to negotiate how to manage the reservoir, but I'm sure it needs an immediate inspection. I rather doubt it's been properly maintained over the last couple of years."

"As I recall, Gamel is a more-than-competent engineer, and he'll know others. In fact, I believe Ronan trained him, and you know what an excellent engineer Ronan is," replies Samuel.

"Isn't Gamel Montfort's tenant now? Assuming he's still alive?" I ask.

"That may be the case," says Samuel. "But don't make the assumption that he wouldn't want to serve you. Free men move from place to place when it suits them. He can always decline."

"Well, that's a little harder to do when it's a king making the request," I chuckle.

"Then ask Laurence to do it. He might be able to give Gamel some assurance about his future once he leaves your service, and that might make the decision easier."

I let the conversation wander to other topics for a bit. When we're not discussing matters of governing the kingdom, Osbert joins in as usual. At midday, we give ourselves and the horses a rest and some food. Once we're back on our way, I broach the topic I've been dreading. "I've saved the worst for last, mates. I suspect the knighthood is in complete disarray. I saw many walk away, back to their lords, and I'm sure those numbers increased as things got worse. Scores were killed before I left – I can't imagine how many more afterward. Were any taken prisoner? How many did John dismiss? Of the ones left, who was conscripted? Who volunteered? Who became a knight as an honorable pursuit? Who for blood lust? Have they been paid? What have they been doing for the last few months? Were they loyal to John personally? The whole lot needs to be sorted out and rebuilt. Rebuilt with honor. As a force for safeguarding the peace, but with the skills to defend the kingdom should that ever be necessary. It's an enormous undertaking."

I urge Star Dancer to a canter to give them time to think about the problem. Slowing him to a trot, I remark, "Louve has to go, of course," and let that hang in the air for a while.

"There's only one person I know that I'd trust to do this right. Samuel, this is asking a lot of you as well . . . but is there any way I could convince you to be my knight commander? I know how happily you've settled into your new life, and I wouldn't blame you at all if you didn't want to disrupt that."

"I think—" Samuel starts to answer but I interrupt.

"One other thing. I'm not asking as a king. This is just a simple question, one friend to another, and I want you to answer in the same spirit."

"I think," Samuel resumes, "that maybe this is part of what both our lives have been leading up to. Yes, I've been content running my little farm. But Ronan can take care of it for a while, and it will be there for me to go back to at the right time. If Tamasine and the family can come to court – like in the old days – then I'll rebuild your knight corps for you."

The horses have slowed to a walk. I reach across and shake Samuel's hand. "Thank you, my friend. It's a tremendous weight off my mind. We are absolutely going to return to a proper court. You can send for your family right away . . . or if you'd rather go tell them in person, that's entirely your choice."

Turning to Richard, I add, "I'm sure you can figure out if the knights have been paid. I'm just as worried about what John may have promised them in the way of pensions or bonuses related to the war or other compensation. It won't surprise me in the least if there's no record of any of it, so you may have to get the magistrates involved to sort out the legalities."

"As I was listening to your litany of questions," Richard replies, "I was thinking about just those things. It's also possible we'll be able to do something with all that excess materiel to put some funds back in the Treasury. It will take us a while to sort that out, Alfred, but we'll work on it. And since you're planning a proper court, I think I will put the proposition to Avelina."

"I know having a proper court will add to the expense for the Treasury, but I'm also convinced it will help rekindle the economy in the town and put people back to work. So I'm looking at the expense as an investment in rebuilding the kingdom overall. Besides, having no one at court is just deadly dull," I add with a laugh.

We let the horses have their heads for a while. Suddenly Samuel pulls up short. "Oh my God! I completely forgot!"

Richard and I rein in our mounts and circle back, wondering what could possibly be wrong.

"I can't be your knight commander, Alfred," Samuel says, a very sad look on his face.

"Why, Samuel? What's wrong?" He has me worried now.

"I have absolutely no idea what I'm supposed to say in that pledge I'll have to make in a couple of days," he replies in all seriousness . . . and then breaks into a big grin.

"That, my friend, can be remedied," I assure him.

"Better write it down for him," laughs Richard, "so he gets it right. Otherwise instead of a knight commander, you'll just have a tongue-tied knight."

How I've missed these easy interactions with my mates! It will be good to have them at court again.

When we reach the border, the roads change dramatically. It's painfully obvious nothing's been done to them since the last time I was here. "We've become accustomed to riding on the verges wherever we go," remarks Richard.

The border control camp lies just ahead. "I suspect they won't do more than poke their heads out of their tents to see if we have any wagons or carriages," says Richard. "That's what happened on the way north. I'm not sure anyone's bothered to tell them this territory is no longer part of the kingdom."

As predicted, two heads look out, study us briefly, then retreat back into whatever warmth the tents provide. "Any of these camps that are left need to be dismantled and the men recalled right away," I remark.

"Father's already disbanded the one on the border with the Territories," replies Samuel. "Gave the men a choice to join the garrison or go back to their homes, wherever that might be. I'll take care of the rest of them straightaway."

The weather has smiled on us, and we've made the journey quickly. Now, as we turn from the Great Trunk Road onto the road leading to the castle, we stop, looking at the imposing presence of the castle before us, each communing with his own thoughts. I recall my father's words in his final letter to me: *You are as well prepared as anyone could be to cope with the coming challenges and to find ways to make things better for our people.* He'd meant during John's reign, and yet I know the challenges of picking up the pieces are at least as great. I recall Grandfather's words long ago: "No one can take what's in your mind, Alfred. And even in the face of what might seem the worst catastrophe, you can use what's in your mind to rebuild." As soon as we pass through the castle gates,

I'll be committed to that rebuilding and to making things better throughout the realm. It's a humbling thought. I only hope their belief in me isn't without merit.

At last, Samuel turns to me and says, "Are you ready?" His words take me back to a day years ago . . . the first time he was sent to bring me home.

"I can't do it alone, my friends, but with your help . . ." I pause. "I think it's time we make a start."

There's a proper watch posted with sentries at the gate, who greet us at attention and immediately send a runner to the inner courtyard. We arrive at the front entrance to a small welcoming party: Matthias, the steward, a knight I've never met, and three grooms from the stable. As I dismount and approach, the knight comes forward, clicks his heels together, bows smartly, and says, "Your Grace." It's the first time I've heard this address. "Welcome home. Sir Tobin at your service. With Lord Rupert's permission, I've taken the liberty of arranging a proper watch, Sire. I hope it meets with your approval."

"Thank you, Sir Tobin. It does. Sir Samuel told me he'd sent for you. I'd very much like a private word with you later."

"As you wish, Sire."

The grooms take the horses, and we follow Matthias up the steps and through the door. "Matthias, my old friend, I can't tell you how delighted I am to see you're still in charge here."

"And we're all ever so glad you're back, Your Grace."

"Matthias, all that Your Grace business was John's way, not mine. Speak as you did with my father, and we'll all be much happier."

"Thank you, sir. I think maybe your mates here are near enough to family I can treat this as a private occasion."

"They are, indeed, Matthias." I give him a broad smile. At least the running of the household won't be a chore for Gwen. The steward will have things back to normal in little time at all.

"Now, sir, Lord Rupert said I was to bring you to the private reception room as soon as you arrived. Osbert, we have your lord's old rooms made ready again. When John told us you'd been killed, sir, he said we had to clear everything out. So I packed it all up for Lady Gwendolyn, but now we've put it all back just as you left it. And Donal brought your things from the manor so Osbert and Donal can finish sorting things out."

"Oh, no!" wails Osbert. "Dinna' tell me those old boots I try so hard to get rid of still be here." Everyone gets a good laugh at my expense.

"I think, Osbert, that it may finally be time to dispose of those boots." Osbert grins and heads off to find Donal.

As we make our way to the reception room, the steward keeps up a steady conversation. "We've done nothing with the king's apartments, sir, other than what Lord Rupert asked. We wanted to wait for the queen."

"She and the children – and the dogs – will be here in a few days. They had to pack and won't be able to travel as fast as we could on horseback."

"Nona brought her things from the manor as well, sir, and things for the nursery."

"She'll be pleased." Then something occurs to me. "Matthias, I do hope you've already gotten rid of the bed where John was killed. I don't want Gwen to have to deal with that."

"'Twas Lord Rupert's first request, sir. You needn't fret. And we've scrubbed the room from floor to ceiling. There's nothing to cause the queen any distress."

As we approach the closed door to the reception room, I take a deep breath. Matthias rushes forward to open it for me. The first thing I notice is that Rupert has restored the comfortable furnishings from my father's time and removed the throne John insisted on having here. As quickly as I take that in, I realize the room is filled with people I hadn't expected to see. All the hereditary lords are here. I freeze in my tracks just inside the door. The murmur of conversation stops abruptly. And then the bishop rises from his seat and says quietly but clearly, "The king is dead. Long live the king."

My uncle walks across the room, drops to one knee in front of me, head bowed, and recites the ancient pledge of loyalty. I reach my hand out to him as he rises, and we embrace. Lord Devereux immediately follows suit and then each of the others in turn, uniting the kingdom once again with their voluntary pledges. Finally, Samuel makes the knight commander's pledge, and when we break our embrace, I announce, "Gentlemen, our new knight commander, Sir Samuel Ernle." His father beams with pride.

Through all the formalities, my mother has sat quietly, the consummate dowager queen. Now I cross quickly to her as she rises to smother me with hugs and kisses. She seems older than the last time I saw her, much as my grandfather seemed to age while I was in captivity. Breaking into my thoughts, she begins asking after the grandchildren. "They're on their way . . . just a few days," I assure her.

"The baby?"

"A girl. Alicia Marguerite. We call her Alicia."

And then the room bursts into a hubbub of conversation. I manage to speak with each of the lords individually, thanking them for their perseverance. Normally sad occasions, coming as they do in the immediate aftermath of the death of a well-loved sovereign, this gathering has a more festive air.

"Ladies and gentlemen," I raise my voice slightly to be heard over the conversation. "If you'll excuse me, I'd like to shed these traveling clothes and the grime of the road. Matthias?" The steward comes scurrying in from the outer chamber.

"Do you think you could arrange a decent supper for all of us? It need not be fancy. But if there's any of father's good wine left in the cellar, we should serve it tonight. The lords have done something quite special today, and I want to honor them for it."

"I hid away as much of your father's cellar as I could before your brother took a personal interest, Sire. I'm sure there's something quite suitable. Where would you like to dine?"

"Perhaps here? It's quite comfortable and easier to have good conversation than in the formal dining hall." I gesture to the others and get nods and "ayes" all around. "Here, then, Matthias."

Rupert follows me out into the corridor. "Welcome home, Alfred. There's something you should know."

"What's that, Uncle?"

"I did no more than send each of them a message that you were alive and that I had sent for you. Everything else was their own initiative. I don't know if it was planned in advance. I do how much confidence and personal loyalty they have for you."

"I must admit I was stunned. Did the surprise show on my face?"

"More than a little," he chuckles. "But I was looking around the room. I think they were all rather pleased by that."

"Uncle, there's so much I have to thank you for and so much we need to discuss."

"There'll be ample time for that in the coming days. Refresh yourself and honor your guests tonight."

"One thing first. Tell me your impression of Sir Tobin. Samuel recommended him to captain the Guard. I'm talking with him before supper."

"Samuel told me why he'd sent for him, but I don't think Tobin knows. He asked my permission first, but he wasted no time sorting out and organizing three troops to man the watch."

"I noticed. That part of coming home felt like the old days. Do you know how the men respond to him? If they respect him?"

"Not firsthand. But those three troops he's organized seem as sharp as any I've seen."

"Good. Now for the first decent bath I've had in days, and then we'll see if Tobin and I will get on."

Walking the corridors to our old apartment feels comfortable and comforting. I find a bath ready, and Osbert and Donal deep in conversation. As I shed my clothes and climb into the bath, they reveal what they've been plotting. "See, m'lord," says Osbert, "we be thinking ye be saying it not be proper ye have two squires. That be too much like yer brother and his haughty ways."

"And it be right and proper," Donal picks up, "that Osbert be yer squire, m'lord. But Osbert be thinking mayhap ye need some extra help with young Geoffrey now ye be king and not have so much time to spend with him. And I be serving Lady Alice these past months, and I think she be liking that a lot."

"So we be wondering," Osbert again, "if mayhap Donal could stay on to serve Lady Alice and when she not be needing him, mayhap Donal could be helping me with Geoffrey . . . and soon with Edward."

"It seems to me," I tell them, "that one thing I *won't* have to do is spend any time worrying about such things. You've found the perfect solution, and I know Mother will be pleased. Geoffrey is feeling his oats as a boy. He needs room to try things and learn, but he also needs to be guided. When Richard's and Samuel's families come back to court, he'll have other boys to do things with. But there'll be the progress and patrols and even state visits, meaning Osbert will be gone as much as I am. If you're up for it, Donal?"

"I be happy to stay with yer family, m'lord," he replies.

"One thing, Donal."

"Aye, m'lord?"

"Geoffrey doesn't know yet about his new status as the heir. He's quite pleased to be a prince, and that's enough for now. Since he's had no experience of life at a proper court, he needs to watch me in my new role before we burden him with what it all means for him later in life. Let's just let him be a boy for now."

"Aye, m'lord," they both reply, and Osbert adds, "But what if other children tell him he be the heir?"

"I wouldn't worry too much about that, Osbert. Children tell each other things all the time. When Geoffrey decides to ask me about it, I'll give him a proper explanation and start teaching him how to behave with that new knowledge. We'll help him take it all in a bit at a time.

"And now," I add, getting out of the bath, "Osbert, if you don't mind allowing Donal to help me finish up, I need you to go find Sir Tobin and bring him here to the sitting room. It's important you go so he understands this is an invitation from the king."

Osbert's smile takes over his entire face. His pleasure in his new status is a joy to see.

I emerge from the bed chamber into the sitting room to find Tobin standing at attention near the door to the corridor. "Thank you for coming, Sir Tobin. I hope I didn't take you away from something important with the troops."

"Not at all, Your Grace. I was speaking with Sir Samuel, congratulating him on his new assignment. Truth be told, Sire, I was rather hoping he might have a place for me." He remains standing, straight as an arrow.

"I'm sure he might, but there's another opportunity I'd like to talk with you about." I gesture to the seating area before the fireplace. "Do come in . . . sit . . . please." He looks rather uncomfortable and carefully waits for me to choose a seat before taking his own.

"Now, Tobin . . . may I call you Tobin?"

"Sire, you're the king. You may call me whatever you wish."

"Let me make one thing clear, Sir Tobin. I'm cut of very different cloth from my brother. The post I'm considering you for is that of Captain of the King's Own Guard. No matter who I choose, the position requires mutual respect. In public, formalities will be required. But in private, we need to be able to converse as two troop captains would – with complete candor. After all, I'm trusting that man with my life and with the lives of the entire royal family. Whoever is captain of my Guard needs to be comfortable with both those situations.

"Now, let's start over, shall we? May I call you Tobin?"

"I'd be honored, Sire," he replies.

"Try sir, Tobin, when it's just the two of us." I smile broadly. "You'll get used to it."

Though he relaxes a bit, I can see he's still on edge. Not surprising, I remind myself. He's being interviewed for a plum assignment by none other than the king.

"Samuel tells me we have something in common."

"Sir?"

"It seems we both found it necessary to abandon the fray in the midst of my brother's battles. I still haven't reconciled in my own mind whether mine was an honorable act or not, especially as I've recently learned that all my troops perished in the battle I was intended to lead. I'm told, however, that you saved the lives of quite a number of men from Lord Ernle's domain by bringing them out with you."

"I've struggled with my actions, sir. You should know, though, that it was your words that guided my conscience."

"How's that, Tobin?"

"They were spoken in whispers throughout the camp, sir, from that very first night when the three approached you about whether it was true they could go home. 'You must each make that decision for yourself,' you told them. When I could no longer stomach the unnecessary loss of life, I decided I had to try to save whatever lives I could. I take no pride in abandoning the field – it goes against all my training and so much of what I believe about honor. But I do take pride in the lives of the men who came with me – and I hope there's some honor in that."

"As I see it, there's no doubt." I like this man. He seems thoughtful rather than rigid – able to evaluate a situation and choose a proper path.

"I was impressed with what I saw of the watch. Lord Rupert tells me you were able to organize those three troops and get them back to proper duty rather quickly."

"All they needed was a good leader, sir. That's true of those men, anyway. Some of the others . . . well . . ." He starts to leave that thought dangling in the air and then apparently remembers my words. "Speaking candidly, sir?"

"Please."

"Sir Samuel is going to have a difficult job sorting out some of that lot. There's many of them that are simply lazy – another bunch that just signed up for the fighting – some that don't know what to do – and some good knights as well. It seems there's been no regular training since they came back from the war. Lots of them are bored and looking for trouble. Too many are drinking too much."

"That's quite an assessment for the short time you've been here, Tobin."

"When you know what well-disciplined troops should be like, it's not hard, sir."

"Perhaps I should tell you a bit about what you'd be signing up for if we go forward. I intend to go about among the people more than John did. Accompanying patrols from time to time. Visiting towns and villages. Even going to market day here or having a drink in the tavern. And I want people to know I'm comfortable mingling with them – not surrounded by guards whose purpose is to keep them away. There's so much we need to rebuild, and I learned from my grandfather that being among the people will give them confidence that we truly are trying to make their lives better.

"I intend to make a lasting peace with the Territories, and that will require that I go there myself as the first gesture . . . and likely go again from time to time. For that, my Guard will need to know how to be restrained and not impulsive.

"Lord Rupert will spend time both here and at the royal manor. His needs must be provided for. My family will visit there on occasion as well. The queen has a cottage in the Kingdom of Lakes. We may choose to holiday there from time to time. And these are just the things I can predict. Do you think you could assemble a suitable Guard?"

To his credit, Tobin pauses in thought before rushing to answer. "Would it be necessary to choose only from the remnants of the knighthood that are here now?"

"Not necessarily. What do you have in mind?"

"I'd like to bring some men from the garrison, sir. And there are a few others I knew well in your father's day – men who returned to their lords when the kingdom was dissolved but who were good and honorable knights. If they were to come back, I know they would serve you well."

"The makeup of the Guard is the captain's responsibility, but I very much like what you suggest. Do you have a wife and family, Tobin?"

"No, sir. I'd like to one day, but as yet I've not found the right lady. Is that a problem?"

"Not at all. I merely wanted you to know they'd be welcome here. We'll have a proper court, so perhaps you'll find that right lady."

"Perhaps."

"Very well, let's not rush to a decision right now. Give this some thought . . . speak to Samuel or to anyone else you care to. But there *is* some urgency. The queen and the children will return in a few days, and I'd like to know someone's looking out for their safety while I'm in seclusion at the monastery before the coronation. What say we meet here at the same time tomorrow to decide?"

"Of course, sir."

"And, Tobin, there'll be no dishonor if you decide to decline. No one need ever know but the two of us. I hope you'll grant me the same consideration if, upon reflection, I decide to follow a different path." I've already almost made my decision – I'd just like a word with Lord Ernle this evening – but want to reinforce the notion of mutual respect.

"Thank you, Sire. I'll be here tomorrow afternoon. Is there anything else?"

"No, Sir Tobin. Tomorrow afternoon." He rises, bows, and leaves the room.

More surprises await at supper. Laurence is here. As we embrace in greeting, Richard, Samuel, and Phillip join us. "You don't think for a minute I'd let these three welcome you home without me, do you?" asks Laurence, getting a laugh all around.

Supper is anything but simple. Two pheasants, a dozen or more squabs, baked apples, lentils, and fresh bread. As the steward serves the wine, I tease him, "Matthias, it looks like you've gone to a lot of trouble for a simple supper."

"Not so much, Sire," he smiles. "When their lordships started arriving, I guessed something might be in the offing, so I sent the lads out hunting. We could keep the birds fresh just by leaving them outside. And the cook was ever so happy to be doing a nice meal for a change rather than feeding all those knights."

"Send the cook my compliments, then. Even before I've had the first bite, those aromas tell me this is going to be tasty indeed."

Talk inevitably turns to the coronation. "This is one ceremony I'm really excited to plan," says Lord Devereux, ". . . as much as the one for your father. I'm just grateful Rupert had to take care of your brother's burial."

"Oh, I think I see now what was behind the dissolution of the kingdom," I tell him. "That's a rather drastic way to avoid funeral planning, though, isn't it?"

Devereux roars with laughter. "Can't fool you for a minute, can I, Alfred?" Then back to the serious. "But I think we should have a proper, traditional coronation."

"My thoughts as well. So after Gwen and the children arrive, I'll go to the monastery for the traditional seclusion. I've one big worry, though."

"What's that?"

"I suspect it's not going to be easy to find a white stallion."

He breaks into a big grin. "You leave that to me, Son. You'll have your white stallion even if we have to paint a brown one."

The evening is everything I'd hoped for. The comfortable interactions and easy banter between my family and the lords are back as if they'd never been interrupted by John's authoritarian ways.

"There's one thing I'd like to ask, sir. At the end of the ceremony, I'd like for us to walk back to the castle. Gwen and me . . . Geoffrey and Juliana as well, though I think Edward's still a bit young . . . the lords and their families, if you're so inclined. I'd like to start by letting people know we see firsthand what their lives are like."

"Of course, Alfred. Besides, it saves us having to organize all those carriages in the midst of what I suspect is going to be a throng of people, even in winter."

Later, I take Lord Ernle aside. "What would you think of Sir Tobin as captain of the King's Own Guard?"

"Samuel told me he intended to suggest that. Tobin is as solid as they come. I put him in charge of the garrison because I knew he wouldn't provoke the Territorial lords. And if they stirred something up, I knew I could count on Tobin for a restrained and measured response. The men seem to respond to him as well. I've intentionally looked for signs of discontent at the garrison and have found nothing of the sort."

"I'm convinced of his thoughtfulness. What I can't get a read on is his willingness or ability to engage in the face of a real threat."

"Well, thankfully, I've never had to see the warrior side of his nature in action. But the men who left the war with him told me they didn't want to fight under anyone else. They trusted him to bring them through a battle successfully and alive.

"I've watched him through the years, Alfred. He's fiercely loyal to the Ernle family. And if he agrees to serve you, it will be because he's made a conscious choice to extend that loyalty to you and yours."

After everyone else has retired, Rupert and I talk late into the night. "The bishop will be here tomorrow for the reading of the will," Rupert tells me. "He said we shouldn't expect much."

"Why doesn't that particularly surprise me?"

He chuckles. "Frankly, I'm surprised there even is a will to be read."

"Are we being too disrespectful, Uncle?"

"Your brother was in some ways a very bad man, Alfred, but in other ways a very sad man. Not that he himself was sad . . . simply that it was sad he never had the capacity to see beyond himself. Even your mother eventually despaired of him. When we buried him, she asked me something quite similar."

"Oh?"

"'Is it wrong, Rupert,' she asked, 'that I have no more tears to shed for him? Somewhere in a corner of my heart there's still a tiny spark of a mother's love. But if this is what it took to end the evil and to save the rest of my family and the kingdom, then I can only be sadly grateful that it's over at last.' Alice is strong woman."

"She seemed older to me today."

"Oh, she's recovering nicely and will be her old self just as soon as Gwen and the children are back."

"Recovering?"

"When John took you off to war, she was terrified she'd lose you both. She never let on to Gwen, but she unburdened herself to Catherine on more than one occasion. The night you came home, you were so intent on following after Gwen that you didn't see her sadness."

"Not my finest hour."

"Alfred, you had just committed treason by deserting your king in the middle of a war and arrived home to discover your family gone and no one knew where. Believe me, Alice didn't begrudge you that bit of self-absorption for even a moment. But the months of not knowing if she'd ever see you or her grandchildren again . . . and then learning that her other grandchildren were lost to the sickness . . . all that was a worry even though she always spoke about a time in the future when you'd return. She's had an extra spring in her step ever since I sent Samuel and Richard to bring you home. And just you watch . . . the minute the children arrive, she'll light up like the sun on a summer morning." We continue talking until the last embers of the fire die away and the last drop of brandy is drunk.

The bishop arrives midmorning, and we gather in the private reception room for the reading of the will. Mother sits beside me. The inspection of the seals complete, the bishop opens the document and reads aloud. "I leave everything from the roof of the highest tower in the castle to the farthest reaches of the kingdom to my son John Gundar."

He pauses, then adds, "That is the complete will and testament of the late King John. Unusual, in my experience, but perhaps not so unusual for the man. I encouraged him on more than one occasion to create a proper will, but he simply admonished me to mind my own business. The day before he marched to war, I confronted him again, telling him it was unseemly for a king to engage in battle without a proper will. So he called for his secretary and dictated that sentence. We affixed the seals, and then he ordered me to leave. The designated benefactor being no longer alive, I believe the tradition is that the inheritance goes to the heir to the throne under the rules of primogeniture. Is that not correct, Lord Rupert?"

"Correct, Bishop."

"In which case, Alfred, the inheritance goes to you. And I suppose it's up to you to decide what other provisions might be in order."

I think we all expected John's will would be out of the ordinary, but this is peculiar even for him. "In which case," I say, "it seems best that the terms of my father's will remain in effect for everything else. If there's anything required to formalize that, Bishop, just tell me what I need to sign."

"As you wish, my son."

After the midday meal, I ask Mother, "Fancy a walk in the garden?"

"If you'll tell me everything that's happened since I saw you last," she replies.

"That's exactly what I had in mind."

"Just let me fetch my cloak."

I tell her first about Gwen's secrets and how they provided a refuge for us. "When she wouldn't tell us where she was going, I guessed there might be a place where she knew they would be safe," says Mother. "But how on earth did you find them?"

She takes my arm to draw me closer to her while I tell the story, and when I'm finished, she says only, "Your father would have been so proud of you."

Despite the efforts of the early afternoon sun, it's still winter, so we retreat to the warmth of the fire in my sitting room before I regale her with details of our life at the cottage. "I'd very much like to visit that cottage one day," she says.

"Well, the children want to go back, so I rather think we'll have little choice but to holiday there occasionally. Just let me get the roads repaired first so it's not such a miserable trip from here to the border," I reply with a laugh. "In the meantime, Mother, I intend to have a proper court, so I want you to choose your apartment before Matthias starts working out the rest of the arrangements."

"I'm quite fine where I am, Alfred."

"I rather thought you might say that." I smile. "But consider this. In a few months, when people are back and the lords and their families are regularly at court, you're going to need a proper place to welcome the ladies for . . . well, for whatever ladies of the court get up to."

She laughs out loud at my ignorance of women's pursuits. "I suppose you're right, Alfred. If I'm to be a proper dowager queen, entertaining the ladies will be part of my role. I'll speak to Matthias and we'll sort it out."

"There's one other thing I need your help with. I'm going to want Rupert here more than he's been accustomed to, so I'd like for him to reclaim the apartment Gwen and I are vacating. I suspect he's going to be as reticent as you were to make any changes, but I want him and Catherine to be comfortable when they're here."

"Leave it to me. I'll talk to Catherine and we'll make the arrangements. He'll be moved in before he even realizes there's a change afoot." Her smile is radiant. Rupert was right about how quickly she's recovering now that she's in her element once again.

The next morning dawns sunny and cold, a good day for a morning ride. All my mates are at the stable, saddling their horses. Elvin finishes with Star Dancer as Tobin walks up leading his mount. "I think I'll be quite safe in the company of this lot, Tobin, if you have other things that need your time."

"With respect, Sire," replies Tobin, "if you've no objection, I'd like to ride along at a distance to observe . . . just to learn your habits, if I may."

"No objection at all. In fact, you should ride with us. It's likely I'll be spending quite a bit of my time with this lot, so you should get to know them. Samuel you already know."

"Commander," Tobin acknowledges Samuel formally.

"Laurence, heir to the Montfort estate. Richard, Lord Devereux's heir. And Phillip, Lord Thorssen."

"Gentlemen . . . my lord," Tobin's manners are impeccable.

"Mates . . . Sir Tobin, the new captain of my Guard. These rides tend to be pretty informal, Tobin. I doubt anyone's expecting court manners." Hands are shaken all around.

Star Dancer is ready, but I pause to check everything before mounting. "No disrespect, Elvin. Just a rule Master Mervyn taught me, and it's stuck with me."

"And don't you or your men ever let him break that rule, Tobin," admonishes Samuel. My friend will never quite get over the fact that my father decided not to check his gear on the day of his fatal accident and no one stepped in to check it for him.

"That be a good rule, m'lord. Me grandda' would be proud." Elvin is all smiles.

We let the horses stretch their legs on a run through the meadows then settle down to a comfortable pace for conversation. I ask Laurence if he knows Gamel's whereabouts. "He's thriving as Father's gamekeeper."

"Any chance your father could spare him for a bit? I'm certain we're going to be in desperate need of engineers for a while, and I'm told he's one of the best."

"Let me talk with him. I've no doubt we can sort out a gamekeeper in his absence if he's willing to take on the job."

"Unless he's adamant in his refusal, Laurence, bring him to see me at the monastery. I know it's traditional that the business of the kingdom takes a pause while the new king is in seclusion. But there's too much to be done – we don't have the luxury of time to waste in getting the kingdom back on its feet.

"You, too, Richard. Whenever you're ready to discuss the state of the Treasury, just ride up. André will be only too happy to give us a place to talk things over."

"It's going to take some time to sort out, Alfred," replies Richard. "But at least I've found a reliable clerk to help."

"Samuel, I need you to join Rupert and me later this morning. I know it's only been a couple of days, but there's something we'll need your knights to do."

•   •   •   •   •

Rupert is waiting for us in the private reception room when we return from our ride. "The bishop and the magistrate should be here momentarily," he says.

"Uncle, is there any reason I shouldn't sign laws before the coronation? There are several that John rescinded that I'd like to put back into effect immediately."

"I understand your motivation, Alfred, but your predecessors have all chosen to wait. There is, after all, that question in the ceremony about whether anyone disputes your right to the crown."

"Alright, then, I suppose I'll just have to be patient." And then another thought occurs to me. "What about proclamations?"

"That's been done before. Proclamations don't carry the same weight and are easier to overturn should it be necessary."

At that moment the bishop and the magistrate arrive, accompanied by another man carrying a small box. "I've brought my clerk, Your Grace," says the magistrate, "in the event that something needs to be recorded. It occurred to me you might not yet have a secretary."

"Another of those tasks I haven't gotten around to, Magistrate. Bishop, my apologies for dragging you back here again. I should have thought to have this discussion yesterday; but I'm only just beginning to sort out all that needs to be done."

"How can I be of service, my son?"

"Tell me . . . are those itinerant priests who were causing so much grief still roaming the kingdom?"

"I haven't heard them spoken of in quite some time. Nor have I seen one here in the town for many months."

"I don't want to take any chances, Bishop. If even one of them is seen preaching in public, I want to hand them over to you to deal with."

"It's not clear I have any authority to deal with them," replies the bishop. "We were never able to determine who sent them or who in the Church hierarchy had responsibility for them. If they believe they're not under my authority, then they'd simply ignore any instruction I might give them."

"I won't have them stirring up trouble again, even if they have to be arrested and sentenced in a civil court."

"That may be your best answer," says the bishop. "If there are laws under which they can be arrested and judged, that's the path you should take. If a clergyman is sentenced in a civil court, I have the authority to demand he be turned over to the Church for punishment. And as punishment, I can assign him to any number of years' penance in a monastery far away from here and he'd have no choice but to obey."

"Magistrate?"

"There's the charge of inciting to riot. In the case of what happened in Abbéville or Great Woolston, that would apply."

"I don't want things to get that far out of hand before some sort of action is taken. Isn't there a lesser charge?"

"Well, there's inciting to mischief, but it doesn't carry a very great penalty. In fact, the magistrate has the right to be lenient in his judgment, even to the point of reprimanding the individual and sending him on his way."

"But there is the option for some sort of punishment?"

"Indeed there is, Sire."

"Then this is what's to be done. I think it requires a proclamation, Magistrate, so if you could help your clerk to draft it, I'll sign it before we leave here today. Any man claiming to be a priest and seen preaching in the public square or on a village green or even alongside the road and who isn't under the bishop's authority is to be detained and charged with the lesser of inciting to mischief or inciting to riot, depending on the circumstances in which he's discovered. No leniency in sentencing is permitted. Every sheriff and every patrol captain . . ." I pause and glance at Samuel, who nods his agreement. "Every sheriff and every patrol captain has the authority to detain such an alleged priest in the circumstances described. Every sentence under this proclamation is to be reported to the bishop. If the bishop demands the individual be turned over to the Church for punishment, then the man is to be delivered into the bishop's custody immediately. We will provide any assistance the bishop might request to ensure that the man leaves our kingdom to take up his ecclesiastical punishment elsewhere."

"Very well, Your Grace," says the magistrate. "If we may be permitted to work in the outer room?"

"Of course. But once you've instructed your clerk, I'd be grateful if you'd return. There's another matter where I need your advice."

As they leave to begin their work, I turn to the others. "I know this seems harsh . . . and my fondest hope is that we never have to take any action under this proclamation. The Church is welcome here, Bishop. But these zealots who try to set people against their neighbors are not."

"There may be some, Alfred," cautions Rupert, "who'll say this interferes with a man's right to speak his mind."

"That's a risk I'm prepared to take, Uncle. There's a vast difference between a man speaking his mind and someone urging people to do harm to their fellow man. It's even more reprehensible when God's name is invoked to justify the harm."

"I didn't say I disagreed with you, Alfred," says Rupert. "I just wanted everyone else to hear your motives."

"The other thing that needs immediate attention – especially if we're to make sure there's no chance for the sickness to return this spring – is dismantling those shack communities everywhere they exist. Samuel, as soon as you can get a couple of reliable troops together, we need them to take this on."

"Even before the roads?"

"I think so. The roads are going to take some time, but I'm not sure this can wait. Even if it's not the sickness from last year, those shacks are breeding grounds for disease. People need proper housing, and the shacks need to be burned and cleared away."

"The problem, of course," Samuel again, "is where to find the proper housing."

"That's what we need the magistrate for. Bishop, I'd venture to guess there are empty dwellings in the towns . . . places where the sickness took the lives of all who lived there and no one has come forward to make a claim on the property."

"That's certainly correct here. And I have reason to believe it's the case in the market towns as well."

A soft knock on the door precedes the magistrate's return. "Just in time, Magistrate," I tell him. "We were discussing demolishing the shacks and getting those people into better housing. I understand there are unclaimed dwellings in the towns. Is there any reason you know of why the Crown couldn't claim those dwellings?"

"If a dwelling has been unoccupied and no one has presented a lawful claim to it for three months, then it reverts to the town, and the mayor can sell it or use it for the common good."

"Bishop, can the Church help us with feeding and clothing these people until they get back on their feet?"

"To the best of our ability, of course."

"Then let's proceed this way. Each mayor is instructed to use the abandoned houses for the common good for a period of one year to provide housing to those who have none. The Crown and the Church will assist with food and clothing for these people until they find work. As soon as they've had work for at least three months, the mayors may begin charging rent to the occupants . . . but initially, the rent must be commensurate with their ability to pay. At the end of a year, if the occupants haven't taken up proper work, then the mayors are free to reclaim the dwelling.

"I think this should be another proclamation so it carries the weight of the Crown. I'd much prefer to have met with the mayors to enlist their support, but once again, we don't have the time to wait. So, Magistrate, if I may prevail on your clerk's time a bit longer, I'd like to write a letter to each mayor explaining why this is so important and so urgent."

"That will get a roof over many of the indigents' heads," says Rupert. "But what about a place to sleep . . . some meager furnishings? And what if there aren't enough houses?"

"Samuel gave me an idea for that this morning. The knights are all moved back into the barracks, so there are all those bunks and simple furnishings that were installed in the old castle. Let's give them to those in need. And the extra can be broken down into lumber for people to build whatever they may be lacking. I'm sure there are blankets surplus to the needs of a properly constituted knighthood. And no doubt there are extra campaign tents as well. Heaven knows there were dozens upon dozens of tents carried on the march. With any luck, some of them came back and weren't left in the field. If there aren't enough vacant houses, then we should set the people up properly in campaign tents while new housing is built. Put the blacksmiths to work melting down some of the surplus arms for whatever metal fittings may be needed. I know it's a tall order, Samuel, but can we get started?"

"I wonder what ever made me think I'd get a few weeks to sort out the knighthood."

Rupert laughs out loud. "Surely you know Alfred better than that by now, Samuel." The bishop and the magistrate chuckle softly, but look a bit uncertain what to make of all this comfortable familiarity with the king.

"Truth be told," says Samuel, "it's good to put the men to work right away . . . and doubly good right now for them to see that a knight's role involves much more than fighting. Will two troops be enough for now? We'll take care of the town here and Abbéville first; then Great Woolston and Neukirk."

"I'll leave it to you, Samuel," I reply. "Very well, I think we've taken care of the most urgent things. Thank you, gentlemen."

They all rise to leave and the magistrate says, "I'll instruct my clerk on the second proclamation, Sire. Then you can dictate your letters. As this is his first time in the castle, you may need to ask someone to show him the way out when he's finished. He's completely reliable and loyal, Your Grace. Whatever he prepares on your behalf will be kept in confidence."

"A word, Lord Rupert, if you will." I wait until the door closes behind the others. "Is it possible to prevail on you, Uncle, to find me a good secretary? That was a detail that hadn't occurred to me in the flurry of the past few days; but it's obviously going to be important."

"Are you sure you want a former spymaster hiring your staff?" he teases.

"Better *your* spy on my staff than someone else's, I should think."

"Then I know just the man."

• • • • •

The next day, early in the afternoon, the tower sentry reports two carriages approaching from the west. Certain that it must be Gwen and the children, I hasten to find Mother and rush to the door of the courtyard to meet them. As Gwen alights from the first carriage, I throw royal dignity to the wind, grab her in my arms and swing her around in a couple of circles before giving her a passionate kiss.

As we break our embrace, she smiles. "Oh, my . . . such exuberance. Is that really seemly for a king?"

"The lords are here, the kingdom is reunited, and my family has arrived at last. What's not to be exuberant about?"

The others are descending from the carriages, and I swoop each child up in turn for a swing and a hug. Geoffrey isn't so sure this is acceptable for his age and gender, but he endures my greeting with only a small grimace.

"Father insisted we bring one of his carriages rather than the wagon," Gwen tells my mother. "I must admit, we were far more comfortable than when we were all crowded into one. He and Mother will bring an extra driver to take it back when they return home after the coronation."

Nurse approaches carrying baby Alicia. "Mother Alice, meet your namesake," says Gwen as Nurse hands the baby to my mother.

"Well, well, little one," Mother coos. "Welcome to your new home."

By now, Catherine and Rupert have appeared and the homecoming is in full flow. Rupert and I decide to go riding while the family settles in. There'll be ample time tonight to spend with Gwen, and we'll make the most of it. Tomorrow, I go to the monastery.

During the first week at the monastery, I observe the traditional rites of seclusion. My "home" is a cell identical to those of the brothers. My days are spent in silence and alone, reading or walking about the grounds or the monastery's fields with only my thoughts for company. I attend services with the monks, sitting by myself at the rear of the chapel. Thankfully, I'm not obligated to interrupt my sleep for Matins, Lauds, or Prime.

I fast during the day. At sundown, a brother brings a small bowl of broth and a piece of bread, silently places them on a table in my cell, and leaves just as silently. The empty bowl disappears each day during my absence. Out of habit, I break the bread and dip it into the broth. How often, I wonder, will broth and bread be what sustains me in this life?

By tradition, the abbot chooses the first book to be read by the new king. Imagine my surprise to find waiting in my cell the small book I'd bought from the bookseller in Great Woolston along with a translation into our tongue. It is indeed a play . . . entitled *The Eumenides* . . . by someone called Aeschylus. While I read, I ponder what led André to this particular choice.

As I leave the chapel after Sext on the eighth day, a brother approaches. "Father Abbot invites you to break your fast with him," he says. "You'll find him in his dining room." To which location I immediately repair.

André greets me warmly. "Alfred . . . please . . . join us . . . let me pour you some wine."

Warin is here . . . something I hadn't expected. "André called me here three months past," he says in response to my query.

"It's my fondest hope," says André as he pours for all of us, "that Warin will succeed me in this post. But as we know, that decision will be out of my hands. If the brothers are to vote for him in chapter, they must already know and respect him. So when our prior passed into the next world, I invited Warin to take his place."

"Brother Frery had long been ready to take over as prior in the west," adds Warin, "and I was happy to give him the opportunity."

Looking at the feast laid out for us, I remark, "Brother Kitchener has outdone himself today, it would seem," drawing laughter from both of my companions.

"I never cease to be amazed," says André, "how a week of fasting can make an ordinary meal look sumptuous to men's eyes."

"Don't let him fool you, Alfred," chuckles Warin. "I assure you we don't eat this well every day."

Over the meal, I ask André about his choice of book. "I've been trying to understand what lesson you intended me to take – what was your purpose in that choice."

"Only one purpose, my son. You found a true gem in that bookseller's stall and were wise enough to recognize it and rescue it. Knowing you had no Greek, I wanted to give you the chance to read it for yourself. Even though Aeschylus was one of the great playwrights, not many alive today have ever seen his works, much less read them."

"I only hope that what we did that day to save the bookseller's life was enough," I reply.

"The brothers are moving your things into my guest room for the remainder of your stay. You'll be more comfortable there, and we three can have more opportunity for conversation."

"Thank you, André. I expect to have visitors as well. I put a number of things in train before coming here and am eager to hear what progress is being made."

Both men chuckle. I pause with food halfway to my mouth. "What?"

"We assumed as much," answers Warin. "In fact, we were both rather surprised how diligently you were observing the rituals of seclusion."

It's my turn to laugh. "Truth be told, my friends, I feel a terrible urgency to make things right in the kingdom once again. The people need to see signs of their lives getting better, and they need to see it quickly or their trust will be strained. But I also understand these rituals exist for a reason. No man has ever truly suffered from a bit of quiet contemplation."

"You're right about the people, Alfred," says André, "but there's so much to do that you can't do it all at once. Have you thought about the order of things?"

"I've thought of little else since Samuel and Richard said those fateful words." I tell them everything I'm planning.

They nod from time to time. "I believe," says André when I pause, "those are precisely the choices your father and grandfather would have made. The people will give you some time, Alfred. Once before, they thought you were lost to them and you returned. You've returned to them again, so they'll have patience as long as there are signs of change."

"Despite everything we *must* do," I continue, "I think it's important for people to have some joy in their lives. The excitement of the coronation will suffice for a while. But we need to be sure the festivals happen in the towns and the larger villages, even if the Crown has to subsidize the celebrations for the first year. I'll never forget how Grandfather used to chide me that every plan I brought forward required some sort of subsidy. He's probably nudging my father and they're laughing together, wherever they are, that I'm still up to my old ways."

"I'm so pleased to hear you say that." André beams.

We spend the rest of the afternoon together, our conversation interrupted only for Nones. André tells me that he's already set the monks to the task of restoring the contents of the castle library to their proper home. I inquire about Brother Eustace. "Is he still here or was he needed in the west?"

"He returned to us in the west," replies Warin. "But the moment I heard you were on your way home, I sent for him. He should be with us tomorrow."

"Thank you, Warin. I want to spend as much time with him as possible while I'm here, since making a proper peace with the Territories is one of the first things we need to do."

I excuse myself briefly to retrieve the most recent pages of my chronicle. "We should bind these into a proper folio," says André.

"Perhaps we should wait until the record's complete," I suggest.

"In what way isn't it complete?" asks André.

"It records the war only up to the time I abandoned it. I want to speak to some of the captains who returned to learn what led to the defeat and retreat. And for it to truly be a factual and objective account of the war, I think I should speak with Lord Egon and learn the opponent's view of those events."

"That would be something quite unusual indeed, Alfred," says André. "It's rarer than rare that such records ever reflect the point of view of anyone but the author."

"I doubt we'll ever know the details of John's murder," I continue. "It seems unlikely that the perpetrators will ever be identified or brought to justice. But we should at least record the facts that are known."

"Very well, I'll keep these pages safe with their predecessors, and we can bind them when you've finished the remainder. In the meantime, I'll begin making a copy. The original will belong in the royal library, but I'd very much like to have a copy here as well."

"Whatever you wish, André. This was, after all, your idea in the first place."

·　　·　　·　　·　　·

The next day, Rupert arrives as planned for the kind of discussions we had previously with Harold and my father. I find it especially poignant that there are only the two of us now to chart a course for the future. As we eat our midday meal, he regales me with events at the castle. "Geoffrey's been chafing at having to move back into the nursery, so Gwen asked me to talk with him."

"I can only imagine. Did you have any success?"

"Well, I told him that he was right about being too old for the nursery and that this was just temporary. I also told him that a wise lad . . . especially a prince . . . would graciously accept his temporary situation and look forward to the change that would be coming."

"What did he say?"

"Nothing at first. He still looked very grumpy. But I could see he was thinking things through, his expression changing as he did. Finally, he said, 'Uncle Rupert, I think maybe you're a prince too. Is that right?' To which I replied, 'That's right, Geoffrey. I've been a prince all my life.'

"So he thinks some more and then says, 'Uncle Rupert, I've never been a prince before. Will you teach me how to be one?' I told him, 'Of course, I'll help you learn. You can ask me any question you have, any time you want to. Don't forget, though, that your Papa knows about these things, too.'"

"I'm curious what he said about that."

"Oh, I think he'll respond to your tutelage just fine; but you *are* his father, after all. What he said next was, 'I think maybe sometimes I might want to ask you first so I don't get in trouble with Papa.'"

"Spoken like a true boy his age," I laugh and then continue in a serious vein, "It seems you'll be for Geoffrey what Grandfather was for me. I couldn't be more pleased, Uncle. Thank you."

"Been wondering what my new role might be," he chuckles.

"Don't get too smug too soon," I chide jokingly. "I'm claiming first rights to your advice. Everyone else can stand in line." Which takes us to the serious business of how to order the roles that must be filled.

"If you want to resume as Port Commissioner, Uncle, the job is yours."

"I think not, Alfred. Laurence is more than ready, and I suspect he'll have more energy for it than I would."

"What about your other job?" A reference to his previous role as spymaster.

"Laurence was already doing most of that anyway. Offer him the whole package and see what he says. I think it's most likely he'll relish the opportunity."

"What about when he inherits? Montfort seemed much older to me than I remembered."

"Cross that bridge when you get to it. And don't forget, the longevity of the Montforts is legendary. So that bridge is probably quite some years away."

"If you're certain, Uncle, then I must tell you, I'm really quite pleased. I want your voice on the Council . . . and I really wasn't joking about laying claim to your advice. In many ways, it should really be your turn to sit upon this throne."

"Don't fret for even a moment about that, Alfred. I long ago accepted my position in the family. Besides," he adds, his sense of humor always at the ready, "I can have much more fun without the weight of that imaginary crown on my head all the time." Then he adds, as something of an afterthought. "I'm assuming, of course, that you're not going to strut around in a coronet all the time like your brother?"

"If I do, you are empowered to force my abdication, exile me to some faraway land, and take the crown for yourself," I tell him with a big grin. "If Gwen doesn't do it first."

Over the course of the next two days, we plan the Council membership and all the other assignments. Richard for Treasury. Philip to reconstitute the Assembly because he has the trust of the commercial interests. Montfort as Ambassador to the Kingdom of Lakes. Ernle, Meriden, and Devereux on the Council with Richard and Phillip. I want to bring Ernle's heir into the room soon, but that requires a conversation with the father first. There are several possibilities for Bauldry, depending on how I sort things out with Peveril.

Peveril's skills are going to be needed in more than one place. "Talk with him," urges Rupert. "I've heard him say more than once that his second son seems to have inherited his aptitude for diplomacy almost from birth. It seems young Emaurri was the one who kept the peace among five brothers as they were growing up."

"Then ask him to bring Emaurri to the coronation and tell him I'd like to speak with them both on the day after." Suddenly, something else occurs to me. "I didn't think of this before I left. Could you also ask Devereux to convene a Council meeting for the second day after the coronation? All the Lords, the bishop, Samuel, Richard, and Laurence."

"Your wish is my command, Your Grace," replies Rupert with a huge grin and a mock courtly bow.

The next morning I'm roused from a deep sleep by a monk shaking my shoulder. "Father Abbot asks you to come to the chapel as quickly as can be, sir."

Rubbing the sleep from my eyes, I ask, "What hour is it?"

"Lauds is just ended, sir," he replies.

No wonder there's no light coming through the window. I get my wits about me and some clothes on me as best I can and make my way to the chapel. André meets me at the door. "I'm not sure what this is about, Alfred, but we found these two huddled in the back here as the brothers departed after the service. Warin is with them now."

We proceed inside where Warin waits near the altar with two men whose backs are to us. As I approach, they turn, and I'm astonished to see Louve and Mauger – John's knight commander and captain of the King's Own Guard, respectively. They both fall to one knee, heads bowed, as I approach. "Well, well. To what do we owe this appearance at such an early hour?"

Slowly, they rise. Louve is the first to speak. "We've come about the death of your brother, Your Grace."

When I don't respond, Mauger adds, "We want to tell you what we know about what happened, Your Grace."

"Very well," I reply.

Louve speaks next. "When we returned from the war, Sire, everything was in chaos. The knights were exhausted from days of riding at a forced pace. Many were angry over our defeat. The king demoted all the captains . . . some he dismissed outright. The troops were then even more confused and angry."

Mauger picks up. "There were rumors, Sire, about plots. We didn't know whether to believe them or if they were just soldiers' gossip."

I hold up my hand. "Let's step back a moment. Tell me about the end of the war and the retreat."

"It was brutal, Sire," replies Louve. "As you know, the late king had his own ideas about how to fight the enemy. We kept charging down that hill for two more days, and on the third day we woke to find that the enemy was gone – their position abandoned. So the king ordered the supply wagons to remain on the ridge and the troops to advance. We descended to where the enemy had been only to find it was a narrow passage at the top of another hill and the enemy was arrayed on the plain below."

"I tried to tell him about the terrain, but he wouldn't listen," I interject.

"The enemy was deployed very wide and not very deep across the plain. The king immediately ordered a charge, and our troops fanned out and started to mingle with their opponents. They seemed to let us penetrate their ranks — in fact, thinking about it later, I was sure that was exactly what they were doing. Once our men were dispersed among them, their commanders organized them into a V formation and started closing in on us like a pincer, herding us back up the hill.

"Our captains couldn't get their men together – couldn't create any sort of organization – so it was mass confusion retreating up the two hills. When we got to the top, we realized they'd diverted the men not needed to pursue us up the hill into positions on both our flanks on the ridge. Then they drove us relentlessly toward the border, day and night. Some of the supply wagons managed to get in our train and come home. Many more were left behind.

"Once we crossed back into our own territory, they stopped following. Not a single man or animal set foot across the border; but they formed a massive line on their side and settled into camp. The king let us have some desperately needed rest that night. When morning came and the enemy was still in position, he seemed to accept defeat and gave the order to go home.

"The journey back was dreadful. The king was despondent, the men in no better mood, and the pace was that of a forced march."

"Once we were back," Mauger now, "the sickness was everywhere. The king confined all the knights to the castle grounds. He wouldn't have anyone around him who'd been anywhere near a sick person. This affected the Guards most of all, but every knight got bored with lack of activity and lack of liberty. That's how both gossip and plots get started, Your Grace."

"Tell me about the night of the king's murder." I choose the word purposefully.

"Even though the sickness had been gone for some months," replies Louve, "the king still hadn't given the knights anything to occupy their time . . . nor had he released them from restriction to the castle grounds. I decided enough was enough and took it upon myself to grant liberty to everyone under my command. In fact, I encouraged them to go into the town and even joined them at the tavern."

"And where were the Guards in all this, Mauger?"

"I gave them liberty as well, Sire. And those who chose not to go into the town, I restricted to their barracks. I thought it would encourage them all to go let off some steam if the only alternative was to be confined to quarters."

"And you, yourself?"

"I stayed in my quarters in case I was needed, Your Grace. I heard nothing the whole night."

"Tell me – why have you come here? Couldn't this have waited until after the coronation?"

The look at each other – hesitating – deciding who should speak first. Finally, Louve offers tentatively, "You see, Sire, we don't know who the twelve were, but we suspect they think we know."

"And?"

"Frankly, Sire," says Mauger, "if they suspect we have any idea, we might well be the next victims. So we came to tell you what we know and to seek your mercy and protection."

I remain silent for a long time, partially thinking about what I intend to say, but equally giving them pause about what might be forthcoming. At last, I've made them wait long enough. "I don't condone either the direct act of killing another person or indirect complicity in the deed. I'm sure you both know that I'm bound by the laws of our land. And as this is a case of regicide, I'm equally honor-bound to my fellow sovereigns to seek out and punish the perpetrators. I won't question your motives in coming here today, but I cannot circumvent the law.

"After the coronation, I intend to issue an order for the arrest of anyone known to be directly or indirectly responsible in the death of King John. Such persons will be tried and, if found guilty, sentenced accordingly. However, I won't waste men or money sending search parties to foreign lands – those men and that money will be sorely needed for rebuilding."

They both look crestfallen . . . and more than a little fearful. Turning to André, Louve pleads, "Perhaps we could request sanctuary here, Father Abbot."

"Are you sure you could really live out the rest of your lives in this chapel?" I ask.

"Then perhaps we could take holy orders," Mauger begs.

"My son," says André, "holy orders are not meant as a path for avoiding justice. If you were to petition to join our community, I could not avoid taking into consideration what I've heard here today. Perhaps, somewhere far away, where nothing is known of your life heretofore, the outcome might be different. But you must examine your soul to determine if the monastic life is really what you seek."

"I intend to honor tradition," I tell them. "No laws, proclamations, or warrants will be issued while I'm sequestered here. That seclusion lasts for another two and a half weeks. My advice to you, gentlemen, is to use that time wisely."

Uncertain what to do next, they stand silently, eyes downcast. Warin reaches out a hand. "Come. The brothers will soon begin arriving for Prime. Let me show you a way out where you can leave unobserved." They follow him meekly away.

When they're out of earshot, André puts a hand on my shoulder. "Very well done, Alfred. They don't yet realize the full extent of the mercy you've granted them."

"It's their good fortune that they chose to approach me here. In other circumstances, my choices would have been more limited."

"You do realize, of course, that they themselves may be the ones responsible for your brother's death? That the twelve knives may have merely been a ruse? The one at the tavern would not have been noticed leaving amid the drinking and revelry . . . and the other one has none but himself to vouch for his whereabouts."

"The thought did occur to me. But I decided it didn't matter if there were twelve or two. I hope they're wise enough to leave and not return. I would much prefer to avoid a trial – to avoid rekindling those emotions. Best to consign John's reign to the past, to be remembered only as an object lesson for those who will follow in my footsteps."

Warin has returned. "I encouraged them that making a new life far away from here was the best way to ensure their safety. Let's hope they leave quickly and take their secrets with them."

"I'll tell Rupert, and we'll decide whether to tell my mother," I say. "But beyond that, I think no one else needs to know anything about this."

"A good decision," says André. "And now I must prepare for the service. Our brothers are beginning to assemble."

As I walk back to my room, the first faint tinges of light are beginning to disperse the gloom of the night. It will be another hour until dawn. Sleep eludes me, so I take quill and paper and write down Louve's account of the defeat and retreat. It will be interesting to hear the tales of others – to see if they tell a common story. Only then will I be prepared to record the facts of the end of the war.

When I describe the encounter to Rupert, he affirms my decision. "People – even history, for that matter – are intrigued by a mystery that remains unsolved. And at this particular time and place, that's probably preferable to the bloodlust a trial would stir up. I rather think, Alfred, that the intentions of those two may have been noble, if misguided. But they're a loose thread. Let's hope their fear keeps them far away and their lips sealed."

·　　·　　·　　·　　·

Three days later, Laurence arrives with Gamel. Before André's warm fire, we talk at length about everything that must be done. "I'm grateful you've been willing to listen to my proposition, Gamel. I've no wish to disrupt your life if you're well settled, but I'm in dire need of engineers and am told you have some talent."

"My life is better than I'd expected it to be, Sire, after losing my knight's pension, but I want to help if I can. The Montforts have been more than generous in offering to preserve my tenancy if I choose to serve the Crown."

"The most urgent problem, Gamel, is getting the port back in operation. I've no idea what may need to be done, but it needs to be done quickly. You'll need builders to help, but I think I know where to find some. Then there's the reservoir. I'm sure it hasn't been inspected since my father's reign. And we all know what a dreadful state of disrepair the roads are in. No doubt some of the bridges need attention as well."

"It's a tall order, Sire," says Gamel, shaking his head.

"Forgive me, Gamel. I didn't mean to make it sound overwhelming . . . even though it rather is. What I propose is that you find a few other good engineers to help. You'd be in charge overall. I can bring you back into the knighthood if you wish, as captain of your group, though I recognize that might be awkward since you were previously knight commander."

"Awkwardness is only among individuals, Sire. I understand Sir Samuel is now commander. There would be no awkwardness between us."

"That would simplify things, if you're agreeable, Sir Gamel. But please understand that I don't expect your men to ride patrols or participate in drills. There'll be far too much else for them to do, and I'm sure you and Samuel can sort out how to pair your men with his to get the necessary work done. Just remember that the port is first priority."

I turn my attention to Laurence. "And if I'm twice lucky today, you just may have a Montfort as Port Commissioner to help get things organized."

Laurence smiles. "Lord Rupert told me you might be making such a request, so I've had a chance to think about it. 'Tis indeed your lucky day, Sire, though I understand I may be in dire need of a place to live there."

I reach out and shake his hand heartily as Warin walks in the door. He stops short as he sees us. "My apologies, Alfred. I didn't realize anyone was here." He starts to retreat.

"Not at all, Warin. Do come in. In fact, you couldn't have arrived at a more opportune time." As he closes the door behind him and comes to join us before the fire, I turn to the others. "What do you think my chances are of being thrice lucky?" They both smile politely, though neither has any idea what I'm up to.

"Last time I was at the western monastery, Warin, there were some immigrants in residence who were expert builders. Any chance they're still there?"

"They were when I left to take up my post here," he replies. "Why do you ask?"

"Well, Laurence is going to take on the job of Port Commissioner, and he's going to need a place to live. I don't want the old residence refurbished. That would only remind people what happened there. So we need the old shell demolished and a new residence built in a different location as quickly as possible. Do you think we could interest those men in doing the work? Sir Gamel here is going to have a team of engineers sorting out what's needed on the docks and could help with any engineering the builders might need."

"I'll send to Prior Frery straightaway," Warin replies. "If those men haven't already found work, I'm sure they'd be happy of it. But they may be anxious about their safety."

"We'll make sure that's not a problem. I haven't spoken to Samuel about it directly, but no doubt he's already realized that troops are going to be needed in the port for a while to prevent the gangs taking over again. Law and order will prevail. I know the builders will have to experience it firsthand before they have confidence, but do your best to reassure them."

That evening, Laurence and I dine in private and speak of the other part of his role. "Rupert mentioned that as well," he says.

"And?"

"And I hope you don't have very high expectations at the beginning. Who knows how many of our old operatives are still around? How many of them may have succumbed to the sickness? And even those that are around . . . will they want to work for us again? Will they trust that we'll protect them after all that happened under John? It really will be starting to build from the ground up again, Alfred. New operatives, new sources, new ways of getting information."

"We have some time, Laurence. There aren't any immediate threats that I'm aware of. Unless you know something I don't." I grin at him.

"What about the Territories?" He's serious.

"Making peace there is my first personal priority. But back to your networks. Build them. Build them well and carefully. I have every confidence you can be as successful as Rupert was."

"If so, it's only because he taught me so well."

"I think he'd be truly delighted if you ever wanted to seek his advice. For what it's worth, he's a great admirer of yours. And I'm grateful to have the job in the hands of a friend."

•   •   •   •   •

Three days later, my luck runs out. Richard arrives just in time for the midday meal. "The news is anything but good, Alfred," he says as we tuck into a hearty potage the brothers have brought us. "I considered waiting until after the coronation to tell you, but decided you might want the time to think about what to do."

"How bad is it?"

"The Treasury is practically insolvent. There's enough money to run the kingdom for three more months . . . four, if we're careful. Despite John's forced collection of taxes, it seems he spent all that and much more on his grand army and his pointless war. Once the sickness began, there was nothing coming in at all. Apparently, the tax collectors refused to go about their task with disease raging everywhere. I can't really say I blame them," he adds with a sardonic chuckle. "And they've only just begun venturing out again."

"All the more reason why we have to get people working again and goods being traded."

"Your instincts are on target there, my friend."

"Actually, I'm about to make things worse for you. Put a stop to the tax collectors' activities right away, if you will. Among the proposals I'm bringing to the first Council meeting is to restore the law under which people pay taxes locally. I've no reason to think the Council will be opposed. And I'm fairly confident we'll get better cooperation that way.

"What about John's personal fortune?" I ask. "It seems only right that some of his funds be given to the Treasury to repay his excess spending."

"It's nowhere to be found, Alfred. And believe me, we've searched everywhere. Matthias has practically torn the castle apart helping Rupert and me look for it . . . in nooks and crannies I suspect very few people know even exist."

"Up the chimneys?"

"Up the chimneys, in the undercrofts, in the gardens, in the stables . . . even in the disused ovens and chimneys in the kitchen of the old castle. There's no sign of it . . . not even a stray coin to indicate that money was once stored nearby."

"It seems unlike John, with his distrust of everyone save himself, but is there any possibility he lodged it with the bankers?"

"I had the same thought. They all claim never to have seen your brother, much less his money."

We spend the rest of the day and much of the evening poring over the details. "If you want to maintain a proper court and help people to get back on their feet, we're going to have to find money somewhere," he says. "And none of this takes into account the cost of your progress."

"Even if I have to fund the progress myself, I won't even consider cancelling it. People need to see their new king out among them."

"It seems," says Richard with a bit of resignation in his voice, "we'll have no choice but to borrow money to carry us through. There are the bankers, of course. Other kingdoms. The merchants. I've even considered whether we should approach the Church."

"That's the one place I'd be loath to go," I tell him. "We have a healthy balance now between the Crown and the Church. Any risk of upsetting that seems particularly unwise."

"Truth be told, that's what I thought you might say, and I agree with you completely. But I didn't want to ignore any option."

"My mind can't take in any more of this in one day." I cross to the sideboard and pour two glasses of André's brandy. "I plan to ask the Council to reinstate the Assembly right away. Phillip may have some ideas about how the merchants might contribute in ways that are different from just an outright loan. Draw up your proposals for the first

Council meeting. If we have to go in debt, I want to do it with their agreement."

The rest of my time at the monastery passes quietly, mostly spent with Eustace, practicing and practicing the language of the Territories. All our other plans might be for nought if I can't make peace with our neighbors.

Coronation Day. The first two words that pop into my mind as I awake. My Coronation Day. It still doesn't seem quite real.

Despite all that's happened since the New Year. Despite spending a month here at the monastery. Despite the fact that Osbert arrived yesterday bringing the finery I'm to wear. Despite the fact that there is a fine white stallion waiting for me in the stable, and Tobin is here with a troop of the King's Own Guard to escort the procession. Despite everything, I'm still in wonder that in just a few hours the crown will be placed on my head. The crown worn by my father. The crown forever linked in my mind to my grandfather. A symbol of their legacies.

As the last ritual of seclusion, I attend Prime with the brothers, dressed in a simple monk's robe, then join André and Warin for a small breakfast. We'll forego the midday meal because the ceremony is timed for the actual crowning to occur when the sun is at its zenith.

Dawn reveals a clear blue sky and a brilliant sun that warms the air with a comforting foretelling of spring days soon to come. Despite the fact that it's winter and travel is difficult, there are people all along both sides of the road as our procession makes its way from the monastery to the church. The dull roar of a multitude of conversations goes suddenly silent when Sir Tobin leads us into the market square and the crowd parts, as if on cue, for us to cross.

As I dismount in front of the church steps, Gwen steps from her carriage, radiant and regal, her gown entirely of cloth of silver with decorations in the blue of our family crest. At her neck, a simple circlet of diamonds – the one worn by my mother as a gift from my father on the occasion of his coronation. Her earrings are the sapphires she received from her mother in celebration of our betrothal. On her wrist, a bracelet of gold, sapphires, and diamonds – my coronation gift to her.

Her golden curls hang long and loose down her back, ready to accept the queen's crown. I take her hand and we ascend the steps together as the processional music begins.

At the altar, we take our positions on the prie-dieux for the ritual prayers and the fateful question, "Is there anyone here present who disputes Lord Alfred's claim to the throne?"

All is quiet for a moment. Then comes the sound of footsteps walking up the aisle. As they approach, a woman's voice, heavily accented. "Here is true king." And again, when the footsteps stop directly behind us, the same voice. "Here is true king." Words that haven't been heard in this kingdom for more than five generations.

Though it's improper for me to look back to see who challenges my claim, I have a pretty good idea what's happening. In whispered tones, I tell the bishop, "Brother Nicholas is here." Was it prescience that led me to ask André to allow all the brothers to attend? No, Alfred, I tell myself. Just extraordinarily good luck.

The bishop calls for Nicholas. "Brother Nicholas, if this woman is who I believe her to be, I seem to recall you have the ability to speak her language. Please ask her to explain her challenge."

While the monk and the woman speak in hushed tones, the bishop signals to his acolytes to bring chairs, which they place facing each other on either side of the prie-dieux. "Perhaps, my children," he says quietly, "you'd be more comfortable seated while we sort out this matter." And once I can see the new arrivals, my suspicions are confirmed.

"My Lord Bishop," says Nicholas loudly enough to be heard throughout the Church, "this woman is Gunhild, youngest daughter of Lord Erik of the Eastern Kingdom, sister of our late Queen Gundrea. I can vouch for her identity, having served as translator when her family attended the last coronation. The boy with her is called Gunderik. She claims he's the son of the late King John. She further claims to be in possession of a letter from King John stating that Gunderik is to be king after his father."

The child is of an age consistent with conception around the time John was crowned. But the bishop proceeds carefully. "Pray ask her, Brother, what proof she can offer that this child is truly the son of our late king."

After consulting Gunhild, Nicholas answers, "Your Excellency, she says that the letter should be sufficient proof. If I may, Your Excellency, there was much gossip among the servants about the queen's sister being seen coming and going from the king's apartments at unseemly hours."

"Thank you, Brother, but we cannot base the future of the kingdom on servants' gossip."

"I only meant to suggest, Excellency, that gossip usually springs from a kernel of truth, no matter how difficult it may be to discern that kernel."

"I need to see the letter," says the bishop. Gunhild withdraws a folded paper from the pocket of her shapeless black gown and hands it to the monk, who in turn passes it to the bishop.

Unfolding it, he remarks. "To my eyes, this is indeed the signature and seal of our late king, but we should have further verification. Lord Rupert? Lord Devereux? If you please?" They come forward and examine the letter in turn, each proclaiming himself satisfied that the signature and seal are John's.

The church bells begin to peal midday, the poor bell ringer having no idea of the drama unfolding here beneath him. The people in the square will be wondering why we haven't appeared. Once the bells are quiet, the bishop resumes. "If further proof is required, I can fetch the late king's will from the vaults for comparison. Does anyone require such proof?" There's utter silence among the congregation.

"Very well," continues the bishop. "The date of the letter is some four months past, approximately the time of the hunter's moon.

To the Lady Gunhild, Greetings.

I write to tell you of the death of your sister and our children. I send my regrets to you and your father on their loss. It is possible that your son may become king one day. Herewith I send you a sum of money for your son if that occurs.

"The letter is signed and sealed as we three have previously witnessed. But as it's written in Latin, I'd like verification that I've rendered the proper translation. Abbot André? Prior Warin? If you please?" Each pronounces the translation accurate.

Now the bishop addresses Gunhild. "My daughter, there is nothing in this letter that says your son is the rightful heir to the throne of this kingdom." Nicholas translates, and Gunhild replies in an emotional fury, stamping her feet and pointing to the letter. The monk tries to calm her.

"My Lord Bishop, she insists that letter is proof that her son is the rightful heir."

The bishop reads the letter once again. "I see nothing in here that so states. Abbot, your opinion?" He hands the letter to André who also reads it again.

"The letter is clear, Your Excellency. It says this lady's son *may* become king. It does not say that he *will* become king. The grammar is perfect and precise throughout. There's no indication of a writer unsure of the tenses of verbs or forms of expression. The writer merely indicates a possibility of such an event – not its predetermined eventuality."

Nicholas has been translating this exchange for Gunhild. She is now almost in tears, pleading with him. "She says, Your Excellency, that this boy is the son of King John and therefore he must be the next king."

"Very well, Brother. Ask her if she was married to King John when the child was conceived or when it was born?"

"She says no, Excellency."

"Ask her if her sister Gundrea was married to King John at the time this child was born?"

"She says yes."

"Magistrate? If you please?" The magistrate comes forward. "Am I correct in believing that the laws of this kingdom exclude a bastard from succession to the throne?"

"You are correct, Excellency."

"And is there any legal way in which a bastard could inherit?"

"If the king signs a law proclaiming a child as his legitimate offspring, that overrides the circumstances of the child's birth. The child would then be legitimate and eligible to succeed."

"And did King John sign such a law?"

"Not to my knowledge, Excellency, though King John often took actions unilaterally, without communicating them to those who should know. The only way to be certain is to examine the official records."

"Then we must do that now," says the bishop. "How should we proceed, Magistrate?"

"My clerk is familiar with the official records. We should dispatch him to the castle to return with the complete folio of all laws signed by King John."

"Summon your clerk, Magistrate. Prior Warin and a member of the Guard will accompany him to ensure his safety and to verify that nothing is tampered with."

So we settle in to wait. I try to give Gwen a reassuring look, though protocol forbids me to display any emotion. For her part, she remains calm and serene . . . a true queen. At long last, the clerk and his companions return and present the folio to the bishop.

"Abbot? Lord Devereux? Magistrate? Please assist me to look at these laws. We must examine each one to determine if any action was taken to legitimize the Lady Gunhild's son." This process occupies no more than half an hour. John did little in the way of creating laws; his reign was more about rescinding those that previously existed.

The bishop turns back to Gunhild. "My child, there is no document signed by King John making your child his legitimate son. Do you have any further proof?" Nicholas translates.

Gunhild can do no more than cry and point to where the bishop has laid her letter on the altar. The bishop waits in silence for a very long time, no doubt with the intention of giving her ample opportunity to produce any other proof. At last, he speaks. "We've examined this challenge to Lord Alfred's claim to the throne and found it to be without merit in the eyes of the law and the eyes of the Church. Brother Nicholas, if you would be so kind as to escort this lady and her child out of the church and to a place of safety, we will proceed with the ceremony."

With small gestures, he invites Gwen and me to resume our places on the prie-dieux and once again intones the fateful question, "Is there anyone here present who disputes Lord Alfred's claim to the throne?" This time the silence is profound.

When the crown is placed on my head, I'm surprised by the weight. Is it really that heavy or is what I feel the weight of responsibility? Perhaps both. I feel nothing but pride as I watch my beautiful Gwen being crowned. She will, I think, be a queen unlike any that has been seen before in this land. Prayers are said for wisdom and long life for the new sovereign and blessings for the kingdom. It is done. The bishop sends an acolyte rushing to the bell tower and soon the bells begin to peal again, our signal to rise and follow the bishop down the aisle.

We gather near the door, preparing to go out and greet the people, Osbert and Letty nearby, helping with our cloaks. "Osbert, we should arrange for that poor girl to spend the night at the castle and then send her on her way."

"No, Alfred, you mustn't." The sharpness of my mother's tone draws my attention immediately. "I know you think to act out of kindness, Son, but you must do *nothing* to indicate she has any place in this family . . . *nothing* to give rise to speculation that there may be any legitimacy to her claim."

Rupert is standing nearby. "Alice is right, Alfred. Even though it may seem cold-hearted."

I kiss my mother on the cheek, clap my uncle on the shoulder, and give them both a big smile. "Thank heaven you two were here to keep me from making a mistake in my first hour as a crowned king."

"It's what mothers do, Alfred," teases mine, "in case you've forgotten."

"Osbert?"

"It be already fergot, m'lord."

As we're about to exit the church Richard taps me on the shoulder. "I sent my squire to find Brother Nicholas and have him question the girl about the money that was mentioned in the letter. We may have our first clue as to the whereabouts of John's personal fortune."

Before I can answer, the riotous pealing of the bells stops, the cue for the church doors to be opened. The cheering is deafening. We pause briefly at the top of the steps before descending to begin a complete circuit of the square. I couldn't be more pleased that the lords have agreed to accompany us. People will see by their presence – not just hear by word of mouth – that the kingdom is truly reunited and the days of uncertainty are beginning to recede into the past.

Tobin's guards, mounted on horseback, are scattered among the crowd, keeping an eye on things, but they're not needed. There's no pushing or shoving, and the mood is entirely of festivity and celebration. Rounding the final corner to complete our circuit, I catch a glimpse of two familiar faces on the opposite side of the square. I turn to Gwen to draw her attention to them, but by the time we look back, the faces and their owners have vanished – as if they had never been there in the first place. Perhaps it was simply my overactive imagination playing tricks on me.

The bells begin pealing again as we make our way up the road – where even more people have gathered – toward the castle. The weather has been kind, and despite the two-hour delay caused by Gunhild's challenge, the air is still warm. No doubt the casks are already being opened in the square. The bonfires will soon follow and the celebrating will most likely continue until dawn. Just before we pass through the gates, my eye is drawn to movement on the main road – two horsemen, alone, riding west. Perhaps it wasn't my imagination after all.

Next comes the formal reception of my fellow sovereigns. As we make our way through the corridors, I turn to Geoffrey. "Now, Geoffrey, when you're presented —" He cuts me off short.

"Don't worry, Papa. Uncle Rupert has told me everything. I know what to do. You'll be proud of me . . . you'll see."

Only Petronilla is here from the Kingdom Across the Southern Sea. "My dear Goscelin has been ill," she tells us. "He's recovering well, but his doctors thought travel would be too taxing just now."

Juliana and Geoffrey play their parts to perfection. I have to resist the temptation to tousle Geoffrey's hair after he's made his bows – he's determined to appear very grown up. So I give him a smile instead, which he returns with a smug, ear-to-ear grin of self-satisfaction . . . the perfect response for a boy his age just learning court protocol.

Formalities complete, all the doors are thrown open, allowing everyone to mingle. Lord Ernle approaches with two people in tow. "Alfred, my boy, I hope you don't mind. I brought two guests of my own."

"Well, Sir Ronan," I address one of his companions, smiling, "it appears you finally found the courage to ask for your lady's hand."

Ronan laughs. "I did indeed, Your Grace," he replies. "My wife, Alienor."

"I think I see in your beauty, madam, why this valiant knight needed an excess of courage." She blushes.

"I'm glad you're here, Ronan. I still maintain my habit of riding every morning when the weather permits, and Samuel often comes as well. Any chance I could convince you to join us while you're here?"

"I'd be honored and delighted, Sire," he replies.

Because of the earlier delay, there's little time before the banquet, which begins just at sundown. Once again, Juliana and Geoffrey are allowed to participate. Devereux has spared nothing to make this a special day. The feast is spectacular, the wine its equal.

At one of the tables in the second row facing the dais are a group I recognize as merchants from the former Assembly. Amelia is not among them. I hope that's only because she wasn't elected this time and not because something dire has happened to her. By inviting them, Devereux either suspects my wish to reinstate the Assembly and is signaling his approval . . . or he's sending me a message that this is something I should consider. Either way, we're in complete agreement, so I'll make it a point to greet them this evening so that everyone knows my intent.

It's after midnight when Gwen and I retire. We walk hand-in-hand back to our apartment, where the doors to the bedchamber have been left open for us. I look around, seeing it for the first time. The bed is our marriage bed and most of the furnishings are from the first apartment we occupied together. My grandfather's small writing desk. My father's favorite chair. "It's perfect, my love," I tell her.

"I'm so happy you're pleased," she replies. "Matthias wanted me to use your grandfather's bed, but I wanted to be reminded of some of the happiest times in our lives. A new canopy and hangings have been ordered, but they couldn't be ready in time."

I take her in my arms and kiss her deeply and passionately . . . something I've been longing to do all day. Releasing her at last, I tell her again, "It truly is perfect. And I know we'll be very happy here."

Letty and Osbert take over, helping us to shed the day's finery. When we climb into this bed again, it feels like home. For the second time, we're starting a new life together here. Our lovemaking is urgent and passionate, and we fall asleep in each other's arms.

The morning is crisp but sunny — perfect for a brisk winter ride. Samuel and Ronan are there, already mounted and ready to go. The big surprise is under my saddle – none other than Sirius, the stallion I gave to Samuel to protect my anonymity as I planned my abandonment of the war. Elvin is grinning from ear to ear, quite pleased with my astonishment.

"What's this, Samuel?" I ask. "*You* should be riding him."

"He's your horse, Alfred."

"I seem to recall giving him to you. Or was that just a dream?"

Samuel laughs. "No dream. And I'll admit I've enjoyed riding him. But he's a king's horse through and through and was meant to be yours."

I start examining the saddle and bridle fittings. "I wouldn't mind, though," Samuel continues, "having one like him. Any idea where I might find one of his brothers or sons? Maybe even trained as well?" We all laugh.

"I'll trade you then. In return for Sirius, you can have your choice of Star Dancer's colts. The training's up to you."

"By the way," says Samuel. "He still does that trick where he pretends to be lame. Mostly these days, though, he only does it when you ask him to. Guess he thinks he's got a pretty good life and doesn't so much need an excuse to go back to the stable."

Later, on my way to meet with Lord Bauldry, I encounter Richard in the corridor. "I've talked with Brother Nicholas, Alfred. The girl couldn't really tell him how much money John sent her. She just said 'many gold coins.' Nicholas said he tried to coax out of her how many, but all she would say was 'much money, many coins.' He couldn't discern if that meant ten or fifty or two hundred, so we don't know much more than we did two days ago. If it's substantial, it would be nice to have it back. But how? Nicholas was certain she had none of it with her."

"I'll think about it."

"The other thing Nicholas told me is that the girl kept asking for her letter back . . . pleading with him, as if it were some sort of treasure."

"Please tell me no one gave it to her."

"Nicholas didn't have it, and the bishop wouldn't see her."

"Then we may have a bargaining tool. Get word to the bishop right away that that letter is not to leave his vault without my express permission."

I find Bauldry waiting in my private reception room. "Lord Bauldry, forgive me. Being late isn't my habit, but I encountered Richard in the corridor, and he's trying to help me sort out the matter of the money mentioned in that letter we heard yesterday.

"Please . . . take a seat." We both do. "We haven't had a chance to talk privately. What I'd like to hear is what you'd most like to do as we try to get things back in shape."

"Since you ask, Alfred," he begins, then quickly stops himself. "I'm sorry, Sire. Old habits die hard."

"Thanks to my brother and his absurd insistence on formal address, I find I'm having to tell everyone the same thing. Speak as you did with my father, and we'll all be much happier. Truth be told," I add with a chuckle, "it's just as hard for me to get used to addressing you as Bauldry."

He laughs out loud. "It's been a strange journey, hasn't it, Alfred? But what I'm hoping is that we can circle back and pick up where we left off with Edward. And what I really want to do is just that. Your father had asked me to mentor John on working out a new scheme for retirement of our knights. We got nowhere with that. Every conversation I had with your brother, it seemed like I had to start over from the beginning. And he was completely unresponsive to anything I knew about how to teach a young man new skills."

"You weren't alone there. It was my father's perpetual lament."

He chuckles. "So what I'd really like to do is start over and do it right."

"I'd like that too," I reply. "Is there any chance I could talk you into doing a favor for me before you get started?"

"If I can."

"I've no idea what shape the justice system is in. How many of the magistrates and sheriffs survived the sickness? I know the port is abandoned. Samuel will have a troop there to suppress the gangs, but that's not a good solution for the long term. We need to get proper authority operating there as soon as may be. The magistrate here is safe, but I don't know about the sheriffs. Nor do we know anything about the other towns. Would you be willing to get my father's system functioning again?"

"With pleasure, sir," Bauldry replies. "May I also ask a favor?"

"Of course."

"Have you any objection to my eldest son Guyat assisting? He needs something to take his mind off the loss of his wife last summer."

"I didn't know. The sickness?"

"Thankfully not or we might none of us be here. Childbed fever . . . she never recovered."

"By all means, have him help. In fact, I intend to pick up where Father left off with bringing the heirs into the room with the lords. And not just my good friends . . . your son and Rainard Ernle as well."

"Guyat will be honored, Alfred. And he'll serve you well."

There's a quiet knock at the door, to which I reply, "Come." The attendant opens the door just enough to get himself inside and says quietly, "Lord Peveril and Lord Emaurri have arrived, Your Grace."

"Anything more we need to discuss, Bauldry?"

"I think not, Sire," the formality for the benefit of the servant. "I'll take up no more of your time."

As he rises to leave, the attendant opens the door widely and stands aside for Bauldry to leave and the Peverils to enter. "Peveril," says Bauldry with a broad smile. "Joining the family trade, Emaurri?"

Peveril grins. Emaurri replies, "Perhaps, sir. If the king will have me." The doors close behind Bauldry, and I invite the Peverils to sit.

Our preliminary conversation is wide-ranging so I can get to know the son. After some initial awkwardness, Emaurri chimes in with his own ideas. His manner of expression is remarkably similar to that of his father – designed to avoid giving offense while still delivering a definitive point of view. "So, Peveril," I finally get down to the real business of the meeting, "I'm sure you'd be the last one to be surprised I need you in multiple places right away. But I think there may be a solution if Emaurri is willing to undertake what I have in mind."

Peveril smiles broadly. I've no way to know how much he prepared his son for this conversation, but it's clear he's pleased with the results. "How can I serve you, Sire?" Emaurri asks.

"What do you think of the post of ambassador to the Kingdom Across the Southern Sea?"

Emaurri lets nothing show in his facial expression, but he does allow a hint of excitement into his voice, "An honor indeed, Sire."

"It won't be easy at the outset. Your first task will be to win back the trust of the great weaving houses and rebuild their demand for our wool. No doubt they've already turned to other sources, but they know and we know that ours is the finest wool in the world. Lord Thorssen will be working on a plan to make some fleeces available immediately – well before the summer wool markets. And your father knows what motivates the weavers. It won't surprise me, though, if they drive a hard bargain, especially if they find themselves in the position of having to cancel arrangements with other suppliers."

"You'll have to lay out for me the terms you're willing to accept, of course. But I agree having some of our best right away will enhance our bargaining power."

"May I take that as your acceptance? I assure you, it won't all be such difficult negotiating. You'll also need to be a proper ambassador to Goscelin's court, which I'm told is not a terrible place to be."

Emaurri finally allows himself a smile. "I spent a bit of time there during my father's last assignment, Sire. Your informants have got it quite right. And yes, I'm pleased to accept the post."

"Well," say Peveril, "now that Emaurri has the tough job, I hope you've got a plum posting in mind for me."

"Depends on your definition of plum," I chuckle. "What I have in mind is something I think may never have been attempted before."

"Now I *am* intrigued."

"The first thing I intend to do . . . just as soon as I get all the wheels in motion to get the kingdom back on its feet . . . is to make a lasting peace with the Territories. The peacemaking, I have to do personally. But then I want to establish a diplomatic connection with them."

"That's ambitious indeed, sir. How does one conduct diplomacy with such a loose confederation of fiefdoms? Is anyone actually in charge there? I mean – where would we even start?" It seems I've truly taken Peveril by surprise; rarely is he at such a loss for expressing a possible path forward.

"There, I think I can help you. Before John turned the world upside down, I was building a friendship with Lord Egon, whose lands border ours. We had developed a mutual trust and were on the verge of expanding that to something that might lead to an alliance. You'd have had no way of knowing this, but my secret negotiation with Egon is what ultimately brought an end to the conflict started by Harold's military exercises and John's unauthorized raid. Egon and his son Goron came quietly to Father's funeral, and soon after, I visited there. I had the foolish notion I could forestall misunderstandings by telling him John would be a very different sort of sovereign from my father.

"If I can succeed in making the peace and the Territorial lords disperse their army, I think Egon may help us resume what he and I had started. It will be a long-term project that may or may not succeed . . . and that may take more than one reign to bear the ultimate fruit. But it's a project that's very dear to my heart. There was no friction between us in my grandfather's time – 'live and let live' suited everyone. But we've disrupted that so many times and in so many ways, that we now bear the burden of undertaking the repair."

Through all this, Peveril has sat with his brow furrowed, obviously deep in thought. "What if the others feel betrayed by Egon? They let him talk them into believing us once and then we turned on them again. His credibility may not be what it once was."

There, I can't help. I can't reveal that it was my message to Egon and Samuel's discussion with him of John's likely tactics that allowed the Territorial lords to repel the invasion. "Maybe I can get a clearer view of that as we discuss the peace."

"That makes sense." He pauses, again obviously deep in thought. "I'm still intrigued, sir. It would be something entirely new that would test the mettle of my skill. One of my biggest concerns, though, is language. I've never before attempted to engage where I didn't have at the very least a modicum of the language easily to hand and a reliable interpreter nearby. Too many things can go wrong when the parties fail to understand each others' meaning."

"Another place I can offer some help. Egon speaks our tongue quite comfortably and is teaching it to his son – at least, he was when I visited. Out of respect, I wanted to learn their language. So Warin found me a tutor among his brothers. Warin and André have both been strong proponents of my efforts, so I'm confident André would allow Brother Eustace to be at your disposal. He's really quite a good tutor. In fact, I intend to try to conduct the peace negotiations in the Territorial language as a gesture of good faith."

"Very well. Let's see how the peacemaking goes. If you still think Egon has influence, then I'll see if I can make something out of the overtures you've already begun. In the meantime, I'll speak to André and see what can be arranged."

●　　●　　●　　●　　●

Tonight, we dine privately with our visitors. The kings will begin their return journeys tomorrow morning. Petronilla and Richenda – her daughter by Harold – will stay another two weeks here in the place that was her home as Harold's wife and as dowager queen.

As everyone starts to retire for the night, I approach Rupert. "A word, Uncle?"

"Of course."

We retire to the library, which – thanks to André's monks – is once again just as it was in my grandfather's day. Settling in with a brandy in front of the fire, Rupert asks, "What's on your mind, Alfred?"

"Money," I reply as I fill my own glass and join him. "Specifically, the money John sent to Gunhild. Richard thinks, from what Nicholas was able to learn, that it may be a rather substantial sum, and heaven knows we could use that right now."

Pausing for a sip of brandy, I continue, "I asked Peveril this afternoon what he thought about our chances of negotiating to get any of it back. We're not in a very good bargaining position. The only tool we have is that letter she's so keen to get back. But he advises against using it, and I agree he's right."

"He's more than right, Alfred. That letter is the only link between John and that boy, and it should be destroyed immediately. Just imagine what could be the consequences of her having it. That boy is going to be raised on mother's milk poisoned with the notion that he was deprived of his rightful place. And when he's a man, he would have a piece of paper that he can't read but that he's been told all his life is the proof of his right to our throne. Do you really want Geoffrey to have to face an angry, resentful adversary who might choose to go to war to get what he thinks is rightfully his?"

"Of course not," I reply. "I'd been thinking how things might play out, but you paint it far more vividly than even my own imagination. The boy is going to be raised on that poisonous milk regardless . . . there's nothing we can do about that."

"But let's not give her anything to which she can tie that vitriol. Where's the letter now?"

"In the bishop's vault."

"Not necessarily a safe place. If she has the imagination to appeal to her own bishop, it's not out of the question some ecclesiastical process would force ours to relinquish it."

"He has my instructions not to release it without my express permission, but I hadn't thought about the possibility of an ecclesiastical appeal."

"I'll retrieve it from him tomorrow."

"It's the only proof we have that John sent her the money."

"There were hundreds of witnesses in the church yesterday that heard it read aloud. Perhaps not as definitive proof as the letter itself, but strong evidence in a court of law, should we ever decide to pursue it. That letter needs to vanish."

"Peveril thinks he might be able to get some of the money back if the Council were to provide him with a writ that it was given illegally."

"Do you really think that's wise?"

We sit quietly, staring into the fire. Finally, I break the silence. "I keep asking myself 'what would Grandfather have done?'"

Gently, Rupert replies, "I know how much we need the money, Alfred. But in your heart, I think you know the answer."

"He would protect the succession first and foremost and find some other way to deal with the current crisis," I say quietly, still staring into the fire.

Rupert's silence is the only reply I need. It also tells me that, once the letter is in his possession, it will never be seen again.

"They be ready fer ye, sir," says Osbert.

I rise from my seat before the fire, where I'd been collecting my thoughts and contemplating how my father and grandfather conducted themselves in Council. It's but a short walk from the library to the Council chamber, but I don't hurry. After all the preparation, all the ceremony, all the celebration . . . when I walk through those doors, it all begins in earnest.

More than anything, I want to do this well. Not the meeting, but the daunting task of being responsible for the future of the kingdom. I want to be a worthy successor to those two men who gave so much of themselves to shape the man I am today. I want to be worthy of everything the lords have done to protect the kingdom. I want to create a legacy that Geoffrey can be proud to build upon. I want to see our people thrive and enjoy happy lives in a land at peace with its neighbors. A lot to want, Alfred, I tell myself, in a world where anything could go wrong.

As I approach, a servant opens the door to the chamber. I hear scrambling and scuffling as of men rising to their feet, so I greet them while walking to my chair at the head of the table. "Gentlemen, please. Keep your seats." Taking my own, I add, "Hmmm. The view from here is not much different than what I'm accustomed to." A reference to the fact that the royal family's representative on the Council always sits at the end of the table opposite the king. "Except that everyone seems to be on the wrong side." There's quiet laughter all around.

"Bishop, nice to see you back at the table."

"It's equally nice to be here, my son."

"I asked everyone to attend today because of the importance of the main topic we have to discuss. But there are a few items I want to deal with first since I'm confident there'll be little need for debate. First, there's the question of the lifetime lords created by John. I haven't seen hide nor hair of any of them and have certainly received no pledge of loyalty. Does anyone know their whereabouts?" Heads shake in the negative all around the table.

Devereux rolls his eyes. "I suspect our late king never asked them for a pledge – probably never asked them for anything. I'll send messages reminding them of their obligations and the consequences of failure to comply." As first lord of the realm, Devereux has a duty to oversee such matters.

"Ordinarily, I'd expect the sheriff nearest their location to deliver your messages," I say. "But as we've no idea where we have sheriffs or magistrates at the moment, Sir Samuel can help you get word to them." Samuel nods his assent.

"That problem is only temporary, gentlemen. Bauldry has graciously agreed to put our legal system back in order with help from his son Guyat. Bauldry, can we expect a progress report from Guyat one month hence?"

"Of course, Sire. He may be a bit anxious about his first appearance in front of the Council, but it's time he had some practice."

"Remind me, Bauldry," I say with a broad smile, "and I'll set the meeting time for early afternoon. That way you can assure Guyat we will have recently eaten and won't be tempted to make a meal of him." More laughter. The easy camaraderie is back in the room.

"If I may, Your Grace?"

I'm curious what all this formality from the first lord is about, but go along with the tone he's setting. "Of course, Devereux."

"The Council members have been consulting in advance of this meeting, and there are some things we'd like to recommend be attended to straightaway. Certain things our late king rescinded should be reinstated as soon as may be: universal education and paying taxes locally. And we'd like to see the Assembly re-established. That experiment was working well and should be continued. None of us ever supported your brother's actions."

"Devereux, I've watched from the other end of the table how expertly you anticipate where king and Council are in agreement. It's almost as if you could read the minds of my predecessors." I pause, then add, "Well, most of them – my brother being a notable exception – though I'm pretty certain most of us would have suspected you of practicing some sort of wizardry had you been able to delve into *that* strange mind." Laughs all around. "But I'm grateful you've been able to read mine. I'm eager to sign those documents just as soon as they can be prepared."

Devereux signals to my secretary, who sits at a small table in the corner of the room recording the proceedings. He collects some papers, a quill, and an inkpot, and places them in front of me. "In the spirit of reading your mind, Sire," Devereux remarks as all this is happening, "I took the liberty of poaching some of your new secretary's time to prepare them in advance. I think we'd all like to witness the signing and celebrate putting the last three years squarely behind us." As I begin signing the documents, my secretary walks back to the table and returns with a wax warmer and my seal.

"Thorssen, it seems to me the most definitive signal we could send to the Assembly that we wish to resume where they left off is for you to continue your role as the Council's liaison. What say you?"

"That I'm glad I don't have to beg forgiveness for asking the merchants to stay after the coronation and convene as an Assembly tomorrow."

"Excellent!" I exclaim, adding, "And by the way, your first priority is wool."

"Wool?" Phillip looks inquisitive.

"Wool. We need every fleece that remains in barns and warehouses from last year's shearing to sell immediately to the great weaving houses. We have to make absolutely certain they know they can count on getting our wool this year and in the future . . . *before* they start renewing and expanding contracts with other suppliers."

"Then wool it is."

"Thorssen, I don't think I have to tell you how important this is. If you encounter resistance, then you have my authorization to tell them that the Treasury will confiscate the wool and pay them ten percent less than the lowest price of the past three years; the Treasury will take on the risk of transport and trade; and the Treasury will collect the profit. I hope you get full cooperation, but use that threat if you must."

Devereux. "And you can count on any of us to help . . . either in the meeting or with private persuasion."

"Thank you, Devereux," I remark. "Now, gentlemen, there's one more thing we have to do to complete putting King John's reign in the past," I resume, "and that is to make peace with the Territories. I've given this long consideration and am convinced that's something I have to do myself."

Meriden. "We all agree John's tactics were ill-advised, but I wonder if we agree that his motives were wrong. After all, King Harold was also intent on dealing with the Territories in some manner."

"And as I recall," Montfort, "there was considerable division of opinion on Harold's intentions."

"Which is precisely why we should re-examine our intentions today." Meriden.

I hadn't expected this. I was certain the disaster of John's foray into the Territories would have put all the old arguments to rest. Reminder to myself: never forget that Meriden likes to stir things up. Have a conversation with him in advance on crucial topics in the hope of satisfying his need to appear important.

Phillip speaks up. "I wasn't part of the original debate of King Harold's plan, but maybe if we examine his motives and John's, we can quickly put those misadventures to rest."

Samuel. "From a military perspective, nothing John did made any sense. So his motivation clearly lay elsewhere."

"There is no doubt in my mind," Devereux, "that John was driven only by a desire to obliterate what he saw as his greatest humiliation. Ironic, isn't it, that that desire led to an even greater humiliation." He pauses. "Is there anyone who disagrees that we can rule out King John's intentions in the Territories as irrelevant?"

Silence around the table.

Meriden once again. "That brings us back to Harold. He seemed so convinced there was an issue with the Territories that affected this realm. And he seemed to have a plan to deal with them. Are we shying away from the problem simply because we don't know what tactics to use to subdue them?"

This has gone far enough. "All fair questions, gentlemen, but not the right questions. Consider this. During the reign of my grandfather and again during my father's, our relationship with the Territories was peaceful. The border was quiet. There were no hostilities between us. There was some immigration, but nothing excessive, and we benefitted from the work done by the new arrivals.

"There's something you're unlikely to know about Harold's motivations. My uncle blamed himself for the fact that I was taken captive during the attack on the reservoir. He knew his life had been saved because he slept in my hut the night before the attack. And he carried an enormous amount of guilt that he was unable to prevent my capture. Once it was known that Ralf had taken me into the Territories, I believe he attached some sort of accountability for my continued captivity to the Territorial lords . . . somehow believing they had either motivation or responsibility to govern Ralf's actions.

"I was there, gentlemen. I can assure you that was *not* the case. We came into contact with only two of the Territorial lords while Ralf held me. The first distanced himself from Ralf's actions and banished Ralf from his land. The second appeared to tolerate Ralf but clearly treated him as a visitor over whom he had no authority. The Territories bear absolutely no culpability in my captivity. Sadly, I was never able to convince my uncle of this."

Rupert has raised a finger indicating a desire to speak, so I pause and nod in his direction. "We all recall that Harold was unable to effectively explain the reasons for his actions. Even to his brothers. As the one here who was closest to him, I truly believe Harold never fully understood his own motivation. What the king says rings true for me."

Phillip sums up. "So the reasons for both previous confrontations with the Territories were rooted not in the best interests of the kingdom but in deeply personal concerns of individual kings."

"My assessment as well, Thorssen." Devereux.

"As to your other question, Meriden," I resume, "about whether we know what tactics to use, let me say this. *If* our intent were to subdue the Territories, I know exactly how it should be done, and it would require cooperation from the Kingdom of Peaks. The first attack should be launched against the western lords . . . over the lowland western border with the Peaks Kingdom . . . and ideally at a time when they're engaged in one of their frequent squabbles among themselves. We could make a good advance in the time it would take them to quit fighting each other and turn their attention to us.

"They would, of course, send to their eastern brethren for help. That's when we would launch an attack over our own border with the Territories. The eastern lords would have no choice but to face us and defend their own lands and couldn't provide reinforcements in the west.

"Once both groups were engaged, a force led by Peaks Highlanders would invade the Territories from the north, over the mountains. That force would prevent the eastern and western lords from ever joining forces . . . and also create a two-front war for both groups."

Samuel nods and smiles as he listens to my recitation. "That, gentlemen, is how one would subdue the Territories." I pause for a very long moment. "*If* our intent was to subdue them." Another long pause. "I submit to you that a far better strategy to serve the best interests of our kingdom is to make a lasting peace with the Territories and develop them as friends and allies.

"And to that end, Peveril has agreed to use his considerable talent to engage our neighbors and devise a way to conduct diplomacy with what he quite accurately describes as a loose confederation of fiefdoms."

Peveril takes up the thread. "When the king first put this notion to me, I was intrigued, even if uncertain how to go about it. After some more thought, I'm actually rather eager to take on the challenge. It may never have been done before, but that doesn't mean it can't be done. Frankly, gentlemen, I like the king's notion more and more each day."

I look down the table to where Lord Ernle has been sitting silently through this entire discussion. "Ernle, what our strategy is for the Territories affects you most directly. I, for one, would like to hear your perspective."

"I've been quiet," he replies, "only because I have nothing to add except my support for your peace-and-diplomacy approach. As you know, I was among those who could never understand Harold's motives and therefore opposed what he was doing. Your insight and

Lord Rupert's make it abundantly clear what was afoot then. I propose we put Peveril to work as soon as we can."

Peveril smiles. "Well, I think we may need to put our king to work on that peacemaking thing first." And all get a good laugh at my expense.

"Gentlemen, nothing would please me more than to go to work in this cause. Do we have agreement on Ernle's proposal?" I ask.

"Aye," "Agreed," and the like all around the table. "I want to be sure we're not missing anything, gentlemen. Does anyone have any remaining reservations? Concerns? Objections?"

This time silence. And I mentally breathe a huge sigh of relief.

"I do have a related question," says Montfort. "If Peveril is busy inventing diplomacy with fiefdoms, who's going to be our ambassador to the Kingdom Across the Southern Sea, to negotiate with the weavers?"

"Why, Peveril, of course," I quip. Most of the expressions around the table are of confusion or befuddlement. At the opposite end, though, Rupert is grinning from ear to ear, thoroughly enjoying my little game. Peveril, ever the diplomat, remains inscrutable.

Meriden. "Not to put too fine a point on it, Sire, but a man can't be in two places at once." He pauses, then adds, "Unless he's practicing some of that wizardry you mentioned earlier."

"I cannot disagree, Meriden. But what would you think of two Peverils?" I see recognition dawning around the table.

"Emaurri?" asks Bauldry.

"Correct," I reply. "I had a very long conversation with both Peverils yesterday and am convinced that Emaurri can represent our interests as ambassador to Goscelin's court."

"I know him well," says Bauldry. "In fact, I had him in mind for my Estrilda until your Laurence," he nudges Montfort, who's seated next to him, "came on the scene and she decided she'd have no one else. A fine man with his father's knack. An excellent choice, Sire."

"Very well, gentlemen. One final thing before we move on to the Treasury. Sir Samuel, how goes sorting out the knighthood?"

"Some progress, Sire," Samuel replies. "All the men who were conscripted – knights, foot soldiers, or archers – have been released and sent home. Four strong troops have been organized under the command of experienced captains. The shack communities have been cleaned up here and they're almost finished in Abbéville Market. They'll move on to Great Woolston and Neukirk next week. The King's Own Guard is fully staffed. Sir Gamel expects two more engineers to arrive any day now. Once they're here, work at the port can begin in earnest."

I interrupt him. "That's good to hear. Our new Port Commissioner is eager to get underway. Gentlemen, I think by now you all know Lord Laurence is taking up that post." Several "Here, here's" around the table, affirming confidence in Laurence.

"The rest, Sire," Samuel resumes, "we're still sorting out, including what, if any, promises of rewards, bonuses, or other compensation may have been made by the late king. There seem to be no records . . . only lots of hearsay."

"Decision on a deputy commander yet?" I ask.

"Soon. It will be one of the four current captains. Another of them will become commander at the garrison. I just have to work out which."

"Bishop, how are things progressing with the Church's assistance to those indigents we're moving out of the shack communities?"

"The priests in each town have my instructions to make sure these people have clothing and enough to eat to survive. And in their homilies for the next few weeks, they'll remind their flocks of the importance of helping our less fortunate brethren get back on their feet not only with charity but also with work and a means to provide for themselves."

"Let's hope the flocks are paying attention," I chuckle.

"Anything else, gentlemen, before we hear from Treasury?" Silence and shaking of heads. "Very well. Lord Richard, please proceed."

"Gentlemen," Richard begins, "I won't mince words. The Treasury is very nearly bankrupt. John's expenditures were devastating. Adding to that the fact that almost no taxes were collected in the year of the sickness, the result is that we're in dire straits, with only enough money to run the kingdom for three . . . perhaps four . . . months. After that, the coffers are empty.

"As we resume collecting taxes, money will come in, but the income will be slower than the outgo. The king offered to contribute some of John's personal fortune to the Treasury as recompense for the damage caused by his policies and actions. With all due respect for the king's noble sentiments, the royal family has its own financial obligations that are different from the Treasury's, and I don't recommend setting a precedent of intermingling the two." He pauses.

Ernle. "None of us doubt the sincerity or generosity of your gesture, Sire. But these policies exist for a reason. Our kingdom's history is not devoid of the occasional unscrupulous king, your brother included." I bow my head ever so slightly in Ernle's direction, acknowledging the truth of his words.

"In any event," Richard resumes, "the point is moot, because John's fortune is nowhere to be found. We can't even determine if he, himself, placed it into the Treasury to fund his war. One thing is certain . . . as controller of the Treasury, King John was abysmally incompetent. Other than the first three months or so, where he carefully recorded orders to cease payments for all manner of things, the records simply do not exist. Not of income from taxes. Not of payments of any sort. It seems John treated the Treasury as his personal purse.

"So we have to start from scratch. The king's emphasis on restoring trade and putting people to work will be a priority for the Assembly, Lord Thorssen."

Meriden indicates he wants to speak. "Lord Meriden?" Richard acknowledges.

"What about the Lords? There's no prohibition I'm aware of against our making loans to the Treasury."

"We've talked about that, sir. But consider this. If you make a loan to the Treasury, that reduces your own funds. In the long run, it's my belief that the Treasury will recover more rapidly if you use those same funds to provide work within your domain to people who need it. You'll be gaining a service . . . perhaps even rents or trade goods that return a profit to you. And the people you employ will be paying taxes.

"The same goes for the merchants, Lord Thorssen. We need them to start giving work to people even in advance of seeing their sales of goods grow. Once people have work, the merchants' profits and the Treasury's income will grow side-by-side." Richard pauses to give the others time to comment or ask questions. No one speaks.

"What I've spoken of so far is all focused on the long-term health and viability of the Treasury. That doesn't change the fact that in four months, we face a crisis. It's my considered opinion, supported by Lord Ernle, that we have no choice but to borrow from the bankers as a bridge to solvency."

Ernle. "Gentlemen, if I understand the silence around this table correctly, it represents both astonishment at the state in which mismanagement has left us and distaste for the idea of committing the kingdom to debt. Lord Richard and I have had longer to take this in and ponder the alternatives.

"The most obvious alternative is to cut everything back to the bare bones. We worked through that scenario. It would get us two – perhaps three – extra months. Merely postponing the crisis. And actually jeopardizing longer-term recovery. What the kingdom needs now, gentlemen, is investment in our future – not suppression of opportunity."

Richard picks up again. "So our proposal, gentlemen, is shared investment. The lords stimulating employment within their respective domains. The merchants taking on staff to help stimulate the increase in purchasing that will occur automatically when people have money to spend. And the Treasury taking on the necessary debt to run the public operations of the realm."

Montfort. "As distasteful as I find going into debt to run the kingdom, I'm not sure I can think of any alternative. It seems our late king took most of the choices out of our hands."

"Gentlemen, are we forgetting there's some money we could go after?" Meriden.

"If you know where we can find money, Lord Meriden," says Richard, "I'm all ears."

"We all heard that letter read two days ago in the church. Our late king sent money to that girl's bastard son. If that money came from the Treasury, it's illegal and we should go claim it back."

Since I've already reached a decision on the lost money, I decide to prevent the conversation going down this path. "The same notion occurred to Richard and to me, Meriden. But I've come to the conclusion that no good can come from pursuing that path. We don't know if the money was from the Treasury or from John's personal fortune. If the latter, it isn't illegal. We'd have to negotiate the money's return, and our bargaining position is extremely weak. We don't know how much is involved. It could be so little that it would have no meaningful impact on our problem. But most importantly, if we engage with the girl and her father over anything related to that boy, we give the appearance that we attach some significance to the boy. That, we must never do. I've made my peace with the fact that whatever money the girl has, it's a small price to pay to protect the future of the realm and the succession to the throne. I ask that you do so as well."

The room is utterly silent. No one moves. It seems even breathing is suspended. Finally, Lord Devereux speaks quietly. "Well said, Alfred." A rare familiarity within the Council chamber, understood by all as shutting down the topic.

"Gentlemen," he continues, "let's all give some thought to Lord Richard's plan. It seems our choices are limited and the plan is well thought out. I freely admit I can think of nothing to offer as an alternative. But let's not vote in haste. Thorssen, that shouldn't hold you back from getting the merchants going on their part. We need that regardless. Everyone else, spend as much time with Richard or Ernle or each other as you need. Examine any ideas you can think of. We'll reconvene two days hence to vote." He pauses. "With your approval, of course, Sire."

"Of course."

"Then we're adjourned," says Devereux.

Much as I want to hear the conversation that follows, it's no longer an option. They aren't free from the formality of the Council chamber until I've left the room. Nor is it traditional for me to linger in the corridor to speak with one or another of them, so I make my way back to the library to assess the meeting.

In short order, Rupert finds me. "Well done, Alfred. They've all gone to your reception room, hoping to find you there. I think everyone wants to congratulate you."

"Did I truly manage it effectively, Uncle?"

"I couldn't have done better myself." He claps me on the shoulder. "Now come along and celebrate your first success."

Everyone is there excepting only the bishop, who's returned to the church to prepare for Evensong. Someone has ordered wine and Matthias is serving. As soon as Rupert and I have a glass in our hands, Devereux signals for attention and raises his glass. "The king!" he toasts, and all follow suit. Then he walks over and puts his arm around my shoulder and raises his glass again, "To our Alfred!"

"My friends, it's been a memorable day. Thank you for what we did together in that room. But I must admit I still haven't quite gotten used to seeing each of you on the opposite side of the table." This time the laughter is raucous.

"Matthias, do you think you could find a bit of food to go with this wine?" I ask.

"Some cheese and some bread, perhaps, Sire. I'll send for it right away."

"Alfred," calls Samuel from across the room, "where did you learn military strategy? That was really quite brilliant."

"I've had a lot of time to read over the past three years," I answer with a laugh.

The conversation is easy and comfortable. At one point, Lord Ernle comes up and puts his arm around my shoulder. "You're off to a good start, my boy." Then realizing what he's said, he shakes his head and adds, "Damn! I've got to stop calling you that."

I give him a warm smile. "Don't concern yourself, sir. You're the nearest thing to a father I have on this earth now."

"Well," he chuckles, "at least maybe I can remember not to do it in front of your fellow sovereigns."

As the late afternoon light is disappearing in the windows, Gwen wanders in and gives me a chaste kiss on the cheek. "My goodness. It looks like I'm interrupting some sort of celebration."

"Not interrupting, my dear," says Devereux. "We're just congratulating ourselves and Alfred on our first successful Council meeting."

"How wonderful!" she exclaims. "But I'm afraid I'm here to tear him away from you."

"Gentlemen," I add, "if you'll forgive me. I'm to dine with my family this evening . . . for the first time in many weeks. And I think I'm looking forward to it just as much as the children are."

In our bed chamber, some privacy at last! I pick Gwen up and swing her around just as I did on the day she arrived back here from our exile.

"Oh, my!" she says. "This is getting to be a habit. To what do I owe today's exuberance?"

"To the fact that your extraordinary husband – who still can't quite take it in that, against all odds, he is an actual crowned king – got through his first Council meeting without doing anything misguided . . . or worse yet, fundamentally stupid." I put her down, grinning from ear to ear, and add, "Not even one misstep."

"Well, of course you did," she says with a bright smile. "You are, after all, extraordinary, as you just reminded me."

"The lords are aligned with my plans, this evening I finally get some time alone with my family, and tonight I'll make love to a queen, who happens to be the most beautiful woman on the face of this earth. What's not to be exuberant about?"

She laughs. Still holding her in my arms, I give her a kiss quite unlike the one I received in the reception room. "I wonder . . ." I whisper in her ear.

She gently disengages. "It will be even nicer later, my love, when we don't have to hurry because people are waiting for us." Then, as she reaches up to give me a more gentle kiss, she presses her body against the stiffening that has started in my crotch, whispering, "Just don't forget what's waiting for you," then turns and walks toward the door to her sitting room.

"I'll be along in a moment." I need time to compose myself before I face her parents and the children.

Food and wine are already arrayed on the sideboard when I join them. I greet my mother and Lady Margaret with a kiss on the cheek and shake hands with Godwin. "Alfred," he says, "I can't tell you how very proud of you I am."

"Truth be told, sir, I'm still trying to take it all in. But every morning, I wake up and it's not just a dream, so I'm slowly getting used to this new life. I must admit, though, I'll be grateful when the rest of the ceremonial part of a new reign is finished and I have more time for our family."

"All in due course, Son. In fact, I think there are three here who are about to burst with excitement."

Sitting on the couch, I hold out my arms and the children surround me immediately. Godwin moves a chair nearby so I can have one child on each side and one facing. Juliana, growing up more every day, takes the chair like a proper lady.

"Papa," Geoffrey taps my arm for attention.

"Yes, Geoffrey?"

"Guess what?"

"I have absolutely no idea."

"Just guess."

"Osbert took you for a pony ride today."

"No. Better than that. Guess again."

"Osbert let you ride a big horse."

"Nooooooo, Papa."

"Well, then, I don't know. Tell me."

"We have the princes' room. Edward and me and Donal and Brumby. All boys. All together. And I can dress myself. And Edward is wearing trousers now."

Edward jumps to the floor and stands with his feet wide apart, hands on hips, to show me his new attire. I tousle his hair, telling him, "Very grown up!" . . . at which he beams with satisfaction and climbs back up on the seat beside me.

Geoffrey continues. "And Donal sleeps with us."

Edward chimes in, tugging at my sleeve. "And Donal helps me get dressed and not get my trousers on backwards."

Geoffrey again. "But Donal isn't our squire. Osbert says a squire helps just one man, and gentlemen don't get a squire until they're eighteen. So Donal is just our helper."

"He's Grandma's helper too," says Edward.

"That's right," I reply. Then looking from one boy to the other, "Do you like Donal?"

"Oh, we like him ever so much," says Geoffrey. Edward nods vigorously. "And we like having our own room," Geoffrey goes on, "and calling it the princes' room. And we made Brumby an honorary prince, even though a dog can't be a real prince."

I reach across to Juliana, take her hand, and bring it to my lips in a proper greeting from a gentleman to a lady. Her smile is radiant; it's clear she likes to be treated as a young lady. "And how is my princess?"

"I don't have my own room yet, but I get to help Nurse take care of Alicia. Papa, she's learning to do so many things," she adds excitedly, clearly pleased with getting to help with the baby. "Today she sat up without toppling over. It wasn't for long – just a moment. But she did it. And Nurse says it won't be long before she can start eating some porridge and then I can help feed her."

"Alicia is very lucky to have such a pretty and attentive elder sister. Does Primrose still sleep with you?"

"Oh, yes, Papa. And Willow sleeps beside Alicia's crib, and if Alicia wakes up in the night, Willow goes and gets Nurse."

Edward is tugging at my sleeve again. "Papa?"

"Yes, Edward?"

"I'm hungry."

"So am I. Let's go see what tasty things Cook sent up for us." The boys bound over to the sideboard; Juliana follows sedately behind as Gwen rushes over to intervene. Geoffrey refuses any help, determined to be grown up – and, surprisingly, doesn't make a mess. Edward doesn't get a choice; Gwen serves his meal for him and gets him settled in front of a low table to eat.

Conversation becomes intermittent as we all tuck into a hearty winter potage and freshly baked paindemaine. Geoffrey inserts himself into one of the gaps. "Pwapwa?" he mumbles through a mouth full of bread.

"Now, Geoffrey," Gwen admonishes, "do we talk with our mouth full?" Rather than risk being scolded again, he shakes his head and begins furiously chewing his bread. "I know you're excited that your father doesn't have to dine with the lords tonight, but excitement is no excuse for bad manners," his mother adds.

A few furious gulps to dispense with the offending bread, and he asks again, "Papa?"

"Yes, Geoffrey?"

"Papa, did you know that Juliana can't dress herself?"

"Geoffrey," Juliana whines. "I've *told* you . . ."

Gwen rolls her eyes. Apparently, this is a new bone of sibling contention. I raise my finger to Juliana, requesting silence and address her brother, "Why do you think that is, Son?"

"Because she's a girl," he replies with great confidence.

"Do you really think girls are less capable than boys?"

"Well, she's a girl and she can't do it, so that must be why."

"Stand up, Juliana," I tell my daughter, and she quickly obliges. "Now turn around," I add, twirling my forefinger in the air.

She rises on tiptoe on one foot and spins quickly in a circle, like a performer in a masque. "Nicely done, sweetheart, but once again, please; and this time more slowly." And then turning to Geoffrey, "Now watch carefully."

Juliana completes her turn. "So tell me what you saw, Geoffrey. What's different about your sister's clothing and yours."

"Well, she wears a dress and not trousers."

"Did you notice anything else?"

He looks at me quizzically. "Juliana, turn with your back to us, please." Once again, she obliges in silence. "Now look carefully, Geoffrey. Do you see how her dress is fastened? With buttons and laces down the back?"

"Yes, sir."

"Do you think it's easy to do up all those fastenings behind your back?"

"I don't know," he admits.

"Very well, then. I think you should try it sometime. One morning, put on your shirt and your trousers and your waistcoat all backwards and see if you can figure out how to get everything fastened neatly and properly behind your back without any help from Donal. You know, your mother needs help dressing too."

"Well, she's a girl too." He's not quite ready to give up on his notion yet.

"Just try my little experiment and then we'll talk."

Before much longer, Donal arrives to fetch the boys. Edward still likes a goodnight hug and kiss from both his mother and his father; Geoffrey tolerates it from his mother, but prefers a good tousling of the head from me. When the door closes behind them, I turn to the others, "Ladies . . . Godwin . . . if you'll excuse me for a moment," and follow them out.

"Donal," I call, "a word, please." He sends the boys on their way, telling them he'll catch them up. I explain the problem and the challenge I've given Geoffrey.

Donal chuckles. "He be lording it over his sister fer nigh on three weeks now. That be right smart of ye, m'lord, to have him figure it out fer himself. Count on me, sir. I not be letting him cheat." And with that, he's off to catch up with his young charges.

As I return to the room, Gwen asks, "What was all that about?"

"Making sure Donal knows what's afoot. I know how young boys think. Geoffrey's going to try my little test tomorrow morning, and I wouldn't put it past him to lace up his waistcoat and then pull it on over his head, so he can claim success. Good thinking on his part, but it doesn't prove my point . . . so Donal will see to it that he does things right." Godwin laughs out loud.

Turning to Juliana, I add, "And if you'll take my advice, young lady, you'll be kind and forgiving when he has to admit that it's harder than he thought. 'I told you so' will just start him looking for more reasons to claim it's just because you're a girl."

"Indeed, my dear," says Godwin. "He'll have to salvage some of his pride, so don't be surprised if he says things like 'So why do girls have to wear dresses anyway if they can't dress themselves?' But if you don't push him, he won't bother you about it anymore. And Edward will learn the lesson just from watching his elder brother struggle."

"It doesn't seem fair," Juliana pouts ever so slightly, "after all his taunting."

"Just think of it this way, my dear," says Margaret. "He's having to learn the hard way something you already know . . . *and* having to admit he was wrong. Being generous in such a situation is the mark of a proper lady . . . and I see before me a *very* proper young lady."

The rest of the evening is pleasant and relaxing. Godwin and Margaret will begin their journey home tomorrow. Not long after, I must go on progress and my peacemaking mission. And then perhaps our lives can settle back into some sort of routine. Surprisingly, Gwen brings up the matter of the progress in our bedtime conversation. "I really want to go with you, Alfred. To be among the people as you are . . . perhaps to find something truly meaningful to do as queen."

"Are you sure? The roads are still a mess and it could well be difficult for a carriage in some places."

"You're going to have to take wagons for your trunk and the gear for your Guard. It won't be any more difficult for a carriage than a wagon."

"You know what the ride was like from the border to here . . . not very comfortable. And I suspect most of the journey will be similar . . . perhaps even worse. It's still winter and we could easily have more snow or storms."

"Is there a rule that says the new king's progress has to happen immediately?"

"Well, I'm not sure it's a rule, though in my experience, it's a tradition."

"But, Alfred, think about it. All the kings we have experience of were crowned in spring or early summer. It would be natural for them to go on progress immediately . . . the weather is fine at that time of year, and it's easy for people to be out and about. Is there any reason you shouldn't wait until spring? It would be easier for everyone. You could even attend some of the festivals . . . maybe present some of the prizes. It wouldn't surprise me if some of the mayors or village leaders were to adjust their usual dates just to be able to have the king present." What she says makes sense in ways I hadn't even considered.

"By then, I suspect there'll be repairs done on some of the roads, and the journey will be less taxing for everyone," she continues.

"I can tell you've given this a lot of thought, my love. I really can think of only one reason why it might not be a good idea."

She cocks her head to one side and looks at me quizzically.

"Alicia. Even by spring, she won't be weaned. And you've always insisted on nursing your children yourself."

"I've given that a lot of thought too, Alfred," she replies. "This is a once-in-a-lifetime thing for us as king and queen. Engaging a wet nurse isn't my preference, but it's necessary for something this important to you and your reign. By then, Alicia will be seven months old, and I'll have given her a good start in life. She won't suffer from the change . . . and your mother will be here to look out for her welfare and be sure she's getting everything she needs."

"It sounds like you have it all worked out."

"I don't want to coerce you, Alfred."

"Oh, I didn't mean that. Only that you've had more time to think about it than I have . . . and I can find no fault with the plan."

"There's one other thing, my love," she sounds a bit more tentative now.

"What's that?"

"I want Juliana to come with us."

"What about Geoffrey?"

"You've said yourself that you want him to be just a boy for a bit longer and get used to court life before you introduce him to his new status. If he goes with us, people will be fawning all over him and calling him the heir and telling him how special he is before you've even begun to prepare him for dealing with that sort of thing. Geoffrey doesn't have the same churlish nature as John, but I worry that all that attention at such a young age might give him an inflated opinion of himself." She pauses to let me think about this, then adds, "The focus will shift to Geoffrey and his position as heir soon enough. I don't want our daughter lost in that shift."

I take her hand and squeeze it gently. "Nor do I. Any idea how to break the news to him? I think I used up all my fatherly imagination earlier this evening," I chuckle.

"That really was quite masterful. I can't wait to hear what he tells you about the outcome," she laughs softly. "But as far as the progress is concerned, it shouldn't be a big problem. Children understand everything about privileges and milestones in life in terms of birthdays. By the time we go, Juliana will be eleven. So we simply explain that one must be at least eleven to go on progress. Just like he has to be thirteen to start his physical training. He'll be unhappy and he'll grumble, but it will make sense to him and fit neatly into his current understanding of the world. We just have to not mention it to either of them until after Juliana's birthday . . . after she's already eleven. He'll have Richard's and Phillip's boys to play with while we're gone, so he'll get over his disappointment easily enough."

"You really have thought of everything."

"What I've thought of most . . ." she reaches out and places a hand in my crotch . . . a gesture she can still manage to surprise me with even after all these years, coming as it does in the middle of a serious conversation. "What I've thought of most," she repeats as my body responds to her touch, "is that I don't want to be away from you for all those weeks."

Two days later, the Council convenes and approves Richard's plan. Meriden still seems reluctant, but hasn't devised an alternative. Richard will need to keep an eye on him. Phillip also has an update from the Assembly. "Emaurri's got his wool, Sire. They were happy for a way to reduce the surplus they'd been expecting this summer. But putting people to work is a different matter. They're unaccustomed to hiring in advance of need . . . at least that's how they phrase it . . . I think it's more likely in advance of profit. So we're still working on that. Right now, they want their taxes reduced as a quid pro quo."

"I needn't tell you, Thorssen, that's something no one in this room would agree to."

"Perhaps," ventures Meriden, "it could work for a limited time."

"With respect, Lord Meriden," Richard replies, "the longer we're in debt, the more it costs us and the more vulnerable we are to unexpected events."

"Gentlemen," I step in, "let's not debate this right now. Thorssen, every man at this table – myself included – is available to assist you in helping the Assembly understand they need to share in the burden of rebuilding."

"Thank you, Sire. Devereux and Bauldry are joining us this afternoon. We may yet require your voice, but not immediately."

As Devereux adjourns the meeting, I tell Phillip, "A word, Thorssen, before your meeting? I'll be in the library."

I've not even had time to take a seat when there's a knock on the door and Phillip pokes his head in. "Alright if I dispense with protocol?"

"You must have run from the Council chamber," I chuckle, beckoning him to come in.

"Very nearly. It's hard to get used to not being able to have a quick word with you in the corridor." He takes a seat. "Thank you for holding Meriden in check back there."

"That's what I wanted to ask you about. Can you manage him if he decides to put in an appearance at the Assembly . . . which, of course, is his right?"

"With Devereux and Bauldry there, probably."

"What would you think of my just sitting in the room to listen, as Father did from time to time? Would it be a hindrance or a help?"

"I'm really not sure, Alfred. I'd like for them to reach the right decision on their own. And I certainly don't want them to back themselves into a corner by recommending something I know the Council won't approve. Right now, though, they're complaining about their taxes already being too high."

"How about this, then? Around midafternoon, I'll drop in casually and just listen. If you want me to weigh in, just give me a signal."

"I like that. But, Alfred, if you see something where you can change the dialog or reshape their thinking, don't feel compelled to wait for me."

"As you wish."

"Then if you've no objection, I want a word with Devereux and Bauldry before we start about how to contain Meriden if he interferes." And with that, he's off.

When I enter the room two hours later, everyone scrambles to their feet. "Please, gentlemen, take your seats. I'm here only as a spectator."

It soon becomes clear that even Devereux's and Bauldry's arguments haven't swayed them at all. Phillip is trying not to look exasperated. He raises his eyebrows as if to indicate that he's out of ideas.

So when a lull in the conversation finally occurs, I take advantage of it. "Lord Thorssen, I wonder if I might offer some observations on what I'm hearing."

"Of course, Sire. I'm sure we could benefit from a new perspective." Phillip pulls a chair up to the table beside him for me.

"Let me start by asking some questions. Who among us has seen their expectations of financial gain reduced during the reign of our late king?" I hold up my right hand and add, "Most assuredly I have."

Every man in the room raises a hand. "More or less as I expected. Truth be told, gentlemen, I should be raising two hands – one on behalf of myself personally and one on behalf of the Treasury.

"Alright. Who here saw their businesses shrink under our late king?" Again I raise my own hand and everyone else in the room follows suit. "My wife and I both found it necessary to curtail our horse-breeding. Lord Bauldry?"

"So many of my tenants were conscripted that it affected production . . . both crops and wool."

"Jolland?" I address the delegate from the castle town.

"With no court, there was no one to buy fine fabrics," he says.

Next I point to a man I think is the new delegate from the port. "Well, Your Grace, some of our businesses are not so classy as yours," which earns him a laugh all around the room. "I can tell you, though, the bars and brothels suffer mightily when there're no ships in port."

"And that brings me to the fact that, once again, I should raise a hand on behalf of the kingdom. We all know how much my brother disdained commerce. That had a direct effect on our trade.

"Now, then. Who here feels they're not as well off as they were before King John ascended the throne?" All hands are raised . . . both of mine.

"Has anyone here failed to make at least a small amount of money in the last three years?" No hands this time. "Has anyone here found it necessary to dismiss any of their domestic servants?" Again, no hands. "Has anyone contemplated having to sell or abandon their home?"

I take my time, allowing them to draw their own conclusions about what their responses reveal. "I think, gentlemen, we may have just discovered that we in this room are all more or less in the same position . . . less well off than we expected to be and all having experienced some setbacks. But none of us are without a source of income. None of us are homeless. None of us lack the creature comforts to which we've become accustomed. We're all still far better off than most.

"Let me pose a business problem to you. Consider taking all your profits and all your reserves and investing them in a venture unrelated to your primary business . . . and losing those funds because this other venture failed. How then would you run your primary business?

"Now, think of managing the kingdom in the same terms you think of managing your business. Consider King John's war as that other venture, with all its costs and its ultimate failure. All our resources squandered. How are we now to run the kingdom?"

I pause for a while to let this sink in.

"The only way to restore the prosperity we relish, gentlemen, is to work together. The lords have already committed to their part – to investing their own funds to provide employment in their domains. And they have reasonable expectations of profiting from that investment. But the investment must come first. The Treasury will invest in the needs of our people, even if it means incurring unusual costs to do so. Accelerating our recovery is *that* important. All you're being asked is to play your part by investing in anticipation of the reward. Nothing more or less than the lords. Nothing more or less than the Crown."

I've no idea if I've made any headway. Their expressions are completely blank. Finally the delegate from Abbéville Market speaks. "With all due respect, Your Grace, what's being proposed goes against all the principles of running a business. One simply doesn't hire people unless there's a clear need arising from increased business. That's why we propose relief from taxes as compensation for our investment."

I decide to try a different tack. "Gentlemen, I'm not a businessman, but I'm reasonably good at simple sums. With your proposal, what we have is zero net contribution from the commercial interests, and one plus one plus zero is only two. What's needed to restore prosperity is three . . . one plus one plus one. I can't compel you to act for the common good. But I can ask you to look into your hearts and do what's right for your community . . . not just for your own personal interest."

The room is utterly silent. "Very well, gentlemen, I'll leave you to your deliberations."

At the end of the day Phillip seeks me out. "I don't know if we made progress or not, Alfred. At least they're not bringing the tax relief recommendation to the Council. I suppose the best we can do for a while is wait and watch."

With the progress postponed, peacemaking has become my first priority. Riding west, we draw nearer and nearer to the border. Our plan is to pass the night in the village there. I want to time our arrival at the camp of the Territorial army about midday, so there are enough daylight hours to determine what our reception might be like and beat a hasty retreat if necessary.

We're a small force, much like an ordinary patrol, but traveling under the king's banner. Samuel, Tobin, and a single elite troop made up of the best of the best from the King's Own Guard and Samuel's knights. We'll unfurl our white banner of peace just before crossing the border.

Knowing there may be spies in the area, we avoid the garrison. Samuel sent Sir Eudo there three days before our departure to learn what's known about the disposition of the Territorial army's camp. Traveling as an ordinary laborer, he'll meet us in the village tonight.

Before our departure, I prepared my will and lodged it with the bishop. I also gave him special instructions. If anything should happen to me before Geoffrey reaches his eighteenth birthday, the throne is to pass to Rupert. When I told my uncle of my decision, he protested that there was no need to include him in the succession. "Not meaning to disappoint you, Uncle," I told him, "but it's not out of generosity to you. If Geoffrey isn't of age, I foresee another attempt by Gunhild to place her child on the throne. A boy king challenged by a boy pretender seems to me to carry far too great a risk of conflict or war."

"There would be a regent protector for Geoffrey," he offered.

"I know. But it's in the nature of many a man to ascribe venality and self-interest to the regent, even where none exists. To my way of thinking, that's yet another spark that could ignite conflict. And even if Gunhild's challenge is rebuffed once again – which I've no doubt it would be – it merely opens the door wider for other mothers of John's bastards to have a go at getting their son on the throne. If Geoffrey isn't of age, the throne needs to pass undisputedly to a man with experience of the world."

"What if something then happens to me before Geoffrey comes of age?"

"My will specifies that Gwen and Richard are to share the role of regent protector. But you, of course, would be free to alter those provisions as you think best for the circumstances that exist at the time."

"It seems you've thought things out thoroughly," he finally acquiesced. "Just know, Alfred, that my fondest wish is that I never become king."

Two nights before our planned departure, my mother asked Gwen and me to dine privately with her. Petronilla was there as well. After we'd eaten, Mother nudged Petronilla gently, "You needn't fear asking them, my dear. You're still very much a part of this family, you know."

"It's a rather important favor," she began tentatively.

Gwen moved to sit beside her. "It can't be that dreadful, dear. What can we do?"

"You know I return home in a week. But I'd be ever so grateful if Richenda could stay here."

"Well, of course she can stay," Gwen said cheerily. "For how long?"

"For as long as necessary." Petronilla was still very solemn.

"Tell them everything, my dear," Mother coaxed.

"She may need to stay here for quite some time. It's the Duke of Lamoreaux, you see. He's made up his mind to have Richenda for his wife and is determined that nothing will stop him. You all know what Charles is like. It was Edward, after all, who warned me about him.

"He's asked his father to betroth her to him twice now, and both times, Goscelin's refused. Then when Goscelin was so ill, Charles twice tried to get her into what he calls his evening entertainments. The first time, I found out about it ahead of time and confined her to her room for two days. The second time, I wasn't so lucky. By the time I learned what was going on, Charles had taken her to his apartments. When I burst into the room, he was there with all his male cronies, half of them dressed in women's attire. Charles himself was doing some sort of lewd dance with each of his women and each of them would turn, bend over, and raise their skirts to him. Charles hadn't exposed himself, but his arousal was obvious, and he was imitating the sex act with each of them.

I'm sure the real thing was next on the agenda. I grabbed my daughter and rushed her out of there while the Duke and his cronies roared with laughter.

"Alfred . . . Gwen . . . I can't take the chance my luck will run out. Goscelin is recovering and can protect her for a time, but what if he falls ill again? Worse yet, what if he dies? I can't let my beautiful girl fall into the hands of a man who has no respect for her and merely wants her as a decorative trophy and an audience for his activities. She would be a queen, but her life would be miserable. I care not how he takes his pleasure, but I care deeply that he doesn't compel my daughter to watch."

Gwen took Petronilla's hand. "Of course she can stay here. For as long as you like. Can't she, Alfred?"

"Of course she can," I replied. Then, having given her my assurance, it was necessary to ask. "What does Goscelin think of all this?"

She reached into her sleeve and withdrew a folded piece of paper, which she passed to me. "We knew you'd ask, so he sent you this letter."

I broke the seal and unfolded the paper.

To my dear friend King Alfred,

My great pleasure in writing those words is matched only by my great disappointment in not being able to witness your coronation in person. However, my doctors insist that travel would be too taxing for me at this moment, so I send my beloved Petronilla and our lovely daughter to stand in for me. I use the word "our" advisedly, for I have come to love Richenda as if she were my own flesh and blood.

I believe my Petronilla intends to make a special request of you during her visit. She will explain the reasons for her request, reasons which I share but do not wish to commit to paper lest this missive fall into the wrong hands. Know that whatever she may ask is with my blessing and my full agreement.

We look forward to receiving your ambassador once again as soon as may be. And I personally hope that a state visit may be arranged as soon as you have made some progress on putting your kingdom in order, for I have no doubt there is much to be done.

Goscelin

I gave the letter to Gwen to read, and when she finished, she folded it and tucked it into her own sleeve. "Richenda will be safe here," I said, "but how will you explain to the Duke that she hasn't returned with you?"

"Goscelin will tell him that we've decided she needs to continue her education in the land of her birth, to master her native language as well as she's mastered her adopted one and to learn the history of her father's realm. Charles will have no choice but to accept the reality of what's already done."

Then, turning to Gwen, she added, "I'd very much like for her nurse to stay with her, so she has someone familiar about her. Would that be too great a burden?"

"It would be no burden at all," said Gwen. "In fact, it would solve a problem for me. Since I gave the boys their own room, Juliana is left behind in the nursery. She makes a good show of things, helping with Alicia, but I know she'd like her own room again, as she had at the cottage. If Richenda's nurse is willing to transform herself into a young ladies' maid, then the girls could share a room with . . ." she paused, not knowing the nurse's name.

"Milla," Petronilla supplied.

". . . with Milla to help them. I just hope Milla likes dogs well enough. Juliana will *not* be parted from Primrose," she finished with a laugh.

"Milla will manage just fine, I'm sure – dogs and all." Petronilla was all smiles by then. We could see the relief she felt just knowing her daughter would have a safe place among people she still thinks of as family.

On the day of our departure, just as we were mounting up, Donal came running into the stable. "Yer Grace, there be three men saying it be urgent they see ye."

"What could possibly be that urgent, Donal? Who are these men?" I asked.

"They say their names be . . ." he hesitated and wrinkled his nose, struggling a bit with the names, "Benoist . . . and Morphew . . . and Puchot."

I dismounted immediately and handed my reins to Elvin. "Gentlemen, my apologies. These are John's lifetime lords come in response to my summons. I'll give them no excuse to delay their loyalty requirements any longer. It should take less than an hour, and then we can be on our way."

I entered the public reception room determined to make this meeting very formal indeed and crossed rapidly to sit on the throne. The three held their bows until I was seated. When they stood up, I was surprised to see that one of them was no more than seventeen or eighteen years of age. One of the older men took a single step forward, apparently the designated spokesman for the group. "Lord Morphew, Your Grace, responding to your summons with Lord Benoist and Lord Puchot. We beg your pardon most earnestly, Your Grace. We didn't know anything was required of us."

"As a lord, Morphew, it's your responsibility to know your duty," I chastised him. "And what of your companions? Can they not speak for themselves?"

The older of the other two stepped forward. "Begging Your Grace's pardon, I also didn't know, Sire."

"And who are you?" I asked.

"Lord Benoist, Your Grace."

Then turning to the third one, "And you, young man? Who might you be?"

Bowing repeatedly, the young one said, "Lord Puchot, Your Grace."

"How can that be?" I asked. "You're not of an age with your companions." He hesitated, looking to the others. "Speak, young man. No harm will come to you."

"My father was the first Lord Puchot, Your Grace. But he died of the sickness, and so I'm Lord Puchot now."

"Is that what your father told you?"

Bowing again, he answered, "Yes, Your Grace. He said the eldest son inherits."

"Your father was either sadly misinformed, young Puchot, or he was deliberately trying to circumvent the law. Only the seven families who joined together with the first king to form the kingdom have the right to pass their titles, privileges, and domains to their heirs. Your father was created a lord for his lifetime only. There's no right of inheritance in such a case, either of the title or of the grants that were made to your father by the late King John."

The young man looked utterly devastated. "But what am I to do, Your Grace? If I don't have my land, what happens to me? What happens to my family?" He was almost in tears.

"Your father should have planned for them, Puchot. But I can tell from your manner that he didn't. The land you currently occupy automatically reverted to the Crown at the time of your father's death. You may petition to become a tenant of the Crown and remain on the land; but we'll have to determine how much land you may work and what rents you'll pay. As you may have been told, I'm leaving today on a patrol. In my absence, Lord Rupert is authorized to make such decisions. If you don't want to be forced to leave your home, then you must speak to my secretary when we finish here and work with him to make the necessary arrangements and secure Lord Rupert's approval."

Then I turned my attention back to the others. "As for you two, if you were somehow of the opinion that you could pass your title and holdings on to your heirs, I hope you've learned from young Puchot's distress. My advice is to begin planning right away for what happens to your family after your death." I paused to let that sink in and then continued, "Assuming, that is, that you choose to retain your titles by solemnly swearing your loyalty to me." They both opened their mouths, about to speak, but I held up my hand to stop them. "Think carefully, gentlemen. I am not my brother. You will *not* hold your title frivolously, owing no duty to your king. If you pledge your loyalty, that's a solemn oath. You'll have given your word. And based on that oath, I have the right to call on you at any time to provide whatever service to the kingdom I may require."

A longer pause to let them fully grasp my meaning. "You may choose to return your title and your grants to the Crown, and there will be no dishonor attached to that choice. You may then become a tenant of the Crown, just as young Puchot will likely do. But once you've given your oath, you are, by law, the liege lord of your king until your death. Now what shall it be, gentlemen?"

I could see them both hesitate, weighing what I might ask of them against the privilege they currently enjoyed. In the end, comfort won out over apprehension, and they each, in turn, went on their knees and spoke the words of the strict loyalty oath required of lifetime lords . . . an oath I doubt they'd ever had to deliver to John.

"Very well," I told them. "You both retain your titles and grants for your lifetimes. Take my advice and plan for your families." I rose from the throne and started to leave the room. Halfway to the door, I turned, "And gentlemen?" All three spun around. "Next time you receive a summons from your king, I suggest you respond with a bit more dispatch." Then I turned on my heel and left. Clearly, I'll need to summon them for something in future, just to keep them on their toes, but the only service I wanted from them at the moment was to be on their way.

Osbert and Samuel's squire, Timm, have ridden on ahead to alert the innkeeper of our arrival and be sure we have suitable lodgings for the whole party and stabling for the horses. Word gets around a village quickly and the green is crowded with people when we ride in. These people still think of me as their special protégé, and I manage to recall many of the names and faces of those gathered to greet us.

After supper, Samuel, Tobin, and I review our plans for the morrow. "I'd still feel better if you'd let me bring the whole troop forward when we approach them, sir," says Tobin.

"I understand your concern, Tobin," I reply, "and am not dismissing it. I just want to make sure nothing we do can be taken as a threat."

"Then at least let me or Samuel be armed," he presses. Samuel says nothing. He may not like the risk, but he understands why I'm willing to take it.

"I know you're only doing your duty, Tobin, but I haven't changed my mind. I know it puts extra pressure on everyone for added vigilance, but I truly think it's worth it. We created this mess. We have to put an end to it."

"What if Egon isn't there? Or if he was killed in the war?" asks Samuel, making sure we go over all the eventualities one last time.

"All the more reason why it's important I negotiate in their language. I know that makes it harder for you and Tobin to have any idea what's going on, but I'll do my best to translate for you when I can."

"I spoke to Eudo just before supper. There's nothing new reported from the garrison troops. Only the occasional horseman appearing near the border and then riding off. They believe the army's still camped half a day away but can't confirm it. No one's set foot in the Territories since your orders were received."

"And if they're not there?" asks Tobin.

"Then we ride to Egon's fortress, still under the white banner."

The next morning, the apprehension among the knights is palpable, all of them wary of the responsibility of protecting their king in a strange land against a full army with such a small force. I don't dismiss their concern – it means they'll be on high alert – but I mount up and ride with confidence, hoping to impart some of it to them. Well before the border, Samuel calls a halt and orders the white banner unfurled. From time to time, we catch a glimpse of movement to one side or the other of the road. Scouts, no doubt. But we ride on at a measured pace, not acknowledging their presence. At midday, we begin to see banners in the distance and, as we get closer, the shapes of tents come into focus. The encampment is still in place. We slow our horses to a walk. Their troops begin taking up armed formations as we continue to approach.

About fifty yards from the edge of the camp, Samuel and Tobin halt our troop. The three of us ride on ahead, slowly. The white flag bearer follows behind, stopping half way between us and the halted troop. About five yards from the nearest man, we stop our horses, drop our reins, and hold out our hands, palms up, to signal that we're unarmed. A single rider gallops from the center of the camp and stops his mount sharply just in front of us, rearing the stallion up in a gesture of intimidation. We sit quietly. His little display complete, the rider speaks curtly, "Who are you and what do you want?"

It's time for all of Eustace's tutoring to come to the fore. I've rehearsed in my mind what I intend to say, but now it all depends on getting it right. "We come in peace . . . unarmed. I am King Alfred. I wish to speak with your lords of peace between our peoples."

The effect is exactly what I'd hoped for – the rider is completely taken aback by hearing his own language from a stranger – a man he thinks of as the enemy. "Wait here," he says and rides away. We sit patiently, watching the commotion near the center of the camp. Various banners are brought together. Men mount up. Finally, the troops facing us part to allow the procession through. Nine men abreast, each of them followed closely by a rider bearing a banner, nine different banners in all. Egon rides at the center, Polaris as his mount. I take his position as a sign that he still has some influence and his choice of mount as a signal to me of his personal intent. Off on the right flank, I recognize Owen, the western lord at whose castle I spent several weeks in a cell.

They stop, facing us. Not a word is spoken as they study the three of us and the group behind. At length, Egon says, "You have come."

"To speak of peace, Lord Egon," I reply. He can't fully disguise his pleasure at the fact that I'm speaking his language comfortably, if not fluently.

A man two places to Egon's left asks, "And where are the rest of your troops?"

"What you see is my personal guard, sir. There are no others . . . as I believe your scouts can confirm."

The speaker nods his head. Egon suppresses a smile, recognizing that I'm trying to meet these men on their own terms as an accomplished warrior but without presenting any sort of threat.

The man to the original speaker's left then asks, "And what of your army?"

"One does not bring an army to talk of peace, sir."

"And who are these two?" The man to Egon's right, pointing to Samuel and Tobin.

I gesture toward Samuel. "Samuel is my friend. We have been friends since we were boys in training together. He is now commander of my knights." Then gesturing with the other hand to Tobin. "Sir Tobin is captain of my guard, an honorable man who took his men away from the field of battle rather than leading them to slaughter in a dishonorable war – one of many who left that war rather than follow a misguided king's bad orders."

"We will talk," says Egon. "But not here. Will you come to my fortress?"

"What of my guard?" I ask. "I don't wish to put their lives at risk by leaving them among an army of men who, for months, have thought of us as the enemy."

Egon consults in whispered tones with the men on either side of him. "They may come as well, if you will allow our men to ride on their flanks."

"As you wish, Lord Egon. Allow me to explain to Sir Tobin." He nods.

Now I have to trust to our planning and the discipline of these men. Both sides know that Egon understands our language. The Territorial lords will be looking to him for any sign that my words convey anything other than peaceful intent.

Tobin remains expressionless as he signals the troop to advance and gives his orders. Discipline prevails – the men all keep their eyes forward. The nine lords and their flag bearers pivot around as the escort surrounds us and two fast riders leave the back of the camp – heading for Egon's fortress, I surmise, to prepare for our arrival.

We ride in silence for the two hours or so required to reach the village below the fortress. As we pass the smithy, the blacksmith grins broadly and waves to me in greeting. Once inside the outer courtyard of the fortress, Egon and his peers dismount, and we follow suit. "Tell your guard, Alfred," says Egon, speaking his own language for the benefit of the others, "they will dine and lodge with the men who escorted us here today. They may see to their horses and will then be shown to their quarters. There is no need for them to be concerned about your safety as you will be under my personal protection."

I translate for Tobin and, though he keeps his features expressionless, I know him well enough by now to detect his anxiety. So I add, for his benefit and Egon's as well, "I have trusted my life to Lord Egon before, Sir Tobin, and I'll do so again tonight. You and Samuel will be with me. That will be enough."

Then I address myself to the knights. "Don't fear for your safety. Be respectful, don't respond to any provocation, but maintain your knightly bearing. That will be respected here, and you won't be slaughtered in your beds. Eat the food you're offered. It won't be poisoned, and partaking of their food is a sign of the trust we want to build. Any questions?" There are none and Tobin gives the order, "Dismissed."

Turning back to our hosts, I see the barest hint of a smile in Egon's expression . . . approval of the guidance I've given. "Come," he gestures toward the inner courtyard. "I believe we are expected in the dining hall. Tonight we will eat together. Tomorrow we will talk of serious matters."

In the dining hall, Egon invites the three of us to sit on a bench at the head of the table as the others immediately take what appear to be well-understood places on the sides and at the opposite end from us. Egon sits nearest us on the side to our right. Why, I wonder, put us in the position of honor?

While the servants fill our tankards, the man nearest us on the left side speaks. "We have the advantage of knowing your names and the land from which you come. But you do not know the same of us. We will now tell you, beginning with Egon, who will translate for your companions."

Rather than going around the table, they go back and forth, from side to side. The man on my left is named Fergal and holds the domain south of Egon, on the other side of the main road. I try diligently to commit the names and faces to memory. And then something important dawns on me. The seating arrangements have nothing to do with honor or precedence but merely geography. These men have no hierarchy among themselves and sit together in the relationship of their holdings. We are in this position only because our lands are to the east of Egon's and Fergal's. I must remember to pass this on to Peveril, for it will profoundly influence how he formulates his approach.

The man sitting two places to the right of Egon is called Narth. He and Fergal were on opposite sides of Egon when the nine rode out to meet us. Looking at the other faces, I think perhaps the arrangement then was western lords on one side, eastern on the other, with Egon in the center not because he holds any position of higher honor but merely because he had the ability to speak to us.

The man opposite us at the end of the table is called Korst. He seems rather more surly than the others as he introduces himself, so I attempt to dispel some of his hostility. "I believe, Lord Korst, that it was in your lands that Ralf abandoned me and from there that I began my long walk home."

"Hmph," he replies. "Are you saying you know my lands?"

"I know that the stable where I spent the night was well-built and warm, showing a great respect for your horses. But I know little else. When I left that stable, I turned my eyes to the east – toward home – and didn't look back."

"You've come a long way, Alfred," chimes in Owen, "from being trussed up like a new-slaughtered stag and locked in my tower to being a new-crowned king." I don't understand some of this and turn to Egon for help, which he quietly supplies.

"It's been a long journey, indeed, Lord Owen. But I'm pleased to have a chance to give you my thanks for feeding me and treating me well while I was in your tower."

He laughs raucously. "Ralf paid me; I fed you. But you were lucky. If Ralf had sold you to me like I asked, you'd have been out on my fishing fleet. And I don't think you were strong enough to survive that."

At a signal from Egon, the servants begin placing platters of food on the table. There is venison, some type of fowl, root vegetables, and the grainy brown bread I've had here before and developed a particular liking for. Over food, the lords begin talking among themselves. I can't follow their fast-paced exchanges, but can manage well enough when someone speaks to me directly. Thus it is that I speak more with Egon and Fergal than with the others. Drink flows freely, and I observe that the western lords, in particular, seem to have a propensity to overindulge. Perhaps this explains their frequent squabbles. I choose to be unusually cautious in my drink – I need all my wits about me to manage the language and avoid saying something inappropriate. I notice that Egon, Fergal, and Narth observe similar discipline.

At the end of the meal, Egon says, "My friends, I think you all know where your beds are located. I will show our guests the way to theirs. Tomorrow morning, we return to this room for talks. I bid you good night."

They all rise from the table more or less simultaneously, and we scramble to do the same. Reverting to our language, Egon says, "My friends, if you will follow me." Samuel has been here before and, like me, is slightly more comfortable. I can still feel Tobin's anxiety and know that, as he and Samuel walk behind Egon and me, his eyes are taking in every detail, remembering every passage, looking for routes of escape or places to hide. In the middle of a short corridor, two doors are open. Osbert and Timm emerge from one of them, both looking anxious. "We be glad to see ye, m'lord," says Osbert.

"Do not fret, Osbert," replies Egon. I'm impressed that he remembers Osbert's name. "Your master is perfectly safe and will sleep here in the room next to yours. You can attend him in the morning."

Osbert looks to me for assurance. "He's quite right, Osbert. Now get a good night's sleep like I plan to do." The two squires retreat into their room and close the door, as Egon shows us into the other room. It's spare, with three beds, a small table for candles, and not much else in the way of furnishings, but this is what I've come to understand as typical here.

Egon turns to Tobin. "I understand and respect your anxiety, Sir . . . Tobin, is it?"

"Yes, sir."

"You feel rather helpless to do your duty to protect your king, having no other guards nearby and being forced to trust to others for his safety."

"And having no weapon, sir."

Egon smiles. "I'm sure you noticed that everyone removed their swords before entering the dining hall. That was not just to make people more comfortable at table but because I do not permit swords inside my living quarters. They will reclaim their weapons when they leave here, as is customary. Most of them, as you will have observed, are too drunk to do more than enjoy a sound sleep. However, if it will make you feel more comfortable for your king's safety," he reaches to his belt and removes his dagger, proffering it, hilt-first, to Tobin, "then you are welcome to my own dagger for the night."

I hold my breath – so much depends on Tobin's response. He looks silently at the proffered dagger for a very long moment, no doubt weighing what would make him feel more comfortable against the purpose of our mission. Finally, he looks squarely at Egon, clicks his heels together, and makes a slight bow, returning his gaze immediately to our host. "That will not be necessary, Lord Egon," he says. "Your generosity of spirit and my king's trust are all the assurances I require."

Egon returns the dagger to his belt. "Very well, my friends. I wish you a pleasant night." And he departs, closing the door behind him.

When his footsteps can no longer be heard in the corridor, I walk over and clap Tobin on the shoulder. "Well done, Tobin."

He's shaking slightly from the tension of the moment. "It may be the most difficult thing I've ever done, sir."

I grin at him. "Well, there's no doubt it was the second wisest thing you've ever done."

"*Second* wisest, sir?"

"Aye. The wisest was when you walked away from my brother's war and stayed alive so you could become my guard captain." The tension is broken, and we all enjoy a little laugh.

As we sit on the edge of the beds to remove our boots, Tobin says, "You told me what I was signing up for, sir . . . and Samuel here warned me that sometimes you've done some surprising things . . . but in my wildest dreams, I could not have imagined what's happened here today."

"Stories to tell your children one day, eh, Tobin?" Samuel laughs. "Now you know how I felt when this crazy mate of mine proposed we waltz into Egon's domain through the back door to talk peace. By comparison, this seemed a whole lot less scary."

"Only because you'd walked out of that other experience alive, Samuel," I tease him.

"Should we have a watch, sir?" Tobin asks.

"You two can do what you like," I answer him. "I intend to fall asleep the minute my head hits this pillow and sleep like a log until morning. I'm completely exhausted from having to speak a foreign tongue for most of the day . . . and I get to do it all over again tomorrow."

"And I'm pretty tired," says Samuel, "from having absolutely no idea what anyone is talking about." Tobin gets the message, douses the candles, and climbs into bed.

I start to emerge from a deep and refreshing sleep as the morning light begins to show in the high windows of our chamber. Shortly after, a knock on the door is followed by Osbert and Timm entering with basins of water and towels. I've absolutely no idea how Osbert manages such things in an unfamiliar place, but I'm grateful that he does.

"Sir," Samuel's squire shakes his shoulder gently to wake him. Tobin begins to rouse himself from slumber as well.

"Sleep well, Tobin?" I ask.

"I never would have believed it could happen, sir, but yes, I did."

Our morning ablutions complete, I gird my thoughts to grapple with whatever this day may bring. "Tobin, perhaps you'd like to spend some time with the guards today . . . perhaps even go riding and invite the locals to go along. If you want to ask them to go riding, the words are *ke marghogeth*. Say it as a question, and it will be understood as an invitation."

"Are you sure, sir? I know the men would be grateful to see me again."

"And I'd like to know what they experienced last night. Besides, a good ride is a way to dissipate any friction that might be simmering beneath the surface. And you can observe how they interact . . . if there's any cause for concern. I have an idea Samuel and I will be sitting at the table negotiating all day."

"Say those words again, sir?"

"*Ke marghogeth.*"

"*Ke marghogeth,*" he repeats, struggling a bit with the unfamiliar sounds.

"They'll understand that well enough," I assure him, and he leaves, repeating the words over and over to himself.

Samuel rises, ready to go. I have a question first. "Before we go down, what's your decision about the garrison?" Certain that the Territorial lords won't disband their army just because I ask them to, I've been talking with Samuel about reducing the troop strength at the garrison as a gesture of reciprocity.

"Eudo talked with the garrison commander. He doesn't like it, but he understands what's at stake. He would want to have some elite knights among the two troops that would remain, and that will make rotations a little more challenging. But it's doable."

"Thank you, Samuel. I don't intend to lead with that as an offer, but it's nice to have a bargaining tool if we need one."

"One thing, Alfred."

"Yes?"

"I'd be a lot happier if you put a time limit on the reduction. Rotations, training, all the duties of patrol . . . all that is more easily managed with three ordinary troops."

"I'll do my best." And with that, we're off to find our way to the dining hall.

I'm pleased we aren't the last to arrive. There's fruit and water on the sideboard, and we help ourselves to some before taking our seats. Korst arrives last, chided by Owen, "Nice of you to join us, Korst. Too much to drink last night?"

Korst merely grunts as he takes his seat. Then, quite unexpectedly, he speaks first. "So where is your army now, King Alfred? Coming to attack across my border with the Peaks Kingdom?"

His belligerence so early in the talks is surprising, but I never expected to proceed without some amount of animosity. "My army, as you describe it, Lord Korst, is in barracks at my castle. Samuel, here, is taking steps to reduce the ranks of our forces to the standard complement of a peacetime knighthood. All of the . . ." I pause, searching for a word, and find it necessary to request Egon's help. "Conscripts?" I ask him. The word supplied, I continue. "All of the conscripts have been sent home. Those knights who joined only because they wanted to wage war are also being dismissed."

"I do not believe you," says Korst. "You are here to lull us into complacency while your army advances in the west."

Fergal speaks up. "Why do you find it necessary to insult this man, Korst, before hearing what he has to say?"

Knowing that some of this bravado must be allowed to play out before productive talks can proceed, I intervene. "Thank you, Lord Fergal. But I do understand Lord Korst's concern. It's a wise man who knows where he might be . . ." Once again, I need Egon's help, "Vulnerable? Weak?"

"*Gwann.*"

" . . . where he might be vulnerable and to anticipate how his enemy might act."

"Humph," is the only acknowledgement I get from Korst.

"But think, Lord Korst. Would you or any of your friends here send an army on a mission with neither yourself nor your commander in charge? Both my commander and I are here. It's therefore logical that our army isn't engaged elsewhere."

"He speaks truth, Korst," says Narth. "But why, King Alfred, did your late king attack us? We did nothing to provoke him."

"That is true, Lord Narth. The fault lies with my brother. In fact, the fault for both of the conflicts between us lies with my brother. We are taught by our religion not to speak ill of the dead. But I must speak truth to you. My brother was an arrogant and selfish man. You already know he was dismissed from the knighthood because of his raid that caused the first conflict. John saw that as a great humiliation. When he became king, he set out to wipe away that dishonor; and with his limited intelligence, the only way he could think to do that was to prove he'd been right in the first place. And the only way he could think to do *that* was to wage war on you.

"I ask you to think back, gentlemen, to the time of my father, King Edward, and to the time when my grandfather was king. There was always peace between us. I want to return to those times."

The discussion goes on for the rest of the morning without ever touching on the matter of their armed camp or exactly how we might live in peace. I sense they're testing my mettle and my motives. They want to know how John was killed and who was responsible. "We don't know for sure," I answer. "The killers have not been found. But if they're found, they will face our justice."

Occasionally, someone wants to address Samuel about the matter of our so-called army. Egon translates. Even though he's understood none of the conversation, Samuel is adept at reading men's intent and acquits himself perfectly with his responses. By the time the midday meal is served, I'm once again exhausted with the effort of communicating in a language not my own and am grateful when Egon calls a halt to the talks. "My friends, now we eat."

Toward the end of the meal, Korst shows signs of belligerence once again. Initially, the men either side of him engage, seemingly trying to calm him down; but eventually all the western lords get into the fray. What I'm seeing is most certainly a verbal incarnation of their frequent armed squabbles. I can't even begin to follow the fast, fiery exchanges.

Egon comes to my rescue. "Korst is spoiling for a fight. He's trying to convince them that the only reason you want peace is because you're afraid of our strength." Listening to Egon, I realize that Korst is a man who respects only strength . . . he has no use for what he perceives as weakness. I've been keeping an eye on the men and the escalating harangue at the opposite end of the table. Twice Korst has stabbed a finger in the air in my direction, shouting *ownek* each time. I ask Egon, "Did he just call me a coward?"

"Aye."

I place my hands firmly on the table, palms down, making enough noise to get the attention of those seated near me, push myself into a standing position, and lean forward, my hands still planted on the table. Then, raising my voice to be heard over the din, "Lord Korst!" The room goes silent. "I . . . am . . . no . . . coward! I know how to fight. And I will fight to the death to defend my people if we're attacked by outsiders. But I have no quarrel with you. I will not fight you." I remove my hands from the table so that I'm no longer aiming my words directly at Korst. Standing straighter, I lower my voice, "I have no quarrel with any man at this table."

"Hmph," from Korst; but he relaxes his aggressive posture a bit. I'm beginning to wonder if that grunt passes for some sort of approval. A brief glance and almost indiscernible nods pass between Fergal and Narth. I sit back down.

"My friends . . ." It has finally dawned on me that Egon has been subtly encouraging me to use this form of address. He smiles in recognition that I've gotten the message at last. Fergal nods in approval. "I have no quarrel with any man at this table. Instead, I respect the way you made a quick end to a war that never should have been started in the first place. I was there at the beginning, and I have talked to men who were there at the end. You forced my brother to be the . . ." I need a word and look to Egon. "Aggressor?"

"*Argasor.*"

"You forced my brother to be the aggressor. You chose an excellent defensive position. You watched his tactics, what orders he gave, how he conducted his war. You watched and learned. It cost you some men; it cost us many more. But you saw his weakness – his stubborn belief that he knew more than anyone else in the field, even when it was obvious his orders were not working. And you used his weakness against him.

"But what gives me hope, my friends . . . hope that we can put a final end to my brother's war and return to our normal way of living side-by-side . . . what gives me hope is that you fought only to defend your lands. You didn't cross into our territory, even though you had good reason to pursue my brother all the way to his castle. That is how we are alike. All of us at this table want only to protect our people and what is rightfully ours. To me, that seems like common ground . . . like a base on which we can live again as neighbors and not as enemies."

Not a word is uttered. At long last, Narth speaks, "My friends, shall we go riding? My friend Egon says men who eat together can talk together. I say men who ride together can talk together." In response, everyone rises from their seat, and I quickly explain to Samuel what's going on.

At the stable, we each prepare our own mounts. Egon has once again chosen Polaris. Narth and Fergal come over to admire Sirius. "A fine stallion," says Narth.

"He was bred at our stables," I reply. "His sire was the son of my grandfather's favorite stallion."

"A very fine stallion, indeed," says Fergal.

"Perhaps," I suggest, "when we're at peace, we can talk of trade in horses."

The weather is fine, and we ride to the meadow where Egon had first tried out Polaris. It's a broad expanse, with hedgerows on two sides and some scattered piles of dried brush that make excellent jumps. Riding up beside Samuel, I tell him what I'm about to do. "Pick up the pieces, mate, if I make a dog's breakfast of this."

He laughs. "You? Mess up on horseback? Not in a hundred years."

Then I ride up alongside Korst. "Lord Korst," I greet him.

"Hmph."

"What say you to a friendly competition of horsemanship?"

"Follow me," he says, and we're off.

I match his skill in a race around the meadow, then follow him over a jump with equal ease. Now I need to work out one thing for him to best me at and one for me to best him. That's how to win this man's respect. I've already spotted my win . . . a spot where two rubble piles are close together with room only for a landing and an immediate takeoff in between. Not many men or horses can manage this, but I'm confident that if I show it to Sirius in advance, he can do it. The win for Korst, however, can't be something where I simply let him win . . . he'd spot that in an instant and perceive it as weakness.

We're making another circuit of the meadow, Korst staying very close to the hedgerow, hoping I won't be able to make the turn at the corner, when I spy the solution for his win. There's a wide puddle of water alongside one of the brush piles. The horse Korst rides is taller than Sirius and should clear both brush and water easily; and Sirius won't be hurt if he lands short in the puddle. Engrossed in my planning, I almost miss the turn but manage it successfully at the last minute, somewhat to Korst's dismay.

By now, the others have got wind of what's going on and have stopped to watch. We slow our horses to a trot to let them rest for a moment, and I slowly circle back toward the jump with the puddle, making sure that Sirius doesn't get a chance to see the whole obstacle. Back at the corner of the hedgerow, I urge Sirius to a canter and head straight for the jump; Korst watches to see what I have in mind. As Sirius takes the jump and spies the water on the other side, I hold him back ever so slightly so he can't quite stretch out enough to clear it, hoping this won't be noticed by the observers. Sirius's forefeet clear, but his hind feet come down in a giant splash in the puddle, earning us jeers and catcalls from the watchers. Korst sees his moment and makes for the jump, clearing both obstacles easily to shouts and cheers from everyone. I bow to him from the saddle, acknowledging his victory.

We take a couple more jumps side by side before I pull Sirius up to a walk to let him cool off. Korst follows suit. I head back toward the far end of the meadow, choosing a route that will take us past the double jump, and pause there briefly to acknowledge our audience, giving Sirius time to appraise the obstacles. The second jump is a bit shorter than the first. This means Sirius won't see it again until the last minute, but it also means he won't need his full power to clear it. I'm about to either make a complete fool of myself and maybe injure my horse, or win the respect of this man who doubts my purpose. As we reach the end of the meadow and turn, I hear Master Mervyn's voice in my head. "Give your horse his head, Alfred, and go with him. He can do it easily without you on his back. Trust him to know how to do it with you there."

Again, I urge Sirius forward and then give him his head. He seems to know what I want and what's at stake. He takes off a bit early over the first jump so as not to land long. And just as soon his forefeet touch the ground, he gathers his hindquarters under him to launch us over the second pile. When we land cleanly on the other side, I suddenly realize I've been holding my breath and release it in a great exhalation of relief. I pat Sirius on the neck in gratitude for his skill and walk toward where the watchers are cheering and applauding. Korst trots up from the other end of the meadow, shaking his head . . . obviously with no intention of even attempting to duplicate my feat. He reaches out his hand to me and we shake. "I do not know if my horse could do that."

Still gripping his hand firmly, I reply, "I admire a man who looks out for the welfare of his mount."

The others gather about, congratulating us both on our skill. When Samuel eases up beside me, he says with a grin, "Remind me never to underestimate what crazy scheme you may get into your head next. I've definitely got to have one of Star Dancer's colts."

By now, the sun is beginning to lower in the western sky. Owen points toward it and announces, "Time for drinks, my friends," and turns his horse's head toward the stable. We follow him, Egon managing things so that we ride side-by-side at the rear.

"That was quite a risk you took, my friend," he uses my language to give me some mental respite from the day.

"A wise man once told me that a man never knows when he'll need to place his trust in his mount."

He smiles broadly. "Korst is a relic of a warrior clan, Alfred. Their land is harsh, and the people had to be harsh to survive there. Korst only respects a man who is willing to challenge him. Whether he wins or loses – though he certainly enjoys winning – it is the challenge that matters. Narth, Owen, and Rusk know how to deal with him on his own terms. Today it seems you have won his respect. I think he will no longer find it necessary to challenge your intentions.

"It may not yet seem so, but you are making progress," he continues. "The most important thing you've done is to speak to them directly. I am quite impressed with your command of our language."

"Well, I had a lot of time on my hands while John was king and a monk who was a most excellent tutor. Still, this may be one of the most difficult things I've ever tried. The concentration necessary to follow the conversation and find the right words is exhausting."

"Then you will most surely sleep well tonight," he laughs, then adds in a serious tone, "I trust you understand why I cannot intervene."

"You once convinced them to trust us, and my misguided brother broke faith with both of us."

"My work will begin after you leave, keeping them mindful of their agreements and of all the signs that you can be trusted."

"I'll do whatever I can to help, Egon, assuming we get an agreement."

"Fergal and Narth are the keys," he continues. "We have no hierarchy among us, but if they are with you, the others will follow suit."

"I've been watching them," I remark. "Some small signs, I think, of progress."

"They will not drag this into a lengthy negotiation. I believe they will make up their minds tonight. I think you know where I stand."

"You honor me by riding Polaris," I reply, pause for a long moment, and then continue. "Egon, it's important to me that you know I kept my promise. I deserted the field rather than be forced to lead an attack on you."

"I know, my friend. My scouts shadowed you until you were safe across the border."

"But I saw no one."

"As we intended. They stayed half an hour or so behind you, their orders to prevent your being overtaken by any pursuit sent by your brother. Oddly, there was none, and the scouts returned as soon as you were safe."

"Your generosity overwhelms me, my friend."

"A small token of gratitude for the gift you gave us of knowing what was coming and how to prepare. Our secret . . . yours, mine, and Samuel's."

"Our secret."

"And Alfred?"

"Yes?"

"It is important to me that you know I have never ridden Polaris in battle." I reach out and shake his hand.

Fergal and Narth are waiting for us outside the dining hall this morning. "May we talk before we join the others?" asks Fergal.

"Of course." I signal Samuel to go on without me.

"Come," says Narth, and he leads us to a small room that looks as if it might be some sort of study or reception room or both. There's a writing table, some chairs, Egon's banner on a stanchion, and a window that looks out over the inner courtyard. "Please, sit," says Narth as he and Fergal each take a chair.

"We want to know what role your lords played in your brother's war," says Fergal.

"None, at the beginning," I reply.

"But are your lords not advisors to your kings?" asks Narth.

"Normally, yes. But my brother believed he didn't need advice. Just as he didn't seek advice from his captains in battle, so he didn't seek the advice of his lords in deciding to go to war. For that matter, he didn't seek their advice on anything. And they had no authority to prevent him."

"You said at the beginning," says Fergal. "Did they play a role later?"

"None of our lords joined the war. I'm the only one my brother ordered to march with him. My friends, I believe his intent was to get me killed . . . he always thought I was some sort of threat.

"But back to your question of the lords. They did play a role. They tried to disrupt the war. They took actions that allowed their men to return home. And they sent messengers to the men of their domains encouraging them to abandon the field. Many heeded their lords and left quietly in the night. I'm sure your scouts reported this to you as desertions. It was, in fact, our lords' effort to reduce John's capacity to fight."

"And do you seek advice from your lords?" asks Narth.

"I do. I follow the custom of my father and my grandfather."

"But as king, you can overrule your Council, is that not so?" Fergal.

"That's true, but it's not something I would do lightly. The lords have pledged their loyalty to me as king, but accepting their pledge binds me to . . . I'm sorry, I don't have the word I need. It binds me to work together with them for the good of the kingdom. I take that very seriously."

"Did your lords advise you to seek peace?" Narth.

"I told our lords that I wished to make peace. They all – every one of them – urged me to do so as soon as possible."

"Why are not some of them here with you?" Fergal.

"They would have come if I had asked. But they don't yet have your language, and so talking together would have been difficult. Besides, my brother created the mess we're in today. I felt a very deep personal responsibility to my kingdom and to you, my friends, to find a way out of it."

Fergal and Narth look at each other, apparently weighing an earlier conversation against what they've heard from me. Finally, Fergal speaks. "We believe you are sincere in your wish to return to our former way of living as neighbors. But we have no authority over our compatriots."

"I'm sorry, Lord Fergal, but I don't know this word."

"The other lords, our neighbors and friends here at this table."

"Thank you."

"We have no authority over them. We can only tell them what we think. They must form their own opinions and make their own decisions."

Narth picks up the thread. "Korst is not an easy man. You took his measure yesterday better than most, and I believe he has a new respect for you. But I cannot guess what he will say or do today."

"Egon has long held a good opinion of you," says Fergal. "I am beginning to understand why."

"Owen," says Narth, "most likely just wants to get all this over with so he can put his fleet back in operation and return to bilking us all out of our money for his fish."

"Be prepared," says Fergal, "for the others to want something in return for their agreement. I am sure you have thought of this and know what you can honorably give. Now . . . they will be waiting for us." He rises, and we follow him out and back to the dining hall.

"Nice of you to join us, friends." Owen grins at his own joke.

Fergal begins. "King Alfred, I like what I have heard from you. I like your manner and how you conduct yourself. I am ready to listen to your proposal."

"I too," says Narth. "Tell us what you propose."

I wait for a moment to see if any of the others raises an objection. "Very well, my friends. My proposal is that we all stop acting as if we are still at war. To that end, I have already removed the border checkpoints and put a stop to the border patrols. The two troops that used to man the checkpoint have been recalled and are now assigned to other duties."

"He speaks truth," says Fergal. "It has been two months or more since we have seen any knights at the border."

"That is not much in return for asking us to break camp," says the man called Rusk.

"They were the only knights we had deployed at the border."

The man sitting to Fergal's left, whose name I cannot seem to remember, says, "That is something, sir, but how are we to know that you will not put them back as soon as we disperse our army."

"You can't be certain, my friend. No man can see into another man's soul. But I've come to you unarmed, offering you my trust, hoping to earn yours. You will have my word of honor. And if you wish, I'll affix my signature and seal to a document that sets out the terms of our agreement. All my kingdom would be bound to honor the king's signature and seal."

"You would have to make a separate agreement with each of us," says Owen.

"I'm not opposed to that," I reply. "Or perhaps we could make one document that names all of you."

"We do not want to disband our army only to have you break your promise and we have to put it back together again. It is disruptive to our way of life." The man to Egon's right whose name, I think, is Durrus. "If we make an agreement, will you agree to five years . . . or ten years even . . . and put that in your document?"

"If that is what you and your friends wish, Lord . . . Durrus? I hope that's correct."

"That is correct."

"But let me suggest something, Lord Durrus. In my kingdom, if we make an agreement that does not set a time limit, the agreement is meant to last forever. Not only will I be bound by the agreement, but so will my heir and his heir and the kings after that. If that's not your way, then I have no objection to making a set number of years part of our terms."

The talk continues back and forth like this for a while. How soon would they break their camp – much discussion among themselves on this topic. Owen, as predicted, wants to pull his men out right away. Durrus wants to go slowly. Narth offers the view that his men are of little use to him when they are just sitting in camp, biding their time. Fergal, "Soldiers with nothing to do get bored and cause trouble." It seems the weight of opinion is leaning toward a quick and orderly dispersal. I try to keep Samuel apprised of how this is developing.

Midday is drawing near when the question I had been dreading is finally broached. From the man to Fergal's left, "And what of your garrison, King Alfred? Could you not launch an attack on us from there?"

"Our garrison has been there for longer than I have been alive, my friend. Its purpose has never been to wage war. Our knights do many things to help our people. They help those in need; they help to keep our roads and bridges in repair; they bring criminals to justice; they patrol within our borders, going from village to farm to town identifying things that need to be done in the kingdom. Our main garrison is at my castle. Most of our knights are assigned there and look after most of the kingdom. Our garrison in the west looks after the western parts of our land, those parts that are many days' ride away from the castle. It's a small garrison, incapable of housing a large army, incapable of waging a war on its own."

Egon has picked up the task of keeping Samuel in the picture.

"How many troops are there?" asks Durrus.

My mind races. I've no choice but to be completely honest with these men. They know we've seen the size of their camp, and it's likely they have spies who've already told them the strength of our garrison. "Three troops, Lord Durrus, on rotation. The commandant is always a senior captain, chosen personally by the knight commander."

"Three troops could mount an attack," says the man to Fergal's left.

I volunteer nothing further. They're quiet for a time. "Perhaps, my friend," says Durrus, "you would consider reducing their numbers . . . say, down to two troops."

I look directly at Samuel, more for their benefit than his, since he and I have already agreed how to play this. He hesitates for quite some time, then nods.

"Perhaps we could consider that, my friends. But here, I have a request of you. It will be difficult to supply the needs of my people with only two troops. But as a gesture of our good faith, we would consider doing that for one year. By then, you will have had time to observe that we're honoring our agreement in all respects."

At this point, the servants arrive with the midday meal. "My friends," says Egon. "Let us eat. We can finalize our agreement on full bellies."

The meal is bread and a venison potage with small ale. The lords eat heartily. I have little appetite, knowing that an agreement is so nearly within our grasp and, at the same time, apprehensive that something might go wrong before we get there. As each man finishes his food, he steps out to relieve himself and then returns to the table.

When all are reassembled, Fergal again begins. "My friend, here is what I am prepared to agree to. I will withdraw my men from our camp and agree to live in peace with your kingdom. In return, you will reduce the strength of your garrison to two troops for one year and provide your signature and seal on a document agreeing to live in peace with us for the duration of your reign and your son's reign after you."

There is a long silence in the room before Narth speaks. "I, too, can agree to the terms described by my friend Fergal."

Egon gives me an almost imperceptible nod, indicating that it's my turn to speak.

"Lord Fergal . . . Lord Narth . . . I, too, can agree to these terms. Thank you, my friends."

Surprisingly, it's Korst who speaks next. "I like you, Alfred. I will agree."

"You'll get no argument from me," says Owen. "I want my men back on my fishing boats."

The others slowly give their consent. When only Egon remains, Fergal turns to him, "And you, my friend?"

"I, too, agree."

"I'm grateful to all of you, my friends. It's a very special thing we've done here," I tell them. "Lord Egon, will you be kind enough to write the documents? We'll need one in your language and one in mine." Egon calls for a servant and requests quill and parchment. While we wait, I explain to Samuel.

No one says a thing as Egon prepares the documents. When both are finished, he reads each one aloud. I take quill in hand and sign both documents, then pour the wax and affix my seal. Narth steps up first, pouring wax and making an impression with his ring. All follow suit. Egon then rolls each document into a scroll, tying it with a leather thong. He gives one to me and the other to Fergal. "Fergal will take our document to the high priest, who will keep it safe for us."

Egon calls for wine. "Let us toast what we have done together."

This has been hard-won, but as good an outcome as I could have wished – perhaps better, for now I know these men and they know me, and therein lies the path to avoidance of future conflict. Already, there's a more collegial, informal atmosphere in the room. I decide that now is not the time to confuse things with talk of diplomacy and ambassadors. The evening meal is raucous and festive. At one point, Korst shouts at me from the opposite end of the table. "Hey, Alfred. I bet you can't make that jump again."

"I'm not sure I even want to try, Korst," I shout back.

He roars with laughter, raising his tankard to me, and I respond in kind.

Toward the end of the evening, Egon takes me aside. "I would like nothing better, Alfred, than to entertain you here for a few more days. But I have some men to withdraw from camp."

"And Samuel and I have new orders for a garrison commandant. We'll also spend a night at the monastery on our way home. I have friends there I haven't seen in almost a year. I trust that will cause no anxiety here?"

"None at all," he replies. "We will ride out at midmorning. It will take that long for some of them to sleep off tonight's celebrating. Ride with us . . . your guard as well."

"It would be my very great pleasure." He turns to leave. "I have one last thing to ask, Egon, if I may."

"Of course, Alfred."

"On the day of my coronation, I thought I saw in the crowd the faces of two men I've come to regard as very special friends. Yet when I looked a second time, they weren't there. I've resigned myself to the fact that this was probably just wishful thinking on my part."

"Perhaps your friends were reluctant to be seen or acknowledged because of circumstances in their world."

"It would give me great comfort to believe that might have been the case."

"Then be comforted, my friend."

• • •

The chroniclers will almost certainly record that we rode home in triumph. I prefer to think that we rode home with the proper order of things restored.

Rupert and Ernle are there to greet us as our procession halts in the inner courtyard, the extra troop from the garrison having gone directly to the stables. "The lords are all waiting in your private reception room," Rupert tells me as Ernle greets his son. "Montfort wanted to hear the outcome before going to his first meeting with the Lakes king, and Peveril is especially eager."

"Very well," I reply. "Osbert?" He opens his pack, pulls out the scroll, and gives it to me. "If you would, please let Matthias know we should have the entire court for supper in the dining hall. And tell him we'll be joined by a troop of knights and Brother Eustace. Eustace, Samuel, and Tobin at my table, please . . . Eustace on my right.

"Tobin, once you've dismissed your troop with an invitation to supper tonight, join us, please. We'll wait for you inside before we go up."

As Osbert and Timm collect our cloaks and gloves, Rupert asks, "Well?"

I'm tempted to keep them in suspense, but the outcome directly affects Lord Ernle since his domain is on the border, so he deserves to be the first to know. "It's done," I reply, holding up the scroll. "But let's none of us give it away when we walk in." Just then, Tobin joins us, and I add with a grin, "I rather suspect these two will have a lot to say about *how* it was done."

Everyone wears a solemn face as we enter the private reception room, where conversation comes to an abrupt halt as we walk through the door. I take my time choosing a seat – king's prerogative to keep them wondering for a little longer. Finally, Richard speaks up, lightheartedly, "Alright, Alfred, you've had your bit of drama. Now let the rest of us in on the secret."

"Gentlemen," I address them, still keeping my expression very solemn . . . and then I break into a broad smile. "We have an agreement. Not only an agreement, but a signed and sealed treaty." I remove the leather thong from the scroll, unroll it, and pass it around the room for all to read.

"You actually got the seals of all the Territorial lords on a document?" Meriden seems a bit incredulous.

"Every one of them, Meriden. But from their perspective, the most important seal on that document is mine. We left an identical one with them, written in their language and bearing all the same seals. It will be stored in the custody of their high priest, which they apparently share in common."

"A remarkable achievement," says Bauldry as he finishes reading and passes the document to Montfort.

"The achievement, I think," I reply, "was in getting them to trust us again. Now we have to prove every day for a while that we're worthy of that trust."

"The achievement," Samuel chimes in, "was actually some pretty spectacular horseback riding by our king, who . . . if you'll forgive me, Sire," his formality a humorous prelude, "can come up with some of the most hare-brained ideas of anyone I know." And so the tale of the riding competition is told, Samuel ending with, "A new one for your bag of tricks, Lord Peveril."

"I've no doubt I'm in for a terrible scolding from Gwen about risking my neck on that jump," I laugh, "but it won Korst over and removed the last of the animosity from the room."

We spend the next hour talking about the details of the talks and why it was important to have a time frame in the formal agreement. "They really aren't belligerent toward us," I tell them. "They only want what we want, which is to protect their lands and their way of life."

Later, in the dining hall following a rather elaborate meal, it's time for some speech-making. Samuel awards the Order of Merit to each of the knights who served as our guard. I award the King's Commendation to both Tobin and Samuel. Eventually, when he retires as knight commander, I intend to make Samuel a lifetime lord, for he has indeed rendered the most extraordinary services to me personally and to the realm. But now is not yet the time for that.

Finally, I turn to Eustace, addressing him first in the language of the Territories. "Brother Eustace, I don't have the words in any language to express the depth of my gratitude to you. Without your tutoring, I don't believe any of this would have been possible." The room goes completely silent, hearing me speak this strange language for the first time.

I revert to my native tongue. "I've been told that the rumor circulating during John's reign about why I was spending so much time with Brother Eustace here was that I was studying to take holy orders." A murmur goes through the room. "Anyone who knows me very well would know that, as much as I lust after this lovely lady," I take Gwen's hand and hold it up in mine as she demurely turns a most brilliant shade of red, "holy orders are unlikely to be in my future." The murmur turns to raucous laughter.

"Now you know the truth. The hours and days and weeks I spent with Eustace were devoted to learning the language of the Territories. When we began, I thought of it only as a way to further the fledgling friendship I was building with Lord Egon. In the end, it turned out to be an essential part of building the trust that led to our agreement. Being able to speak directly with these men made it possible for us to come to know one another as individuals.

"Brother Eustace, I know that medals and royal commendations aren't part of your way of life. So I want to reward you by presenting you with a horse from our stable."

Eustace begins to protest, "But I can't accept—"

I cut him off. "I know, Eustace, that your order doesn't permit individual ownership of such valuable possessions . . . that they're owned in common by the entire community. Knowing this gift will become part of the monastery's common property, I give it with the proviso that, whenever you need to travel for any reason, this horse is to be at your disposal."

"My gratitude knows no bounds, Alfred," replies Eustace.

"See Master Elvin tomorrow. He'll help you select a mount that suits you." Then I turn back to the assembled court. "Ladies and gentlemen," I pause and raise my glass. "To peace. May our children and our children's children never know the horrors of war." Only time will tell if this hope is futile. But having seen those horrors first-hand, I know that it's something most fervently to be wished.

Waiting for spring to go on progress is turning out to be an inspired choice. Montfort and Bauldry – the first two stops on our grand anti-clockwise tour of the realm – both eschew the formal royal banquet in favor of expansive lawn parties to which they invite all their tenants and the villagers within their domains.

Our third stop is Abbéville Market, where they've moved the spring festival two weeks earlier than usual to coincide with our visit. "I hope you'll forgive us, Your Grace," says the mayor, "that the decorations are a bit shabby. Money's scarce, with all the rebuilding we had to do after the fires. And it still isn't finished."

"I was actually quite impressed, Mayor, with what you've accomplished. It looked to me, as we rode in, like there were only a handful of structures yet to be rebuilt. It can't have been easy with so many men conscripted into the army. Did any of the immigrants ever venture back?"

"Sadly, I don't know what happened to them, Sire. I fear they must have perished in the sickness."

As Amelia curtseys to me for the first time, I realize that, with the change in my circumstances, that bridge I'd pushed to the back of my mind is now entirely different from what I'd imagined. And I'm suddenly consumed with an overwhelming desire to be alone with her.

Which we manage, after a fashion, when it's her turn to be my partner at the dance this evening in the market square. "I was devastated when the news reached us that you'd been killed in the war." She keeps her voice quiet, almost a whisper.

"And I when you weren't in the first Assembly meeting. All I could imagine was that you'd succumbed to the sickness."

She laughs softly. "No, I just decided it was time to give someone else a chance. And now look at us. We're both very much alive and dancing together."

"I suppose we'll have to be content with that for tonight."

When the dance ends, she takes my arm as I escort her back to the area designated for the dignitaries. In the shadowy light of the lanterns, she contrives to press her breast against my arm, and I have to suppress my body's instant reaction. "I cherish the memory of what it's like to hold the skylark in my hand," she whispers. "And long to do so again." All I can manage with so many people around is to linger just a little longer than necessary as I kiss her hand when she takes her seat. In spite of my better judgment, I know, should the opportunity arise, I'll cross that bridge.

•　　•　　•　　•　　•

We spend a night at the western monastery before going on to the border village. It's the first time Gwen has been to either of these places that have figured so prominently in my life. From time to time she takes my hand and squeezes it tightly, imagining, I suspect, what those experiences must have been like for me.

Earlier, I had contemplated inviting Egon and Fergal to join our celebration in the village. A chance, it seemed, to show them a different side of our people. In the end, I abandoned the notion. Despite my good intentions, I couldn't be sure how it might affect the villagers, some of whom are immigrants themselves and others who've given shelter and succor to those fleeing their lords. The sight of horsemen arriving who might be those very lords would almost certainly have put a damper on the festivities. Life on the border won't change instantly just because I'm trying to forge better relations with our neighbors. So I simply sent messages to Egon and Fergal informing them of our arrival and its purpose. I'll take no chances that the presence of the king at the border with a troop of armed guards could be in any way misconstrued.

As always, arriving at Ernle Manor is like coming to a second home. And we finally get a break from the rigors of travel – two days to rest before we resume our journey. Samuel and I take one day to visit the garrison. "We're managing with only two troops," the commander tells us, "by changing the rotation to half a troop at a time. We're also limiting the number of men who go into the village at any one time, whether it's for supplies or to help the villagers or just for the occasional afternoon or evening free from duty."

"What about your drills?" Samuel asks.

"One troop at a time, sir," he replies. "And always to the east. Your brother Rainard has given us one of the hayfields for this year and is planting his hay on our usual training ground. In my opinion, the drills are rather less effective when two half-troops are pitted against each other. But it does keep the men on form. As long as there's no disturbance at the border, sir, I think we'll be fine for the one year."

We share the midday meal with the troops, seated among them rather than at some formal head table. Samuel rises and raps on the table for attention. "Most of you know," he says, "that I place as much value on honesty as on respect for command. Our king is of like mind. This is your chance to tell him anything you think he needs to know. Speak candidly – even if it's about your captains or commanders. Just don't complain about the food." He grins. "I doubt even the king can do much about the skills of our cooks." Which gets him a laugh and serves to put the men more at their ease. Their concerns are predictable, mostly about their role if the peace doesn't hold.

The next morning I spend with Ernle and his eldest son Rainard. At one point, conversation turns to the dissolution of the kingdom during John's reign. "All the heirs were part of the decision, Your Grace," says Rainard. "Knowing there was no way to predict how long that state of affairs might last, Lord Devereux wanted to be sure we were all committed to the path. When Lord Rupert told us what he'd heard from deserters, we knew it was the right decision." So my uncle was not without assets, despite having been deprived of his base of operations. "By then, we understood it was as much about denying territory to any conquering force as about opposition to King John.

"I must admit, none were more relieved than my father and me when things unfolded as they did. Not that I wish death for any man," he rushes to clarify. "Simply that the entire kingdom is now better off, if I may say so."

"I'm just glad that's all behind us," I reply. "Have you given any thought, Rainard, to what role you might like to undertake for the realm? I'm sure your father's told you I intend to engage the heirs more directly."

"Father's told me I can speak freely with you, Sire," he begins hesitantly.

"I'd expect no less."

"Then you should know I'm quite content as things are. You see, I'm not an outgoing sort like Samuel. Perhaps that's why I've never found a wife to suit me. And I'm pretty sure that would make it difficult for me to adapt to life at court. I know eventually, I'll have to, but for as long as Father's able to represent our family at court, I'm much better suited to managing the estate."

"I appreciate your candor, Rainard. And to the degree that I can respect your wishes, I'll do so. By the same token, consider how much more difficult that eventuality you alluded to will be if you find yourself plunged into it with little preparation and no real experience of it."

"I hadn't thought of it quite that way, Sire."

"Not every role requires a regular presence at court. One example is Warden of the King's Forests. There are others – even some that, once the task is complete, there's no further need for the role. Give it some serious thought, and let's talk again before the end of the summer. Consider what things interest you, and then we can discuss what's possible."

Just at that moment, Rainard's squire interrupts. "Begging yer pardon, m'lords . . . Yer Grace . . ."

"What is it?" Rainard is overtly unhappy with the interruption.

"Begging yer pardon, m'lord, there be some problem with the arrangement of the pavilions fer the party tomorrow. M'lady Ernle be napping so they canna' ask her, and so they tell me ye be needed at once. I be ever so sorry, m'lord."

"Why not wake Her Ladyship?"

"Go, Rainard," I intercede to spare him more embarrassment. "There's no need to wake your mother. These things never happen at an opportune time; and it's my experience they're easier to sort out early than after someone's made a mess of things. I think we're finished here anyway."

"Thank you, Sire," he rises. "You're right about the sorting out. I'll think on what you've said."

Ernle and I are left alone. "You handled him well, Alfred. He's always been quiet and shy. But he has a quick intellect, and there's no man better at managing a great estate. He'll be a capable and loyal asset if you ease him into the role. I only wish I'd had more success at finding him a wife."

"Is he simply not inclined to marry?"

"He would answer that by saying he finds most women too interested in society – too interested in social gatherings and making him part of such things – too interested in romance. As far as I know, it's not that he isn't attracted to women. It's simply that he needs a very special type of woman that I've been unable to find – someone more interested in quiet contemplation or helping him run the estate than in the trappings of being lady of the manor. I've no doubt that if such a woman could be found, he'd do his duty and produce an heir for the family . . . and even be happy. But his mother and I are beginning to despair of finding the right match."

"It's not out of the question that Gwen might have some ideas."

"Now that's a most welcome suggestion. When this progress is complete and life at court has settled back down, I might just have to have a talk with your lovely lady."

The day of the party dawns cloudy and blustery, and there's much scurrying about trying to work out how to move the festivities indoors with so many people invited. Fortunately, the west wind blows the clouds away by midday, taking itself along with them and leaving behind a delightfully sunny spring afternoon with only an occasional gentle breeze. The party is a huge success. It seems both the gregarious Lord Ernle and his shy son have a knack for gaining the loyalty, admiration, and even love of those who call this great estate their home.

Fulk, the blacksmith who removed my chains when I returned from captivity, seeks me out as he does every time I visit here. "Ye be looking in fine fettle, Yer Grace." He makes an awkward little bow.

"As do you, Fulk. How's the smithy these days?"

"Me son be in charge now, m'lord. Lord Ernle, he tell me, 'Fulk, ye not be needing to work yerself into an early grave.' Me youngest son be the one interested in the trade, so when he become a master blacksmith, I put him in charge. But I go there most days and do some light work. I watch, too, and make sure everything be done perfect fer his lordship. And Lord Ernle, he be a kind man and keep paying me."

Gwen chooses this stop, with so many herdsmen present, to announce she's making Juliana Deputy Patroness of the Royal Kennel – a surprise for Juliana. Some of the herdsmen have brought their prize dogs with them, and Juliana fawns over the lot of them while one explains to Gwen, "Ye see, m'lady, this one be me favorite on account of I be able to trace his lines all the way back to Luna and Cedric." Two of the three foundation dogs of the Royal Kennel. "He be me best herder too."

When Gwen told me of her intentions, I was hugely pleased. But then something occurred to me. "You'll be setting quite a precedent," I said.

"In what way?" she asked.

"Well, when Geoffrey turns eleven, I now have to find some equally prestigious title for him."

"Don't be silly," she laughed. "When Geoffrey turns eleven is most likely when you'll start telling him what it means to be the heir. Nothing we do for Juliana can ever hold a candle to that."

I smiled at her. She was right, as usual. "Very well, you've set the precedent for Edward then."

"Well, we have a few years to work that out, don't we? And besides, I rather think you have some small grasp of what it means to be a second son."

•   •   •   •   •

Our brief respite from travel over, we take to the road again with a destination of Lord Meriden's seat. I expect this will be a very different sort of experience. Meriden lost his wife during the last years of my grandfather's reign. His only surviving child, a daughter, acts as lady of the manor now. She's a rather plain woman, but her husband clearly dotes on her.

We're to be treated to the most formal of royal banquets – completely in keeping with how Meriden would think to convey his own stature by entertaining the king in the manner to which he believes all kings must aspire. Afterward, he invites me for brandy in his study.

"A most impressive evening, Meriden," I tell him as he hands me a glass. No reason not to let him feel good about himself. "Both the food and the entertainment were superb."

"Thank you, Sire. Mary was at least as responsible for the preparations as I myself."

"Then I'll make a point of thanking her personally as well."

It's a cool, late-spring evening, and there's a welcoming fire in the hearth. He gestures to chairs facing it, and I choose first, as protocol demands.

"You know, Sire," he says, with a tinge of longing in his voice, "it rather saddens me that all this will go to my nephew on my death. Mary is exceptionally competent – she manages all the accounts for the estate as well as running the household. I do believe she could run the estate single-handedly, given the chance. But it's not the way of our world . . . or even of our laws."

"You're a Councillor, Meriden," I remind him. "Quite entitled to propose new laws if you're so inclined."

"I've actually spent many an evening thinking about just that. I don't know if our world is ready for such a drastic change. I also don't even know how to think about what it would mean for future generations. Would the Meriden line be pushed aside in favor of descendants of my son-in-law's family? It's all extraordinarily complicated. But it does trouble me that my daughter will be passed over."

I'm truly surprised by his depth and thoughtfulness. Father always said he was a good man. It seems that the goodness is at least in equal measure to the meddlesomeness. We spend an hour or so reminiscing about the last years of my grandfather's reign and all that's happened since. When he offers to fill my glass for the third time, I demur. "If I have any more of that marvelous stuff, there's a chance I might embarrass my host by falling asleep in the middle of our conversation."

He chuckles, pours a single sip into my glass, and raises his own. "To the new reign. May it be all we could possibly hope for." I raise my own glass and we drink the toast.

The next morning, we depart for the royal manor, where we'll spend one night. Rupert, Catherine, and Mother are waiting there and will go with us to Great Woolston and Thorssen Castle.

We arrive in Great Woolston on the second day of their spring festival. The afternoon is devoted to music, dancing, a pageant presented by the local children, and endless eating and drinking from the food pavilions set up in the square. The next day is the annual horse race, and wagering is already at fever pitch. The favorites seem to be the local baker and a farmer from the nearest village to the east. I let Juliana place a small wager, and she chooses the stable master's son, primarily, I think, because he let her give his horse a handful of oats.

Race day dawns sunny, if a bit chilly, but that will only serve to make the horses livelier. The course is set up in a hay meadow south of town. A shallow stream crosses the meadow, and the riders will have to decide if leaping over or pounding through is the fastest choice. There are three hurdles set up with hay bales, so the horses can't injure themselves if they miss . . . these "race horses" are, after all, essential to the livelihood of their riders. The last hurdle is half again as high as the first two. A long straight stretch on the west side leads to a sweeping curve at the near end of the meadow that takes the riders toward the stream and then the hurdles. The race will most likely be won or lost, however, by what happens in the two sharp turns at the far end of the course. If the riders get bunched up there, anything could happen. Seven laps of the course will decide the winner.

The mayor has talked me into giving the people an added treat. After the main event, I'll join the mayor, the sheriff, the stable master, and the local priest – who, it turns out, is quite the horseman – in a three-lap race around the same course. I've agreed only on condition that it's an honest race – there's to be no letting the king win. And just to be sure, I've added the incentive of a gold coin for the winner.

The big race is to start at midday, but people begin crowding around the edges of the meadow an hour or more before. A small viewing stand gives the local dignitaries and our party an unobstructed view over the heads of those bunched near the finish line. When horses and riders assemble for the start, there must be twenty or so trying to get the best position. Eventually, the starter gets them organized and holds up his white flag. When it drops, mayhem erupts. The first three laps are chaotic, and, as I'd expected, they all get bunched up in those tight corners at the far end. Down the straight stretch, even those who came last out of the turns seem to catch back up to the leaders. In the fourth lap, those turns begin to make a difference. The best horses and riders are able to put more distance between themselves and their chasers as they approach the long sweeping bend. The baker and the farmer seem to stay neck and neck, with the stable master's son not far behind and another rider, who I'm told is the blacksmith's son, keeping pace with him. As the final lap begins, it's really down to these four, and the baker's horse seems to be tiring. Coming out of the final turn, the farmer is in the lead followed by the stable master's son. The blacksmith's son lags a bit, but once on the straight stretch, he gives his horse its head, and they quickly catch the others and win by half a length.

The crowd cheers and rushes out to congratulate the winner as the remaining riders come home. There'll be more cheering and moaning this night over wagers won and lost, but it will all be in good spirits with large doses of ale. The prizes are given, but the crowd shows no sign of leaving – word has spread quickly of the extra event to come.

As our horses are brought up, I notice the pride with which Osbert is leading Sirius. He must have spent all morning polishing my saddle – it fairly gleams in the sunlight. In the finest tradition of chivalry, I bow to Gwen, and she ties her scarf around my arm. Then the five of us mount up and walk to the start line.

On the first lap, I let Sirius decide what to do about the stream. He leaps it without a thought then clears the hurdles effortlessly. When we get to the sharp turns, I hold him back a bit to watch how the others are going to handle things, knowing we can catch up on the straight. True to their word, the others are running an honest race, and we're all pretty much together at the end of the second lap. By now, though, I've no doubt Sirius can win handily, so I decide to adopt the blacksmith's son's strategy. Coming last out of the final turn, I let Sirius catch his breath as the others begin their rush to the finish. When I give him his head, he catches them easily; but I hold him back ever so slightly so that we win by only a nose ahead of the priest.

We dismount, shake hands all around, and I invite them to return to the viewing stand. When the crowd finally quiets down, I turn to my fellow racers. "A delightful competition, gentlemen, for which I thank you. But now I have something of a dilemma." I pause. They look a bit puzzled. I turn to the crowd. "You see, I had offered a gold coin to the winner of the race, but I can hardly give it to myself." Polite twitters of laughter run through the crowd.

"And I'm not quite sure how to reward a priest for coming in second." The priest makes as if to offer some sort of protest, but I hold up my hand.

"So here's what I'm going to do." Gwen gives me the coin, which I hold up for the crowd to see. "Mr. Mayor." He steps forward. "A gold coin for your town's treasury. For giving us a most pleasant entertainment." The mayor bows deeply, the crowd cheers, and then everyone begins to disperse. It's been a good day.

•   •   •   •   •

Phillip seems to be out of favor with the weather gods. As we draw closer to Thorssen Castle, the clouds we've seen all day at a great distance over the sea seem to be closing in, and the skies are heavy when we arrive.

Age may have put a damper on the dowager Lady Thorssen's stamina, but it has in no way blunted her tongue or her disdain for protocol. As I dismount, she's already down the steps, completely ignoring the tradition that the lord is first to greet his sovereign. Her cane in one hand, she puts the other on my arm and looks me up and down. "Well, well, Alfred. I wouldn't have given a mug of ale for your chances of ever being king, and look at you now!" By this time, Mother has descended from the carriage, and Lady Cecily turns to her, "Alice, my dear, what a pleasure!" She takes Mother's arm and lowers her voice ever so slightly in pretense of not wanting to be overheard, "Quite a handsome king, isn't he? Almost as handsome as his father." I smile at her in appreciation as she bustles on to greet the others. Phillip and Addiena join us.

I kiss Addiena's hand in greeting. Phillip and I embrace, and he shakes hands with Rupert, who chuckles, "I'm glad to see your mother's in her usual fine form."

"I quite imagine she'll one day be telling St. Peter there's absolutely no need for her to talk to him – that it's God she's come to see." Rupert laughs out loud. "Actually," Phillip continues, "she's been looking forward to this for weeks. Once she heard that Catherine and Alice were coming, she's spared no effort to arrange the best rooms for them and every comfort you can imagine."

Addiena glances anxiously toward the sky. "I think we'd best get indoors before the rain," she says as her mother-in-law returns with Juliana in tow.

"Quite right, my dear." Then, turning back to Juliana, "Come along, young lady. I'll show you and your grandmother and your aunt to your rooms. They have quite the best views of the sea." She pauses and looks up at the sky. "If these annoying clouds will just cooperate."

We've been indoors barely a quarter hour when the skies open in a great deluge, the rain so intense we can barely see the courtyard wall from the windows of the sitting room where Rupert and I have joined Phillip while the ladies get settled. "It's the price we pay this time of year for living on the coast," says Phillip. "The southerly breezes that bring warmer air have a nasty habit of bringing the clouds along with them."

"Not too bad a price, I should think," says Rupert, "for the views you have most of the time."

"Indeed, Lord Rupert," Phillip replies with a broad smile. "I truly cannot complain."

Situated on a cliff overlooking the Southern Sea, Thorssen Castle was – in the days before my great-grandfather formed an alliance with Goscelin's ancestor – a watchtower to guard against enemy ships approaching the mouth of our river. Its position on a point extending into the sea provides unobstructed views east, west, and south. Legend says that, on a really clear day, one can see from the top of the tower all the way to the far coast, though that does stretch the imagination a bit.

In those days, a reinforced troop of knights and archers were garrisoned in the castle. At the first sign of a threat from the sea, the troops would rush to the place on the river bank where they could raise the massive chains to prevent intruders from sailing upstream. Disembarking from a warship at that point in the river was a tricky business indeed. A few fire arrows into the rigging of the ships were usually enough to discourage would-be attackers and send them scurrying away. Any so bold as to try to disembark would find the fire arrows redirected to the poor souls trying to scramble down the sides of the ships, with any arrow that missed its human target lodging in the wooden hulls where it could wreak real disaster. Trying to disembark on the offside was even more treacherous, for among the salt marshes are many hidden pools of quicksand.

There's been no need for a garrison at Thorssen Castle in my or my father's lifetime. Instead, the castle is known for its spectacular scenery. But it remains a perfect defensive location, and the legacy of the Lords Thorssen is their duty to the defense of the realm.

In less than half an hour, the rain has slowed to a steady drizzle but the clouds show no sign of dissipating. When the ladies join us, it's evident Lady Cecily has taken Juliana under her wing. "Let's see what sort of refreshments we can find, my dear. And after that, I shall show you all around the castle. I'm an old lady, mind you, so I can't go as fast as I used to, but I'll show you all the best spots. Would you like that?"

Always polite, Juliana replies, "Of course, my lady. And we don't have to go fast."

"Good. Then we'll finish our circuit in the nursery where you can meet my own young granddaughter. She's much younger than you, but she's a very sweet child . . . much like her mother." It's nice to see how much the dowager has warmed to Addiena over the years.

"I'm afraid we'll have to move the festivities indoors tomorrow," Addiena laments. "And I don't know how many of our tenants will brave this foul weather, but we'll just have to make the best of it."

And that's exactly what we do. More of Phillip's tenants come than I would have expected. It seems the rain is stalled here on the coast, and the weather is quite fine a mere hour's ride away. "It happens like that sometimes," Phillip tells us. "The clouds just rain themselves out here, and Great Woolston never sees a drop." Despite the weather – or perhaps even because of it – the day is a huge success.

Our departure next morning is in a pea soup of fog and mist, so Rupert and I opt to join the ladies inside the carriages. True to Phillip's prediction, though, before we reach Great Woolston, the sun is high in a brilliant blue sky with nary a cloud in sight. We spend a night at the manor, then say good-bye to Mother, Rupert, and Catherine before moving on to the port.

The first order of business there is to meet with Gamel and Laurence. To my great surprise, the dock repairs are nearly complete. "Another two weeks of good weather, and we should be finished," says Gamel. "Things were not nearly so bad as either of us feared. And those immigrant builders have been a godsend – truly master builders all. They worked out a system for doing the underwater work that improved on what my engineers had devised. Things are going so well I've already diverted men to begin work on the Port Commissioner's house."

"The foundation is nearly complete," says Laurence. "And the head builder tells me that, if we don't get an early frost this autumn, he thinks they should finish by late spring next year." Good news of this sort gives me hope that we really will get the kingdom back to normal.

"As soon as we finish here," says Gamel, "I'm putting most of my men onto the roads. Sir Samuel has been requiring the patrols to make full reports, so we'll have their assessment to start with. Then we'll have to hire road builders. From what I've seen, I can tell you now, it won't all get done this year, Sire."

"I didn't expect it would, Gamel. And I've come to realize that may be quite a good thing, since it will provide lasting work for the men involved – not just a few weeks' pay and then nothing."

"I'm glad you see it that way, Sire. It helps me to know how many men to hire and how to organize the work. As for the reservoir, I want to inspect that myself . . . with Ronan's help, if I can tear him away from his farm for a couple of weeks."

"I don't think you'll have any problem there. That dam is his baby just as much as it was Harold's. He'll be keen to know what state it's in."

We take our evening meal at a tavern in the town – not one of the more unsavory ones farther down the docks. Afterward, Laurence invites me to his room in the inn for brandy. "No word from Emaurri yet," he begins, "but it's only been a month since he sailed."

"Why the delay?" I ask.

"When the wool arrived, the bales were clearly marked 'Best', 'Mixed', and 'Good.' That's when Emaurri recognized that his knowledge of the wool trade could be improved. We sent for Rupert's estate manager, and he explained how it's done. Apparently, the traders bargain more freely on the 'Mixed' bales. That allows them to keep the prices up for 'Best' and sets a benchmark for what they can get for 'Good.'

"The ship was provisioned and the wool loaded. On the day they were to sail, two wagons arrived filled with crates and bearing a letter from my father. It seems the King of Lakes was eager to sell some of the linen they had been accumulating while they had little or no access to a port. Reading between the lines of Father's diplomatic language, I translated 'eager' to 'desperate.' And Emaurri thought having both wool and linen would give him an even better negotiating position. So we took the time to offload most of the 'Good' bales of wool and load the crates of linen. The wool is still in our warehouse."

"Sounds like Fortuna is on our side for the moment, my friend. I've been concerned about how quickly we could open trade routes for the Lakes, so I'm delighted it's already underway."

"What we need now, Alfred, is to get more ships refurbished. Only one master shipwright survived the sickness, and he desperately needs apprentices. I've written to all the mayors telling them work is available here, but so far only one man has come."

"Be patient, Laurence. Men don't easily uproot themselves from their homes to go to a strange place for work they don't know if they're suited for. Just keep spreading the message that there's work here. Once a few have come and start sending word – and more importantly, money – back home, more will arrive."

"I hope you're right."

"Mark my word. All too soon, you'll have the opposite problem."

"Maybe one or two of them will be suitable as clerks if they don't take to shipbuilding," Laurence chuckles. "I'm managing just fine on my own for now, but as soon as we have more shipping on a regular basis, I'm going to need help."

"How goes your other little enterprise?"

"Slowly but steadily. So many were lost to the sickness, Alfred. Rupert maintained a few agents even through the worst of John's mayhem, and they're working for me now. I've not had time to rebuild my innkeeper network, but I have two men among the dock taverns and brothels."

"Alf?" I feel compelled to inquire after the tinker who found Ralf's family and recognized his sons in our stable at the time of my father's fatal accident.

"I haven't heard from him, sad to say. But he hasn't been confirmed dead either, so I haven't given up hope that he's biding his time somewhere and will eventually turn up."

"You know, Laurence, I've just had an idea."

"Oh?"

"That wool that's in the warehouse. Do you know if our own woolen mill is operational yet?"

"No idea."

"Me either. But what I want you to do is this. Get with Phillip and see if he can convince the merchants to put the mill into operation now. They can use the wool we have for their first run. That will give some more people work."

"What if they won't go along? You know how reluctant they are to spend in advance of profits."

"Don't pressure them. Just tell them the Crown will put the mill back in operation and will take the first run of cloth as payment for its investment. Actually, I rather hope that's how things play out."

"Richard won't like spending the money. But you've obviously got some scheme in mind."

"I've been trying to work out what trade goods Peveril could take on his first trip into the Territories. This would be perfect. The few sheep

I remember ever seeing there were pretty scraggly, so I suspect woolen cloth comes very dear to them. Even our cheapest quality would be welcome – maybe even prized. But it wouldn't be ostentatious or offensive as a first gesture."

Next day, we take a walk through the town and down to the docks in the company of the mayor and the newly appointed sheriff. The port town is all about commerce, not festivals, so they're eager to show us the progress that's being made on getting their own world back in order.

$$\bullet \qquad \bullet \qquad \bullet \qquad \bullet \qquad \bullet$$

The day after, we depart for Peveril's estate. It takes three ferry crossings to get our entire party to the other side. Even so, that's a pleasant change from my last time here.

Peveril's domain is in the hills that border the Eastern Kingdom. Their wealth is derived not from farming or grazing, as on most of the other estates but from the stone quarries they operate in the mountains. Their building stone is of good quality, but their real treasures are the extraordinarily beautiful flagstone for floors and the two quarries that produce the stone favored the world over by carvers of decorative ornamentation for great houses and cathedrals. The family has become expert at very conservative quarrying, in part to keep demand and prices high, but more importantly because they know that once the stone is gone, it's gone. All that will be left to them then are the vast forests that cover these hills, and that, too, is an expendable resource.

A valley between the northern and southern ranges gives them access to convey their stone to market. The roads here haven't suffered from the neglect evident in other parts of the kingdom. The Peverils have always maintained these roads to a higher standard than elsewhere – a necessity for transporting the heavy loads from the quarries. This is my first trip here, and I find the scenery quite beautiful indeed.

Peveril Castle is breathtaking. Perched on the highest spot for miles around, it looks across the valley to the northern range. The village here lies at the foot of the hill, and a narrow track with numerous switchbacks snakes up the hillside – a vertical rise of two hundred feet or more – to the main gate at the east end of the promontory.

We're met in the village. The carriage and wagon will remain here, as they can't possibly negotiate the track to the summit. Pony carts are waiting to carry the ladies and our baggage up the hill. Only two people are allowed in a cart so that the pony isn't overburdened on the climb. The driver leads the pony up and then drives the cart back down, using the brakes extensively to keep the cart from overrunning the pony. Gwen and Letty go up in the first cart; I join Juliana in the second. Osbert and the guards are advised to lead the horses up if they're unaccustomed to such a climb. Even though the numerous switchbacks are intended to keep the slope of each individual section as manageable as possible for the ponies, each section still makes a considerable ascent. As we make the second turn back to the east, I observe how our trunks are being brought up in two carts. Each is pulled by two ponies, led by a driver. In the back, two men push, to help the ponies out, and a lever has been rigged so that one of the men in the back can operate the brakes if the ponies need a rest or things otherwise get out of hand.

Once at the top, there's even more at which to marvel. The southern side of the hill is a sheer precipice that drops even more than two hundred feet from the foot of the castle walls to the easterly flowing river below. We learn that a gorge at least as deep as the southern precipice runs along the western wall, prohibiting access from that direction. A drawbridge from the second level of the keep can be lowered as an escape route into the dense forests on the other side of the gorge, should that ever be necessary. I knew that Peveril Castle had never been taken and only rarely come under assault – and now I understand why. Its defensive position is almost unassailable.

In the southwest corner, the original keep rises above everything. Two wings extend from the keep, one along the south wall, the other along the western wall. The stable and some lower buildings that appear to house the kitchens line a portion of the northern wall. Even the inner courtyard is on a slope, with the only somewhat level ground being along the southern side. Clearly, the servants and villagers here must be very fit, coping with this extraordinary landscape every day.

Osbert and the guards go off to attend to the horses and the baggage. Peveril and four of his sons greet us at an entrance to the southern wing. "I must say, Peveril, this is quite spectacular!"

He smiles broadly. "One of my ancestors did seem to choose rather well. I must admit, though, when I'm coming home after a tiring journey, the prospects of climbing that hill can be rather daunting. More than once I've been tempted to call for a pony cart, but what kind of image would that be for the lord of the manor?" he laughs. "You must come again in autumn sometime. The hunting is almost as spectacular as the scenery. Now, though, the ladies are waiting for us inside."

A servant opens the door, and we enter a corridor that extends to left and right, with doors indicating several rooms opening off it. Peveril pauses in the corridor. "Before we go in, Sire, I should explain. My wife was injured some years ago. When our youngest was but two, she was watching him one day while the nurse attended to something else. As toddlers will do, he was dashing about, exploring everything in sight, fearless as you please. He darted down a spiral stair and, fearing for his safety, Emmeline rushed after him. He came to no harm, but she lost her footing and fell terribly, breaking both her legs. The barber tried to set them, but he wasn't very skilled, so they didn't heal correctly. She can walk with her canes or someone to help her, but she can't manage stairs at all. She insists on walking some each day – fearful that if she doesn't, she'll lose whatever ability she still has – but it tires her.

"That's why she hasn't been to court in many years. She simply doesn't want anyone to be bothered with having to carry her up and down stairs. But more than that, she especially doesn't want to be pitied. She has an incredibly strong spirit. I offered to relocate our home to our cottage across the valley. I thought it would be easier for her, and she could get out more. But she would have none of it. 'This is *Peveril* Castle,' she told me, 'not just some castle on a hill. And it's my home too.'

"So we reconfigured everything so that our living and dining quarters are in this wing where things are relatively flat. Leaving our guests, of course, to cope with the stairs."

"She sounds like a remarkable woman," says Gwen. "I'm eager to meet her."

Peveril leads us to a door and makes as if to enter first, but I stop him. "Allow me." The servant opens the door, and even before I have one foot over the threshold, I'm speaking, "Ladies, please keep your seats. It's been a long day on horseback, and my most fervent wish at this moment is to sit on a soft chair rather than in a saddle." I make my way quickly to the chair that's obviously been designated for me. As Gwen takes a seat beside me and Peveril crosses to sit beside his wife, she beams at him with pleasure. "Your Grace . . . My Lady," says Peveril, "my wife, Emmeline . . . Lady Peveril." I rise from my chair, cross to her and kiss her hand, then return to my seat, making a bit of a show of sinking deeply into it.

She laughs quietly at my antics. "My husband has told me, Sire, what a fine man you are . . . much like your father, it would seem. Welcome to our home . . . and you, My Lady. We're so pleased you're making a proper visit. Allow me to introduce my daughters-in-law."

I watch and listen in fascination as she introduces the others. She is stunningly beautiful. Small and delicate, with hair the color of ripe chestnuts and warm brown eyes that have glints of gold when the light hits them just so. Her voice has the song-like rhythms of the Kingdom of Lakes. The combination is mesmerizing. When she finishes, Gwen presents Juliana, and ends with, "And please, call me Gwendolyn. It's what the lords' wives have done for so long that I don't want to change it other than for formal occasions."

"Thank you, My . . . Gwendolyn. We took it from your letter there was no reason this progress had to be a formal event, so we've planned it more like a family gathering. We'll dine as our family does—"

"Don't let her fool you," Peveril interjects. "We should all be so lucky as to dine as well every day as the feasts she and the steward have cooked up."

Emmeline laughs. "Well, I didn't say the food wouldn't be nice, Pev – just that we'll dine as family.

"Tomorrow is market day. I thought it would be fun for us all to go down to the village. I've ordered the pony carts for an hour before midday. The men can make their own way down. There's a nice tavern for our midday meal, and then we can explore the market. It might not be quite as expansive as later in the summer, but it's still quite delightful and one of my favorite outings."

Emaurri's wife inquires after her husband. "I know he's been gone only a month, but it's been almost two since he left here."

"I asked Lord Laurence exactly the same question when we were in the port. No word yet, but I'm sure there will be soon," I try to reassure her.

"I'm trying to help her adjust to being a diplomat's wife," says Emmeline. "I know it's not easy at first; but it's *so* worth the effort since you eventually see places and meet people that others only dream of." Turning back to me, she adds, "Thank you for giving Emaurri the opportunity, Sire."

While the ladies explore the market the next day, I linger in the tavern with Peveril and his heir, Ademar, enjoying the exceptionally good ale. It turns out Ademar is the businessman in the family, running the estate on his own now. They kept the quarries working, albeit at a much slower pace, during John's reign. He doesn't plan to up their production for a while, not wanting to create a precedent by selling their stone at less than its true value. But they've kept all their people in work throughout the last three years, so a slow return to normal will be a detriment to no one.

Our time here is far too short. Gwen and I have both grown quite fond of this family even though we'd barely known them before. But leave we must. Richard and Avelina will be waiting for us in Neukirk Market and from there we complete our progress at Devereux Castle.

· · · · ·

In Neukirk, the innkeeper takes me aside. "Yer Grace," he speaks in hushed tones, "if ye be so kind, I be hoping to be working fer Lord Laurence again. If ye be seeing him, mayhap ye be telling him fer me?"

"That I will, my good man," I assure him. It will be interesting to hear how Laurence reacts to this approach.

It's market day here as well, and we all enjoy a day mingling with the people and eating from the food stalls. I'm surprised to come upon the bookseller we saved from the mob in Great Woolston a couple of years ago. He has nothing particularly special at the moment, but I buy a volume from him anyway as a memento of the occasion.

As we draw nearer to Devereux Castle, Richard and I ride out ahead of the rest of the train. I sense Tobin is nervous about this and invite him to send a guard on ahead as a scout. He demurs; he's learning my habits and learning to trust my mates to keep an eye out for danger. But I notice he keeps himself and another guard within shouting distance of us.

"I had a chat with Laurence on the way here," says Richard. I try to put on my best air of nonchalance. "Am I the one who has to pick up your grandfather's role of chastising you for always wanting to spend Treasury funds?" he tries to sound cross.

"That may be," I chuckle. "So chastise away. But don't forget, he always backed me in the end."

Richard roars with laughter. "That he did. Actually, I don't think this latest scheme of yours is such a bad idea. Not that we can actually *afford* it at the moment . . ." He lets that thought hang in the air for a time. "But then there's very little we can afford, so why not? It seems like a good investment in the future. And it can't hurt to challenge the merchants to be a little more altruistic in helping us get the kingdom back on its feet. Not that I have much confidence in their actually taking the point . . ."

"So you'll back Phillip to move quickly if they even hesitate?"

"I will. We'll never get out of debt unless we get people working again. I've no idea what the Territories might have of value to us, but we won't know until we try."

As we ride from the village up to the castle, I recall the terrible state of agitation I was in the last time I was here. Then, I wasn't expected. Today, I'm calm and happy, and Lord Devereux is in the courtyard to greet us. As the ladies descend from the carriage, he takes charge of Juliana, treating her like a proper lady of the court and seeing to her every need.

"Don't spoil her too much," I tell him. "After all, we do have to return home and resume our normal lives."

"I shall spoil her as much as I like, Alfred, while she's my guest. Come, my dear," he turns back to Juliana and offers her his arm. "Let me show you around my home, and then we'll find the room we've prepared just for you." Juliana is over the moon.

Over supper, we tell the others of our delightful visit with the Peverils. "I can't believe that, in all this time, I didn't know about his wife," I remark.

"Such a lovely girl," says Devereux. "Daughter of a Lakes merchant. Peveril's father met her when he was ambassador there and was determined to win her for his son. I think he was rather in love with her himself, though he acted completely honorably. When they first wed, my late wife helped her adjust to life on a great estate, and we visited often when they weren't away on some posting or other. So sad about her accident. I do wish she'd come back to court. I know how welcome she'd be."

We have three days here, so Devereux has arranged that each day we ride to visit various of his tenants where they live and work – a rather special way for me to see more of his estate and to mingle with his people. It's clear he's taken steps to ensure they have work, a commitment to his duty as first lord that's greatly to be admired.

As we start our journey home, I recall something my grandfather once told me. "Next to the birth of his heir," he'd said, "a king's first progress is probably the most memorable event of his life." I understand now what he meant. A newly crowned king, traveling among the people, is the personification of their hopes and dreams. A weighty responsibility, to be sure. But that responsibility can in no way overshadow the sheer joy and wonder I've experienced these past few weeks.

Our arrival at home coincides with Emaurri's return. "It was an interesting negotiation, Sire," he reports, "but I think the outcome will work to our advantage. At first, it looked like our plans would come to naught. The weavers are unaccustomed to purchasing wool off-season, and their schedules aren't built around having it available this early in the year. But as they inspected our best quality bales, they couldn't disguise their pleasure at the prospect of having such fine fleeces. Though they never said it outright, I got a clear sense they had pent-up demand for the very finest woolen cloth. The prices weren't what we'd get in the summer markets, but no one expected that. The merchants may grumble a bit for show, but I doubt they'll really be dissatisfied."

"What about this year's shearing?" I ask him.

"They were cagey. No one willing to discuss contracts, but I'm not surprised. The manager of the third most important house did say he might place an order with a trader he's dealt with in the past. I let it go at that. Letting them work out among themselves how to compete for the best fleeces seemed a better way to maximize our sales."

"I like the way you think, Emaurri."

"It was an easy choice, Sire. They were practically salivating over what I had to offer. I've always heard our finest wool was the best in the world, and now I've seen the truth of it with my own eyes."

"Did we do as well for the King of Lakes?"

"I think so, Sire. The brokers were happy enough to pay full price with no bargaining. If the Lakes weavers are smart and release their backlog carefully, they should be able to demand top prices for at least another year. Lord Montfort is meeting me here tomorrow to collect their profits before he returns to the Lakes at the end of the week."

"Well done, Emaurri. Congratulations on your first successful mission."

"Thank you, Sire. I'm starting to see why my father likes this work."

"Speaking of your father, I should tell you we had a delightful visit at Peveril Castle during our progress. And one of the women there is most eager have you back by her side."

He smiles. "I sent word to her the moment we docked. As soon as my business here is finished, I'm going to collect her, and we'll both be headed back to Goscelin's court. He was most welcoming and seemed very eager for my return."

"Your mother will be pleased. She's been painting lovely pictures for your wife of the joys of diplomatic postings."

The timing of Emaurri's return is fortuitous, for the Assembly is here once again. I'm just leaving the stable to join Gwen and Mother for a quiet family supper when Osbert finds me. "Lord Phillip say he be grateful if ye could find some time fer him, m'lord."

"Any idea what he wants, Osbert?"

"Nay, m'lord, but he be in a right foul mood."

"Then best we see what can be done to cheer him up. Tell him I'll meet him in my private reception room straightaway. Be sure there's some wine there for us, if you will. Then see if Letty can arrange enough food for him and Addiena to join us for supper. That should cheer him up even if I can't."

Phillip is pacing the room in frustration. Before I can even greet him, he starts in, "I swear, Alfred, there is *no* satisfying them."

"Whoa, my friend. No satisfying who about what?" I take a seat, but it's obvious Phillip needs to continue to work off his current pique.

"I brought Emaurri to the meeting this morning to deliver their proceeds from the wool and tell them what to expect for this year's markets. They sat there completely stone-faced. Not a word of thanks to Emaurri. No questions. Nothing. In the face of all that silence, Emaurri excused himself. And then all hell broke loose.

"Why were they only getting a pittance for the finest wool in the world? Every one of them said he could have gotten better prices if he'd done his own negotiating. When will we learn that the king's lackeys don't know anything about business? They actually said that, Alfred.

'The king's lackeys.' They'd just squandered their future. Prices would be forever depressed. It went on and on. I had to shout to get their attention."

"So what did you tell them?"

"Well, I reminded them that just a few short months ago, they were delighted – even eager – to sell their wares so the surplus wouldn't drive down prices this summer. And I told them they couldn't have it both ways."

"And?"

"More protests. Finally, I asked them if they had heard what was said about the weavers being unable to disguise their near desperation to get our wool. Didn't they think that was a good omen for business to return to normal in the summer? That quieted the protests, but they were still grumpy." He finally stops his pacing and takes a seat.

"I know it's a risk we took when we established the Assembly, Alfred, but we've never had such a quarrelsome group before. They're like children – self-absorbed and wanting everything their way – not a single voice of reason among them. What I wouldn't give to have Madame Greslet or Mister Ouistreham in the room right now."

"Can you tell how much of it is just impatience with the fact that all this takes time?"

"That would be easier to read with a couple of level heads as benchmarks. Right now, they're just feeding off each other and don't believe they need to be part of the solution."

"Have you taken up the matter of the woolen mill yet?"

"Oh, yes. I decided while we were on the subject of fleeces, we might as well finish it off. I suppose the good news is that you got the result you wanted," he chuckles.

"Tell me about their reaction."

"So it started with 'The Crown can't tell us how to run our business. That mill is our business, and we'll operate it when and how we want to.' One man even had the temerity to suggest there were no workers available to operate it."

"Pretty extreme," I remark. "Clearly they aren't listening."

"So I laid it out again – so simply my son could understand. The Crown is not running your business. The Crown is suggesting you prepare for this summer by putting the mill in operation now using the leftover wool from the trade mission. It will put people to work; it will give you cheap cloth to sell now; and it will ensure the mill is fully operational when you need it in late summer. They all adamantly refused.

"So I played my trump card. For a moment, the room was so silent you could have heard a pin drop. And then chaos broke out again. 'The Crown can't confiscate our mill' was pretty much all that was said, though everybody used different words, and someone claimed we were trying to go into competition with them in cloth sales. They were all raising their voices to be heard above each other. When I finally shouted for silence, they had spent enough of their fury to at least shut up for a moment. So I told them, 'The Crown is confiscating nothing. We're investing in your business in advance of when you say you need it and taking a very modest return on our investment. For the late summer milling, *you* will pay the workers, *you* will take the production, and *you* will sell the cloth, making whatever profit you're able to.' There were a few feeble protests attempted, but I shut them down immediately. My parting remarks before I adjourned them for the day were that they'd had their chance, they declined it, and the Crown would therefore act in the best interests of the kingdom."

He quaffs his glass of wine in a single gulp. "I'm so looking forward to tomorrow. They want to talk about taxes again."

"I just had a funny thought," I remark while he refills his glass.

"Tell me," says Phillip. "I could use some amusement about now."

"I wonder what Meriden would have made of today's proceedings?"

Phillip laughs out loud. "I think even he would have been appalled."

"Then let's hope we get Greslet or Ouistreham back in the next rotation."

"Better still, both of them," he laughs.

"Agreed, my friend. Let's go in to supper. I might just drop in on your little gathering tomorrow and see if their manners are any better for my presence."

I wait until after midday to put in an appearance. When I step through the door, everyone scrambles to their feet, and this time I make no effort to stop them. Once seated in the back of the room, I gesture to Phillip, "Please carry on, Thorssen," allowing them all to resume their seats.

"You were saying, Corbon?" says Phillip.

"I was saying, your lordship, that the purpose of this Assembly is for us businessmen to tell the Crown what we need to improve our business, and what we need right now is lower taxes. That's the only way to get our profits back to where they were before King John."

I signal to Phillip that I want to respond to this.

"Gentlemen," I rise and proceed to the head of the table, indicating with a hand motion that they should remain seated. "I'm curious how many of you share Mister Corbon's assessment of the role of this Assembly?" All the hands go up, though a couple of them seem slightly more tentative than the others.

"Then may I recommend that you re-read your charter. I'm assuming, naturally, that you've read it sometime in the past. As you re-read, you'll be reminded that this body exists to advise the Council on matters of commerce and trade and to bring to the Council proposals that would benefit the kingdom as a whole."

"With respect, Your Grace," Corbon interjects, "lower taxes will help business."

"There is nothing in the charter of this Assembly that prohibits your binging forward a proposal to reduce the tax rate, Mister Corbon. I've only just arrived and so haven't been privileged to hear your prior discussion. If it includes a clear delineation of the benefits across all segments of our society, then I encourage you to draft it and bring it forward. If, however, it's framed in the narrow context of what all of you just indicated you believe your purpose here to be, then I recommend that you reassess it within the framework of the charter." No one responds.

"Perhaps, gentlemen," says Phillip, "this would be a good opportunity for one of those private discussions we always make time for during these gatherings. I'm sure you have a lot to consider among yourselves. Would an hour be sufficient?" No one objects. "Very well. I'll return in an hour, and we can conclude our agenda."

Phillip and I rise and make for the door. Once again, I let them scramble to their feet. As Phillip opens the door, I turn back to them. "By the way, gentlemen, are your tax rates lower than they were last year?" There is a general mumbling of "Yes, Your Grace."

"And do you remember how long it's been since they were as low as they've been set this year?" I glance around the table, looking directly at each man, then head out the door with Phillip right behind.

He's grinning from ear to ear. "I wish I had your knack for timing."

"Blind luck, my friend." I clap him on the shoulder. "I was only hoping my presence would make them a bit more civil, but Corbon really put his foot in it."

He laughs. "That little bit of drama at the door made everything I've put up with this morning worthwhile."

"A king has to take his fun where he can get it."

Later that evening, Phillip reports that the Assembly backed off their strident insistence on more reduction of their taxes. His opinion is that they've merely gone away to come up with a different tactic to get what they want. Our best hope is that things start to improve enough to tone down the rhetoric from this group and that next year's Assembly is more balanced.

Life is settling into something of a routine. Gwen is starting to plan for next year's breeding of her mares. She's had half of them brought back here from the manor. "Actually," she told me, "I've decided it's a good idea to have them in two different places. If anything terrible should happen in one place, we'd still have half our breeding stock.

Elvin, too, has turned his attention to breeding, giving more and more of the daily running of the stables to his son. He's taken an interest in improving our draught horses, acquiring a broodmare from the Peverils. While we were away on progress, he traded a stallion from one of my grandfather's lines to the King of Peaks for one of the type they use to pull heavy wagons in the lower slopes of the mountains. Elvin's hope is that crossing these two lines will produce an animal of particular strength and stamina that will be valuable not only to us but also to those who might wish to buy them from us.

The children begged for a holiday at Gwen's cottage this summer. Despite how nice I know it would be for them – for all of us, for that matter – I don't believe it would be wise – or even moral – for us to be holiday-making in a foreign land when our people are still struggling and my time on the throne is yet numbered in weeks and months rather than even a single year. "Besides," I reminded Juliana, "I believe you have a royal obligation to preside over this summer's herding competitions." It's not too soon for my children to start learning that royal duties often take precedence over personal desires.

Juliana and Richenda have become inseparable, despite the four years' difference in their ages. Whenever I see them together, I'm always astonished by how alike they are – one might easily mistake them for sisters. Richenda is tall for her age – something she inherited from Harold. Both have long, wavy, dark hair and brilliant blue eyes – the dominant combination in our family. Recently, Gwen tells me, Juliana has asked Richenda to teach her the language of the Kingdom Across the Southern Sea.

Geoffrey is getting his first full-size horse this summer. Elvin chose a seven-year-old gelding that he tells me is completely reliable. After riding him myself, I agree. Things that would spook a more high-strung animal have no effect on him; and when I pretended to fall off, he simply stopped in his tracks and came back to nuzzle me and see if I was alright.

I've asked Donal to bring Geoffrey to the stable at the end of my morning ride. Elvin has his new mount saddled and ready for him.

"Donal said we were going riding, Papa," he says. "Where's my pony?"

"What would you think," I ask him, "about riding this horse that's already saddled?"

He can barely contain himself. "Can I, Papa? Really?"

"Elvin, do we have a mounting block somewhere?"

"Aye, m'lord," he replies, reaching into Sirius's empty stall where he's stashed it in advance. "Here ye be, Master Geoffrey. I think mayhap ye be able to climb aboard from this."

While Elvin helps Geoffrey into the saddle, I mount Sirius. "Now, we're just going to ride around the arena a bit for you to get a feel for what riding a big horse is like."

We walk the horses side-by-side into the arena and then make a full circuit around, Sirius on the outside and Geoffrey on his horse next to the rails. "What do you think?" I ask him. "Would you like to trot him a bit?" I know how smooth this horse's gaits are and that there's little danger of his falling off.

That's all the encouragement a young lad needs. He's off at the trot, zigzagging back and forth across the arena. When he slows back to a walk, I call him over. "You did quite well. Seems like you've learned a lot on your pony. Now let's go back to the stable." I watch him struggle not to beg for a longer ride.

Elvin is waiting with the mounting block. "So what did you think of him?" I ask after giving Sirius into the care of one of the grooms.

"He's nice, Papa. Can I ride him again sometime?"

"Would you like to have him for your very own horse?"

His eyes get as big as saucers. "*Would* I? Oh, can I, please, Papa?"

"Then he's yours." I get a big hug.

"Oh, thank you, Papa, thank you, thank you, thank you."

"There are conditions, Geoffrey." He suddenly goes quiet, anxious about what might be coming – my indication that I have his attention. "You must take lessons from Master Elvin. And you must do exactly what Master Elvin and Donal tell you. Do you understand?"

"Yes, Papa."

"No galloping until Master Elvin gives you permission. And absolutely *no* jumping. Is that clear?"

"Yes, Papa." He hesitates, trying to decide whether to say what's on his mind. "Papa, can't you teach me to ride him?"

"Master Elvin will have more time than I will, so you'll learn faster with him. You know, Master Elvin's grandfather taught me, and I think I turned out to be a pretty good horseman."

"Very well." He turns to Elvin. "Will you teach me to be as good a rider as Papa, Master Elvin?"

"I be thinking mayhap ye turn out to be an even better rider than yer da' if ye be putting yer mind to it."

"There's just one other thing, Geoffrey."

"What's that, Papa?"

"I want you to be kind to your horse. Look after his needs. Brush his coat. Master Elvin will teach you how to take care of him. Give him a treat from time to time. And if you take good care of him, he'll be your best friend."

"I will, Papa." His face lights up with joy. "I promise. And I'll be his best friend too." He reaches up, and the horse lowers its head to be stroked. "Master Elvin?"

"Aye?"

"What's his name?"

"Methinks 'twere yer grandda' what give him his fancy name. He be called Nestor."

Richard and I have planned this together. Geoffrey and William – Richard's eldest – have become best friends, just as their grandfathers did. William is getting his horse later today, and Elvin has agreed to teach both boys. A missed holiday at the cottage will soon be a distant memory.

Edward, at his own request, is learning to fish this summer. He begged Donal to teach him. No doubt he'll want all of us to sample his catches. I only hope the cooks don't mind. "Of course they won't," Gwen assures me. "They're quite fond of spoiling all the children. Think back to when you and your mates were lads."

"True. But we wanted fruit pies, not fish suppers," I grimace.

She laughs. "I just hope they have some imagination when it comes to how to cook them."

The summer wool markets, by all accounts, are successful. Prices are neither as low as everyone feared nor as high as anyone wanted. But the traders buy every fleece they can lay their hands on.

As Emaurri predicted, competition between the great weaving houses works in our favor. Buyers arrive in the port from all the main houses, seeking both our wool and finished linen from the Kingdom of Lakes. Laurence reports that the bargaining is fierce, with buyers trying even harder than usual to drive down the prices – assuming, perhaps, that we're still in dire straits and beholden to them. Our traders are up to the task, however, congratulating themselves on their cunning . . . and the tariffs and port fees contribute to our slow replenishment of the Treasury.

Not surprisingly, a portion of the wool is held back for our own woolen mill. I can't help but be amused at how the merchant-owners have no thoughts of gratitude that the mill is already fully operational. Human nature is a peculiar thing indeed.

Lambing and shearing seasons complete, the herdsmen are ready for some relaxation. The herding competitions are happening for the first time since my father's reign, and it seems the enthusiasm for these events permeates every town and village. Not wishing to overshadow Juliana in her new duties, I've decided to attend only the event in Great Woolston, the last round, where the King Edward Prize for the overall best in the kingdom is to be awarded.

As we arrive at the field where the trials are to be held, Juliana very properly offers to let me present the prizes. I politely decline and am rewarded with a smile that glows as if it were Christmas, her birthday, and a new puppy all rolled into one. The moment we alight from the carriage, she's off, seeking out all the entrants, inquiring about their dogs, and wishing each of them good luck.

"She's really become quite accomplished at this," Gwen remarks. "And the herdsmen are all in love with her." A fact that I get to observe firsthand after the last prize is presented. All the herdsmen gather round her with their dogs, and the conversation turns to blood lines, training techniques, who would like a dog from the Royal Kennel to augment their stock – anything and everything herding dog.

I see the wisdom of Gwen's choice to give our daughter an official role. She's an ambassador from our family to the people and is learning through something she loves what it means to be a lady of the royal house. I also fancy I see in her something of what Gwen must have been like at this age – a stark reminder that my task of finding a suitable husband for my daughter will be not unlike Godwin's.

At the height of midsummer, Rainard Ernle comes to court, ostensibly to visit his father and brother. Three days later, he asks to speak with me. I invite him to the library, a place that seems more in keeping with his personality than the often bustling reception rooms on the floor above.

"This is really quite amazing, Sire," are his first words after Osbert shows him in. "I'd heard, of course, what an impressive collection it was, but I've never been in this room. One could spend hours here among such treasures."

"So perhaps I've found a way to get you to court more often," I chuckle.

"Perhaps, indeed, Sire."

I describe the system for those in residence to borrow books. "When the room isn't in use for a meeting such as this, it's open to anyone with a desire to read." I give him a few more moments to explore the shelves and then invite him to sit.

A bottle of wine and glasses are on the table between us, my glass already filled. "Wine, Rainard?" I offer.

"Thank you, Sire," he replies, filling a glass for himself and tasting it. "Quite good. Quite excellent indeed." He takes another sip.

"I've been thinking, Sire, as you asked, about a role I might fill in your court. And I think maybe I've hit on something that would suit me quite well if it meets with your approval."

"I'm eager to hear."

"Well, you see, Sire, I've always been a great admirer of the system of magistrates that your father set up. And I've had an interest in how justice has been dispensed by various rulers throughout history. So when the time comes for Lord Bauldry to move to a different role, I'd very much like to take on that position.

"I still have a lot to learn, so I'll have to study before I'd consider myself ready. I took the liberty of broaching the topic with Lord Bauldry. I hope you don't mind, Sire?"

"Not at all. And, Rainard, when we're in private, 'sir' is sufficient."

"He's more than willing to help me prepare. Even to introduce me to the magistrates so I can observe how they conduct their proceedings."

"I admire the thought you've put into this, Rainard. It reminds me of one of my father's best traits. And your idea makes very good sense." I pause for a sip of wine. "Mind you, I want to leave Bauldry in his current position for a while. I don't want to disrupt things until there's confidence throughout the kingdom that life is on an even keel."

"As I said, sir, it will take some time for me learn."

"Might we see you here, then, from time to time, as you prepare?"

"I expect that will be necessary, sir."

"Good. I want to hear what you think about what you're learning. When you take the role, we're going to have to be comfortable discussing the details of cases that are appealed to the king. So some conversation in advance would prepare us both. I promise we won't overwhelm you with all the trappings of the court right away."

He smiles. "Thank you for that, sir. Now that I know I can come here as a refuge, I think the prospect of being at court might be somewhat less daunting."

Not long after, Sir Gamel is back to make a report. "We found some small problems at the reservoir, Sire, but nothing that couldn't be readily repaired. Mostly, it was things that just happen with lack of attention. You might remember, the sluice gates are supposed to be tested and lubricated once a month. I don't know when it was last done

- the troop on duty didn't even know they were supposed to do that. When we did our test, one of the gates stuck partially open. It was a blessing Ronan was there – he knew how to free the gate without having to dismantle that section of the dam.

"We found a few places where some patches to the mortar were needed. The lake was a bit over-full since the gates hadn't been tested regularly, and the extra pressure from that water meant that any weak spots were starting to deteriorate. But aside from that, things were in pretty good shape. I left an engineer there to help them re-establish their inspection protocol. I also intend to send someone out with each rotation for a while, just to supervise the handoff and look about for anything unexpected. When I'm confident things are once again routine, we can discontinue that practice."

"It sounds like we've had another lucky break, Gamel."

"We have, indeed, Sire. I have two crews inspecting the canals now – one north and one south – an engineer and two masons on each crew so they can deal with any repairs as they go along. How long that takes will depend on what they find."

Bauldry has asked that I put Guyat in sole charge of the proposal for reforming our practices for retiring knights. "He's a veritable magician with finances, and I'd like him to get full credit for the work he's doing."

"I presume he's engaging with Richard before he brings anything to the Council?" My only concern.

"Every chance he gets. I swear, sir, they're like two bankers, those two, when they put their heads together."

"Then perhaps Guyat's next assignment will be in Treasury."

This leaves Bauldry responsible only for oversight of the magistrates. One day each month is designated for judicial appeals to the king. So far, there've been none. Most of the cases, he's told me, have been petty thefts of food. With my full agreement, he's urged the magistrates to be fair but light-handed in sentencing people who don't have enough to eat. Usually, they sentence the thief to just enough work to repay the victim for what was stolen. Despite this practice, there's an appeal of just such a case this month – and, surprisingly, it's the victim appealing and not the thief.

These proceedings are very formal, held in the public reception room with the king seated on the throne, and open to any lord who's at court. Bauldry presides, summarizing each case and the magistrate's verdict.

"Your Grace," he begins, "this case comes from Abbéville Market. A lad called Hutch was accused by the baker of stealing two meat pies from his shop. When brought before the magistrate, Hutch admitted what he'd done and was found guilty of petty theft. The magistrate sentenced Hutch to work for the baker delivering pies for a week as recompense for what was stolen. It's Master Ros, the baker, however, who brings the appeal."

He signals to the three who've been waiting near the door: the magistrate, a man I met the day of the Abbéville fires, who offers a formal bow; a bulky man who must be the baker awkwardly struggles to decide whether to kneel or bow and ends up doing a bit of both, which comes off rather like a botched curtsey; and a small boy who falls to his knees with his head bowed. The lad can't be a day older than Geoffrey, and he's thin as a rail. Despite how threadbare his clothes are, someone has taken pains to be sure he's clean, with his hair neatly combed, to come before the king. I address him first. "I'm told, young lad, that you're called Hutch."

Without moving a muscle, he murmurs, "Aye, Yer Grace."

Reaching down to touch the low platform on which the throne is set, I tell him, "Then, Hutch, please sit here." I want to be sure the baker has a good view of the lad throughout these proceedings.

Uncertain what to do, Hutch raises his head to look at the magistrate, who smiles kindly at him and nods. The lad scrambles up and sits on the edge of the platform just to the right of my feet. The baker looks as if he's about to protest, but has the good sense to heed Bauldry's signal not to speak.

"Magistrate, I trust the lad has been in your care on the journey here?"

"Yes, Your Grace. He rode with me on my horse and shared my room at the inns where we stopped. Also, Sire, these events happened just over a week past, so he wasn't long in the sheriff's care before we set out for the castle."

"Very well. Now, Hutch," I address the boy again. "Since you've admitted taking the pies from the baker, I wonder if you'd tell me why you did it." Again, he looks to the magistrate for guidance. "Hutch, look at me," I say kindly. There's fear in his eyes when he does so. "I assure you . . . no harm will come to you if you tell me the truth. I only want to know what it was that made you take the pies. Was there a reason? Or are you just a little thief who goes around taking things for the fun of it?"

This loosens his tongue. "Nay, Yer Grace. I be not a thief. I never afore take anything 'tweren't mine. Me ma, she be taking us all to church and she be teaching us what be right and it not be right to steal, Yer Grace. I knew 'tweren't right, but . . ." He looks down at his hands.

"But what, Hutch?"

"But me ma get sick, see. She do washing fer the ladies of the town and she get money to buy us food. But she get sick and she canna' work and so she get no money and so we be having naught to eat. And when it be three days that the littl'uns not be eating, they be crying on account of they be so hungry. And me ma still be sick. And me being the oldest, I have to do somat' fer the littl'uns so they not starve. I ask at every shop if there be somat' I can do fer a coin or two but there be nothing. So I ask meself if it be more wrong to steal or to let the littl'uns die. And so I take the pies. And I not be wanting me ma to know, so I tell her I get work and buy them. Me ma, she get better and can work again. But the sheriff, he see me in the street and take me to the magistrate. And me ma come and she be crying and begging for mercy and she promise she punish me right so. But the magistrate, he say I have to work fer the baker to pay fer the pies. I dinna' mind working, Yer Grace, but the baker, he dinna' want me to. And that be the truth of it, Yer Grace. I swear it be the truth." He's almost in tears, but seems determined to be brave.

"That was a very difficult decision you had to make, Hutch. I hope you never have to make such a decision again." Next I address the magistrate. "I've no doubt you've looked into the truth of the matter, sir."

"Indeed, Your Grace. The sheriff knows the family. There are four younger children, each of them about a year and a half apart, the youngest just three years old. The father disappeared soon after the youngest was born, and the mother does indeed do washing for several of the merchants' wives. Nevertheless, the family lives hand-to-mouth, with each day's pay going to buy that day's food. The sheriff spoke with the merchants' wives and verified that the mother was indeed sick and unable to work during the week in question. They're a law-abiding lot, Sire. None of them has ever been brought before me until young Hutch here. That – and the circumstances surrounding the theft – are what led me to the sentence of simply repaying the baker by working for him."

Throughout all this, the baker has grown increasingly fidgety. I rather suspect he thinks I'm taking Hutch's side in the matter. Time to relieve his misery. "Well, Master Ros. This all seems very clear, and the sentence seems appropriate to the crime. I must admit I'm somewhat puzzled as to why you'd appeal to the king's justice."

"It all be well and good fer the boy, Yer Grace. But it dinna' help me. I need money to pay fer what was stolen. Ye see, I be living hard times too."

"What hard times are those?"

"Me business be good in King Edward's time, Yer Grace. But when we had the riots and the fires, I almost lost me shop. The fire be stopped just afore it take me shop, but not afore the front corner be part burned."

"I was there that day, Master Ros. Many people lost all they had. You were one of the luckier ones, it seems."

"Aye, mayhap, Yer Grace. But it cost me dear to fix things. And then me business not be so good on account of people dinna' have so much work and so many gone to the war. And then me kitchen boy, he die of the sickness and so I be having to do it all meself. People only just now be starting to buy a mite more."

Looking from the bulky Ros to the emaciated Hutch, I'm tempted to comment on the relative degrees of hardship each has endured but decide that's not directly pertinent to the judgment I have to render. Instead, I put my hand to my chin in a gesture of thoughtfulness. "Perhaps I don't understand, but it seems to me that if young Hutch here delivers pies for you, then you can keep your shop open and not have to close it while you do the deliveries yourself. You'd be making money by having the shop open, and you wouldn't have to pay Hutch.

Don't you actually gain twice from the arrangement? It seems to me the magistrate has hit on a rather satisfactory solution."

"But that be the problem, Yer Grace. See, I canna' trust a thief not to steal more pies, so I have to close me shop anyway and go with him on the deliveries. So I not be getting any . . . re . . . recom . . . I not be getting any payment fer me pies."

"Ah, I think I see the problem." Ros's face lights up as if he thinks I'm now completely on *his* side.

"Master Ros, why do you think Hutch would steal from you again?"

"Once a thief, always a thief, Yer Grace."

"Hutch," I address the lad. "Is it true you've never stolen anything before?"

"Aye, Yer Grace."

"Do you intend to steal again?"

"Nay, Yer Grace. Me ma, she be working now. The littl'uns have food. And I be wanting to look for work – after I pay back Master Ros – so we be having a bit of extra money in case me ma get sick again."

Turning back to Ros. "I'm still puzzled, Master Ros. The lad seems very earnest. And yet you don't trust him."

"Nay, Yer Grace, I dinna' trust him."

Time to try a different tack. "If I understand what you've told me, Master Ros, you would prefer not to have to close your shop to deliver pies, but without a kitchen boy, you can't do this. If you had a kitchen boy, you could keep your shop open . . . what? Another hour every day? Perhaps more?"

"An hour fer certes, Yer Grace. Mayhap more some days."

"And how much money would you make in that hour, Ros? Just roughly. One coin? Two?"

"Some days, naught, Yer Grace. But most days, at least one plain coin. And on a good day, two or three."

"So with a kitchen boy, you could keep your shop open six more hours every week, right?"

He starts counting on his fingers. "That be right, Yer Grace."

"Very well, now let's say you don't have any really bad days or any really good days in this normal week, so you make one plain coin every day. That's six coins in a week, right?"

"That be right, Yer Grace."

"And what would you pay a kitchen boy for a week's work?"

"Me last kitchen boy, I be paying him two coins a week."

"So you could pay the kitchen boy and still have four coins left over as profit. Is that right?"

The magistrate and Bauldry have quickly grasped where I'm going with this – I've caught their exchange of glances as I look from Ros to Hutch and back. Ros is now furiously working his fingers again. "That be right, Yer Grace. Four coins."

"So having a kitchen boy again would be rather valuable to you?"

"Aye, Yer Grace."

"Very well. Hutch, would you please go stand between the magistrate and Master Ros?" He goes reluctantly, uncertain what's coming next.

"Lord Bauldry, please have what I'm about to say placed into the records."

"Yes, Your Grace."

"It is the king's judgment that the original sentence was fair and appropriate to the crime. I will therefore not overturn it. I do, however, amend it as follows. Master Ros, you will not accompany young Hutch on his deliveries but instead, will keep your shop open during that time. If Hutch steals even one pie from you, you may bring accusation against him, but you *must* be able to prove without question that it was Hutch who took the pie. If this occurs, I charge the sheriff to investigate the matter thoroughly, and if the lad is found guilty, I direct the magistrate to impose a sentence appropriate to an ordinary thief.

"If, on the other hand, young Hutch renders you good service, then I direct you to give him work as your kitchen boy and pay him two plain coins each week. This will allow you to make more profit from your shop and restore your livelihood to what it was like before the fire.

"Further, when autumn comes, Hutch should be in school, along with any of his siblings who are of the proper age. Hutch, I'm directing you that you and any brother or sister who is at least seven years old must attend school. And Ros, you must allow Hutch to work for you after school. You may not force him to work into the night on school days. You may, however, pay him only one coin per week when he's attending school and works only a partial day.

"Finally, magistrate, I charge you with ensuring that all these arrangements are carried out according to this judgment. Any party who fails in their duty is to be fined one silver coin." That should be enough to ensure that Ros complies – and perhaps learns some compassion and a bit of arithmetic at the same time.

The magistrate smiles, Ros looks grumpy, and Hutch bursts into tears. The first two, I expected; the third is a surprise. I beckon to him. "Come here, Hutch. Stand beside me and tell me what's wrong." He almost trips over the platform as he tries unsuccessfully to restrain his sobbing. I place a hand gently on his shoulder to comfort him. "Try not to cry, lad. Tell me why you're so unhappy."

He gathers himself up. "Ye be kind to me, Yer Grace. Ye let me repay Master Ros. And ye get me a job. And I be ever so grateful. But I canna' do all what ye ask and we dinna' have a silver coin to pay a fine, so I dinna' know what be happening to me." He snuffles back more tears.

"And why do you think you'd have to pay a fine?"

"I be wanting to go to school, Yer Grace. But if me sister have to go too, there be no one to look after the littl'uns. But if she dinna' go to school, then we be failing our duty and have to pay a fine. And we never once ever had a silver coin, Yer Grace."

I put my arm around his thin shoulders. "You won't have to pay a fine, Hutch. Think for a minute. If you work for Master Ros, your family will have extra money. So your mother can pay someone to look after the little ones while you and your sister are in school . . . and your sister can care for them after school while you work. Your mother will know how to arrange these things."

As happens so easily with children, his mood shifts from despair to joy. His face lights up, and the tears are replaced with an enormous smile. "I never think of that, Yer Grace. Yer Grace be ever so smart and ever so kind."

"Just promise me, Hutch, that you'll study hard in school and that you'll never again steal from anyone."

He goes down on his knees again, but this time he gazes up at me. "I promise, Yer Grace. I swear . . . I promise."

"Very well then, off with you . . . and be a good lad."

The magistrate knows the proceedings are complete, makes his bow, and leads the others from the room. "There are no more cases, Your Grace," says Bauldry. My cue to exit, stage left, into my private reception room. I'm grateful this first case was no more difficult. This, to me, is the most daunting task of wearing the crown – I've no idea if I'm up to the more difficult cases. I can only pray that the necessary wisdom will come in advance of need.

"I've decided on the first thing I want to do as queen." We're enjoying some quiet time in Gwen's sitting room before joining the court for the evening meal.

Too late, I recognize I should've suppressed the chuckle that escaped along with my query, "And what might that be?"

She bristles immediately, almost glaring at me. "Are you mocking me, Alfred?"

"Not at all, my love. It's only that I've been wondering what was taking you so long, but didn't want to ask." It's been quite some time since we returned from progress and already the early harvest is beginning.

Her pique subsides immediately. "I formed the notion while we were on progress, but I needed to be sure it was possible."

"Tell me."

"Everywhere we went, Alfred – in the small villages or the large towns – everyone wanted to talk to me about the sickness. They were all still distraught about not being able to do anything to help their loved ones or prevent their deaths. Some even asked me why you were spared and their loved ones were not."

"That must have been hard to answer."

"I tried to offer them some comfort by telling them no one could know the mind of God. It seemed like telling them it was Father Bartholomé's medicine that saved you would only add to their distress. It wasn't just the past they were concerned with, either. So many mothers spoke of their anxiety when a child gets sick and they don't know what to do. And I realized how lucky we've been, with the monastery and its infirmerer nearby. Most of our people are too far away from any sort of help and have to rely on what little they know." She pauses.

"What I want to do, Alfred, is to bring healing skills and medicines closer to the people. Infirmaries in the larger towns as a start. Healers trained by the monks of St. John's. Beyond that is beyond my vision at this moment."

"That's ambitious indeed!"

"It can be done, Alfred. I have a plan. All that's left is consent from the Council, and I don't think that will be difficult."

"Really?"

She smiles knowingly. "I'm certain of most of them. Richard may hesitate because of the cost, but I also have a plan for that."

"What makes you so sure?"

"You'll see. Will you bring this to the Council, Alfred?"

"I have a better idea. Why don't you bring it yourself?"

"That's rather out of the ordinary, isn't it?"

"My dear, I doubt anyone would ever describe you as ordinary," I laugh. This time, my humor is appreciated.

"Be that as it may, I do understand protocol."

"And who's to say I can't dispense with protocol occasionally?" I pause briefly. "Actually, I think you've chosen exceptionally well. It sounds like an enormous undertaking, but the people's welfare is exactly the sort of cause a queen should champion."

"I'd really like to do that, Alfred."

"Then I'll tell Devereux to expect a request from you. I can't imagine he'd object, but it doesn't hurt for him to know in advance that I agree."

Two weeks later, this is the main topic for the regular Council meeting. We deal quickly with Bauldry's updates on the situation with the magistrates and sheriffs, then Devereux invites Gwen to speak.

One would think this was something she'd done many times in the past. Her explanation of the need and how she wants to address it is as cogent as any I've ever heard. "My Lords, I can't do this alone, and it won't succeed if it has to rely on random charity. It will certainly fail without the help of St. John's Abbey, but we have the abbot's support. May I read you his letter?" Devereux nods.

My dear Gwendolyn,

I know you will have been anxious for a reply to your letter, but it is my considered opinion that efforts of the magnitude of what you propose are best not undertaken in haste. I find myself drawn to the vision you have for the welfare of your people, for it reflects a generosity of spirit and true caring for one's fellow man that is so often lost when one ascends to positions of great power. My brother in Christ, André, confirms that your intentions are indeed born of a pure spirit and not of a selfish motive. And Father Bartholomé has nothing but praise for you.

What you propose is in keeping with our calling as healers of the sick. But as it would divert some of our brethren, for a time, from the work we are pledged to do here, I felt it appropriate to discuss the matter in chapter. There are some among our community who urge caution – who fear that our ability to respond would be inadequate if disease should break out here while some of our number are away. I do not dismiss their concerns. But I am more inclined to agree with those who have the view that our knowledge and skills have been given to us not to hide away as sacred treasure but to share with those in need.

And so I have made the decision to offer you our support and to assign two of our brethren to guide you in creating your first infirmary. There are two conditions, however. The first – which I'm sure you will expect – is that I may recall our brothers at any time if there is an urgent need here. The second, however, is the most important. You must turn no one away. Rich or poor – whether they can pay or not – no one must be denied if they are sick and need the help of a healer.

Write to me again, my dear Gwendolyn, when you are ready to begin. I will, in the meantime, give due consideration to what you will require and which of our brothers are best suited to the task.

Yours in Christ,

Abbot Stephen

She pauses at the end of the letter, giving everyone time to absorb what they've heard. "So, gentlemen, there's one final thing needed. Commitment of the Crown to ensure we can meet the abbot's conditions. And that's my request to you here today."

Bauldry speaks first. "My daughter's been onto me several times in the past month about how important she thinks this is."

"Mine as well." Meriden.

"And mine." Rupert.

"Your daughter's been doubly busy, Lord Rupert." Richard. "When she hasn't been bending your ear, it's been mine or my father's."

Phillip. "Addiena's also mentioned it more than once over the past few weeks."

Samuel. "And I hear little else from Tamasine these days."

Ernle chuckles. "Nor I."

"I have here a letter from Montfort," says Devereux, "that he's asked me to read to you."

My dear Devereux,

I write to you on the matter of the queen's proposal to establish infirmaries in our towns. Both my daughter and my daughter-in-law have sworn not to give me a moment's peace until I lend my support to the queen's project. I beg your indulgence, for I'm keenly aware that I have no vote on the matter at present. That said, what I've heard on the subject makes me inclined to agree that taking these steps would be of incomparable benefit to the people of the kingdom. Knowing that there are questions of cost and other considerations, I don't presume to advise on how to vote. If, however, you authorize this plan, know that you'll have my full agreement as to its merit.

"He added a postscript below his signature," Devereux continues. "'You'll also have my eternal gratitude for giving me back some peace and quiet.' I gather we might all echo that sentiment. Gentlemen, we are in the presence of a master tactician . . . as good as we've seen since King Harold's day." He nods approvingly in Gwen's direction.

In the ensuing conversation about the merits of the idea, the Bishop is surprisingly silent. "Bishop, I can't help but notice you haven't spoken," I remark. "Do you have some reluctance? Some objection from the Church?"

"Not precisely," he replies. "The monks of St. John's are known and respected for their skill. In fact, they have a papal dispensation from the divine offices when such observances would impede their ability to relieve people's suffering. There are some, however, who would argue that sharing those skills with lay people is not in the best interests of the Church."

"And what say you, Bishop?"

"It seems to me that those who make such arguments may not themselves have witnessed the anguish and suffering wrought by terrible illness like we saw here last year. I'm personally inclined toward the views expressed by Abbot Stephen. But I feel it's my duty to caution you that some may not embrace this project in the same way."

"As you know, Bishop," says Gwen, "I have trouble understanding how anyone could believe a caring God would want people to suffer just so Church leaders can control this knowledge." I hold my breath. Surely she knows that engaging in a debate over her modern ideas and conservative Church doctrine won't advance her case with the Council.

"Calm down, my dear," says the bishop. "You know you have my personal support. But I also have a duty to this Council to inform them of the risk."

"Rightfully so, Bishop." Now I can exhale. "But I'm convinced it's worth the risk," she continues, "especially when I think of how many could have survived last year if only we'd had the skill and medicines that saved Alfred."

Richard changes the subject. "I'm as enthusiastic as any of you about the notion of saving lives, but let's not forget that costs money. What you propose, My Lady, will cost a lot of money, especially when it comes to honoring Abbot Stephen's condition. With the Treasury in its current straits, we've no choice but to weigh our priorities for using what little money we have."

"Of course," Gwen replies. "But as you and I have discussed, the costs don't occur all at once. My Lords, consider this. It will take at least a year for the teaching of the first healers, so we have that much time to fully establish the first infirmary. And after that, more healers must learn. As much as we might want this dream to become reality overnight, the truth is, that's impossible. We won't be bearing all the cost up front. It will be spread over many years." I notice she's subtly making everyone here part of her cause. "The longer we wait to begin, gentlemen, the more distant is the day when everyone can benefit. All we need to find money for immediately is the first step."

"And where would you begin, My Lady?" asks Ernle. "How would you choose one town over another?"

"The castle town is closest for you to oversee the effort," Bauldry remarks.

"I've given that a great deal of thought," Gwen replies. "Proximity is a possible factor, as Lord Bauldry says. But is it really right that the people nearest the castle should have all the advantages? Aren't we trying to bring healing to the people who are most remote from it today? I have an opinion, My Lords, but we should choose together."

"I think we'd all like to hear your opinion." Ernle again.

"Very well. I've considered the difficulty and time to travel from each of the towns to one of our monasteries. On that basis, I recommend we put the first infirmary in Neukirk Market. No other town requires several days of travel complicated by a ferry crossing to reach help. And when one considers the extra distance for the people of Lord Peveril's domain, Neukirk seems the only logical choice." Well done, my dear! Unassailable logic. Sufficiently off the beaten path to avoid too much attention from Church naysayers, and squarely in the domain of the first lord and the treasurer – where those who can most influence the continuation of your experiment can see the results firsthand.

"My Lady," says Meriden, "I joined in the praise for your idea. But given the cost, I find it necessary to ask why we can't continue to rely on our barber-surgeons and delay the expense of this project until we can better afford it?"

"To which I would ask, what do they know of a child's fever? And, Heaven forfend we should ever see the sickness again, but we know such things are completely beyond their abilities. Yes, they can remove an arrow gone astray, sew up a cut, remove a damaged limb, extract rotten teeth . . . But even for those things, some lack the needed skill. I don't expect you to take my word for it, My Lords."

She signals to my secretary, who opens the door to reveal Lord and Lady Peveril and Father Bartholomé. Everyone in the room rises as Emmeline makes her way slowly to the seat Gwen has vacated for her. "You all know the Peverils," says Gwen. "Our other guest is Father Bartholomé, the priest who saved Alfred's life. Lady Peveril, I was attempting an inadequate explanation of the limitations of the healing skills of our barber-surgeons."

Emmeline says nothing for a moment, apparently waiting to be invited to speak. "We welcome your words, my dear," says Devereux.

"I never thought to be addressing the Council – nor even to be back at court," she begins a bit tentatively. "But I've been in correspondence with the queen and knew I had to add my voice to hers.

"When I fell so many years ago, the only help anywhere nearby was the barber-surgeon in the village. He wanted to remove both my legs at the knees – claimed it was the best thing to do. I was certain I could never survive that, so I begged and pleaded until he finally agreed to attempt to repair the damage. You've seen just now that his skills were inadequate. I mean no disparagement of the man – he couldn't do more than what he knew. And I'm grateful to be alive and able to walk, albeit with some difficulty.

"While the barber was hesitating, my husband suggested taking me to the monastery here. But I knew I could never endure the pain of that long journey. Had there been help in Neukirk, I might have been able to make it there."

She pauses and looks around the room, clearly now at ease. "It's natural you'd be asking yourselves why bother with even a short journey if the outcome wasn't going to be good. Gentlemen, over the past couple of days, I've had the pleasure of traveling with the good Father here. We met him on the road just before the ferry. On the first evening, he examined my legs and explained what was done wrong after my fall and what should have been done. And his assessment is that if I'd received proper care, I'd have been able, as he put it, 'to dance into the room to greet you today' . . . but more importantly for me, to dance with my husband at so many celebrations in the years past and those to come." She turns to Father Bartholomé.

"Lady Emmeline does not exaggerate, my friends. The healing arts I learned from the monks of St. John's are far advanced over what even a skilled barber-surgeon knows. And I know that with better medicines and more healers in your midst, the toll of the sickness on your people would have been much reduced. In my small corner of the Kingdom of Lakes, we have not had a single child die of a fever in the past year. It's true not all can be saved – not every illness can be cured. Some things are still in God's hands. But every year, thanks to the good monks, more and more people in our land survive illnesses that would once have taken their lives."

I now know the answer to my silly question about what was taking Gwen so long. She's corresponded with the necessary people, created her plan, and built her case in such a way that any man opposing it would be thought either an imbecile or a hard-hearted curmudgeon.

The expression on Meriden's face softened to one of fatherly kindness as he listened to Emmeline. "My Lady," he addresses Gwen, "my intent was only that we not fail to answer the question one way or the other. And I, for one, have my answer."

Richard brings things back to business. "As the queen said, she and I have discussed this at length, and I think there's something to what she's proposing that goes beyond even the benefits of just having better medicines for people. We're making a lot of investment in getting things back to the way they were before John, but that takes time and patience on everyone's part. If we could start showing that some things will be even better than they were before, then it's my opinion people will be less likely to get discouraged if the pace of recovery isn't as fast as they'd like it to be. For that reason – if we can agree to take it one step at a time as the queen suggests – then I think this is as good an investment in our future as fixing the roads."

"And you know how to finance it?" Ernle.

"And I've already worked out how to finance it." Richard.

No one else seems to have anything further to add. "Very well, gentlemen," says Devereux. "Are we agreed on the queen's proposal?" There's a uniform chorus of "aye's."

"There you are, My Lady. I must say, I'm impressed. Will you come back from time to time to let us know how you're getting on? I think we'd all like to hear how this experiment unfolds."

"It would be my pleasure, Lord Devereux."

"Very well, gentlemen, if there's nothing further, we're adjourned."

"Just one thing, Devereux," I interject. "I intend to break with protocol on this occasion. Whatever you gentlemen may have wanted to talk about after I leave the room will just have to wait for some future time." I go to Emmeline and kiss her hand. "My dear, I've seen knights in battle whose courage was not a match for yours. It's an honor to have you in this room."

The others crowd around to greet her, and I step back with Peveril. "She's spoken of little else since Gwendolyn first wrote to her about this," he says. "I haven't seen her so excited about anything in years. She's already making plans to help with the outfitting of the Neukirk infirmary. I'm glad there was no opposition."

"Will you dine with us this evening? I know Mother will be overjoyed to see both of you."

"That will be Emmeline's decision," he replies.

I step back into the group that's now talking with both Emmeline and Father Bartholomé. "I wonder, Lady Emmeline, if you and your husband would join our private family supper this evening? You too, Father."

"I don't know what to say, Sire," she replies. "We wouldn't want to intrude."

"It'll be no intrusion at all," Gwen chimes in. "The court dinner is tomorrow evening. And the ladies of the court usually spend the afternoon in my sitting room ahead of time." I can only imagine what a celebratory session *that* will be. "Please say you'll join us for both."

"Well," Emmeline still hesitates.

"I've already arranged your quarters just across the corridor from Mother Alice's – on the same level as our apartment," says Gwen.

"And it would be my pleasure to assist you to your room," I add.

"That's not necessary, Sire. Pev can do that."

"I don't doubt your husband is quite capable. But it isn't often I get the opportunity to carry a beautiful lady up the stairs."

She smiles brightly. "How can any woman resist such gallantry? Very well, I accept your invitation. Truth be told, I really *am* eager to see everyone again."

The whereabouts of John's personal fortune and the peculiar phrasing of his will continue to weigh on my mind. Having watched my brother's penurious treatment of his own family, I can give little credence to the thought that he sent it all to Gunhild. Certainly he sent no more than what he considered the absolute minimum to appease Lord Erik for the violation of a daughter. Nor was he the type to spend lavishly on himself. Unless he poured it all into his war – which, to me, makes as little sense as sending it all to Gunhild – there should have been quite a substantial sum left behind. But where?

In what spare time I have, I've been conducting my own search. Not with doubts for the thoroughness of the one conducted by Rupert and Richard, but trying to get inside John's mind . . . trying to see through his eyes. What would he have considered a safe hiding place? Or places?

I looked first in the secret passage from the king's bed chamber to the undercroft. As far as I can tell, John never knew of its existence. The two torches I doused in the sand bucket at the top of the stairs when I used the passage to surprise John and free Richard from his clutches were exactly as I left them. Removing them from the sand and shaking off any loose grains still clinging, I stood them upright in the box with the others, ready for whenever they might next be needed.

I've wandered through the old castle looking for anything that might appear slightly amiss or awry. But it seems equally unlikely he would hide a fortune in a place used as a barracks, where it might be discovered quite by accident. Matthias mentioned John's suddenly taking an interest in the wine cellar. An ideal hiding place, one might think, but I find nothing there. And perhaps, after all, too obvious a location. Had there been anything amiss in the library, the monks would have noticed it when they started returning the collection. Still, from time to time, I remove the contents of entire shelves looking for anything that might be so subtle as to be missed by someone unaware there was anything to find. So far, nothing.

Then there's the wording of the will. "I leave everything from the roof of the highest tower in the castle to the farthest reaches of the kingdom to my son John Gundar." Was that simply a typical flamboyant gesture – the type John was so fond of? Or is it a clue? I've scanned the sentry tower from the outer courtyard. It would be impossible to access the roof by ladder, even from the battlements at the top of the wall. Some sort of scaffolding would be required . . . and that would have drawn attention and been remembered by Matthias and others.

Access to the sentry tower is through the gatehouse. From there, two flights of stairs lead up to the first fighting level. Arrow slits open onto the outer courtyard and onto the open land beyond the castle walls. A dozen or more bows are stacked in one corner, crossbows next to them. Beside each arrow slit hang two sacks of arrows, ready for the archers. In another corner, boxes containing hundreds of arrows and still more boxes full of crossbow bolts. Near the hearth, enough wood to fuel a hot fire for several hours, the fire intended less for keeping men warm than for preparing the deadly fire arrows. In the event of an attack, this room would be a beehive of activity. Archers firing, boys preparing the flights and reloading empty arrow sacks, other boys preparing the fire arrows, men loading crossbows, and a second team of archers ready to spell the first when their muscles require rest from the constant repeated effort of drawing the bow. Chaotic, perhaps, to the untrained eye, but carefully orchestrated to ensure no lull in the rain of arrows and fire pouring down on an attacking force.

A door gives access to the battlements and would, in battle, be open to allow men and arms there to be replenished. But should an enemy actually succeed in scaling the walls, the door could be secured by three heavy iron bars, making it difficult to breach and even more difficult, should a breach be achieved, for men to rush in and overwhelm the defenders.

I've found nothing at this level that could serve as a cache. No loose stones that could be removed. No hidden niches or mechanisms inside the hearth. I've even walked the walls looking for the slightest hint of a hiding place.

This level, however, is still well below the roof. Another flight of stairs inside the tower leads to the second fighting level. It's identical to the first except there's no door to the outside. This level feels more confining than the one below, having only a single exit by way of the stairs. Using a heavy wooden pole, I've poked at every board in the ceiling, looking for one that might give way, revealing access to some hidden space under the roof. All to no avail. Every one is solidly nailed in place. Nor are there any clues inside the hearth.

I've spent what must be hours staring again and again through each arrow slit on both levels, looking close and in the far distance for any sign of a hut or an unusual grove of trees or a gully that might conceal a small cave or something unusual in the walls or the castle itself that would be discernible only from these heights. More than once, I've picked up a bow and arrow, drawn the bow, and sighted along what would be the flight of the arrow, looking for clues. Nothing. Tempting as it might be to loose an arrow and follow its flight, I've no wish to risk harm to who or what might lie in its path.

But I won't give up. My brother wouldn't easily part with money. Perhaps there's something in the reference to "the farthest reaches of the kingdom." That will take some time to puzzle out.

Throughout the summer, the entire kingdom – noble, merchant, and peasant alike – has been in a state of mixed anticipation and anxiety about what the harvest would bring. My relief, when it proves abundant, is immeasurable. By all accounts, it's the best we've seen in several years. To avoid having prices fall too low, the lords are buying the surplus, which they'll sell slowly over the coming year to keep prices moderate and their people well fed. It falls to the Treasury to do the same for the traditional lands of the Crown. Richard isn't happy with the additional expense. "Just remember," I remind him, "you'll get the money back as we sell it off."

"I never thought of myself as a grain merchant," he says with a chuckle and a shake of his head. "But I suppose it will keep my clerks from being bored."

Observing family tradition, we go to the manor for the harvest festival and the hunt that follows. While we're there, a messenger arrives from Prior Frery. They've learned there's to be an important event in the Territories. Egon's son Goron is to marry Fergal's daughter – his firstborn, whose name is Kensa. By their tradition, such dynastic marriages always take place at high noon on New Year's Day.

I reveal the news at our evening meal. "I think you all know I have to go."

"But you'll miss New Year's and Twelfth Night with us," says Gwen.

"I know. But Egon has come here for all the ceremonial events in my life since we first began our friendship. It would be unconscionable for me to miss such an important event in his, regardless of what our own traditions may be."

"You're quite right, Alfred," remarks Rupert. "It's the next step in cementing the peace and building that alliance. Gwen can host a beautiful New Year's court for those who aren't celebrating at their own estates."

"Of course you're right, Alfred," says Gwen. "It simply came as a surprise. You will, I hope, be with us for Christmas?"

"That I shall, though it may be wise to leave on Christmas afternoon. Even then, it'll be a hard ride to get there in time. But I won't spoil the children's Christmas."

"Will you take Samuel with you?" asks Rupert.

"I'd like for him to go. It's been the two of us on all the important visits there. But it will be his decision. I won't order him away from his family at this season."

As it turns out, the entire Ernle family has chosen to spend Christmas and the New Year on their estate, Lady Ernle having been unwell and wanting to be in her own home for this special time. Since this allowed Samuel more time with his family, he agrees to meet us in the border village when we arrive the night before New Year's Eve. Prior Frery is there as well.

"As in our tradition," Frery tells us, "the woman goes to live in the domain of her new husband, where the wedding is also held."

"What about gifts?" I ask him.

"It's traditional to bring a gift to the groom of something suitable for the wedding feast. I've brought you a pair of pheasants that the brothers managed to capture. They've been hanging for two days, so should be perfect for cooking when you present them to Goron tomorrow evening."

"What about for the bride? Gwen has sent something."

"In their society, women are permitted to receive gifts only from their husband or from other women. If the queen were here, she could present her gift directly to the bride. As it is, you must present it to her husband and ask that he give it to her. Whether or not he does is his decision entirely."

"It's only a small packet of lace – quite obviously a gift from one woman to another, which seems safe enough. And of course we'll honor their tradition."

"I'm told," says Frery, "that if the gift is open when you present it to the husband – so that all can see it is purely women's business – then he'll most likely give it to her straightaway, as there can be no question of an inappropriate gift from another man.

"Just remember – you must never address a woman out of the presence of her husband or father and never by her name. To do so implies an intimacy that would be dishonorable to both the woman and her family."

I can imagine how disturbing Gwen would find these male-dominated customs. And it reminds me that the only women I've ever seen there are servants.

Tobin is hardly happy with my decision that Samuel, Osbert, and I will go on alone to the wedding. "Just this once, Tobin," I try to assure him. "A reflection of Egon's choice when he came to my father's funeral with only Goron to accompany him. Once we've reciprocated the gesture, there's no reason not to have a proper guard on future visits." But I can tell he's in no way reassured.

"If we're not back in four days," says Samuel, "then come looking for us. But just you and the guards. If Egon doesn't know where we are or if Egon isn't at his fortress, then return to the garrison. The commandant has my orders for how to proceed."

"I understand what I'm asking, Tobin," I tell him. "But don't worry. We'll be back in four days' time."

"See that you are, sir." Tobin's fatherly tone is clearly meant to mask his unease. "I wouldn't like to have to be the one telling either the queen or Lord Rupert that something dreadful happened to you on my watch."

I clap him on the shoulder. "Then we'll just have to make doubly sure you don't have to face either of those dragons."

The winter days are short, so it's already sundown when we arrive at Egon's fortress. His greeting is joyous, as always. "But I wish I had known you were coming, my friend. As it is, it will be quite difficult to rearrange the guest accommodations."

"We expect no special treatment, Egon," I reply. "We're simply ordinary guests, just as you and Goron have been to me. A campaign cot in the gatehouse is more than adequate. And I insist you make no fuss over us. We came only to honor Goron and Kensa."

He seems pleased that I remember their names. "You are exceedingly generous, Alfred. And I know Fergal will be pleased as well. He is staying with Kensa in the village tonight and will bring her to the ceremony on the morrow."

"Speaking of the ceremony," I reach up to my saddle and remove the pair of pheasants hanging there. "A gift for Goron. I hope it's appropriate."

"Very appropriate indeed," says Egon. "But you should present it to him directly. Come . . . join us in the hall."

The next day – New Year's – dawns clear and fair, a perfect day for a wedding, despite the winter crispness in the air. As the sun nears its zenith, all the guests assemble in the inner courtyard, where a small arched bower of evergreen has been erected. A priest stands in front of the bower. Just at midday, Fergal escorts his daughter through the gateway to the inner courtyard. Goron comes from inside the hall, and they meet in front of the priest. Ritual words are spoken by the priest. A cup of some beverage is shared by the couple. The priest then leads them through the bower, and when they emerge on the other side, the assembled guests break into cheers. It's done.

The wedding feast is unusual in my experience. Men and women are seated separately. Only the bridal couple sit side by side, between their respective fathers – Egon on Goron's right and Fergal on Kensa's left – the bride thus sheltered by her father on one side and her new husband on the other. It's a stark reminder of how very different the customs of these people are from our own and how very careful we must be in our rapprochement with them.

Near midafternoon, during a lull in the feasting, I approach Goron and Kensa. Holding Gwen's small packet of lace open for all to see, I proffer it to Goron. "My wife sends her best wishes to you both. She asked that I bring this gift to your bride on her behalf."

Goron lifts the edges of the lace and looks underneath, apparently to show those watching that he has inspected the gift and found nothing offensive. "You may give it to her yourself, as it is from your lady wife," he says. Perhaps there's reason to have some hope for this young man about whom I know so very little. Kensa accepts the packet, taking great care not to touch my hands in doing so. There may be hope, but there's still a very long road to travel.

Fergal's pleasure at our presence, when we at last have an opportunity to speak, is equal in measure to Egon's. We drink a toast with him in honor of his daughter's marriage and then fade into the background among the other guests. The next morning we depart quietly. All according to plan. All in accordance with Egon's prior appearances at my important ceremonies. From now on, I hope that such occasions will become more of the type I share with my fellow kings and allies.

Tobin is waiting for us in the stable when we ride back into the border village. I can imagine him pacing in front of the stalls, wondering how long to give us before saddling up to come in search. Even were Samuel himself the captain of my guard, I could not have a better man looking out for me and my family.

The anniversary of our peace agreement with the Territories has come and gone. The garrison is now at full strength, with no sign of reaction from the other side of the border.

Just after Easter, Peveril leaves for his first mission to the Territories, accompanied only by his squire and Brother Eustace. My presence, we both agree, would place too much pressure on the Territorial lords. Instead, he takes with him a letter of introduction under my seal. He'll visit Fergal first. We want to avoid any appearance of favoritism in our dealings.

Just before we leave to enjoy the May Day celebrations at the manor, we have surprise visitors. Laurence arrives from the port with news that operations there are returning to normal. Three more ships are now fully repaired, and the master shipwright has promoted two of his apprentices to journeyman, allowing them to supervise more of the restorations.

Rebuilding the intelligence networks is going more slowly. Alf has been found, thankfully. His days as a traveling tinker are behind him, but he's agreed to help teach new recruits. I ask about the innkeeper in Neukirk Market who was so keen to let me know he wanted to work for us again. Laurence chuckles, "Ah, yes . . . Diggory. A bit full of himself . . . and I chided him severely for revealing his role, even to the king. But he's the one who identified Ralf and his sons when they were wandering about in those parts. He's reliable . . . just needs to have his own sense of importance reinforced from time to time."

The main reason for Laurence's visit arrives the following day in the form of Estrilda and the children. The new port commissioner's house is nearly complete, so the family can be together again. It's an opportunity for something we've not done for far too long. "Just like we used to, Osbert," I tell him. "A stroll through the market and then supper at the tavern – that big table in the corner if the innkeeper can manage it."

"Dinna' ye fret, m'lord. I be making sure it all be like ye be wanting."

"I suspect the ladies will want to do some shopping in the market, so the men can get in an early round of drinks. But Osbert, tell the others I'd like us all to arrive together. I don't want to make any more fuss than necessary over my presence in the party."

"Oh, there be a fuss, m'lord. Not be much ye can do about that, now ye be king and all."

"Just tell the innkeeper I'd be grateful if he'd go about his business as usual."

"Aye, m'lord."

"And Osbert," I add, pulling on my boots. "I'm buying."

Osbert grins. "Yer mates be liking that, sir."

The evening is the most fun we've all had in years. When my mates and I arrive at the tavern, the usual noisy conversation goes instantly silent – followed immediately by the scraping of stools and chairs on the floor as people rush to get to their feet. "Please, my friends," I raise my hands and signal them to remain seated. "We're here for a drink just like you and maybe a bit of supper. Innkeeper, a round for everyone on my bill, if you please."

We make our way to the big corner table where Osbert has full tankards waiting. Ever so slowly the noise level returns to its usual state. When the ladies arrive, the conversation turns to Laurence and Estrilda's new home. "There's still work to be completed in some of the formal reception rooms," says Laurence, "but the family quarters are finished. Those builders of yours have been nothing short of remarkable, Alfred."

"I suspect the mild weather didn't hurt either," I remark.

"Now, Alfred," begins Estrilda, "Laurence and I have come to a decision. We know the Treasury can't afford to furnish the house properly at the moment, so we want to do it ourselves."

"You'll get no argument from me," chuckles Richard.

"That's generous of you," I tell her. "But the house belongs to the kingdom. It should be furnished at Treasury expense. You won't always be the occupants, after all."

"Be that as it may," Estrilda is firm. "We've made our decision and intend to follow through. Later, when Laurence leaves this post, the Treasury can pay us back for what we choose to leave there."

"I learned long ago, Alfred," adds Laurence, "that when Estrilda makes up her mind about something, it's best just to go along."

That earns him a laugh from all the men. "I do seem to recall," chimes in Phillip, "her father said almost exactly the same thing about her choice of a husband."

Undaunted, Estrilda turns to Gwen. "I'd really like it, Gwendolyn, if you could find the time to come down and help me. Having another woman's eye on the selections would be helpful – the girls aren't really old enough yet to have good taste."

And so it is that after our two-week sojourn at the manor, when most of us return to the castle, Gwen departs for the port, taking Juliana and Richenda with her as company for Estrilda's daughters. I'm looking forward to Peveril's return and his assessment of what's possible with diplomacy in the Territories.

André was ill during the winter. At one point, we feared he might not recover; but he's rallied, though the illness took a toll. Every couple of weeks, I make a point of riding up to visit with my old friend. The chronicle of John's reign is now as complete as I can make it without more conversation with the Territorial lords. We've decided to bind this version and create a companion volume at such time as Peveril or I assemble the rest of the history. On a recent visit, André gave me the bound folio to add to the collection in the library.

Returning from just such a visit, I'm surprised to be met halfway by Tobin himself, riding rather more rapidly than I would expect. He turns his horse and falls in beside me, ahead of the guards, slowing to the gentle trot Sirius has been maintaining. "We have to hurry, sir. There's been a messenger from the queen. Juliana has been kidnapped. The queen begs you to come right away."

I pull Sirius up short. "Say that again, Tobin. I'm not sure I heard you correctly."

"Your daughter has been taken, sir. I don't know any more than that. Nor did the messenger. He'd ridden hard from the port – said the queen was in great distress and you need come at once."

"My God, Tobin! How could such a thing happen? Didn't they have guards?"

"Of course they did, Sire," he reverts to the formal address, uncertain, I suppose, if I somehow intend to blame him.

"What's being done?"

"I don't know that either, Sire. The messenger said only that the port's being turned upside down looking for her." He pauses for a moment. "Before I set out to meet you, Sire, I took the liberty of organizing some things. Osbert will have your gear and fresh horses ready for us by the time we get back. I also told Sir Samuel. He's organizing a troop of knights to ride with us."

"Let's go," I tell him, and we all put spurs to our horses, riding hard the rest of the way back to the castle. The procession is already mounted and waiting for us – we need only change horses and be on our way. Samuel has taken personal command of the knights.

At the port, the turmoil seems to have subsided, but people are more deferential even than usual, quickly stepping to the sides of the streets and bowing as we ride through. Giving my horse's reins to Osbert, I bound up the front steps and through the door, Samuel and Tobin hot on my heels. A servant jumps up from where he's waiting and rushes to open a door on the left of the entry hall. Gwen is up from her seat even before I set foot in the room and practically falls into my arms. Uncharacteristically for her, she's clearly been weeping, and the tears flow again as I hold her close.

Leading her back to a couch, I sit beside her. Estrilda hands her a fresh handkerchief and returns to sit beside Laurence. I try to muster as much calm as I can. "Now, tell me everything that's happened so we can work out how to find her."

"The girls were sewing – making fancy pillows for their rooms. They wanted some lace and ribbons, so I asked Milla to take them to the shop. The guards went along, of course. Milla has taken to her bed. She blames herself. She was helping Richenda choose some lace at the back of the shop while Juliana looked at the ribbons in the window.

"It seems the men burst in suddenly and grabbed Juliana. Milla turned when she heard Juliana scream, but the men were already rushing out. Even though Milla ran, she couldn't catch up to them."

"Where were the guards in all this?" I ask as gently as I can.

"There were two of them right outside the shop, like always. But Milla says there were at least six men, and they managed to subdue the guards."

"Richenda?"

"She's alright, but she's terrified and thinks it was somehow her fault since she had Milla's attention. Alfred, do you think they could have been trying to kidnap Richenda and took Juliana by mistake?"

"It's possible." I look across to Laurence. "What's been done?"

"The sheriff's men turned the town upside down, and we put an embargo on any ship leaving the docks. There was one ship anchored in the middle of the river that got underway while they were searching in the town. One of the ship captains noticed it starting to slip downriver on the tide and raised the alarm. Once they realized they'd been spotted, they wasted no time hoisting sail and putting men to the oars. I dispatched men to raise the chains, but they were too late. The ship had the advantage of the rapidly falling tide, a good northwesterly breeze, and strong oarsmen. By the time my men got there, the ship had cleared the chains and was making its way strongly toward the mouth of the river."

He pauses to let me take it all in. "These men knew what they were doing, Alfred. That ship had been anchored there for the past two weeks. We thought they were just lingering until they finished filling their hold with trade goods. They'd done everything properly . . . paid their anchorage fee right away . . . brought their goods ashore and sold them . . . paid their tariffs. They didn't cause any trouble in the bars. Nothing to make anyone suspicious."

"Why were they anchored mid-river?"

"They arrived at night when there was no one to help them dock. We offered them a berth the next morning, but the captain said he didn't want to bother . . . said where they were, his men who had the watch wouldn't be tempted to leave their post for the brothels. That seemed plausible enough."

"Do we have any idea where they might have gone?"

"No way to know. What we do know is that the cargo they brought in was wine from the Lamoreaux estate."

By now, there's no doubt in my mind. "I believe Gwen's right. They were sent to kidnap Richenda and took the wrong girl. Now what we have to do is go get her back." Gwen has managed to regain some of her composure in my presence. My own emotions, despite my efforts to appear calm, are boiling with a mixture of fury and fear. Who knows what Lamoreaux might do when his minions return with the wrong parcel.

"How soon can a ship be ready, Laurence? Commandeer one if you have to, but make sure it's a fast one."

"Make sure it can carry a troop of knights and their mounts as well," Samuel chimes in.

"There's an old troop carrier that's just been refitted for trade. The shipwright told me just this morning that it's finally seaworthy. I've no idea how fast it is, though."

"Save that in case we need to send for more troops," says Samuel.

"In that case," replies Laurence, "we'll have to offload some of the linen that's on the *Constance* to make room for the horses. She's already provisioned, so that will save time. We can have her ready for you by morning, and you can sail with the late morning tide." The irony isn't lost on me that it's the same tide that took my daughter away.

"Do it," I tell him, a little more perfunctorily than I'd intended. "Samuel, I need you here. I sincerely hope we don't have to turn this incident into a major conflict, but I *will* go to war if necessary to get my daughter back."

"With all due respect, Alfred, my deputy is perfectly capable of organizing an invasion force if it's needed. I'm here, and it would take too long to send back to the castle for a troop captain."

"I'm going too," says Tobin, "along with the two guards from here. They'll be mortified that this happened on their watch and will want to redeem themselves."

Before I can protest, he goes on. "I ordered a half troop of guards to follow in our wake. They'll be here before morning and will take over duties here. Your family and Lord Laurence's will be properly protected."

There's nothing more we can do until the morning – a feeling of helplessness unlike any I've ever experienced before. Supper is a morose affair, no one having any appetite except the children. We've managed to reassure Richenda that she's not to blame, but Milla is inconsolable. It will take time for her to accept that this wasn't her fault.

Sleep doesn't come easily for me or for Gwen. My impatience grows as I imagine all the things that could be happening to my little girl. Dawn can't come soon enough. When eventually it does, the place becomes a beehive of activity. Good-byes are said, the horses are loaded, and we're on board well before the tide turns. The captain raises sail as soon as we're in the channel and puts a few men to the oars as well. Once the tide begins to ebb, our momentum increases noticeably. 'Juliana, my little one,' I think to myself. 'Papa is coming. Be brave.' And then I say a heartfelt prayer than no harm should come to her.

My impatience is evident in my pacing of the deck for the first hour we're underway. Samuel eventually comes to stand beside me as I pause to gaze at the horizon, hoping – foolishly, of course, at this point in the voyage – for some sight of our destination. "There's nothing you can do until we get there, Alfred," he says quietly.

"I know," I reply, "but it's not much comfort."

"You know," he continues, "Tobin is taking this almost as hard as you are. He feels like he's let you down."

I say nothing for quite some time. "At times, my gut says the same thing, I fear. But my reason tells me he's not to blame."

"Then tell him so when you can," says Samuel. "He'll be of much more help to us with his mind at ease."

The three of us spend the rest of the voyage working out options for what to do once we arrive. It's all likely futile planning, since we've no idea what we'll find, but it's calming and helps to pass the time. As soon as we dock, we send a fast messenger to Goscelin and Emaurri. Perhaps they'll already know something of the situation. Regardless, they need to know that our presence with armed knights is not a threat.

When we arrive at his castle, we find Goscelin already preparing troops to ride with us. He and Petronilla are both devastated. "We had absolutely no idea, Alfred," he tells me. "Presumably, they sailed directly to the southwestern port. It's closer to Charles's estate, after all."

"I considered doing the same, but we're going to need your help, I think."

"My son can be very unpredictable. Most of the time, he'd rather hold court with his cronies on his estate. He shows a remarkable lack of interest in governing the kingdom for someone who is the heir. But on the subject of Richenda, he's been single-minded in a way I've never seen before. There's no doubt in my mind that his intent was to grab her, force his priest to marry them, and then present it to me as a fait accompli. Frankly, Alfred, my greatest fear is that he won't believe he has the wrong girl."

"I've no doubt Juliana will make that known."

"But will he believe her?" he voices the doubt that's been plaguing me since we first set sail. "I'm coming with you, Alfred. Whatever sway I may yet hold over him as his father is at your service."

Emaurri offers to come as well. "I'd rather you stay here," I tell him. "If we need to send for more troops or get word to Gwen, I'll need someone to organize that."

It's five days' ride to Lamoreaux's estate – five days in which I must wage war with my imagination. Thankfully, the long days in the saddle mean we're tired at the end of each, and sleep comes more readily than I would have thought.

Word of our procession has clearly preceded us, for we're met by an armed troop of men outside the village nearest the manor. The leader shows a modicum of respect to Goscelin, but then immediately adopts an air of command and orders us to follow them. When we arrive, they bid us halt and wait outside the gate to the courtyard while they ride in. I look to Goscelin, thinking he might override the order. "It's perhaps best," he says, "to humor him for the moment. Let him show his hand to us rather than put him immediately on the defensive."

And so we sit on our horses and wait – a full half hour before we see any signs of activity inside. Eventually, the armed troop returns, this time with the Duke of Lamoreaux – in splendid regalia – riding in the lead. They halt before us. "We have invited no guests," he announces haughtily, "and were expecting no visitors. We're in no way prepared to receive you, so you will camp in the meadow just there," he gestures to an open field at some small distance from the gates. "Once you've made your camp, I will return to learn your business." And with that he wheels the troop around and rides back through the gate.

Samuel and Goscelin's captain get underway with the business of establishing our camp. In what it now seems may have been a stroke of genius, Goscelin had ordered the inclusion of two massive royal tents, complete with proper banners and campaign accoutrements. Once the camp is complete, it looks like the legendary meetings between kings recounted in the poems of the troubadours. "My son requires a strong dose of intimidation from time to time," Goscelin tells me as we meet in my tent to wait.

Just before sundown, Lamoreaux and his entourage return. They dismount and enter my tent without invitation. The Duke bows his head perfunctorily toward Goscelin, saying only, "Father," and then turns his attention to me. "What gives you the right to come onto my estate without an invitation, sir? And with armed troops in your train?"

"I've come for my daughter, Lamoreaux," I reply.

"You've lost her?" he seems to think this is amusing. I say nothing. "I've no idea why you would think she might be here. On the morrow you can break camp and look for her elsewhere."

"I think she's here, sir, because she was stolen from us by men sailing on a ship that came from your estate to trade with us. I think she's here because you ordered those men to kidnap Richenda. Those men took the wrong girl. And I think by now, you're well aware of that."

He pretends to look thoughtful, pacing back and forth in front of us, one hand on his chin. "And why would I have any need to kidnap a girl? I believe it's well known, even to you, sir, that I have little interest in the feminine sex."

"Don't play games where my daughter is concerned, Lamoreaux. Bring her to me, and we'll be on our way at first light tomorrow."

"If, as you suggest, there is a young girl who is a guest in my household, how do I know she's your daughter?"

"Bring her, and it should be as plain as the nose on your face."

"But would not a true father be prepared to fight to get his daughter back?"

"I presume you've noticed," I put a bit of a sneer in my voice, "that I didn't come alone."

"Oh, I'm not talking about having other men do your work for you," he says with a dismissive wave. "From what I've heard, a true father would wage a personal battle for his daughter's honor."

"Lamoreaux, if you've harmed even a single hair on her head, you will indeed answer to me personally."

"And to me," Goscelin adds.

The Duke resumes his studiously thoughtful pacing as the tension grows in the tent. Finally, he stops in front of me. "Here's what we will do. On the day after tomorrow, at midmorning, you and I will meet on the field of honor. We shall fight with swords. If you win, you may see for yourself whether there's any girl here and if that girl is indeed your daughter. If I win, this entire menagerie," he gestures broadly all around him, "will leave immediately."

"This is nonsense, Charles," Goscelin's tone is forceful. "Your quarrel is with me and not with Alfred. If you want to fight someone, then fight me."

The Duke turns to his father. "I'll gladly fight you, old man," he sneers. "And once I've dispatched you, then I'll fight Alfred as a peer – king against king."

"Leave your father out of this, Lamoreaux," I tell him. "If there's to be a fight, it will be between you and me." I pause for a moment. "But there's no need for a fight. I renew my offer. Bring my daughter to me, we'll depart at first light, and I'll have nothing further to say about this incident." I'm intentionally leaving Goscelin the opportunity to discipline his son if he sees fit.

Charles turns back to me, his eyes steely, staring me down, attempting intimidation. "You and me. Midmorning on the day after tomorrow. Swords. The winner keeps the girl."

I stare back, unblinking. "Swords. No daggers."

"As you wish," he replies, then turns on his heel and marches out of the tent.

When we hear the hooves of their horses leaving, Goscelin looks at me. "Alfred, do you have any idea what you just signed up for?"

"Not really, my friend, but I hope you can tell me."

"It's said that my son fights with a poisoned sword."

"Is there any proof of that?"

"Not directly, but there are those who've died after fighting him from wounds that didn't seem all that serious."

"That happens sometimes, if the wounds aren't tended properly," I offer.

"But this happens far too frequently for my liking. It's one of the reasons I prefer to let him go about his business down here rather than force him to be at court. He's hot-tempered – always ready to pick a fight – and a pretty fair swordsman. I've no wish to put others at risk if the rumors are true."

Samuel and Tobin both look extremely worried. "It might be better, Sire," suggests Tobin, "just to ride in with an armed force. Do we know how many retainers he has, Your Grace?" This question directed to Goscelin.

"I can't be certain, Sir Tobin, for he might well have recruited additional men locally to add to those he brought with him."

"I don't like to think what he might do to Juliana if we attack in force," I muse.

The tent is quiet. We all seem to be out of ideas. It's up to me to be resolute. "So here's what we'll do. Samuel, Tobin . . . you have one day to make a better than average swordsman out of me. It was never my best skill, but I promise to be your diligent student. I want to practice with several of your men so I don't get attuned to any one man's style of fighting. I want you to throw at me anything you think Lamoreaux might try . . . and teach me how to defend against it. Starting early in the morning. We'll work all day if need be."

"Are you really sure you want to do that here, out in the open?" asks Samuel. "Shouldn't we find some place away from prying eyes?"

"Actually, I want reports to get back to the Duke that I'm practicing. I want him to be supremely over-confident. And to that end, whenever we have an audience, I want you to let me lose more often than I win. Let's give him every reason to believe he has the advantage. But there's one thing I do want to do out of sight."

"What's that, Sire?" asks Tobin.

"I want you to teach me how to disarm him. If he really does poison his blade, that may be the only way I can come out of this alive."

"We'll clear everything in this tent to the side," says Samuel, "and when it looks to our audience like you've come in here to rest, you can work on that skill. But I'll tell you, Alfred, it isn't easy. We can teach you the technique, but in the end, he may not give you an opportunity." Samuel's concern is palpable. "Are you sure, Alfred? Isn't there some other way?"

"I have to get her out of there, Samuel . . . as quickly as possible. Every minute she's in his clutches, she's in danger. And there's one thing Lamoreaux is right about: a true father is prepared to fight for his daughter. I'm sure you'd do the same for yours."

When Osbert finds out what I'm doing, he can't contain his dismay. "I know it be fer Miss Juliana, m'lord, but I be thinking there must be some other way. What good be it fer her if ye be getting yerself killed getting her back?" I try to show him more confidence than I really feel.

And so it begins just after first light. By midmorning, the first spectators appear – servants and villagers, by the look of them. They seem primarily interested in the diversion from their ordinary day. Late in the morning – as I'm growing more comfortable with routine fights – two of Charles's armed retainers show up, no doubt sent to assess my skill. I win against the first opponent and then intentionally make a stupid mistake with the next man. Just before midday, Tobin calls a rest. He and Samuel follow me into my tent.

Our midday meal is dried meat and bread. We wash it down with small ale – I'll have nothing to dull my senses. The meal finished, we rest for a bit, no one speaking. Finally, Samuel breaks the silence, "Shall we demonstrate for him, Tobin?"

"We might as well. I don't think he's likely to abandon this foolishness."

They both rise and pick up their swords. A bit of ordinary thrust and parry. Tobin appears to be taking control, then backs off a bit. Suddenly Samuel lunges forward, his sword arm outstretched. Tobin closes in rapidly and before I can even see what's happening, Samuel's sword flies from his hand and lands a few feet away. Samuel raises his hands in submission, and Tobin bows and sheaths his sword.

"I couldn't even follow your moves, Tobin. It appeared as if Samuel simply dropped his sword."

"Then I did it right, sir. Sir Samuel was in full control of his sword and of his moves in the duel."

"The key, Alfred," says Samuel, "is speed and follow through. When your opponent puts himself in a position where he's off balance and lacks leverage with his sword arm, you must act quickly . . . and forcefully . . . and not back off on either until he's disarmed. Come, Tobin, let's show him again more slowly."

Samuel raises his sword and lunges forward, arm and sword outstretched to their maximum length. Tobin parries on the inside of Samuel's blade. Then, maintaining contact with Samuel's blade, he steps in and brings his own sword almost vertical. Samuel is now even more off balance with his sword arm in an awkward position. Tobin then pushes his blade over, sort of wrapping it around Samuel's, never losing contact. Initially, this twists Samuel's wrist backward. Tobin then applies all the force he can muster and flings Samuel's blade. Samuel can't recover, and his sword slips from his grasp.

"There are some," says Tobin, "who advocate grasping your opponent's wrist, dropping your own sword, and taking your opponent's from his hand. I think that's too risky. If your opponent has more arm or grip strength than you, you might not succeed . . . leaving you as the one who's disarmed."

"I agree," says Samuel. "Especially in this situation, with the possibility that Lamoreaux's sword is poisoned."

"Once you commit to the move, sir," Tobin again, "you *must* follow through. And you'll likely get only one chance. Any good swordsman will realize what's afoot and won't put himself in a vulnerable position twice."

"I've noticed both times that you start with Samuel's sword arm extended," I remark.

"That gives you the best chance of success," replies Samuel. "You need to advance on him enough to convince him you're willing to keep attacking and then back off just enough that he has to reach out if he wishes to attack without exposing himself to another advance from you."

"We're going to spend a few more minutes here letting you practice the maneuver slowly," says Tobin. "Then we'll go back outside so we don't draw too much curiosity from our spectators. Outside, you're going to practice drawing your opponent into that attack position."

"None of our men know what you're trying to learn," adds Samuel. "So their reaction to your moves will be completely natural. Just don't try disarming any of them. That would give the game away, especially if anyone's watching. We'll practice the final move when we take a rest break later this afternoon."

After they walk me through the maneuver a half-dozen times, we leave the tent. I have no success at all drawing my first two opponents to attack me arm outstretched. But with a couple of pointers from Tobin, I finally succeed with the fourth one. About that time, some villagers and two more of Lamoreaux's retainers wander up to watch. So I begin to mix up what I attempt in each duel, once again losing as often as I win. Despite the pretense for the audience's benefit, I'm feeling increasingly confident that I can draw my opponent into a vulnerable position. Samuel confirms this with a subtle nod whenever I get it right.

As the sun begins to lower, Tobin steps up as my opponent. He comes close, sword raised vertically, apparently saluting his king as an opponent, and whispers quietly, "Samuel and I are going to take turns putting you through everything we can think of. Do your best, but don't be surprised when you lose. We need it to look as if you're tiring and need to rest." I nod my understanding.

The duels that follow are clearly with master swordsmen. I know they're giving me a taste of what I might face on the morrow. When I lose to Samuel, he puts an arm around my shoulder and leads me to my tent as Tobin calls a rest break for the others. I notice the audience drifting away.

For the next hour, I alternately face Tobin and Samuel and attempt to disarm them. Initially, I have no success. "You're hesitating, sir," says Tobin. "When you commit, move fast and with all your strength. You can't let your opponent have time to realize what you're doing."

My next few attempts are a little better, but still I have no success in disarming either of them.

"Start from the beginning this time," says Tobin, when Samuel steps up again as my opponent. "Fight him a bit, then draw him into position and disarm him."

This feels more natural. And when I finally succeed in getting Samuel to lunge toward me, I move in instantly and, much to my surprise, actually disarm him.

"You let me do that," I challenge him.

"Not at all, Alfred. That was well executed. Faster than you've moved so far, and you followed the maneuver all the way through. There was even that jerking motion at the end that's been missing from all your previous attempts. Remember what that felt like. That's the way to do it."

They continue to alternate as my opponent, each time starting the duel from the beginning. Three out of four times, I succeed in disarming them.

"I think that's enough," Tobin calls a halt to things. "You know what to do. Continuing to practice now is not going to teach you anything new. And you need to let your sword arm rest." He pours mugs of small ale for all of us. The refreshment is welcome.

The three of us rest in silence for a full half hour. Then I pick up my sword and head outside for more practice. The knights scramble to their feet and buckle their sword belts about their waists. Sir Thomas steps up. We salute and begin to duel. I'm surprised to lose to him when I'm not doing so intentionally. Samuel comes out of the tent and steps in at the end of the duel.

"Come, Sire. I think it's time we call a halt for the day. Supper will be served soon, and we should find out from King Goscelin what he's learned today."

Not wanting to put Samuel in an awkward position, I acquiesce. Samuel dismisses the knights, and we return to the tent. Once inside, I turn to my friend in no small amount of dismay. "I need more practice, Samuel. Thomas beat me handily back there. I wasn't even trying to lose."

"What you need now, Alfred," says Samuel calmly, "is rest. Think about it. You've fought every bout today. You're exhausted. If you're to be at your best tomorrow, you need to rest."

I sit on my cot, head in my hands, realizing that Samuel is right about how tired I am. But I can't succumb. It's Juliana's fate that's at stake. To their credit, Samuel and Tobin leave me to my thoughts.

Not long after, Goscelin's squire appears at the door of our tent. "King Goscelin say you come." He has none of our language so is merely repeating the words Goscelin gave him. Turning on his heel, he beckons us to follow, and we oblige.

The scene inside Goscelin's tent is a world away from ours. Candles have been lit, a sumptuous meal has been laid out, and a servant is pouring wine. "Sire, this is quite a surprise," exclaims Samuel. "How did you manage it?"

"I stopped by the kitchens and asked Charles's cook if she could arrange a proper supper for us. That fine woman is not the sort to disregard the wishes of her king, no matter what someone else might tell her." He gestures to the food arrayed before us as his squire places a full plate in front of him. "Please, gentlemen. Eat. Enjoy!"

Samuel and Tobin fill their plates. Out of politeness, I also put food on a plate, though I have no appetite. The servant gives each of us a glass of wine. I set mine aside. Samuel and Tobin tuck into their food ravenously, as does Goscelin. When his plate is half empty, Goscelin suddenly realizes I'm not eating. "Is the food not to your liking, Alfred?" he asks. "I'm sure we can find something else if it's not."

"The food is excellent, my friend," I reply. "I simply don't feel much like feasting at the moment."

"But my boy," Goscelin, too, falls into the old habits Lord Ernle chastises himself for. "You must eat. You need your strength on the morrow."

"He's right, Sire," says Samuel, observing the formalities in the presence of my fellow king. "The first thing a knight in the field learns is the importance of nourishment and rest. Without food, your strength wanes. Without rest, your senses aren't at their peak. Eat well and drink some of this extraordinary wine. It's what your body is used to and will help you rest and recover from today's exertions. Just don't overindulge."

"Very well," I pick up my plate and start to eat slowly. After the first few morsels, I'm surprised that I really am exceedingly hungry and finish the rest with gusto.

Goscelin laughs. "Hungrier than you thought, I see."

Feeling somewhat restored, I find it easier to join in his laughter.

"Now drink that wine," he admonishes. "Even if I do say so myself, the wines from this region are some of the best in the world. And I pilfered this from Charles's private cellar, so it's the best of the best."

Tasting it, I reply, "You'll get no argument from me there. This is really quite remarkable."

The servant clears away our plates and the remainder of the food, leaving us alone in the tent with the rest of the wine. "Thank you for supper, my friend," I tell him. "I have to admit that went down much better than hard bread and camp potage."

"The least I could do," Goscelin replies. "For I've not had a very successful day. While you spent the day preparing for tomorrow's fight, I spent it trying to put a stop to this madness. Unfortunately, with no success. My son is rational and cogent in discussing any other topic; but on this one, some sort of lunacy overtakes him. I tried to reason with him . . . I cajoled, begged . . . I even bribed him to release your daughter without a fight. He's implacable."

"He did admit to me that the girl is here. She's being held in one of the guest rooms on an upper floor. It seems that a kitchen maid takes her food and attends to her needs once each day. But the room is locked from the outside, and a guard stands watch at the door day and night."

"At least he doesn't have her in some basement cell." I'm certain my relief is apparent in my voice.

"We arrived just in time, though, Alfred. As I feared, he was planning to make the best of the botched kidnapping. His intent was to marry Juliana next week and then bring her to court as his wife. We'd have had no trouble getting the pope to annul the marriage on the grounds that he'd stolen her and you hadn't given your consent; but I fear restoring your daughter's spirit would've been a far more difficult task. I must admit, though, I'm somewhat surprised, since he was so fixated on marrying Richenda."

"When you see Juliana tomorrow, you'll understand," I tell him.

"Which brings me to something I must ask of you, Alfred. I have no quarrel with your teaching my son a lesson. His actions were and are reprehensible, and he deserves to be punished for them. But for the sake of our friendship, I ask that you not kill him. If you did, my personal honor and the respect of my people would require that I wage war to avenge his death – and that is something I have no wish to do. I'm grateful for the way you've handled this. A lesser man would have arrived with an army, intent on punishing the entire kingdom for the actions of one man. And so I ask you to stay the course of your measured response. Get your daughter back – but don't create further strife."

"That's all I want, sir – to take my daughter away from here and safely home."

"Then we shall say goodnight," he replies. "Rest well and may God be with you tomorrow." He reaches out his hand and grasps mine strongly. "I may have accomplished at least one small thing today," he adds with a smile.

"What's that?"

"I kept him occupied so he couldn't practice his own swordsmanship," he chuckles. "Just before I left, his spies returned with the report of how soundly Sir Samuel and Sir Tobin had bested you in the last two bouts. He was calling for wine to celebrate his victory even then. Perhaps he will not be as wise as you in his indulgences tonight."

With that, we return to our own tent. Sleep doesn't come easily; but when it does, it's the deep, dreamless sleep born of total exhaustion. Far too soon, I become aware of Osbert shaking my shoulder to waken me. Samuel and Tobin are already dressed. "Well," teases Samuel, "nice to see we won't have to forfeit because our principal was still asleep in bed."

"Like *you've* been up since before dawn," I taunt back at him as I swing my legs over the edge of the cot and rub the sleep from my eyes.

"Actually, he has, sir," chimes in Tobin. "Dragged me out of a deep sleep. Insisted we walk the grounds twice over, looking for booby traps or anything Lamoreaux might have done in the night to trip you up or give him an advantage." Samuel is indeed my guardian angel.

"The grounds are clean, Alfred. And our men have been on guard since we made our rounds. No one can tamper with the area without our knowing about it."

I step outside to relieve myself and return to find Osbert uncovering a tray containing bowls of porridge. "It not be very hot, m'lords," he says, "seeing as how it be brought all the way from the kitchen." He hands me a bowl and a spoon. "Best ye eat, m'lord. Ye be needing all yer strength this morning." Remarkably, a bit of honey has been poured over the top of the porridge.

"Osbert, how?"

"I try telling His Grace's squire, but he not be understanding. So he take me to His Grace, and I be telling him what I want. His Grace, he say, 'Ye be leaving it to me, Osbert,' and this morning his squire bring this tray."

The porridge is surprisingly good – a sign, no doubt, that I'm really hungry. As Osbert helps me dress, he's uncharacteristically quiet. He won't say that he's fearful, but I can tell it from his manner. Samuel, on the other hand, is all easy conversation – doing what he does best by making an extraordinary situation seem like a perfectly ordinary day. "Get your boots on," he says, "and let's go for a walk. There's no better way to loosen up and get ready for a match."

With Samuel and Tobin on either side of me, we make several circuits of the meadow and criss-cross the dueling field twice. I watch their eyes checking everything – looking for anything they might have missed before or anything that might have slipped past our guards. "Just remember," says Tobin, "to take a good measure of him. Let him make the first move."

"You know, Alfred," says Samuel lightheartedly, "you really are a better swordsman than you give yourself credit for."

"John was the one skilled with the sword," I reply. "I'm the horseman."

"John was a brash fighter . . . all bluster, intimidating his opponent, winning more often by scaring them into mistakes than by excess of skill."

"Really?" I ask incredulously.

"Really," he replies. "You, on the other hand, are more thoughtful. In the long run, that's the better way to win. In case you didn't notice, you really made Tobin and me work to beat you yesterday," he adds with a grin.

He may just be trying to boost my confidence, but it's working. Tobin rushes to help. "That's right, sir. You were too busy concentrating on what you were doing to notice how much better you fought than at the start of the day."

"Well, my friends," I put an arm around each of their shoulders, "let's just hope it's enough."

We've arrived back at the tent. There's just one more thing to be said. "I intend to win this bout and secure Juliana's release. But nothing's certain. If Lamoreaux should succeed in killing me, Samuel, you know what to do. And I believe Goscelin will help you. Free Juliana and take Lamoreaux your prisoner. Take him back to our kingdom for trial. The people must see him brought to our justice for the crimes he committed. Once he's been tried and sentenced, if Goscelin demands his return . . . well, that won't be my decision to make."

As I buckle on my sword, Samuel says, "That's not a duty I care to fulfill, Alfred. So you get out there and make sure I don't have to."

As the village church bell chimes midmorning, Lamoreaux rides up at the head of a group of retainers, all decked out in fine regalia and followed by grooms on foot. They dismount, give their horses to the grooms, and assemble on one side of the field. Our knights return from their guard positions to assemble on the other, and the three of us walk over to join them. Goscelin and his guards take a position at one end of the field, showing favoritism to neither opponent. The Duke removes his fancy coat and plumed hat and gives them to his squire.

We face each other across the field, neither moving for several minutes. Finally, Lamoreaux draws his sword and begins to advance toward the center of the field. I follow suit. As we salute each other, I notice that his eyes seem red and puffy. Overindulgence last night?

Stepping back, we circle one another cautiously. Remembering Tobin's advice, I watch his eyes and wait. When he attacks, his maneuvers are simple and predictable, and I defend against them easily. For a full five minutes, we continue with simple sword play . . . more like a demonstration than a duel. Is this the skilled swordsman I was warned about? Concentrate, Alfred, I tell myself. Don't get lured into overconfidence.

Then Lamoreaux does something totally unexpected. He lowers his sword to his side, turns his back, and walks away. This is not how one cedes the victory to an opponent. What's he up to? Is he encouraging me to attack him from behind? Surely he would be ready for that and would parry any attack with ease. I follow him slowly, my sword at the ready.

Suddenly, he swings around, his blade held flat at shoulder height, both hands on the hilt. I duck just in time to hear the swish of the blade slicing through the air mere inches above my head. Half a second later and the blade would have lodged in my neck. Propelled by Lamoreaux's strength and the momentum of his spin, it might even have severed my head.

I never take my eyes off him as I gather my wits and regain my footing. He steps back several paces, his sword down at his side leaving himself completely unguarded, and laughing out loud – a sound that's equal parts self-satisfaction, amusement, and malevolence. "Better swordsmen than you have fallen for that trick," he calls out.

He's taunting – hoping to lure me into an angry charge that would undoubtedly get me impaled on his sword. Concentrate, Alfred, I remind myself yet again. Ignore the theatrics and circus tricks. Stick to the plan.

Finally realizing that I'm refusing the bait, Lamoreaux takes up the en garde position, and I quickly follow suit. "Very well," he pronounces, "enough of schoolboy fighting. Let's have a proper duel."

Not wanting to show my hand too soon, I withdraw, and let him decide his next move. This time he attacks more aggressively. I defend, and then take the attack to him, putting him on his guard that he won't get a quick, easy victory. As I let him bring the fight to me, I remind myself that if I can hold my own with Samuel and Tobin, then I *do* have a chance of besting the duke.

We continue in this vein for what seems like an eternity but in reality is likely no more than ten minutes. It's time. I take the attack to him; he defends; I withdraw. Again, I take the attack to him, but this time I don't withdraw quite so far. I allow him to attack next, but defend quickly, then withdraw and attack him. When he defends successfully, I withdraw a bit more than usual, watching his eyes and imagining what he must be thinking. I feign intent to attack again, and he falls into the trap. He lunges forward, sword arm outstretched . . . and I am ready. The maneuver seems to come naturally. Whether that's from skill or from my determination to rescue my daughter, I'll never know . . . and in truth, it doesn't matter. In the blink of an eye, his blade is flung from his hand, and Samuel rushes over to retrieve it.

Charles stands before me, his hands up, my blade pointed at his chest. I signal to Samuel, who brings me the Duke's sword. I switch my own sword to my left hand and take the Duke's in my right. "Now kneel, Lamoreaux," I order in the most commanding tone I can muster. He hesitates and backs up a step. I advance and repeat the order. "Kneel if you value your life." Slowly, his hands still raised, he complies.

His retainers all draw their swords and advance a few steps forward. Our knights follow suit. From the end of the field, Goscelin shouts out "Hold!" in both languages.

With Lamoreaux's blade just inches from his face, I tell him, "Now, send for the girl."

Still defiant, he replies, "Why should I do that?"

"Because I've won, and that was the agreement." I wave his sword so he can see its movement. "Would you like me to scratch your face with this? It would only be a small scratch."

Through all this I'm aware that he hasn't taken his eyes off my own sword, which I'm holding down beside my left leg. Is he considering reaching out to grab it? I take one step closer to him and raise my own blade to point at his crotch. If he moves now, there's no doubt some portion of his skin will come in contact with his own sword. But for effect, I taunt him further, "Or would you like me to rearrange things so that you can play the part of the woman in your little entertainments?"

His eyes have moved to my face now, and I see the terror in them. "Bastien!" he shouts. One of his retainers comes running, sword in hand. At his approach, I point Lamoreaux's blade toward him and order, "Drop your sword!"

The man stops in his tracks and hesitates. "Do as he says," shouts the duke. When Bastien has laid down his sword and moved to his master's side, I point the poisoned blade back toward Charles's face. "Fetch the girl, Bastien," he orders.

"Make it fast," I add. "Your master wouldn't want me to decide you're not coming back."

Bastien runs for his horse and gallops at top speed toward the manor. While we wait, Goscelin brings his guards to the middle of the field and orders the duke's retainers to sheathe their swords. Samuel orders ours to follow suit.

Sooner than I would have expected, we see horse and rider returning from the manor, at a slower pace this time to accommodate the young girl who sits in the front of the saddle. As they approach and slow to a walk, I drop the swords I'm holding. Goscelin orders his guards to take charge of the Duke as I run to the horse's side and lift Juliana down. I hold her in my arms, squeezing her tightly, until finally she says, "Please, Papa . . . I can't breathe."

Samuel and Tobin have come up to join us, each of them giving Juliana a hug. In the background, I hear Goscelin ordering his men to take the duke and his retainers back to the manor and keep them there. Suddenly, he's come to join us. He bows to Juliana and brings her hand to his lips. "You, my dear, are a very brave young lady. Will you allow me to escort you to my tent where we can have food and prepare for your journey home?"

Despite everything she's been through, Juliana doesn't forget her manners. She curtseys to Goscelin and then replies, "Thank you, Your Grace. I'd like that very much."

As we make our way to Goscelin's tent, he drops into step beside me. "I see what you mean, Alfred. They could be twins." And then, after a pause, he adds, "That was well done, my friend. I thank you for your forbearance. I must admit . . . in the same circumstances, I do not know if I would have been able to stay my sword."

Once inside his tent, Goscelin is all business. "Alfred, I want to be away from here as soon as we can. I'm leaving my men here to hold Charles in check until you're safely aboard ship and on your way home. Can your men break camp and accompany us back to my castle?"

Tobin doesn't hesitate. "I'll give the order now, Your Grace. We can be on our way in an hour." And he's off to put things in train.

Before we leave, there are some things I want to know. I sit on the edge of a cot and invite Juliana to sit beside me. Putting an arm around her shoulder, I speak as gently as I know how. "I need to ask you some questions, my sweet. But before I do, you need to know that you've done nothing wrong . . . absolutely nothing. And if your mother were here, she'd tell you exactly the same thing. None of this was your fault. Do you understand?"

"Yes, Papa," she says quietly, looking down at her hands in her lap.

I take her chin in my hand and turn her face up to look into my eyes. "I mean it, Juliana. You've done nothing wrong. I need to know that you believe me."

"I believe you, Papa. You've never told me an untruth. It's just that . . ." She stops.

"Just what, my sweet?"

"It's just that, I've been so scared. I kept praying you would find me, but I didn't know how."

I take both her hands in one of mine and caress her hair. "Well, it seems your prayers have been answered."

She's struggling to be brave, but it's all more than she can take. She buries her head on my chest, wraps her arms around me, and weeps. I hold her closely and gently, hoping to impart my strength to her and assure her that she's safe once again. When her turmoil is spent, she dries her eyes and looks up at me. "What do you want to know, Papa?"

"Did the duke harm you in any way, Juliana? Did he or any of his men lay a finger on you?"

"No, Papa."

"On the boat or here?"

"On the boat, they put me in a tiny cabin with some bread and fruit and didn't come in or let me out until we docked."

"And here?"

"No, Papa. But the duke came into my room every day."

"Did he touch you?"

"Once, he touched my hair. He scared me, Papa. He looked at me like . . . like he was hungry and I was his dinner."

"But did he touch you other than that one time?"

"No, Papa."

"Very well." I kiss her forehead. "You're safe now. We'll go back to Goscelin's castle, and Petronilla can get you some new clothes. Then we'll board our ship and be home before you know it."

Goscelin brings her a bit of fruit pie. "I thought you might like this, my dear."

"Thank you, Sire."

"Now, will you and your father travel with me in my coach?"

"I'd like that, Sire, if Papa agrees."

I tousle her hair. "Thank you, my friend."

The men are ready to strike Goscelin's tent, so we make our way to the carriage. Tobin urges us to be on our way . . . the supply wagons will follow as soon as the tent is loaded. "Tobin, can we spare a man as a courier? I want to get word to Gwen that we have her safe and sound."

"Already done, Sire. He should be with Emaurri by nightfall day after tomorrow, and a fresh courier will be dispatched to cross the sea in a small, fast boat."

"Thank you, Tobin."

We spend a day at Goscelin's castle, where Petronilla takes Juliana under her wing. I'm assured that new clothes are just the thing to lift a woman's spirit and make her feel happy and beautiful. Knowing that Gwen will be receiving the courier any moment now and that a break in the journey will be good in any event, I'm happy enough to accede to these feminine pleasures.

Emaurri has kept the *Constance* in port in anticipation of our return. She's provisioned and ready to sail when we arrive, but a storm at sea delays us for two days. When the weather clears, the sea is calm and smooth, and our crossing is actually quite pleasant. I take this opportunity to give Tobin new instructions. "Juliana is not to leave the castle walls without a full troop of guards accompanying her. The same goes for Richenda."

"Yes, Sire," is all he says, a reply that quite surprises me by both its formality and lack of enthusiasm.

"Something's wrong, Tobin. What is it?"

"You once told me I should speak candidly, Sire. But your tone and manner indicate there's no room for discussion on this topic. I accept my responsibility in the matter of your daughter's abduction."

"Come, Tobin," I encourage him. "This isn't like you. You know I hold neither you nor your guards to blame."

"I did believe that, sir. But these new orders . . ." he lets the comment hang in the air.

"The new directions have nothing to do with the past, Tobin. Don't you know how much I rely on you? Without you, I'd never have succeeded in bringing her home. Don't ever forget that."

"May I speak candidly, sir?"

"Always, Tobin."

"Sir, these new orders. I can't reconcile them with how you've always been. You've always wanted yourself and your family to go among the people. What will the people think, sir, when your daughter and Lady Richenda are always surrounded by guards?"

"I suppose they'll think I'm trying to prevent either of them from being taken from us again."

"I hope it's no more than that, sir," he replies. I can tell he's still unconvinced.

"I'll think about what you've said, Tobin. But know that I'm unlikely to change my mind. I lost my daughter once, and I don't intend that it should ever happen again."

"It's your decision, of course, sir. Perhaps when you've talked with the queen . . ." he lets that thought, too, hang in the air.

Laurence must have posted a lookout, for everyone is on the dock to greet us when the *Constance* arrives. As soon as we disembark, the hugs begin. When her mother releases her, Juliana runs straight to Milla for a long embrace. Gwen's eyes are brimming with tears, but I recognize them as an expression of relief and happiness. Rupert and Catherine have also come.

My uncle takes me aside as we make our way to Laurence's home. "Emaurri sent a letter to me by the courier with some of the detail of what happened. I haven't told Gwen about the duel."

"I'm not sure whether to thank you for that or not, Uncle," I chuckle. "Leaving me to face her wrath all alone?"

"Why should I deprive you of the pleasure?" he laughs. "You'll have to tell me the whole story once all the excitement subsides."

Much as I try to resume normal daily life, there seems to be no end of problems arising from Juliana's kidnapping. Two weeks after we returned home, I was taken aback when Gwen stormed into my private reception room, interrupting a conversation with Richard.

"Whatever you're discussing can wait," she announced. "Richard, would you excuse us, please?" Her demeanor was so uncharacteristic that Richard immediately gathered up his papers and left the room.

"What could be so urgent?" I didn't hide my displeasure.

"I'm trying to plan for the herding competitions, and Tobin tells me he hasn't enough men to send with us. When I pressed him, Alfred, he said we couldn't go without a full troop of guards. What's the point, Alfred? Juliana wants to preside over the events again this year, and you know how much the herdsmen enjoy how she engages with them. She can't do that with guards all around."

"You'll just have to find a way to make it work. I don't want to take a chance she could be stolen from us again."

"Alfred, we can't 'make it work,' as you say, if we can't even go. Tobin says there simply aren't enough men to dedicate a whole troop to such long trips. Or were you planning to hire more men? If so, you'd best tell him soon."

"Perhaps it's best Juliana not preside this year. It's not worth the risk, Gwen."

"And how do you intend to explain that to her?"

"We simply tell her it's for her own safety. That should be reason enough."

"Do you really believe that, Alfred? Or is this all about your own sense of inadequacy to protect her?" I've never heard such accusations from my wife. Nor have I ever seen her so angry.

"It's nothing of the sort. I'd think you'd be pleased that I'm doing everything possible to guarantee her safety."

"I'd be pleased if you'd let her live her normal life," she retorted, marching into our bed chamber and slamming the door behind her.

A week later, while he was helping me dress, Osbert surprised me with his own comment. "Milla be telling me it not be easy anymore to take her girls to the shops. She say all the guards be always hurrying them along. There be no time to look at cloth or ribbons or trinkets . . . no time to decide what they be wanting."

"And why was she telling you this, Osbert?"

"I dinna' know, m'lord. I be thinking she just be talking about what be different these days."

"Some things are different, Osbert. It can't be helped."

The need to ensure Juliana's safety is taking its toll on other parts of our lives as well. Though Gwen calmed down somewhat from her outburst, she brings up the topic from time to time, always suggesting that I'm being overprotective and urging me to relent on my strict rules. We've never been in such complete disagreement on any matter, and it's affecting how we are with each other. More and more frequently, Gwen retires early and is asleep by the time I climb into bed. Our lovemaking is strained, when it occurs at all.

Today Juliana comes to me in the library. It's obvious she's been crying, but she's trying to put on a brave face for my benefit. "Papa, I want to go see Brother Adam, but Mama says I can't."

"Why do you want to go, my sweet?"

"Brother Adam said we could breed Primrose this summer, and it's time, and I need to take her up to the kennel and talk to Brother Adam. But Mama says I can't go without a troop of guards, and Sir Tobin says he can't spare a troop until the end of next week, and by then it will be too late."

"Couldn't Brother Adam come get Primrose?"

"I suppose he could. But I want to see the other dogs. Like in the old days, Papa."

"Well, you'll just have to decide which is more important – breeding Primrose or seeing the other dogs. If you want to see the other dogs, you can go later and let Brother Adam come get Primrose."

Her frustration gets the best of her, and she bursts into tears. "Is that really any reason to cry, Juliana?" I find myself surprisingly impatient with her. "We all learn as we grow up that we have to make choices sometimes."

That only seems to make things worse. "Papa, why are you punishing me?" she asks plaintively through her tears.

"I'm not punishing you."

"But you are, Papa. You won't let me do any of the things I used to do. You said I didn't do anything wrong, but I must have. If I didn't, why are you punishing me like this? And why does Richenda get punished, too, when she wasn't even taken away?"

"I'm just looking out for your safety, Juliana . . . yours and Richenda's. It's what parents do."

"It's not what you and Mama used to do. We used to be happy." She runs from the room still crying. My heart breaks to see her so upset. But that's nothing to how it would break if we were ever to lose her again.

Gwen is even more subdued than normal tonight at supper and as we say goodnight. But she doesn't bring up the topic of Juliana's tears or her wish to go to the monastery.

In the morning, I take my usual ride. Returning from the stable near midday, I'm surprised to see two carriages in the courtyard. Nurse, Alicia, and the boys are in the second one, Letty, Milla, and the girls in the first. Donal sits beside the driver of the wagon behind, which is loaded with travel trunks. Three mounted guards bring up the rear. Gwen is just coming out the door, making her way to the front carriage.

I rush to her, catching up just as she's about to step into the carriage. "What's all this?" I ask.

"The children and I are going to the manor, Alfred."

"You haven't enough guards."

"We have the usual complement of guards for that trip, Alfred, and I'll have no more."

"What's this all about?" I'm trying not to cause too much of a scene here in the open, but I can barely take in that she's decided on this without even mentioning it to me.

"You know what it's about, Alfred. I'm taking the children for some time in the country. When you come to your senses, perhaps you'll join us. Nothing would make me happier."

She ascends the carriage, then leans out the window and calls to the driver, "Drive on." I watch in complete dismay as their little procession leaves the courtyard and drives out of sight.

•　　•　　•　　•　　•

Despite the fact that court life continues and the business of running the kingdom goes on as usual, the atmosphere around the castle is palpably different. My interactions with the lords are cordial enough, and yet they're distant. I spend time with Phillip, Richard, and Samuel – even going to the tavern occasionally – but I don't feel as much pleasure in their company as usual. Rupert tries to encourage me to go to my family and put things back to the way they were before Juliana was kidnapped. I miss my family desperately, and this only serves to reinforce my fear of failing to protect them as I should.

Every time I think of the duel with Lamoreaux, I'm seized with anxiety. The outcome could so easily have gone the other way. What if I should have to fight for her again? Could I possibly be so lucky twice? The memories of that morning only serve to strengthen my resolve never to be in that position again.

When the Assembly meets, Amelia is once more among the delegates.. She attempts to engage me, even suggesting a ride in the woods. I'm disinclined to be alone with her and keep her at arm's length. What if Juliana's abduction was some sort of punishment for my dalliance with her? I can't risk my daughter's safety for my own personal pleasure.

I begin training a new horse – a son of Sirius – a pastime that usually gives me great pleasure – but somehow, I can't put my heart into it. The horse recognizes this and is often uncooperative as a result. After initially trying to cheer me up, Osbert has settled into his own version of my moroseness; we talk very little as he goes about his duties. He seems as unhappy as I am, but I don't know what to do about it. Some days, I don't care.

The knock on the door is so quiet that I wonder if perhaps I've imagined it, engrossed as I've been in the pages of the book that lies open in front of me. The library has become my refuge, these books that have been my friends for so much of my life providing a kind of solace as I struggle with feeling abandoned by my family and my friends. While I'm trying to decide if there really was a knock, the quiet tapping is repeated. It takes me quite by surprise when my mother enters in response to my rather unenthusiastic, "Come."

"I'm so glad I found you here, Alfred," she says. "I really wanted to talk with you without prying eyes knowing about it."

She seems genuinely disturbed about something. I close the book and return it to its proper place on the shelf. "Now," I say, taking the chair nearest hers, "you have my undivided attention."

"I, uh," she begins hesitantly, quite uncharacteristically for her. "I'm actually here, Alfred, to seek your approval." This is unexpected, but I wait for her to continue. "You see, Lord Devereux has asked to pay court to me. I really don't know if we would ever be more than good friends, but I'm rather inclined to spend some time in his company. And so, I'd like your approval."

I reach over and take both her hands in mine. "Mother, you're a free woman. A woman whose judgment of people is impeccable. You don't need my approval to pursue your interests."

She smiles. "That may be. But I'm the dowager queen, and protocol dictates I should seek the king's approval for any liaison that might result in anything more than a casual friendship."

It's my turn to smile and shake my head. Now I understand her reluctance to broach the subject. "Oh, my. How far we've come! It seems like only yesterday that I needed to seek your approval or Father's for things I wanted to do." Still holding her hands, I bring both of them to my lips and kiss them. "Mother, I can't imagine your ever doing anything that would warrant my concern. For the sake of protocol, you have my approval. And you should assume that goes for whatever interest you wish to pursue."

She leans over and kisses my cheek. "Thank you, Alfred, for not making this any more awkward than it is."

"There's no reason it should be. Lord Devereux's wife has been gone for many years. And I know Father would want you to be happy."

"I don't know if anything will come of it. I've told Emrys as much. But I do enjoy his company, so we've decided to see if it leads anywhere. I really don't know, though, if I could ever be with another man as I was with your father. He was kind and loving and generous.

"He wasn't without fault," she continues. "But he only ever had one dalliance that I know of." She rushes on, apparently expecting me to question or contradict her. "Oh, he never told me; he respected me far more than that. But I knew. He was," she pauses, searching for a word, "distracted during that time. She wasn't a lady of the court, and I don't think anyone else ever knew. I was grateful for that – and for the fact that it didn't last long. And it was very long ago. We had a good marriage, and he really knew how to please a woman in the bed chamber."

"Why are you telling me all this, Mother?"

"Truth be told, what I'm embarking on is a bit unnerving. And I needed someone to talk to. Gwen's been gone for ages, and Catherine's gone down with Rupert to see to the estate."

"I'm surprised you didn't go with them. Why *did* you stay?"

"I stayed to look after you, Alfred. You've been so sad of late. I was thinking – hoping even – that you might need someone to talk to as well."

"Oh, I've talked," I reply, exasperated. "For what little good it's done me. I tried to talk to Gwen. Since she left, I've talked to Richard and to Samuel and to Phillip. They all think I'm being foolish. But like I told them, no one here has had a child stolen from them; so why should I expect anyone to understand why I think certain measures are necessary for my children's safety?"

"There, you're wrong, my dear." Her voice and facial expression are soft and kind and gentle. I look at her inquisitively. "Your father and I had a child taken from us."

"Mother, I was a grown man with an expectant wife at the time."

"Alfred, you will always be my child. And as your own children grow into adults, you'll understand that parental feeling never goes away. When you were taken, Edward and I were absolutely devastated. We had no idea where you were or if we'd ever see you again."

"I'm sorry, Mother." I'm truly contrite. "I didn't mean any disrespect to what you and Father suffered."

"Alfred, when you came back to us, your father's instinct was exactly like yours. He wanted to provide extra guards for you and not allow you to go anywhere alone. He wanted to avoid any risk that you could be taken from us again.

"It was your grandfather who interceded. He said the best way for you to recover from your ordeal was for your life to be completely normal. To his credit, Edward listened to that advice. And as he watched you thrive – how quickly you recovered in both mind and body – he was grateful that he hadn't imposed restrictions on you."

"You, also, think I'm being foolish with Juliana?"

"Not foolish, Alfred. Just a loving father, consumed with fear for her safety. That fear and the measures you took to combat it were making Juliana fearful too. And as long as she feels fear, she'll never quite relegate those events to the past.

"The other thing your grandfather told Edward was that there were other ways to keep you safe. Keeping track of and dealing with any threat, he said, would be far better for you than restricting your freedom. Together, they decided to make you part of those efforts. I've often suspected that was yet another way to help you put the trauma of your captivity behind you." She smiles. "Perhaps that's how you should look out for Juliana."

"Mother, I . . . I don't understand. Why didn't you tell me all this sooner?"

"You weren't ready to listen. If Gwen couldn't get through to you . . ." She leaves the thought hanging in the air.

"So you think she was right to go?"

"She was right to give Juliana a chance to return to her normal life. It wasn't easy for her. And I've no doubt she's cried herself to sleep many a night, longing for you to join them."

"You can probably guess that our ability to keep track of threats, as you describe it, was thoroughly disrupted during John's reign. We've had to start completely over."

"But in this case, it might be easier than you think. You have Emaurri already in Goscelin's court. Send an agent to him. I suspect Goscelin would have no objection to someone keeping track of Lamoreaux. He might even be grateful for the help."

"I wish I'd had the wisdom, Mother, to think this through myself."

"Don't chastise yourself, Alfred. Remember – your father couldn't see it without help either. And I seem to recall your grandfather telling you that wisdom comes only with time and with learning from our experiences." She reaches out and touches my cheek. "Now, I've invited Emrys to join us at the manor for a bit of a holiday. We'll be going down with Richard and Avelina at the end of the week. Will you go with us?"

"I'll think about it, Mother. And thank you."

The next day, I summon Rupert and Laurence to discuss how we keep track of Charles. "You know that brandy you like so well, Alfred?" queries Rupert. I'm puzzled by his abrupt change of subject, but know my uncle well enough to wait and see where this is leading.

"It comes from a small estate that borders the duchy of Lamoreaux on the north – Saint Didier, it's called. Their vineyard's not large, and their production isn't enough to bottle wine in sufficient quantities for trade. So they sell their grapes to Lamoreaux. Their soil is the same as the Lamoreaux north vineyards, and the vines come from the same ancient stock. So it's an ideal way for Lamoreaux to add to the quantities they can bottle.

"In return, Lamoreaux sells wines from their best vintages to Saint Didier, from which they distill their remarkable brandies. As it happens, I'm down to my last two bottles. But as we've had no trade with them since the beginning of John's reign, I've no idea if the quality is the same. It occurs to me that the only way to be sure is to visit and sample their current offerings."

"A splendid idea," says Laurence. "I've been thinking about asking you to send for Emaurri, Alfred, for us to discuss trade. But it occurs to me I might learn more by paying him a visit."

Listening to these two master spies weave their plans before my eyes reminds me of the times Rupert and I conspired to keep track of Ralf – and brings back the same feeling of control and contentment I remember from those days. I feel the tension in my body and my mind start to recede as I let go of a burden I had thought necessary to bear alone.

Rupert lingers after Laurence leaves. "Now this is the Alfred I remember," he says with a broad smile.

"I don't know what came over me, Uncle. It was like I completely lost my mind. Why didn't someone speak to me sooner?"

"The lords have been asking me exactly that question," he chuckles. "Alice and I talked about it often. She was convinced you wouldn't listen – would only go deeper into your sadness, as she called it – unless there was something to get you to think about someone other than yourself. This business with Devereux proved to be just the thing."

"So that was contrived?"

"Oh, no, that's quite real. Devereux's been in love with your mother for a long time. I suppose he finally decided Edward had been gone long enough that declaring himself wouldn't dishonor his friend."

"It's like a terrible weight has been lifted off my mind. I just don't know how I'm going to face Gwen."

"She loves you, Alfred. It won't be hard."

Over the next day or two, everything seems to change. A comfortable camaraderie returns to the court. Osbert is his old talkative self. I know the difference is in me and not the people about me, but the atmosphere is contagious and boosts my spirits even further.

At the end of the week, I'm in the carriage with Rupert, my mother, and Lord Devereux, on our way to the manor, Richard and his family in their own carriage behind ours. "I can't tell you how happy we all are that you finally returned from your dark place, my boy," says Devereux.

"No one could be happier than I am," I reply. We have a delightful conversation on the journey, and I'm keenly aware how attentive he is to my mother.

As we drive up the lane to the manor, some of my apprehension returns. Sensing this, Mother reaches over and pats my hand. "There's nothing to worry about, Alfred."

Nevertheless, I allow them to alight first. Only Catherine and Gwen are there to greet us. When I step down, Gwen rushes into my arms. "My love, I am so very, very sorry," I tell her.

She releases her embrace and puts her finger to my lips. "Say no more, Alfred. You're home now." Yet again, I'm reminded how lucky I am to have the love of this woman.

"The children are on the terrace. I couldn't have borne seeing their disappointment if you hadn't come."

"Gwen, what do I say to Juliana? She must despise me."

"Tell her that you love her, and say no more about it. Let her tell you what she's been doing."

"What about Geoffrey and Edward? How has this affected them?"

"I've told all of them you had business of the kingdom to attend to. Mostly, they're just children having summer fun in the country."

When we emerge from the house onto the terrace, I see immediately that she's right. Edward spies me first, and both boys run to greet me. Reminding myself that Geoffrey considers himself too old for a hug, I just tousle his hair. Edward, on the other hand, says, "Swing me around, Papa. Swing me around." A request happily fulfilled. Seeing this, Alicia runs as fast as her short little legs will carry her, crying, "Me too, Papa. Me too." And she squeals with delight as I swoop her into the air and swing her around and around. Richenda, too, approaches, and I kiss her hand gallantly before she reaches out to me for a hug.

Juliana hangs back. I hold out my arms to her, and she comes slowly into them. "I've missed you, my sweet."

"I've missed you too, Papa." She's still rather hesitant.

"If you're not too busy, how about we walk around the garden, and you can tell me everything you've been doing."

"I'm not busy, Papa." She takes my hand and we set off together.

"I'm glad you're here, Papa. Primrose is going to have her puppies any day now, and I wanted you to see them born."

"So you figured out a way to get her bred. I'm impressed!"

"I remembered that Mama said we would breed her to Brumby if we stayed at the lake cottage. So I asked her about it, and she said yes." My beautiful daughter beams with pleasure at her good idea.

"We may have a problem," I try to sound terribly serious.

"What, Papa?" I sense her anxiety.

"Remember when we were at the cottage, and Edward wanted a boy dog in the nursery, and I promised him if Primrose ever had puppies, he could choose one for himself?"

She laughs happily. "Oh, yes, Papa. So does Edward. He reminds me every day."

"Is that alright with you?"

She smiles. "I don't think we have much choice, do we?"

"I suppose we don't." We continue our walk in comfortable silence for a few minutes.

"Papa?" I hear anxiety in her voice again.

"Yes?"

"Papa, we went to the herding competition in Neukirk."

"Did you enjoy it?"

"Papa, we went without a troop of guards. Mama said it would be alright."

"Your Mama is very wise. That wasn't my best idea. Are we going to Great Woolston next week?"

Her face lights up as if I've just given her the crown jewels as a personal gift. "Will you go with us, Papa?"

"I wouldn't miss it. Let's just hope Primrose has her puppies before then – I wouldn't want to miss that either."

Gwen and I are alone at last. When I climb into bed, she snuggles close as if nothing had ever come between us. "Gwen, how can I ever make this up to you?"

"The minute I saw you, my love, I could tell you were back to your old self. That's all I ever wanted. Well, maybe that and . . ." She caresses my cheek and kisses me passionately. Our lovemaking is urgent and intense . . . and repeated again before morning.

Two weeks in the country push the dark days even farther away. Watching Juliana at the competition in Great Woolston, I wonder how I could ever have thought that constraining her joyous spirit and the people's love for her was a good idea. If the people love her, they will protect her far better than I alone ever could.

Too soon, it's time to return to the castle. The weather being nice and the carriages rather full, Richard and I decide to make the journey on horseback. Approaching the castle, I find myself thinking how majestic and beautiful is this place I call home. As I look up at the ramparts, my eye is drawn to the sentry tower – and I'm struck by a sudden realization.

"Richard, I know what John did with the money. Come with me!" And I'm off at a gallop, my friend hurrying to catch up.

Slowing to a walk as we get closer, I point toward the top of the tower. "There!"

"What are you talking about?" asks Richard.

"Up there . . . at the top of the tower. I've never made the connection before."

"What connection?"

"Don't you see? On this side of the wall, there are three levels of arrow slits. On the inside, just two. And there are just two fighting floors . . . the one at the top of the walls and the one above. So how does one get to the third level? That must be what John figured out."

"Calm down, Alfred," Richard shakes his head. "We thought of that before. Apparently there were three fighting floors in the distant past . . . in your great-grandfather's time and earlier. Rupert said the stories are that the archers didn't like going up there . . . wouldn't volunteer. They told their captains that they couldn't get the right angles for their shots. But when they talked among themselves, they talked of their fear of being trapped up there. It seems the access was difficult, and with only one way out, they worried that if an enemy breached the castle they'd either be left up there to starve or the floor beneath their feet would be fired.

"At some point, the floor of that topmost room collapsed, and the archers took it as an omen. To a man, they swore they'd never go back up there again. So the access was sealed off, and the repair was made by putting a new ceiling in at the second level."

"I've often wondered why there are no beams visible in that upper room," I remark.

"I suppose they just nailed the planks of the ceiling to beams above and never bothered with the uppermost level," Richard replies.

"I'm not convinced," I shake my head.

"Alfred, that second level is nothing but stone walls with arrow slits and a stone hearth. You said yourself that you couldn't find any loose planks in the ceiling."

"I know. But think about it, Richard. John's will said 'from the roof of the highest tower.' That third level is as close to the roof as a man could get on his own."

"What if John was just speaking metaphorically?"

"My brother was not that poetic. He always wanted to be thought smarter than those around him, and yet he was always being outsmarted. He would have relished the notion of leaving behind a riddle that none of us could work out. I can just imagine the smirk on his face as he dictated those words to the bishop. He found some way up there, Richard. I'm sure of it."

We ride through the gates into the outer courtyard, and I'm off my horse in a flash, rushing into the gatehouse and bounding up the stairs to the second fighting level. When Richard catches up with me, I'm standing in the middle of the room, turning slowly in a full circle, surveying everything in sight. "Both flights of stairs circle around the chimney and come out in the fighting rooms in roughly the same place, right?"

"Right," he answers.

"So," I walk over to a spot on the wall not far from where the stairwell opens into the room, "that must mean that the door to the battlements is roughly here."

"It seems so," Richard is still skeptical.

"Go down to the lower level. Find a pole or use your sword or one of the bows and tap on the ceiling in front of the center of the door."

He's not gone long before I hear tapping and Richard saying, "The door is right here, Alfred." To my surprise, the sound is muffled. And I don't feel the tapping on the planks under my feet as I'd expected. It's almost as if the sound is coming from beyond the wall.

I walk to the top of the stairs and call down to Richard. "How many paces is it from the door to the opposite side of the room?" I hear his boots pacing off the distance on the floor below, even as I do the same in this room. In another minute, he appears at the top of the stairs. "Eight paces, Alfred," he announces.

"So that's it!" I exclaim. Richard looks puzzled.

"This room has always felt more confined to me than the one below, but I put that down to the fact that there's a solid wall in place of the door below and that means only one exit. But Richard, this room really is smaller. It's at least a foot shy of seven paces." I point to the solid section of stone and mortar. "There's something beyond that wall."

Moving quickly back to the wall, I start examining the mortar joints at eye level but they're all as solid as the day they were made. Pushing on the stones has no effect – everything is strong and immovable just as the masons intended. Looking lower, I finally find what I'm looking for – a mortar joint that looks worn away. "Richard, look here." I take out my dagger and poke it into what looks like a surface crack between mortar and stone. It goes in well beyond the surface. Withdrawing it, I push on the stone. It gives ever so slightly.

Now Richard helps scan the mortar joints. We find several that have clearly been tampered with – not so much that one would notice, especially scanning the room at eye level, but enough that we're convinced those stones have been removed in the not-too-distant past.

"How are we going to get them out?" I ask. "We don't have the right tools. But I'm convinced John wouldn't have had a mason to help him."

Richard is still scanning the wall, looking ever closer to the floor. Just above the lowest row, there's a spot where a narrow stone was used to fill an odd space between the larger ones. "Alfred, look," Richard exclaims, pointing. "That one is ever so slightly misaligned with its neighbors." He reaches for it and is able to just barely grasp its edges in the tips of his fingers. Being careful to keep it level and straight, he tugs

. . . and it slowly moves out of position until he can take it firmly on both hands and slide it completely out of the wall.

We both stand there silently, awestruck, for several minutes. "Now what?" he finally asks. "If we remove the stones in the wrong order, we could wind up crushing one or all of our hands."

"We could also bring the whole thing down on our heads," I give voice to what I'm sure we're both thinking.

"Maybe we should send for a mason."

"Not yet. If John could figure this out, then I'm sure it's not beyond our ability."

We spend the next quarter hour studying the wall. Which mortar joints have been opened. How the stacking of the stones alternates from row to row. Trying to work out which stone to remove first. Based on the number of stones that appear to have been freed, the hole will be small – barely enough for a man to slither through. "We're going to need something for light when we get this open," I remark. "I don't think the light from the arrow slits will be enough."

"Let me go get a couple of torches," replies Richard. He returns with one torch lighted and places it in the holder beside the stairway, keeping the other in reserve.

I'd worried that the stones would be too heavy for the two of us to manage . . . but then, I remind myself, John wouldn't have had help. And as we remove the first one we've selected, it becomes obvious why. These stones are much smaller – perhaps only a third the thickness of those in the outer walls. The masons were merely patching over a hole – not building fortifications – and none of this needed to bear more than its own weight – the frame of the previous opening was designed to handle all that load.

Despite working slowly and carefully, we have all the loose stones removed in less than half an hour. Richard hands me the torch. "You figured this out, Alfred. You should be the first to look inside."

Lying on the floor and extending the torch through the hole in the wall, I see a small chamber inside. Bits of construction detritus – chipped stones, bits of wood – lie here and there on the floor. I pull the torch out of the opening and had it to Richard. "Since this is my hare-brained idea, as Samuel would call it, I should go in first. If I fall through the floor to the room below, pick up the pieces, will you?"

Richard shakes his head in dismay. "Now I understand why Samuel says you need a minder on all your little adventures."

It's a tight fit. I have to twist my body so that my shoulders work their way through the diagonal of the opening. But once my chest is through the hole, there's enough room inside to bend easily and pull my legs through. It's not completely dark inside – a faint light shows through a hole in the ceiling. "Pass me the unlit torch," I call to Richard. "I'll hold it out so you can light it."

When the torch is lit, I can see the chamber is a little more than one pace wide, from our hole to the outer wall, and about two – maybe two and a half – paces long. A ladder that looks to be quite ancient is propped against the outer wall. The floor looks solid, with a bit more of the construction detritus in the corners – almost as if it had been pushed there. I walk around a bit, testing each step before putting my weight on it, but the floor seems sturdy, so I call to Richard, "Aren't you going to come join in the fun?"

He eases himself into the chamber and cautiously gets to his feet. At first, he doesn't move. "It seems safe enough," I tell him. "Take a look around." I hold the torch high so we can both examine the little chamber then lower it behind me so that we can better see the opening in the ceiling.

Handing Richard the torch, I take the ancient ladder and move it toward the opening. With a bit of experimentation, I find I can prop it against the lip of the opening above, giving us a way up. I start to climb. The fourth rung seems like it might give way, so I shift my foot to the side where it joins the ladder rail and try to avoid putting any more weight on it than absolutely necessary. Despite its age, the ladder is up to the task, and I'm quickly able to poke my head through the opening and into the room above.

The light from the arrow slits is brighter here, illuminating the old fighting room. The collapsed portion of the floor is on the far side of the room; the nearby planks seem intact. Hoisting myself slowly through the opening I first sit on the edge and test the nearby area by leaning on my hands. Then, reminding myself that, if I'm right, John walked about up here, I stand and call for Richard to join me. "Watch that fourth rung," I remind him, as he begins to climb with torch in hand. As he reaches the top, I take the torch and put it in the wall bracket nearby.

"No wonder the archers didn't want to come up here," he comments, getting to his feet, "if that was the only way up and down."

We walk carefully around the near edges of the room, where the floor seems safest, looking for niches in the wall, loose stones, anything that could be a hiding place. Nothing. "I've an idea," I tell him. I take the torch from its bracket and, getting down on all fours, crawl toward the edge of the collapse. When I've gone as far as I dare in this fashion, I lie on my belly and inch toward the edge.

"What are you doing, Alfred?" Richard's voice is anxious. "You're going to fall through and get yourself killed."

"Remember they nailed the new ceiling below to the bottom of the beams. That means there's space between floor and ceiling that could serve as a cache." As I approach the edge, the planks seem less stable than those behind me; but I have to know if there's anything hidden under them. Easing my shoulders over the edge, I hold the torch out and look down and into the gap. Once again, nothing.

Growing increasingly disappointed, I slither slowly back to the solid part of the floor. Getting to my hands and knees when it feels safe, I realize Richard is standing stock-still, starting at something as if mesmerized. "What is it?" I ask him as I get awkwardly to my feet trying not to drop the torch.

"There," he points toward the ceiling. "In the rafters." Gazing upward, I see what's caught his eye. A plank placed across the rafters. On it, two boxes – strongboxes, by the look of them – each draped with some sort of cloth. We both stare in silence. Finally Richard says, "The roof of the tallest tower."

"Let's find out what's up there." I move quickly to the opening and pull up the ancient ladder. Taking care that its feet are on a safe part of the floor, I prop it against one of the rafters where the boxes are perched, grab the torch, and start to climb. In my eagerness, I almost forget about the rickety fourth rung but remember at the last minute to adjust my footing.

The boxes are indeed strongboxes. The drapes turn out to be banners. One is John's personal banner from when he was the heir, the other the three lions rampant, symbol of the king. I remove the latter. "It's a Treasury strongbox," I shout to Richard. "The Treasury seal engraved on the top, the lock sealed with wax and embossed with the Treasury seal."

"Melt the wax," Richard orders. "Then come down here and let me get at it. I just hope it's the same key." The wax melts easily in the heat of the torch. But before I descend, I take the banner from the other box. The lock is old and loose, and I can pry it open with my dagger. Inside, sacks of gold coins. John's personal fortune. I close the lid carefully and descend the ladder.

Richard climbs up. He takes from around his neck the chain bearing the Treasury keys. I've often teased him about whether or not he actually wears them to bed. But today, I'm grateful for his habit. He gets the lock open quickly. More sacks of coins. "Gold and silver," he reports and scurries back down the ladder. "And the other?" he asks.

"The remainder of John's fortune," I reply. "Most of what he inherited, in fact. He must have sent very little indeed to Gunhild. How much of the Treasury?"

"I won't know until we sort it out. Not enough to get us completely out of debt, I suspect, but it's a start."

And then I realize something. "Richard, I don't think John was protecting Treasury funds. I think he stole that money for himself."

"Why?"

"Remember his will? Everything from the roof of the tallest tower left to John Gundar? And the king's banner covering the Treasury strongbox? He resented Father's giving me half of the family fortune, and I think he took that money as what he considered his just compensation, intending to leave it all to his son."

"You might be right," replies Richard.

"From this moment, it belongs again to the Treasury," I tell him.

We embrace for a moment, overcome by the enormity of what we've just found. Stepping back, Richard says, "We're going to need help to get this down."

"We have to get ourselves down first," I chuckle. I grab the ladder and reposition it in the exit, and we begin the process of reversing what it took to get up here. I slither out of the hole in the wall on the second level and shout, "Guards!" There's the sound of boots scampering up the stairs, and a sentry emerges on our level just as Richard crawls out of the wall. The sentry's jaw drops and he's still standing there, dumbstruck, when two of the King's Own Guard arrive seconds later. Managing to recover from his astonishment, the sentry executes a belated bow and says, "Your Grace."

"At ease, men. Not what you were expecting, I take it?" None of the three know quite how to respond. By now Richard has stood up and shaken the dust from his clothes.

"Lord Richard and I have been on a scavenger hunt, and we've had rather a bit of success. Would one of you kindly fetch Sir Tobin here?" One guard scurries away. "We'll also need a mason with his tools, and two tall ladders . . . tall enough to reach from the ground here to the top of the battlements with perhaps a rung or two to spare." The second guard scurries off, and I tell the sentry, "See what you can do about rounding up a hand cart."

When he's left, I turn to Richard. "A good afternoon's work my friend. Are you comfortable with letting Tobin supervise the movement of all that money?"

"Aye, Alfred. I need to get to my clerks and tell them what to prepare for."

Shortly after, Tobin bursts breathlessly into the room, having quite obviously run the entire distance and up the three flights of stairs. "They told me you'd crawled out of a hole in the wall, sir," he gasps. "What the devil is going on?"

I clap him on the shoulder as he struggles to catch his breath. "Sounds like you've mastered the candid speaking bit, Tobin," I chuckle.

"No disrespect intended, sir," his breathing becoming a bit less labored. "I was just afraid something dreadful had happened."

"None taken, Tobin. Richard and I are just in a particularly jovial mood. We've found some hidden treasure and need your help to retrieve it."

I explain our little adventure and watch as he tries, unsuccessfully, to control his expression of dismay. "You should've asked our help with that, sir. You could've been hurt quite badly."

"You should know me well enough by now, Tobin, to know I can't let everyone else have all the fun," I tell him with a big grin.

"Believe me, Tobin," laughs Richard, "I now fully understand what you and Samuel have had to put up with around this one's crazy schemes."

"I've sent for a mason." My voice is serious once again. "We'll have him take down the rest of that patch of the old doorway. Then your men can walk in rather than sliding through that tiny hole. That will also allow you to get two proper ladders inside. The one that's in there is quite old and has a rung that could give way any minute. You'll need one ladder to access the third level and the second one to get up into the rafters. The part of the floor that isn't collapsed seems sturdy enough, but you might want to decide for yourself how many men it's safe to have up there at one time. There were only the two of us. Richard can give you instructions on where to take the money. I trust you'll have your best men protecting it. Now, I'd like to go tell Rupert that we solved the riddle."

"Off with you, Alfred. I can finish getting things underway here," says Richard.

Crossing the two courtyards, I notice a spring in my step reminiscent of the carefree days when my father was alive. While I wear the crown, I'll never be truly free of care. But watching the bustling enterprise of people going about their business here, remembering the optimism of those in Great Woolston and the village near the manor, and thinking on what we've accomplished in barely more than a year and a half since I rode through these gates for the first time as king, I'm filled with a sense of pride. There's much yet to do, but we've made a start. A very good start indeed.

And then I hear Grandfather's voice in my head. "Celebrate your successes, Alfred. Revel in them. They're the source of much of the joy in a man's life. But never forget they're not the sum total of life. There will always be surprises. Some will lead to new successes; some could bear the seeds of your undoing; some will break your heart. But for now, Alfred, well done. Very well done indeed."

It takes me back to the day he spoke those very words to Samuel – the day my friend brought me home from captivity – the only other time I ever heard him utter them. The memories of that day and of the man are palpable.

We celebrated on that day. We'll celebrate now. And tomorrow will bring what it will.

Author's Notes

When I reached the point in the narrative where it was apparent that at least a modicum of the Territorial language would be required for believability, I had a decision to make. Throw together a few random syllables and hope it doesn't actually have some unintended meaning in a legitimate language that's unfamiliar to me but might be known by some readers? Take the trouble of creating a language for the Territories? Find a suitable language to use?

I discarded the first option based on the risk of potentially offending someone. The second option seemed way too much trouble for just a few phrases. That left me with finding a suitable language – one that would be ancient enough to be realistic for the time and for a people that had been living rather isolated from my main characters – but at the same time, something that wouldn't be sufficiently well known to be recognizable by most readers.

Welsh and Gaelic are old enough, but their use in everyday life is fairly widespread and expanding. I settled on Cornish and found some excellent resources to make sure I got it right. When all I needed was a single word, Gelyver Kernewek (cornishdictionary.org.uk) was my primary source and I found a good cross-reference at: https://archive.org/details/EnglishCornishDictionary/page/n63.

Context was critical for the phrase Alfred gives Tobin to use as an invitation to go riding. I wanted it to be simplistic, as one might use if they know very little of a language and are trying to make themselves understood to native speakers. My thanks to The Cornish Language

Partnership, which offers a translation service and provided exactly the short phrase I needed. Check out their web site at: https://cornwall.gov.uk (which is available in both Cornish and English) to learn more about this ancient language.

As in previous volumes of this series, I've used contractions liberally to provide a more natural flow and allow my readers to more easily identify with the characters and feel a deeper sense of immersion in the story. (Contractions have been part of the language since the days of Old English.)

I've tried to be diligent about avoiding linguistic anachronisms, but I've made a couple of concessions to modern understanding. In Alfred's time, people would have used "wain" to refer to what we now call a wagon. Since "wagon" came into common usage in the mid-1500s, I've opted for the more recognizable word.

On the other hand, I've explicitly chosen to use some period-appropriate words for authenticity and flavor. "Paindemaine," the term for the finest bread, made with flour that had been sifted multiple times to eliminate as many as possible of the husks and stones left from grinding. Besides being correct for the time, it's a really delightful word.

Occasionally, there just isn't a period-appropriate word or phrase that is "fit for purpose" for the modern reader. One set of such words: "diplomat," "diplomatic," and "diplomacy." They came into the language much later than Alfred's time – (nineteenth century for the first two, slightly earlier for the last). I simply couldn't find suitable synonyms that instantly convey all the nuances we understand today from these terms; and writing an elaborate, period-appropriate explanation seemed an unnecessary distraction from the narrative.

Most names of characters (both forenames and surnames) are authentic for the period, the exceptions being Durrus, Korst, and Narth, which I made up.

This novel is a work of fiction that tells the story of what might have been in a world that doesn't precisely correspond to the one we know. Readers will note similarities with northern Europe, but my decision to fictionalize the setting was a matter of practicality for my characters. European history from this period and its major actors are too well known for it to be plausible that a different set of kings and nobility might actually have existed. The fictional setting also gave me the freedom to embed the allegory of our own times within Alfred's story. *Upon This Throne* explores national debt, engagement with other cultures, alliance building, the role of women, health care, and post-traumatic stress. The period-appropriate depiction of Charles's sexual orientation sets the stage for exploration of those issues in a subsequent volume.

For those who prefer to read the Second Son Chronicles solely as entertainment, I hope you get as much enjoyment from immersing yourself in Alfred's world as I've had in bringing his tale to life.

Shadows

Isabella wants to come home – a seemingly innocuous request. But when you're the king and Isabella is the aunt whose mental instability caused so much trouble that her own father banished her from the kingdom, the prospect is anything but innocuous. Her arrival, unbidden, on the steps of the castle opens old wounds and sets in motion a series of events that will test Alfred as he's never been tested before.

Note from the Author

Word-of-mouth is crucial for any author to succeed. If you enjoyed *Upon This Throne*, please leave a review online — anywhere you are able. Even if it's just a sentence or two. It would make all the difference and would be very much appreciated.

Thanks!
Pamela

About the Author

Pamela Taylor brings her love of history to the art of storytelling in the *Second Son Chronicles*. An avid reader of historical fact and fiction, she finds the past offers rich sources for character, ambiance, and plot that allow readers to escape into a world totally unlike their daily lives. She shares her home with two Corgis who remind her frequently that a dog walk is the best way to find inspiration for that next chapter.

Thank you so much for reading one of Pamela Taylor's novels.
If you enjoyed the experience, please check out the rest of the
Second Son Chronicles!

Second Son   My Father, My King   Pestilence

It is the dawn of the Renaissance, a time when new ideas are just beginning to emerge. Alfred – the eponymous second son – comes of age in the enlightened court of his grandfather convinced that his life will be unremarkable, spent in diligent but mundane service to the kingdom. His grandfather, however, foresees for him a special destiny.

The Chronicles follow Alfred's journey to discover what that destiny might be. Peace and stability are tenuous in this era, and threats can arise from unexpected quarters. Renegades intent on revenge, a brother with a particularly difficult personality, looming military conflicts, the rise of a merchant class demanding to be heard, a king's Councillor who likes to stir things up, and the usual vagaries of medieval life – just a few of the challenges Alfred will encounter. How he deals with each obstacle will affect not just Alfred, but those closest to him and, in some cases, the entire kingdom. And just what will that special destiny turn out to be?

www.ingramcontent.com/pod-product-compliance
Lightning Source LLC
Chambersburg PA
CBHW011130100726
47898CB00009B/2921